ABOVE US THE SKY

Newly qualified teacher Phyllie Saunders is evacuated with her school to Dorset. As she struggles to control the crowd of tearful children, she sees Sammy. Her oldest and dearest friend is on the way to join his submarine, and as he kisses her goodbye, everything changes for them. But now that war is tearing them apart, is it too late? Phyllie throws herself into village life, determined to protect and nurture the children in her care. But war leaves no one untouched, and Phyllie will need all the support of the community, as she waits and prays for Sammy's safe return...

ABOVE US THE SKY

ABOVE US THE SKY

by

Milly Adams

Magna Large Print Books
Long Preston, North Yorkshire,
BD23 4ND, England.

British Library Cataloguing in Publication Data.

Adams, Milly
    Above us the sky.

    A catalogue record of this book is
    available from the British Library

    ISBN   978-0-7505-4285-2

First published in Great Britain by Arrow Books in 2015

Copyright © Milly Adams 2015

Cover illustration © Colin Thomas

Published in Large Print 2016 by arrangement with
Arrow Books who is one of the publishers in the Random House
Group Ltd.

119152316

Magna Large Print is an imprint of Library Magna Books Ltd.

Printed and bound in Great Britain by
T.J. (International) Ltd., Cornwall, PL28 8RW

To the gorgeous girls of the Downley Village
Evening Women's Institute.
And my very own ex-submariner.

Acknowledgements

My dear friend, Kaila Shabat, led me to a wonderful friar in Jerusalem who explained how closure could be brought to Jake. Thank you both.

The Women's Institute was formed in Canada in the late 1800s, and arrived in the United Kingdom in 1915. During the First World War the WI encouraged countrywomen to become involved in growing and preserving food to support the war effort. The WI did the same in the Second World War but also collected herbs for medicines, and salvage for all sorts of things. Bravo, I say, and to the Guides and Scouts who did their bit. Let's hear it for all their unsung efforts.

Today we think of the WI in terms of jam, Jerusalem, and perhaps a saucy calendar. As a member of the **Downley Village Evening Women's Institute** – bring it on. But we're more than that. As a movement we care for one another and the community, we have monthly speakers who add to our knowledge, and every year we choose resolutions that could bring about real change at local and national level on the issues that matter.

Also, I write of submariners. My husband, Dick, was a peacetime, well, cold war, submariner, and has been an invaluable source of information, though all faults are mine.

I bow my head to the memory of all those who served, and still serve.

Above Us the Sky is my tribute to all these organisations. It is written from the heart.

Chapter One

Friday 14 June 1940, Waterloo Station

Phyllie gripped her clipboard, red pencil poised, then hesitated, mesmerised. Her two classes – one of seven-year-olds, one of eleven-year-olds – had transformed themselves into a seething mass intent on competing for noise with the troop train arriving on the adjoining platform. For heaven's sake, she had been a teacher for six months; she was too young, too inept, too everything to be taking these children away. And for how long?

She braced herself and shouted, 'Children, I need your attention; now, not when you're ready.'

It was a lost cause, and she took a moment to draw a deep breath for another go, but clearly it was a breath too long. Further along the platform Mr Stevens, the headmaster, rose onto his toes beneath the banner bearing the words *Ealing Close School*. Similar banners, with names of schools throughout London, festooned the station.

'Miss Saunders, take your registers at once,' he bellowed at her. His children, aged twelve, were lined up like well-behaved skittles, the boys in their grey shorts, the girls in their red dresses. There was barely a word between them all. How did he do it?

'I have, Mr Stevens. I took them when we first arrived at Waterloo, and, anyway, I have the Class

11

B seven-year-olds as well as my Class A eleven-year-olds, while you have just the one class.' She stopped, then added, 'Sir.' This, though, was swallowed up by the shriek as the train opposite eased to the buffers. The other classes had been evacuated a few days earlier – where to was anyone's guess. Sulphuric smoke, smuts and dust caught in her throat.

'Take them again,' Mr Stevens ordered, in a voice that would carry over a volcanic eruption. 'One of your charges could have been dragged off by a hysterical mother. For goodness' sake, Miss Saunders, do keep up.'

Stevens was usually impeccably dressed, but this morning his homburg was slightly awry. What would he think if he could see himself? It was said he had been yanked out of retirement a year ago to take the place of young Mr Taylor who was – well, where?

Train doors were swinging open opposite. The walking wounded and the weary spilled onto the platform – the remnants, she assumed, of the evacuation of Dunkirk.

The children turned and started to clap. The men just shrugged and walked, or limped, towards the barrier, with a sergeant bellowing, 'Head for the clock on the main concourse where the good ladies of the Women's Voluntary Service might even have a cup of tea, though I've never seen such a bunch of ne'er-do-wells in the whole of me bleeding life. Assemble there, and get rid of that damned dog, Braithwaite. How you got it on the boat in the first place, I'll never know. How you kept it with you while they sent us towards Aldershot, and then bloody decided to send us on up here after bloody all, when we should be at Victoria, I don't know either. What a bloody pig's ear, that's all I've got to say.'

Phyllie heard a terse reply from a pale young private. 'Couldn't leave it, Sarge, could I? Scared to death it was.'

'You'll be bloody scared in a moment. I'm worse than any beach being bombed to buggery.'

Phyllie knew her mother would have whispered: 'Language, if you please.' She tucked her clipboard beneath her arm, rammed her pencil in the pocket of her grey cotton jacket and put her wicker shopping basket at her feet.

A guard blew a whistle nearby. Why hadn't she thought of that? She put two fingers in her mouth. The children swung round, the soldiers too, as her whistle pierced the chaos. She waved the clipboard as the children moved nearer, but then the soldiers started wolf-whistling back at her and the children turned again. It was like a pantomime. The chatter restarted.

To her left, Mr Stevens shook his head in apparent despair.

Phyllie adjusted her grey beret, which had slipped, feeling sad for the lads, and unsure, because if this was the general state of the British army, what was to stop the Nazis from jackbooting their way over the British or bombing them to smithereens? It was all so unreal, panic stirred, as it had when the cinema news had shown the Dunkirk beaches. Had her friend Sammy, the one who'd taught her to whistle, been out there, his captain watching helplessly through the submarine's periscope?

Phyllie whistled once more. 'Pay attention, children. The train isn't ready for us quite yet, and we still need to tick off names.'

'Not again, miss.' It was Ron Cummins, standing at the back, showing off in front of the passing troops, one of whom was smoking a cigarette just behind the lad. Wasn't that the pale young man with the dog? Yes, there it was, barking. Poor creature. What would happen to it now?

Phyllie dropped her pencil. Young Jake, who lodged with his father next door to her, in Sammy's home, dodged forward, and handed it to her. Ron shouted from the back: 'Oooh, teacher's pet is at it again.'

Phyllie smiled at Jake. 'Thank you.' It was unbearably hot. Her girdle was hitched up, and her left suspender unsafe because the rubber button was perished and she feared it wouldn't last the journey to ... wherever they were heading. They had not been told – evacuees never were, it seemed.

Mr Stevens stabbed a finger towards her clipboard. She nodded. 'All right, children,' she said, her voice strong, 'I will call your names and when I have ticked you off, you are to move to the left and form a line.'

A soldier with a bandaged head yelled as he limped past their group, 'You do what your teacher says now. She'd make a good sergeant major, so she would.' His mates laughed. She half waved and smiled, beginning to call – almost to scream – the names as their train gushed smoke and steam. Across from them, the last troops were

14

slamming doors as each carriage emptied. The WVS women were visible now, directing the men to the main concourse. The WVS had also arrived to help with the evacuees and could be seen dotted about amongst the various schools but they had not reached Ealing Close School yet.

She began to tick the names. The cinema news had said the Nazis were near Paris. It had also announced that children who hadn't gone in the first wave of evacuation in September were being given the chance to move to safety now. A headache was beginning.

She was well over halfway through her list of names, and the children were moving to the left. She continued ticking but found the familiar questions bothering her. Why wouldn't her mother evacuate too? Why did she insist on moving into the East End to help Phyllie's brother Frankie at his Roman Catholic presbytery? She ticked the last name, and smiled at the children, who were in lines as immaculate as Mr Stevens'.

They looked so small standing quietly in groups, their gas masks huge somehow, even on the eleven-year-olds like Ron and Jake. Now that the train opposite was quiet, they were watching their cases, which had been stacked further along the platform, and were being put in the guard's van. A porter called across to the children, 'You'll enjoy your holidays.'

'It is the seaside where people go for holidays, isn't it, miss? I've never been.' Melanie was seven, and her ankle socks were perfectly white, as usual.

'Sometimes it is,' Phyllie said, hunkering down to talk to her, brushing back strands of the child's

15

ginger hair that had escaped from her single plait. 'But sometimes they go to the countryside, and I think that's where we might be going. They have lambs in the countryside.'

'I like lamb, when it's had its throat cut and been cooked. It's best with mint sauce,' said Ron, looking round for approval. His friends' laughter was loud. Melanie's lip quivered.

Phyllie whispered to her, 'If there are lambs, you'll see how they leap in the air.' She stroked the child's face, and then rose.

She'd have to deal with Ron, yet again, but not here, not now, and fat lot of good it would do anyway. Melanie was starting to weep and if it caught on, then there would be hysteria. 'Melanie, I'd like you to hold my pencil, and Jake, I need you to make sure you stay by her side. If you pull that face, my lad, and the wind changes, you'll stay like that. Is that all right, Melanie? It's a very important job.'

Melanie swallowed, brushed the back of her hand across her eyes, and took the pencil. 'Yes, miss.'

Jake stood beside the smaller child who reached for his hand. He folded his arms. Phyllie checked her watch. Fifteen minutes before departure. Would her mother get here? She'd said this morning she wanted to make sure that Phyllie had a key to their Ealing home, which they were letting. 'You must have one, just in case,' she'd said.

'Just in case' had become a phrase as common as breathing since the war began. Her mother had also taken the opportunity to slice in between Phyllie's ribs as usual, saying, 'Especially

16

as I won't know where you are for ages, what with you running away when you should be here, bearing whatever comes.'

The fact that teaching was considered essential war work for women and older men, and that Phyllie's request to transfer to one of the services had been refused, had not impressed her mother.

Phyllie snatched a look towards the barrier. There was no sign of her, but there were many parents waiting, and all along the platform were bustling WVS, and the press of other schools, banners and porters.

The parents would be allowed through only when the children were embarked and the train leaving, to prevent last-minute scenes. A few troops were still hobbling up the platform on the other side, their eyes to the front. She heard barking again. A small girl tugged at her flowery cotton skirt. 'Please, miss, I'm tired.'

'Yes, I'm sure you are, Dorothy, but soon we'll be sitting down, leaving London behind and finding lots to look at out of the windows.'

She heard a shout then, a loud one, and one she recognised but couldn't believe. She swung round and her heart leapt. It was Sammy.

'Hello, hello; where's my lady friend?' Two sailors were running towards her, dodging and sidestepping their way through the crowd, leaping over several cases.

Phyllie snatched a look towards the headmaster, who was further down the platform and deep in conversation with the guard. 'Sammy,' she cried, 'what on earth?' But he was here, swinging down his kitbag and pulling her to him.

'We're going up north, from down south.' He winked. 'Can't say any more. Got to get to Euston. Isaac wanted to see Jake as we came through, so I thought I'd come and see you too. No time to get to Ealing to say goodbye to Mum and Dad.'

Sammy Williams and Phyllie had formed their own gang since the time they could walk, playing Cowboys and Indians, and swinging on the ropes his dad, Bill Williams, and her own, Cyril Saunders, had hung on the oak tree at the back in the allotments. Four years ago, at the age of nineteen, Sammy had joined the submarine service. A year later, when she reached nineteen, Phyllie started teacher training. She pulled away and looked at him. 'You be careful wherever it is you're going, do you hear me, you great dollop? And while you're being careful, have a bath.'

He roared with laughter. 'Can't do anything about the smell of submarine diesel so don't you start being a fusspot, Phyllie. Talking of fusspots, where's your mum?'

She grinned and slapped him, then saw Ron Cummins staring at them. Phyllie remembered where she was, and turned to Isaac, Jake's father. Rachel and Isaac Kaplan had arrived in England in 1934. Originally from Krakow in Poland, they had worked in Germany for a few years, before lodging in the attic flat of the Williams' house. Isaac had joined the submarine service at the same time as Sammy. The Williamses had let their house from today, to fit in with Jake's evacuation, and were probably on their way to Wales, so Sammy would have missed them anyway.

Jake ran towards his father, and Isaac held him

18

tight, his face alight with joy. Releasing him, he crouched down and dug into his kitbag. He pulled out a parcel and handed it to Jake as though it was the crown jewels. Phyllie and the children watched as Jake unwrapped it slowly. Then he threw the gift to the ground. Not just that, but he stamped on it, screaming, 'Why, Dad, why? No one knew.'

The porters stopped in their work, the children were silent but, next to her, Sammy cursed quietly. Phyllie was frozen, unable to believe what she was seeing until, at last, as tears streamed down Jake's face, she moved towards him. Sammy, though, pulled her back. 'I told him not to,' he ground out. 'He doesn't understand that the fascist buggers he left in Europe are here too. That's the trouble; he thinks England's so bloody marvellous.'

Isaac was picking up the soiled Jewish shawl, the precious family tallit, which he had just given his son. He looked pale and shocked. In spite of the station noise, and the activity of the porters who had returned to work, it seemed as though a silence remained. A silence that was broken by Ron, his mousy hair long and unwashed, elbowing his way through the others to the front and bellowing, 'Jake's a bloody four and two, a Yid, that's what he is. My mum and dad would have a bit to say about us being evacuated with the likes of that.'

'Dad,' yelled Jake, beating at his father. 'You see, now you've ruined it.'

Sammy was still gripping Phyllie and now he whispered, 'We've got to do something. Ron's father's a fascist, you know – a blackshirt – and I expect some others have grown up that way too.

19

Their leader, Mosley, might be in clink, but it's not going to stop this bloody Jew baiting.'

All she could think was that he was wrong; these were children, so surely they didn't... But then she saw the expression of hate on Ron's face. Behind him the other children were whispering. His best friends, Ernie and Jonny, jeered: 'Bloody hell, it's a four and two, a bloody Jew's coming with us. Bloody disgusting, it is.'

She started towards the boys, but Sammy's grip was firm. 'Work with me,' he demanded. 'We need a distraction because anything else will escalate the whole damn thing, and it's Jake who'll suffer.'

He released her and leapt across to Jake, pulling him close. He reached for a few others. Sammy then flung himself down on one knee. Out of the corner of her eye, she saw Isaac still holding the tallit, his face deeply sad as he looked across at her. He mouthed, 'Please, Phyllie, take care of my boy.'

'Always,' she answered and he nodded. Near him Ron spat on the ground. Phyllie felt as though she'd been slapped and a wave of anger surged over her. She simply did not know what to do, because she feared she'd do too much, and that would be of no help to anyone.

'Miss Saunders.' It was Sammy, shouting at her, yelling in fact. 'Miss Saunders, the lovely fair-haired, blue-eyed Miss Saunders.'

He was still down on one knee, the children he had gathered around him were grinning. Sammy turned to them. 'Shall I?' he asked. By now all the children were watching, curious and puzzled. They drew closer, the tallit forgotten. The porters were watching, too. Would they never get the wretched cases on? She checked her watch. They should have left four minutes ago, which would have prevented any of this from happening.

'Well?' Sammy yelled. Melanie and Jake nodded. 'Yes,' they said, the others nodded too. Ron and the other two loudmouths were watching, nudging one another.

Sammy continued to shout, 'Shall I? Really?' Although Mr Stevens was approaching, irritated, tapping his watch, she paid him no mind. Instead, she listened as Sammy sang, 'Even if you weren't the only girl in the world and I wasn't the only boy.' He stopped, grinned, flung out his arms and continued, 'I'd marry you, so will you marry me? Truly you must, mustn't she? The children say you must, don't you, children?'

They shouted as one, 'Yes.' Even Ron and his mates looked at one another and joined in what was becoming a chant. 'Yes, yes.'

Her mouth had dropped open. Three soldiers were limping along the platform heading for the concourse, and one called, leaning on a crutch, 'Aw, go on, miss; he's off to war. Don't be cruel.'

The children looked from one to the other, then to the soldier, then to Phyllie. 'He's off to war,' they repeated, in a ragged chorus.

Melanie came right up to her. 'Yes, miss, you must.' The porters waited.

Mr Stevens was strutting nearer, but then saw Isaac refolding the tallit. Phyllie watched her headmaster pause and then nod at her, smiling slightly. She had told him that Mrs Kaplan had journeyed to the Krakow Jewish quarter, Kazimierz, in 1939 to try to persuade her parents to

21

leave for the safety of Britain. Then the Germans had invaded and Rachel Kaplan had not been heard of since. Jake never spoke of his mother, and the joy had gone from the child.

The guard was signalling with a green flag right down at the front of the train, as though he was using some sort of semaphore; the soldiers were calling, 'Come on, miss. Come on, miss.'

The porters threw on the remaining cases. The children were chanting again. For once, Jake's face was alight with fun. Melanie was laughing, Sammy was grinning, his arms spread wide. 'Come on, Phyllie, get with the plot,' he said with a smile. 'Me knee's killing me.'

'Yes.' She laughed. 'Yes, I'll marry you.'

Sammy leapt to his feet, the children cheered, and the soldiers too. One of them shouted, 'Give her a kiss, then.'

So Sammy pulled her to him, and planted a kiss on her mouth. The shock of it took her breath away; his mouth was soft, he was so close. He was her friend, and she'd always followed his lead but never thought of him as a boy, and then a man. Now, though, his mouth was on hers and she didn't want it to end.

He drew away, opened his eyes, and looked into hers. For once in his life he said nothing. She could feel his breath, he was so close; she could see his long lashes, the lips that she had not noticed before, his dark brown eyes that matched his hair and which said ... what?

It was Isaac who broke the moment, calling, 'We've got to go.'

Behind Sammy, Jake ran to his father and

hugged him, before walking back to Melanie. Once there, he let her hold his hand.

Sammy backed away, his eyes holding hers. He grinned, then ruffled Jake's almost-black hair. 'You look after her, you hear.' He came back to Phyllie, and she longed to feel his mouth again. He leaned close, and spoke against her ear. 'Move along to the next carriage or you'll have them tiddling out of the windows. You need a corridor, you daft doughnut. Be safe, Phyllie. Above all, be safe.'

The two men swung up their kitbags and headed back through the crowds, passing her mother who was staring at Phyllie. Phyllie groaned as she heard Sammy say, 'Hi, Mrs S. or should I call you Mum?'

She saw Isaac pause to speak a few words to her mother and hand something to her. It was the tallit.

Sammy turned and called to Phyllie over his shoulder: 'Remember what we used to say when we climbed the pear tree, right to the top, Phyllie. *Above us the sky, and it always will be, over us both.* It's still there, over us, and you too, Jake. It's the same sky over us all, wherever we are. So your dad and me, we're not so far away after all.' Suddenly he looked young, tired and frightened, and it was as though she was looking at herself. But then he grinned, turned into the crowd, and was gone.

Her mother was beavering towards her, head forward, scowl in place, her headscarf worn like a multicoloured turban. She was wearing her usual mackintosh even on a hot day like today.

'What a disgraceful display, Phyllis, here in front of these children, when you should be setting an example. Kissing in public, indeed, and that lout too. You will write and tell him the heat got to you.'

Phyllie held up her hand. 'Just a moment, Mum. Stay here, children, I'm just having a word with Mr Stevens.' She hurried to the headmaster and brought up the problem of the carriage.

He smiled. 'A wise young man, Miss Saunders. I'll move down, you follow. I'll mention the change to the guard who will notify the WVS ladies who are to travel with us. Ah, and felicitations on your engagement.'

She shook her head. 'It wasn't real. It was to distract the children ... because of the tallit.'

'Ah,' he murmured again and then looked over her head, as though to somewhere distant. He sighed, then waved her away. 'Best go and say goodbye to your mother, then follow me with your tribe.'

She explained the story behind Sammy's proposal to her mother, who nodded with relief, saying, 'You need to marry up. You're a teacher, he's a sailor, with a police record.'

'Hardly, Mum. He was only cautioned when he heckled the blackshirts at a meeting.' Phyllie stopped. Her mother was thrusting Isaac's tallit at her, as though it was something contagious. Her whisper was fierce as she leaned towards her daughter. 'The Williamses had no right letting their top floor to Jews. Ours is a nice neighbourhood. They killed Christ, you know.'

Phyllie leaned forward, whispering just as fiercely, 'I think you'll find Jake and his father weren't alive then. This sort of talk isn't Catholi-

24

cism, Mum, it really isn't. It's just horrid and Frankie wouldn't care for it.'

The guards at either end of the train whistled, and called, 'All aboard.'

Phyllie picked up her basket, smiled reassuringly at Melanie and Jake, then shepherded her classes along the platform. Her mother followed, complaining that if Phyllie had converted to Roman Catholicism when her brother had the call, then they might see things in the same light.

Mr Stevens flagged them to a stop, and instructed her to embark her children mid-carriage. He would take the near end. She thanked whoever was up there, because soon she would be on board, and her mother would not. She called Class A's leader, Simon, to her, and asked him to check the children as they boarded. She stood aside. The children were leaping into the train now, Simon ticking frantically.

She returned to her mother. 'Come with me to the country, Mum. I want you to be safe. Frankie has the presbytery housekeeper to help him.'

Her mother straightened her turban, her lips drawn thin. 'I'm staying at the presbytery to do my bit, with Miss O'Brian.' Behind her the mothers were being allowed through the barrier to wave farewell now that the children were almost all on board. The engine was shoving out steam for a quick getaway. All along the platform the porters were slamming the doors shut.

Her mother added, 'The WI is to have extra sugar off ration from the government, to make jam from surplus fruit, but they'll be stocking up their own larders while they're at it, of course.

25

You can send some to London for us, that's if you can be bothered.'

Simon tapped her arm. 'I haven't ticked off Ron Cummins.'

'*What?*'

'I'm here, miss,' Ron called from a window to her right. 'I got on through this door. Don't worry, I'm coming with you.'

For one glorious moment she had thought Ron's mother had arrived and whisked him away but then she saw him searching as the parents arrived. She watched his face fall. Mrs Cummins probably wouldn't come, she never did, and what did that do to a child?

'I'm glad you're with us, Ron,' she called.

The WVS ladies were boarding now. Somewhere a dog barked. Had one of the mothers taken on the soldier's stray?

Phyllie turned back to her mother. 'I'm sorry, Mum. It's just a bit frantic. At twenty-two I'm finding this – well, you know. I didn't mean it, about your Catholicism. I'm glad you have an interest. I expect Dad would have been too.'

The guard called, 'All aboard, please, miss.'

Her mother stood there, presenting a cheek. Phyllie kissed her, but longed to be held. She whispered, 'I love you, Mum. I'll miss you. Please be careful.'

Her mother nodded. 'It's not me you'll be missing, it's the train, and for goodness' sake, wear your gloves. At least go through the motions of respectability.' She handed her the key to the front door. 'Keep this safe, just in case.'

'Oh, Mum, make Frankie look after you. I've

26

written to him to wish him luck at his first mission.'

Phyllie walked away, tucking the key into her basket, patting her pockets, finding her gloves, but not putting them on. What was the point, they'd be on and off until they arrived.

She heard her mother call, 'We call your brother Father Francis, don't we, Phyllis? Take care of yourself, and remember you're a teacher – you need to set standards.'

'All aboard, miss,' the guard shouted again and Mr Stevens called from the window, 'At once, Miss Saunders.'

Phyllie turned but her mother was walking away.

Chapter Two

Phyllie climbed on board and into a compartment containing ten seven-year-old girls and boys, sitting as though pinned to their seats, staring at nothing. They tugged at her heart, and she smiled at them before placing her basket on the overhead baggage rack. The netting sagged. 'Not long now, then we're off on holiday and it will be lovely.'

The usual advertisements above the seats had been replaced with wartime posters, some exhorting everyone to keep 'it' under their hats. A guard slid back the corridor door. 'If you'd just put the window up, miss.' It was not a question.

She did so, securing the thick leather strap on the brass button. The sudden quiet was extraordinary. The guard turned to the children, tipping back his cap and scratching his sparse grey hair. 'Now, I'm sure miss'll let yer at the window to wave to your mummies, but never, never open that window unless she says, or you'll be grabbed by hobgoblins and mashed into jam by the wheels. D'you understand?'

Phyllie groaned inwardly as the children turned to her, their eyes even bigger, and now it was a named horror that stalked them. She said, 'Why, thank you, Mr Guard, I'm sure they'll sleep well tonight.'

The mothers were hurrying along the platform, peering in the windows, trying to find their children.

The guard grinned as he left, whispering, 'Works a treat with the little ones. There'll be no fiddling with that strap, mark my words. Not so sure about that lot further along, the ones with the dog. I've told all the children to keep the corridor doors open, as per your headmaster's instructions. He said something about aural aids, but he lost me there. But you'll know about that.' She did, but she knew nothing about any dog, and a horrible thought was brewing.

She said, 'It means that if we keep the doors open we can hear them, that's all.'

He tipped his finger to his cap, winked and moved along the corridor.

Phyllie stood behind the children as they clambered onto the seats to wave to the mothers congregating on the other side of the glass. She realised now that Melanie was not amongst them, and her heart failed. She checked the clipboard

Simon had returned but everyone was ticked off, so Melanie must have moved into one of the other compartments with Jake.

'Mummy,' Marjorie Spencer wailed, as she knelt on the seat, her breath condensing on the window. 'I want me mummy.' The other children began shoving one another, shouting and crying now as their mothers and a few fathers waved.

'Steady now,' Phyllie called, acting as backstop. The train lurched a fraction and the children almost fell, the wheels ground on the lines, found purchase and then they were off, with the parents walking briskly alongside, some in cardigans, some in jackets, some in their best frocks, all waving and blowing kisses. They began to run as the steam and smoke built, along with the noise, until they ran out of platform, and at last the train was clear of the station.

The children scrambled and huddled around Phyllie, who dragged some onto her knees, while others stayed standing on the seats with their arms around her neck. She let them cry themselves out, trying to wipe noses before her jacket did the job. The heat of the day was building, and she told the children to remove their cardigans and pullovers. They did, but then clustered back in her arms.

In other compartments the WVS ladies would be doing the same, and their uniforms would be taking a bashing too. Would Mr Stevens? She thought perhaps he would, because she had seen a glimmer of kindness for the first time ever over the tallit episode. Perhaps he'd had a bad Great War, which locked him into severity? Well, if he hadn't, her dad certainly had. The gas had finally killed him in 1932 and every day she missed him. She thought it was his absence that had driven Francis to the Roman Catholic faith, but why, when it meant he could never marry? For a moment she thought of Sammy. Felt his lips. If only he'd meant it. Or had he? How much was an act?

'Miss, will we see them again?'

She said, 'Yes, of course. Until then, I'm here.' At last, with the resilience of children, the seven-year-olds slipped from the shelter of her arms, ranging themselves on the seats. They fiddled with their clothes, kicked their legs, then looked out of the window, deciding that perhaps they were hungry.

Phyllie shook her head. 'It's only eleven o'clock, so too early for our picnics. How about in an hour or two? Now, I'm just slipping along the corridor to check on everyone else, but I will be back. In fact, I will be wandering up and down most of the day, so listen for me, and I'll pop up and surprise you.'

Thomas, who lived near Ealing Common, looked up, uncertain. 'Just like the hobgoblins?'

Phyllie stood, fluffing out her skirt with its mass of small flowers, and brushing down her cream blouse. It was her good outfit and she was glad Sammy had seen her in it. She stopped. Sammy, the touch of his lips...

'Hobgoblins, are *only* to be found in books, and our guard's head. When we arrive we will find a book about them, but for now, let me tell you that hobgoblins are friendly if a little naughty, a bit like some of you children. However, you are real, but perhaps I might need to poke you to prove it.' She

30

waggled a finger at Marjorie, diving in for a poke, and then Alice, who was sitting next to her, and Thomas. All the children laughed, leaning forward, their eyes alight.

Phyllie continued, 'As hobgoblins don't exist, I can't poke them, so we must forget about the little rascals. However, we must not forget the window. We do not touch it, unless I say. I'm going to open it just a little bit now, because I'm hot, and I think you are too?' They nodded. She opened the window, catching its strap on the brass button. The noise whipped in, along with some smuts, but the breeze was welcome.

'I am off to see all the others, but I will be back.'

She turned, and then thought she heard a bark. Oh Lord, the dog. Where was it? Who had brought it? Why did she think immediately of Ron? Because he hadn't embarked through the right door, and because he was Ron, that's why.

She stood in the corridor, looking left and right, steadying herself as the train rumbled and lurched past the backs of grimy terraced houses. It was further along, wasn't it, that Ron had stuck his head out of one of the windows?

She walked along, peering into the next two compartments, smiling at the children, and thanking the WVS helpers who were reading to their charges, and supplying biscuits, or so it seemed from the mass of crumbs on the floor. So far, no dog; so far, no Ron. And where was Jake? And Melanie? It was so hot that she opened the corridor windows a notch, too. The houses were thinning. There was a clutch of shops, with women standing in queues. There was an air raid shelter at the corner of one street.

Ahead, she saw that the door of the third compartment was shut. She moved closer, peered through the window. Ron was sitting under a stark black-and-white poster of a drowning sailor. At the top was the word *Someone,* at the bottom, *Talked.* Her heart twisted but she forced herself to concentrate on the matter in hand.

Ron's grey socks drooped around his ankles. A rope was looped around his left leg; the other end of the rope was attached to a brown dog. Ron was showing a ten-bob note to his sidekick, Ernie. Jonny was sitting on the left of Ron, his thighs clenched together to prevent a small pile of coins from sliding between them onto the seat. He held up one. 'Bugger, Ron, it's a bloody Frenchie. He's ripped us off.' The glass muffled his voice, but Phyllie could hear perfectly well.

By the window Jake sat with Melanie, the only seven-year-old amongst several older children, all of whom were sitting silently, watching Ron. Jake was staring at the poster, anxiety in every rigid muscle in his body. No doubt he could see his father in that deep dark water, just as she had seen Sammy. But what on earth were Jake and Melanie doing in here, in the equivalent of the lion's den?

'Gimme it, I'll have a butcher's.' Ron snatched the coin, letting the ten-bob note flutter to his lap.

Phyllie slid open the door. The dog barked, and struggled to sit, but the rope was pulled too tight and he choked. 'Perhaps you won't have a butcher's after all, young man,' she said. 'I think you should give that money to me, and an explanation.' Phyllie braced herself against the doorway as the train altered pace, slowing to ease through a station.

'Nothing to do with us, miss. Bloody dog was in here, with 'im.' He jerked his head towards Jake. 'That's right, ain't it, lads?'

Ernie and Jonny nodded, smirking, and all three were digging their hands into their pockets. Magically, the money had disappeared.

'Stand up, and turn out your pockets,' Phyllie insisted, gripping the doorway again as the train switched points and took a long curved bend. The pale embankment grass was charred. Smuts and sparks threatened to create new fires. Behind the embankment were silver birches, with fluttering leaves.

Ron slouched to his feet, loosening the rope from his ankle, discarding it, kicking the dog to one side. The dog yelped; the coins in Ron's pockets clinked.

Jake grabbed the rope, pulling the dog away from Ron. 'I didn't bring the dog in, miss. Honest.'

Melanie slipped from her seat, her white ankle socks still pristine, her face red and sweaty. 'No, he didn't, miss. It was Mr Stevens sent us in 'ere, cos you said I was to stay near Jake. The dog was here, hidden behind them boys. Mr Stevens didn't see the dog. Mr Stevens said it would be good for Ron to get to know Jake better, but I don't think Ron wants to, so we've just been quiet and looked out of the window, like the others.'

Some of the other children in the carriage nodded and Phyllie smiled. 'Sit down, Melanie. I will–'

'But the seat's prickly, miss. I don't want to sit any more, and I want to do a wee, but he said we was to sit tight.' She pointed to Ron.

Phyllie kept her eyes on Melanie, but she could see Ron nudging his friends and edging towards the door she was blocking. What did he intend to do, ram her? 'Melanie, the train is swaying about a bit so it will be safer to do as I say until I sort this out and then we will find the toilet and somewhere else for you and Jake to sit. Hold out your hands, boys.'

Ron, Ernie and Jonny removed their hands from their pockets, holding them out for her inspection. 'Ain't got nothing, miss,' Jonny said. Ernie nodded. Ron just glared.

She patted their shorts, and felt the clutter of coins. 'That's not nothing. Show me.'

They produced a medley of pennies and Ron a crumpled ten-bob note as well as a franc, a florin and two half-crowns.

She looked at them, and at the cowering dog, which was about the size of a spaniel, shaggy and nervous.

'So, that poor tired soldier paid you to take the dog, boys? What would your mothers say?'

As she finished speaking she heard the sound of water, a stench of urine and at the same time Ron yelled, 'The bugger's peed on me leg.'

Indeed, the dog was standing, his leg cocked, a steaming puddle forming at Ron's feet. Phyllie's fondness for the dog knew no bounds. Melanie laughed. Ron cursed and punched the dog, who yelped and fell.

Jake barged him then and Phyllie shouted, 'No.'

Ron dominoed into Ernie and Jonny, and they crashed to the floor. Jake, Melanie and the dog were in a bunch by the external door. The other children had lifted their legs clear of the spreading puddle. Phyllie sidestepped the urine, as the three boys scrambled to their feet. She reached Jake and said, 'Take Melanie and the dog to my compartment, the third one down, the one with Marjorie in it. Stay in there and keep that animal under control. I'll take you to the toilet soon, Melanie, but if you can't wait, ask a WVS lady. You other children, off you go, too. There are spaces in the compartments between here and mine. Joseph, you bring me back the newspaper in my basket.'

She pressed herself against the seats as the children passed her, tiptoeing around the urine. The money was all over the floor, the ten-shilling note soaked through. Ron, Ernie and Jonny stared at their loot. Joseph returned with the newspaper, and hurried back to find a spare seat.

Phyllie divided the newspaper, handing out sheets to the three boys, but keeping one for herself. 'First you will rescue the money and place it here.' She spread her sheet of newspaper on a seat. 'You will use the rest to sort that out.' She pointed at the puddle.

Ron started to object but she wagged her finger at him. 'One more word and you'll be cleaning it on your own.'

When the floor was almost respectable, she marched them along to the toilet, the boys holding the newspaper at arm's length, dripping. It went in the bin. Ron washed his sock, shoe and his leg. The money was also washed, and finally their hands. They were marched back to the same compartment, leaving the note and coins in Phyllie's care. She opened the window a notch. They sat, holding their hands out for their money. Phyllie shook her head. 'Oh no. This goes to whoever takes on the poor wretched animal, one that you will have nothing more to do with.'

'I'm telling ya, the Yid brought the dog on, didn't 'e lads? You know how they'll do anything for money. Paid he was. Gave it to us to keep safe.'

The other boys said nothing, just looked at their feet. Phyllie shook her head at Ron. 'Be quiet. It's not nice, true or clever, it's just something you've heard and are copying.' She stopped, taking a deep breath, striving for calm and somehow finding it. 'Now, boys, this is a bad start, but it can improve. I won't tell Mr Stevens, who as you know all too well will resort to the strap. But if I have more of your nonsense it will go further. Do you understand?'

She waited. No one said a word, or looked at her. Ron kicked out at an imaginary something, his arms crossed, his chin on his chest, glowering. She waited. At last they nodded, and said, 'Yes, miss.'

'You'll stay in here except for toilet use. I'll come along frequently, and if not me, then one of the WVS. You won't know when the visits will occur. This door remains open so I can hear any shenanigans.'

As she left she heard Ron mutter, 'I'll get the Yid. I'll get him, you hear me.'

She hesitated. Had she done more harm than good?

'Oh, put a sock in it,' Ernie grunted. 'Fed up with the whole thing, we are, ain't we, Jonny? Stinks of bloody pee in here and no money in me pocket for all the hassle of it and it weren't the Yid. And if miss tells me mum, I'm for it.'

She half smiled to herself, calling into the next compartment, explaining to the curious children who had witnessed the comings and goings, that yes, there had been a bit of a problem, but it was sorted now. On she went, until she reached the guard's van. The guard was unscrewing a flask. 'Tea, miss?' he asked, gesturing to a canvas stool next to his own. She accepted. He smiled. 'No sugar, mind.'

'I'm lucky; I can't stand it in tea.' Phyllie sat, rocking with the train, sipping the tea, and it was better than brandy.

'You can come again then, miss.' His laugh was long, and he removed his cap. His windows were wide open and the draught was glorious. Phyllie relaxed at last. He said, 'Bit of a hullabaloo going on in the corridor. Everything tickety-boo?'

Phyllie nodded. The children's cases had been piled to the ceiling but seemed as solid as a wall. She drained her tea to the dregs, and then explained the whole situation, finally asking for a mop. He insisted he would sort it, and the toerags too, if he heard any more bloody nonsense from them. He'd make it his business to be passing frequently.

'You're very kind,' Phyllie said, rising, returning her enamel mug.

He shook his head. 'Poor little buggers, the lot of them. Can't be much fun leaving everything you know, and your mum and dad. Even those toerags, you know, are probably as miserable as sin and just kicking off.'

She walked back along the corridor, knowing he probably spoke the truth. How sad Ron must feel, she guessed, because his mother had not come. She balanced as the train rattled and swayed. The silver birch had given way to open countryside baking beneath a sky pale with heat. Scythed hay lay in rows. In one field men were pitchforking hay onto a cart already piled high. One load fell short and tumbled to the ground, but they were past before she knew what happened. Yes, poor little devils, the lot of them.

She lingered, leaning on the rail, studying her reflection. She touched her lips, remembering the reassurance of Sammy's presence, the look in his eyes, the feeling in her heart. She felt such a longing, a longing that was turning minute by minute into a great loneliness. She remembered his grin as he perched on one knee, heard his whisper, 'Me knee's killing me.' If he had meant it, what would she have said? She felt herself relax. If he had meant it, somehow her world would have opened out into something different, something she had never even imagined. If he'd meant it, that was, but he hadn't, or not to begin with, but his eyes had said...

'Miss, miss?' It was Melanie. 'I need to do a wee. I told you.'

When Melanie came out of the toilet she held her dripping knickers in one hand. 'I'm sorry, miss. I was too late.'

It was one of those days. Again the sink was deployed for washing before Phyllie hurried along to the guard's van. He looked from the pile of cases to her. 'I've no idea which is hers,' he said.

She took Melanie's hand and they returned to their compartment, where she said, 'I'll be back to deal with the question of the dog soon, Jake.'

'Francois,' Jake said.

She rooted around in her bag. 'Who is?'

'*Le chien*,' he said. The smaller children were looking from one to the other, giggling.

Jake looked at them and nodded. They said in unison, '*Le chien est magnifique.*'

'I decided that he hasn't got a family so he should have a name to feel less alone,' Jake explained.

She laughed and said, 'My word, I think you'll have to wear a hat that says "teacher" soon, my lad. Now, everyone, don't get too attached. We'll have to find someone to take care of Francois. You might be lucky, Jake, and go to the same home. We'll have to wait and see.' She watched the boy's expression change from despair to relief.

'Can I say he's mine, for now, miss?'

'Why not? I'm going to go and find Dan. You must be missing him?' The other children were stroking Francois now. He sank to the floor, his tongue lolling. There was a fine layer of sand on the compartment floor. Dunkirk. Poor everyone who had been there. She pulled the dog's ears gently. 'You're safe, lad,' she whispered. 'For now at least.'

She found a cotton headscarf in her bag, and a safety pin. She also tucked the tallit beneath the clipboard, her notebook and the kitchen sink, sneaking a look at Jake, who was holding the rope, and counting the strokes that Francois received. 'Not too many, now, Sarah, just three for everyone; I think he has fleas.'

Oh joy, she thought. Yet again she took Melanie by the hand, and trudged out of the compartment, stopping at the next and asking the WVS woman, who introduced herself as Shirley, to swap half the seven-year-olds in Jake's compartment for some of her eleven-year-olds, including Dan, Jake's best friend.

Phyllie peered into Ron's compartment as she passed. The smell was unable to compete with fresh air from the window. She spoke to the WVS lady in the next-but-one compartment, and passed the guard, who muttered, 'On patrol, I am, miss. Not having that sort of Nazi nonsense, I'm not. He's been to the lav, but that's all.'

She touched his arm. 'You can stand down now. We have the WVS babysitting.'

He laughed. 'Even better, lass. Wouldn't like to cross them on a dark night, or in the daylight, come to that.'

In the toilet she and Melanie giggled together about wearing a nappy, and as she finally led Melanie back to the compartment, she checked her watch. A mere hour had passed. Just let her mother tell her she was running away right now and she'd have a proper answer ready. Indeed she would.

Jake and Dan sat with Francois at their feet. The others were talking quietly, and Phyllie had strolled along the corridor again. Jake had seen circles under her arms, now she'd taken off her jacket. She was sweating but didn't smell. His dad did, when he came back from the submarine. It was a smell of diesel and sweat and lots of other things. His dad said they couldn't wash on the submarine, but that he always had a bath before he came home.

He was glad Sammy was going to marry Phyllie. His mother would be pleased. He stopped. He didn't like to think of her. He'd heard them talking before she went. His dad had said, in Polish, 'No, stay with us, we're happy and safe here. You should think of our family, our boy.'

His mother had cried as she said, 'But they're my parents. Have you forgotten that in Berlin, they cut off my cousin's beard before the war, making him wipe the pavement with it? These Nazis will not stop. They and the communists will take Poland. Don't think for a minute I don't love you, and Jakub. You are my world.' She said she would be back, so she would be. But it was still best not to think about it.

Dan said, 'I'm hungry'

Jake replied. 'I've got Marmite sandwiches, what about you?'

Dan had Marmite and tomato. They opened their Oxo tins, undid the greaseproof paper and swapped their sandwiches, half and half. Francois sat up, sniffing the air.

'You can have one, Francois,' Jake said. 'It's very salty but it'll be all right if I pour some water from my flask into the tin so you can have a slurp.'

He eyed Phyllie's basket, knowing the tallit was there. Melanie looked at him. 'I've got egg in my

41

sandwiches; my auntie queued,' she said. 'Francois can have one, instead of Marmite.'

Jake tapped the lid of his Oxo tin. 'Thank you, I think Francois would like that. So you can have two of my Marmite to make up for it.'

Melanie shook her head. 'You're older than me, with longer legs, and my dad said before he went to the war that legs need to get filled up to the top.'

Phyllie came back and sat next to Dan, taking out a small tin from her basket and passing wet flannels around all the children. 'When we've all wiped our hands, we can begin, and what's all this about legs?'

After they'd explained Phyllie said, 'Tell you what, let's give Francois two of my sandwiches, and you children keep yours. Then we can give him water in one of the empty tins.' So that's what they did.

They had to let Francois out when they came to a station at which they stopped. He did a number two along the embankment, as well as a long number one. Leaning from the window to make sure Phyllie brought him back onto the train, Jake heard Phyllie say to one of the WVS ladies that if she had to deal with anyone else's bottom today, she'd scream.

He told Dan and they laughed, but then, when the train started moving again, and the wheels clattered, Jake's eyes closed. He dreamed of his dad, in his submarine, and when he woke, as the train's brakes screeched to a stop in a station hours later, he thought of the poster of the seaman in the water. He hoped that no one talked and sank his dad and Sammy.

42

Chapter Three

Phyllie counted up her children yet again on the platform of Little Mitherton in Dorset, or so the billeting officer, pristine in her WVS uniform, had called it in a posh voice as she welcomed them. Shirley, the WVS helper, murmured to Phyllie, 'All the signposts have just been removed just in case the Nazis arrive. Disturbing, one feels.' With that, she clambered back on the train, wishing Phyllie well.

Phyllie ticked the last name, tucked away her clipboard, picked up her case, and waited for Mr Stevens, with his crocodile of children and their suitcases, to leave first. It was seven o'clock in the evening and still daylight. Mr Stevens said as he passed her, 'I would pay a great deal for a gin, wouldn't you, Miss Saunders?' He did not wait for her reply, but marched on briskly, calling, 'Left, right, like soldiers, please, but without the language.'

Phyllie was so surprised that she laughed aloud. 'Come along then, children,' she called to her charges, 'I know you're tired but the lady said we'd have sandwiches, cake and barley water at the village hall.'

They followed in the footsteps of the billeting officer as she led them out through the exit and onto the narrow lane that led to the village. The children wore their mackintoshes rather than carry them. Melanie walked at Phyllie's side, and Jake the other, Francois at his heels. The smell of urine was high. She'd have to wash Melanie again and perhaps her dress. Had some splashed on that when she had her accident? What she didn't want was for the child to be the last to be chosen because of it. She'd heard that that sort of thing had happened during the September 1939 evacuation.

They passed hay fields in which men still worked. Somewhere sheep were bleating and the children hesitated, scuffling their feet, dropping their cases, looking back at her. Jonny shouted, 'What's that noise, miss?'

She explained.

Ron started to yell, 'We need mint–'

Ernie elbowed him. 'Put a sock in it.'

As the clouds gathered and the light faded Francois barked as bats flew across the track and the children screamed.

Ron sniggered, 'It's all right; they're after the Yid.'

'Silence,' roared Mr Stevens from the head of the column. He stopped and turned to face the children. 'Any more of that and you'll be up here with me, Ronald Cummins, so no one needs to think they will copy such nonsensical rubbish.' He marched off again.

'Come along, we need to keep up with Mr Stevens,' Phyllie insisted. They continued, their gas masks banging against their sides. Melanie was amongst the many who dragged their cases in the dust, for that's what the lane was, an earthen track. Silently, Jake took Melanie's case from her, managing Francois' lead and his own case, and

44

Phyllie gave her a piggy-back. Marjorie was crying, and now Dan took her case, while Phyllie carried Marjorie, on her hip, feeling like a camel and as though she would stumble full length at any moment. All along the crocodile the strong were helping the weak and she straightened her back, touched by the goodness of them all.

At that moment she heard a man's voice booming, 'Stand to the side, for pity's sake, and let m'cart through.' It was only then that she heard horses' hooves, and the grinding of wheels coming up behind them. At the head of the column, Mr Stevens swung round, the billeting officer too. The cart came alongside Phyllie, and the billeting officer barked, gesturing towards the verge, 'Yes, yes, into the side, everyone. Come along now. We don't want to lose any of you under the wheels. Mind the nettles. About time too, Joe Bartlett."

Marjorie slid from Phyllie's hip and scuttled for the verge. 'You can fall under lots of different wheels in a war, can't you, miss? Do cart wheels make jam of us too, and are there hobgoblins?'

'No one is going to make jam of anyone, and I've already said that there are no hobgoblins. Come along, quickly now.' Melanie, Jake and Dan headed for the verge, lugging the cases behind them. Soon they were all hard up against a beech hedge. Some yelped.

'It's bleedin stinging nettles,' Ron yelled.

Quite, Phyllie thought as they stung her through her stockings, which were laddered by now. She called, 'We'll find some dock leaves. Do not step into the roadway, no matter how much you are stung, until the cart has passed.'

She watched the cart trundle along, heard the billeting officer as she stood in the road waving the cart to a halt. 'You should have been here ages ago, Joe Bartlett.'

The cart creaked to a stop in front of her. 'You can keep your gob tight shut, an' all, missis, just cos you've got a bleedin' uniform. I've hay to get in and I don't need to be taking me cart to gather up a load of perishing kids, just you think on that.'

Jake looked at Dan, and then at Phyllie. They all grinned. Dan whispered, 'That's her told.'

Mr Stevens called, 'All the seven-year-olds, bring your cases to the cart. There'll be a bit of room for the kind gentleman to take the tired ones.'

Phyllie shooed Class B past those who had now moved back onto the track. The cases were heaved on board by Mr Stevens, while Joe Bartlett remained seated, lighting a limp cigarette he had taken from behind his ear. The horse eased itself from foot to foot, swishing his tail. Marjorie said from the cart, 'I don't want you up here, Melanie Adams, you smell horrid.'

'Jake can help me up, and he smells too,' Melanie said. 'But it's because Francois is French and doesn't understand manners. I expect Ron smells worse.' Jake's sigh was loud as he stood next to Phyllie. She realised Melanie was correct. There was a smell coming off Jake, or was it her own jacket from the piggy-back?

Ron called, 'Sweet as violets, I am.'

Only a few spaces remained, so the smallest put their cases onto the cart, and the column continued to lug their own. The billeting officer waved them ever onwards, coughing through Joe

46

Bartlett's dust. Phyllie felt he enjoyed every tiny particle he threw up.

Fifteen minutes later they came to the first cottages, mostly thatched, with women and elderly couples waving from their gates. Children emerged from the gardens to run alongside the column, yelling, 'It's the vacees.' The villagers came to take the children's cases, and chattered as they headed for a large hall in front of which stood a war memorial.

So many names, and no doubt, more to come, Phyllie thought. But, please, not Sammy. For a moment she smelled the diesel, and felt his arms.

The billeting officer called from the entrance to the hall, 'Well done, everyone. Now, the Women's Institute has prepared a delicious tea, though we were expecting you much earlier, so the sandwiches are no doubt dry and curly. I dare say you'll remember Mr Manners and smile nicely, though. After refreshment, you will meet your new foster parents. These are the people who will take care of you until your parents collect you, which might take some while, no use pretending it won't.'

A woman next to Phyllie who was carrying two cases muttered to her friend, 'Oh, let's just get everyone in a state, shall we? Curly sandwiches and reminders of absent parents, I ask you. Our Miss Featherstone will have covered the sandwiches with greaseproof paper, you mark my words. The children will just have to take it day by day, so don't let's remind them it could be years. High time Hilary de Bere took her smart uniform off to her big house in Swanwick village, and let us get on with it. Thank the Lord she is off to Amer-

47

ica any day now to sit out things there.'

The billeting officer waved them through the door into a hall bedecked with bunting. Phyllie saw trestle tables set up, loaded with plates covered, indeed, in greaseproof. At the end of the hall was a stage. It was here that the cases were taken.

A tall elderly woman in brogues and a tweed suit stood in the centre of the room, holding a clipboard. She was flanked by others who wore aprons and headscarves tied as turbans, as well as the broadest smiles. At the windows were blackout shutters; low-watt electric lights cast a yellow glow.

The billeting officer, Mrs de Bere, marched towards the women. 'Miss Featherstone, at last we land. I'm orf in a moment for my dinner because Harold will be famished and ratty as hell. I will be back in one hour at which point the foster parents will draw into harbour to collect their charges. I'll take Mr Stevens; he could, I know, do with a gin and some succour.'

She turned on her heel, almost bumping into Ron who was charging towards the food tables. Miss Featherstone dodged to head him off. 'Back you go, young man. I'll let you know when we're ready for the off.' She led him by the ear back to his friends and stood, surveying what Phyllie felt must seem a motley crew. Silence slowly fell amongst the children. The woman oozed authority and Phyllie wished she had just a teaspoon of the stuff herself.

Miss Featherstone smiled at Phyllie, and then the children, and it was as though the sun had come out. Phyllie felt her shoulders drop from around her ears for the first time that day. Miss

48

Featherstone tucked the clipboard under her arm and turned towards the food tables. 'Ladies, covers off please.'

She swung back to the children who were milling, talking, even crying. 'Children, on your left you will see Mrs Speedie, who most certainly is. You will note she has a bowl of warm water. You will wash your hands. Miss Deacon stands next to her with a towel.' There was utter silence in the room. Even Mr Stevens stood stock-still and not once had Miss Featherstone raised her voice.

She continued, 'Miss Deacon will dry said hands. Children, you will then progress towards the food. The first child will go to the left end of the tables, the second to the right, and so on. You will then move towards the middle of the tables. Miss Harvey is the middle point.'

Miss Featherstone gestured to a small plump woman of about sixty who stood at the midway point along the trestle tables. 'As you move along, the kind ladies of Little Mitherton Women's Institute will place upon your plates a selection of sandwiches, which, please note, Mrs de Bere, are moist and possess not a curl.'

Miss Harvey grinned. Mrs de Bere, standing next to Mr Stevens, shuffled her feet, no longer smiling as Miss Featherstone continued: 'We have sausage rolls, courtesy of our Pig Club; lettuce and tomatoes, courtesy of the allotments; cakes and biscuits. When you reach Miss Harvey, you have completed the food run, so return to these tables, here.' She gestured to the tables on which glasses and jugs of barley water waited. 'In one hour you will be whisked off to a nice comfortable bed, by lovely kind people, which I'm sure is quite the thing when you're tired and a mite fretful. You may begin.'

The children, looking dazed, headed for the bowl of water, queuing neatly, even Ron. Phyllie felt as though she should salute. Miss Featherstone came to her. 'You, my dear Miss Saunders, will have a nice cup of tea because we don't rise to gin. Go to our little Mrs Dewar over there, and she will sort it all out.' She pointed towards a door labelled 'Kitchen'.

Phyllie found her voice. 'I think I'd rather stay here, if you don't mind, just to keep an eye on things.'

'Why should I mind? I applaud you. I see that your headmaster has retired from the fray, heading for more salubrious fare. Higher ranks are so often a complete pain in the arse, are they not? The good thing, however, is that for at least an hour they will not be here, meddling. I include myself in with meddlers, of course, being the headmistress with whom you will be working. No doubt you will find me a similar pain in the arse.'

With that she swept away, conferring with Miss Harvey, gesticulating with a sweeping gesture that took in the hall. It was then she spotted Francois.

Oh Lord, thought Phyllie as the headmistress headed in her direction again, brogues clipping the wooden floor, and brown lisle stockings wrinkled at the ankles.

'Dogs are not permitted.'

Phyllie shook her head. 'I'm sorry, Miss Featherstone, this one is. He's survived Dunkirk. Jake will take him for a walk, but I insist that he is permitted to remain with us, just until we can sort out something else. He has earned it, and so have we. It has been a trying journey and I'm not in the mood for argument.'

She had to look up to meet Miss Featherstone's eyes. Good heavens, the woman must be nearly six foot tall. Jake was standing nearby, flanked by Dan and Melanie, the rope wound round his hand, his face determined. Phyllie could almost see his heels digging into the floor.

Miss Featherstone looked long and hard into Phyllie's eyes, then nodded, turning away, saying over her shoulder, 'I see. I did wonder about a rather ghastly pong. I presume it's the dog? Well, young man' – she bent to speak to Jake – 'off you go then, take him for walkies. I dare say Miss Harvey will save a few morsels for you and your friends, and perhaps even for the dog.'

Melanie was with Jake. She had removed her mackintosh and hung it on the back of a chair, but now she reached for it again, as though to follow him and Dan, but Phyllie grabbed her, saying, 'Thank you, Miss Featherstone. Melanie, to the bathroom, just for a moment.'

In the village hall bathroom, which comprised one toilet for the use of everyone and one sink, she sniffed around the child. There was barely any smell, so she guessed it must be the dog. She washed her nonetheless and scooted her out, to have some tea, dragging her own jacket off. No, there wasn't much smell if any.

Within an hour the villagers were arriving and Phyllie was amazed to see Ron gliding from one family to another, talking and smiling – it was a

51

side of him she had not seen before. Soon, the billeting officer was back with Mr Stevens in tow, weaving his way through the crowd of adults and children towards her. 'I'm off now, back to the station, Miss Saunders, or shall I say, Phyllie?'

Phyllie, who could smell the gin on his breath, stared. 'Off? Where to?'

'It seems I'm being sent on to Somerset where our other classes are installed. Don't worry, Phyllie, you have Miss Featherstone as your superior and she is clearly most able, although a touch scary. I think she'll keep even Ron in order. I am sorry to go. I feel I would have enjoyed this village, and working with you. You are a good teacher, never forget that.'

For a moment he looked exhausted, but also sad. He turned and left, but then hurried back, leaning close and speaking quietly. 'My dear, just watch that Ron Cummins. Far from doing daring deeds in the Middle East, as the boy believes, his father is actually doing time for grievous bodily harm to a Jewish socialist who had the temerity to heckle at one of those awful Mosley blackshirt meetings. I feel concern for Jakub Kaplan because the Cummins boy has certain inherited beliefs. Do you understand?'

Phyllie nodded. 'Yes, I do.'

Mr Stevens was checking his watch, and turned. 'Good luck,' he called.

Thanks a bunch, she thought, but didn't say.

By nine thirty most of the children had gone with their foster families. The cases had been cleared from the stage, all but Melanie's and Jake's. Miss Featherstone was deep in conversa-

52

tion with an elderly couple who were preparing to leave with one of the boys. Finally they shook their heads and left.

Miss Featherstone came to Phyllie, taking her to one side as Jake and Melanie sat on chairs, swinging their legs, their heads sunk in weariness, seeming so small in this large hall. 'A young man – Ron someone – has been letting it be known that these two are inveterate bed wetters and the boy is a Jew with strange eating habits, which is clearly untrue, as he has enjoyed several sausage rolls. What's more, the dog goes where he goes, apparently, which again is untrue, as I know you intend to sort something out. The thing is, our foster parents didn't know. I apologise, I wasn't on top of the situation.'

Phyllie frowned. She should have suspected something was wrong when she saw Ron circulating. How stupid she was, because it was she who should have been on top of it all.

'I've lived next door to Jake for a few years; he'll eat anything and he's not a bed wetter, neither, as far as I know, is Melanie. What on earth is the matter with these people? What is it doing to these two to be left, unwanted?' Around them the ladies of the WI were clearing up the debris. Francois had done very well out of the bits dropped on the floor.

Miss Featherstone drew herself up to her great height. '*These people,* as you call them, are on the whole kindly folk, opening their homes to strangers.'

'As long as they're no trouble,' Phyllie snapped.

Miss Featherstone shook her head slightly, and

a faint smile appeared. 'Perhaps you're right, but they're also concerned at their ability to cope with someone "different". It's not religious, I'm sure. We've never had any of that nonsense here in Little Mitherton. It's just one problem too many when rationing has hit, when bombers or jack-boots are expected, and they have been asked to take in children for what could be years. I will be talking to everyone at the next WI meeting, never fear.'

Miss Harvey approached, a tea towel in her hand that she flapped towards the two children. 'This is insufferable, the poor wee mites, and not like our villagers. But do you notice, Audrey, there's a wee bit of a tiddle smell around them? It's sort of stale and not like a child's.'

Audrey Featherstone drew closer to the children, crossed her arms and returned to Miss Harvey and Phyllie. 'As always, dear Catherine, you are the master of understatement. It's not a wee anything. It's a pong and that dog needs a bath.'

'Well, I'm taking that poor wee girl home. Miss Deacon has already taken Dan, but neither of us can take two, or a dog.' Catherine Harvey tapped Audrey Featherstone on the arm. 'But that is not a problem because I can see you're already thinking about how you can clear the boxroom for the lad.'

Phyllie had been listening carefully and now she left them and approached the children. Melanie and Jake's mackintoshes hung over the back of their chairs, and around and about was the heavy urine smell. She sniffed, honing in. She felt in the pocket of Jake's mackintosh and drew out a damp crumpled wad of stinking newspaper. She could see that it was *The Times,* which she had given Ron and his cohorts to clean the carriage. It had soaked the inside of Jake's pocket. She found the same in Melanie's.

How could any child behave with such cruelty to others? she wondered. Well, if you had a father like Ron's, she supposed, and a mother who cared not one jot, how else would you be?

Melanie and Jake had turned in their chairs and were looking at her, and the newspaper. 'It's that Ron and his gang,' Melanie said, beginning to cry. 'Why, though, Miss Saunders?'

'It's my fault.' Jake almost tipped back the chair as he stepped away from the table, dragging Francois to his feet. 'It's my fault and my dad's fault because Ron knows I'm a bleedin' Yid now, and because Francois peed on him. So I'm going.' He dragged Francois towards the door.

Miss Featherstone and Miss Harvey paled with shock, frozen to immobility. Not Phyllie, though. She tore after Jake, snatching the dog's rope from his hand, and held the hot, sweaty and weeping boy to her. 'You're not going anywhere. You're staying with me, and I never want to hear you call yourself by that disgusting name again. We'll find somewhere together. I don't know where, perhaps a little cottage, anywhere. You and me, Jake, with Francois, do you understand?'

Miss Featherstone came marching up to them then. 'Absolutely no need for dramatics, Miss Saunders. You were to billet with me anyway, and yes, Miss Harvey is quite right, I have been thinking about how to clear the boxroom. So now I will have two billeted with me; and in the morning you will take young Francois to stay at Joe Bartlett's farm, where he can romp with the other dogs, and you may visit him daily, young man. So that's that. Have we a plan?'

Chapter Four

The next morning, Phyllie woke, her head splitting as the light from the early dawn poured through the window. For a moment she couldn't imagine where she was. She eased herself upright. She was at the table, in Miss Featherstone's kitchen in Myrtle Cottage, and had been sleeping with her head on the table. She remembered then that she had been woken in the early hours by Francois who they had settled on a blanket in this large kitchen. He had clearly disapproved and whined, endlessly. She had wrapped a blanket around her shoulders, lifted the bedroom blackout blind just five inches so she could see her way to her door in the moonlight and joined him downstairs, concerned that he would wake Miss Featherstone.

She looked for him now, and there he was, curled up by the old leather sofa that stood against the wall, at right angles to the Aga. There too, stretched out on the sofa, was Jake, sound asleep, his arm hanging down to touch Francois. The door into the hall opened and Miss Featherstone stood in her tartan wool dressing gown, which looked remarkably like Phyllie's father's, viewing them all. Phyllie hoped she hadn't dribbled onto the oilcloth that covered the table, and surreptitiously wiped it, and her chin.

'What a sorry little group you are.' The voice was grumpy but the smile warm. 'Well, get dressed, and I'll sort out some breakfast. Joe Bartlett will have been up for hours, getting in the cows for milking, so you can nip off there with Francois. Then, Miss Saunders, you can borrow Maeve, my bicycle, to check on your charges and make sure that all is well. I've been thinking of young Ron. I wasn't paying attention and I see that the Andertons have taken him on. You might want to cast your eye closely over the situation, paying heed to their two ghastly boys. Eddie, in particular, is a ne'er-do-well with a gang. His father's in prison.'

Phyllie's heart sank, but Miss Featherstone said no more, just nodded towards the folder on the table that contained Miss Harvey's notes on who had gone where.

Phyllie and Jake walked through the village with Francois. It was only six o'clock and few others were about. Phyllie had memorised Miss Featherstone's directions. They turned left just beyond the Church of St James's and kept going for half a mile along a track heavily rutted by carts and tractors. They carried milk bottles that needed to be left with Joe Bartlett for sterilisation, and which would be exchanged for two fresh pints.

They passed cow parsley growing in the verges and honeysuckle in the hedgerows. Cobwebs shone in the early sun. Larks flew overhead and the sky was a pale blue. Through a gate they saw a field with cut hay still lying in rows. Work would begin later today, Miss Featherstone had said, after Joe Bartlett and his son Andy had cut down pitchforks donated by the villagers. The vicar, Jack Thompson, had decided it would help to integrate evacuees and village children if they all assisted with the haymaking. 'What's more, it'll give us a chance to keep an eye on our Ron and have a quiet chat,' Miss Featherstone had murmured for Phyllie's ears only.

As they walked, Phyllie pondered the idea of Miss Featherstone having any such thing as a quiet chat. Somehow her voice had an extraordinary carrying quality.

The lane, however, *was* quiet. The whole world was quiet in Dorset, compared to the hum and clatter of London, but was it more peaceful? She ground her teeth at the thought of Ron, and the meanness of the villagers. Was Miss Featherstone right, though? Perhaps it was just uncertainty on their part? Beside her, Jake was talking to Francois. Soon the lane opened into a farmyard and Phyllie saw a large stone house covered in roses.

To the left was a long low building from which came the sound of cows mooing, and on from that an old barn with great holes in its corrugated-iron roof. To the right stood a stable block, with buckets at the entrance, a bridle hanging on an upright, and a new barn nearest the house. Geese rushed across the straw-and-muck-strewn cobbles of the yard, their wings back, squawking at the visitors. Francois bared his teeth and growled, straining at the leash. Phyllie reached down and helped Jake to restrain him. A few chickens and a couple of ducks were pecking at the ground near the stable.

Two sheepdogs rose from the kennels outside the front door and slouched towards them. Behind her some of the WI ladies she'd met the night before cycled into the yard, towing carts in which were large preserving pans. They rang their bicycle bells and Phyllie pulled Jake to the side, into the lee of the long low building from which came the lowing of cows, and the clank of pails. Ah, the milking parlour.

Together they watched the chaos as the geese ran at the women, who fearlessly kicked out with their feet, ringing their bells and laughing, before parking outside one end of the farmhouse. They heaved two pans each from the carts, which clanged together. Miss Deacon and Mrs Speedie waved at Phyllie and then disappeared through a doorway. Had she really thought it was quiet? It was a madhouse.

At that moment Joe Bartlett stepped out of the entrance to the milking parlour, wiping his hands on a towel. 'That be the dog, then? Miss F said you'd be coming when I popped round last night. Partial to a few rabbits, and really partial to pheasant, she be.'

A blond young man, about Sammy's age, came out of the front door of the house. He was pale, with his arm in a sling, and a blood-stained dressing on the end of his arm where a wrist and hand should be. He limped across the yard towards them, kicking away the geese. 'I told you we don't damn well need another dog, Dad,' he yelled. 'He'll never settle, he's not a farm dog. It's best to shoot the bugger. It'll be kinder in the long run. He'll chase the sheep; you know he damn well will.' Under his good arm he carried a shotgun.

The women were back at their carts, unloading more pans. Mrs Speedie, called, 'Don't be such a grouch, Andy. Miss F's been filling us in, and the boy's been bothered enough. We all feel badly.'

The young man looked from Phyllie to the door through which the women were disappearing. 'And why do we have to have the bloody WI Preservation Centre setting up in the big kitchen?'

Joe walked to meet him, taking the cigarette from behind his ear and fiddling with it. 'Because we never use the bugger, Andy lad, and the ladies need it for the war effort, which is important, as you well bloody know. They use the odds and sods of fruit that'd only go to waste. Work their fingers to the bone they do, what with that, the salvage they collect, the kids they look after, the vegetables they grow, so less of your lip. We have a good old kitchen in the snug, which your ma was more'n happy with.'

The two men faced up to one another. Next to Phyllie, Jake stirred and called, 'I won't leave him here. You'll kill him, and he's had enough of that. He was at Dunkirk, brought back by a soldier who wouldn't leave him. He should be safe, that's what he should be, like you are now, Mr Andy. He shouldn't be listening to all this shouting. Here, look at him. He doesn't understand English. He's French. You're loud and mean and he can tell that. I'm taking him away, back to London, anywhere.' Francois was cowering against the wall and Jake was down by his side, tears threatening.

Andy Bartlett glared at his father, at Jake and finally at Phyllie, before turning on his heel and limping back across the yard, kicking at a goose. He slammed back into the house.

'Pay him no mind,' Joe called to Phyllie and Jake. 'He's in a bit of a do. Now, lad, my Mollie'll take care of him. Born mother she is, ain't ya, girl?' The sheepdog sat at his feet, looking up. 'It'll be best for the dog, being with his own kind, and my boy will calm. He's not taken things well.'

Phyllie leaned over Jake, saying softly, 'We'd better give it a try. Miss Featherstone really thinks it's better for him.'

'But why?' shouted Jake, his arms around Francois' neck.

Joe was with them now. 'Ah well, dogs like to be with dogs, it's a pack thing. What's more, be painful for her to have him, y'see, tiddlin. Looks a tough old nut, our Miss F, but she lost her Sandy a coupla months ago. Nice little dog she were and Miss F said she'd not ever let herself feel like that again. Give us the rope, lad.'

Jake looked at Phyllie, his large dark eyes full of despair. He seemed too vulnerable for all that was happening, and for all that had happened over the past few years. Her mind raced, but what else could they do? She straightened, facing the old farmer. 'If you let that boy of yours hurt the dog I will hunt you both down.'

She could hear Miss Featherstone's voice saying, Enough of the dramatics, but she damn well would. Joe took out a match, scratched it on the wall behind Phyllie, and lit his cigarette, speaking through the smoke. 'Happen you will, lass.' He took the rope. Francois went to him. Jake rose and clung to Phyllie's hand.

Together they walked back, neither speaking.

Phyllie cycled around Little Mitherton, Great Mitherton and Forton, then Swanwick where she saw Mrs de Bere's mansion, and the convoy of taxis that were already taking her family to safety. She would not allow herself to replicate her mother, and sniff in disdain. All morning she checked on her charges, ironing out problems with the foster parents, which often meant just foster mother as the father was away in the forces.

In Great Mitherton she braked outside Ron's billet. The Andertons' devastation of a front garden was not reassuring, with its rusty bikes and toys, and a dog chained to the corner of the house. On her approach the dog strained at the leash, barking and growling. She surely didn't need to knock, as Mrs Anderton must have been forewarned unless she was deaf, which she wasn't because the door swung open. A middle-aged woman stood there, in a summer dress with a low neckline and too much make-up, or perhaps Phyllie *was* becoming like her mother. She was invited into the council house. There was lino on the hall floor, but it was ripped and dangerous. Mrs Anderton said, 'Yon lad's in there with my two boys. They get on right well.'

The three boys were lounging on the settee. One, Bryan, who was bigger than Ron who was tall for his age, looked at her. 'You're the one with the Yid for a neighbour, then?'

She frowned and said, 'We don't use that term, ever.'

He said, 'Maybe Great Mitherton does.' She made a mental note to move Ron the moment she could find another billet, or was this attitude typical, in spite of Miss Featherstone's fine words? The other, Anderton boy, Eddie, was thirteen and at school in Great Mitherton, while Bryan was eleven, and at Little Mitherton. It had been deemed best to separate them, according to the notes. Eddie ran a gang, but this had *not* been noted. Yes, Ron must be moved.

That afternoon Miss Featherstone and the young vicar, Jack Thompson, gathered up the evacuees and the village children. Phyllie hiked with them to the hay field, singing 'This Old Man'. All afternoon they turned the hay with the cut-down pitchforks, the evacuees being shown how by the village children, and Miss Featherstone and Phyllie waited to see what happened between Jake and the Anderton crew. After an hour or so Bryan Anderton and Ron rested on their pitchforks, and as Jake came alongside they turned the hay, but flipped it at him as well. Bryan laughed, 'Grow horns, do you, like the other Yids, like Ron's dad says?'

Phyllie darted towards them, as Dan moved to stand alongside Jake, but the Reverend Jack Thompson moved even quicker and caught both boys by the ears. 'I was a boxer before I was a parson. You are eleven years old, with mouths and minds like guttersnipes. It stops here, do you understand? Ron, you will be living elsewhere from now on. I know just the family. You, Bryan, will go back to your mother with Eddie, and Miss

Featherstone will talk to you, very soon.'

Eddie flung down his pitchfork and stalked off, his hands deep in his pockets, kicking at the row of hay as he went. Phyllie could cheerfully have put him over her knee, if he hadn't been too big.

As the vicar marched the two younger boys through the gate, they passed Andy Bartlett arriving with the horse and haycart. He showed no interest in the lads, but why would he, Phyllie thought, his face creasing in pain as he jolted in and out of ruts, heading for the southern side? It was here that the hay had been turned and dried sufficiently, and where the carting had begun yesterday, according to Joe, who waited with two of the farmhands.

The children continued to turn the hay under the leadership of Phyllie and Miss F who took over Ron and Bryan's shortened pitchforks. Phyllie was impressed that even with her great height, Miss Featherstone never paused, though her back must feel like breaking, even more than hers did. After an hour, the children stopped for water, and Andy Bartlett passed with a full load, heading out of the field. He called down to Phyllie, 'Bit of a lightweight, your lad. Couldn't sort that bit of trouble himself, eh?'

Miss Featherstone caught Phyllie's arm, but she shrugged her off and ran after him, keeping pace with the cart, and calling up, 'How dare you? No one should have to put up with bigoted rubbish. You didn't even hear what was said; that he was asked if he had horns, because he's a Jew. His mother's lost in Poland, his father's in a submarine. Proud of yourself, are you?'

Andy shrugged. 'You know nothing about any-thing. Now get out of the way of the cart or you'll end up–' The cart slipped into and out of a large rut. The man paled; sweat broke on his face. Phyllie saw his bandage was dripping blood. 'Oh, never mind,' he finished.

She marched back, ignoring Miss Featherstone's raised eyebrows, not wanting to hear about un-necessary dramatics, or any such thing. Even though someone was in such pain it didn't mean they had to be so foul. She worked on alongside the children, moving from one group to another, wanting to do nothing more than lie in a cool dark room. She pretended, though, that it was the best fun she'd had in years.

At last it was time for tea at the village hall and there were bowls for hand washes, and towels, with Mrs Speedie, Miss Deacon and Miss Harvey in attendance.

'Do you ever stop?' Phyllie asked. 'You must have come straight from the jam making.'

'It's the end of *our* jam shift, and the start of this one. Miss F, our WI president, has things worked out to a T.' They grimaced and then laughed.

At six o'clock, the children were collected and taken home. Phyllie and Jake stayed, to help clear up. Melanie stayed too with Miss Harvey, and Dan, with Miss Deacon. The children dragged the chairs and benches to the side, and then pulled a face when they were handed tea towels. Melanie now asked Jake if he really would grow horns, and he shrugged and said he didn't under-stand what Bryan was talking about, not really, but what he wanted to know was how Francois was getting on.

Miss Featherstone called across from the cupboard in which she was stacking plates. 'Don't
you worry, he'll be fine. Mr Joe will keep an eye
on things.'

'How can he?' Jake countered. 'He's doing things
in the hayfield or somewhere else, while Mr Andy
is driving the cart back to the farm. How do we
know what he's doing when he's at the farm?'

Phyllie waited for the answer, wanting to know
it herself. Miss Featherstone tufted. 'Regular
little worry guts, you are, lad. My WI ladies have
been there, on shift, all day, and this continues
into the evening. They're better than guard dogs,
you mark my words. Besides, young Mr Andy has
a good heart. It's pain that does it, pain and... Oh
well, never mind, we must hurry up.'

They arrived back at Myrtle Cottage at nine,
exhausted and covered in hay dust and grass,
their hands blistered, their faces burned. All
Phyllie and Jake wanted was to crash into bed.
Jake asked for a glass of water to take up with
him. Miss Featherstone nodded, 'Of course.'

Phyllie sat at the kitchen table, examining her
hands, while Jake started to open the corner
cupboard door. 'Not that one,' Miss Featherstone
shouted, rushing across and slamming the door
shut. Not before, however, Phyllie saw bags and
bags of sugar neatly stacked.

Miss Featherstone was still shouting, 'That's
nothing to do with you, and is not to be spoken of,
do you understand?' They both nodded, startled
and confused. Phyllie stood now, her sore hands
forgotten. Miss Featherstone reached into the next

cupboard and handed two glasses to Jake. He filled both with water from the tap, and gave one to Phyllie, who took it and sat down again. 'Goodnight, Miss Featherstone, and you too, Phyllie. Thank you for having me, Miss Featherstone. I expect Francois is happy, with other dogs and the geese.' His tone was forlorn as he left the room.

Phyllie stared at her glass of water, and then at Miss Featherstone, who was pulling down the blackout blind at the back of the sink. She then busied herself at the sink, her back firmly to the room.

'I think it's time we all turned in. It's been a long day. We will find out in the morning where the vicar has settled Ron,' the headmistress said.

Phyllie stood up again, feeling like a jack-in-the-box. 'You're right, I'm very tired. Thank you, Miss Featherstone, for your kindness.'

She climbed the stairs, and sat on her bed. So much sugar, when it was so scarce. Had her mother been right, was it being given to the WI and was some being pilfered, and by the WI president? After Jake had been in the bathroom, he called goodnight. Phyllie entered the little boxroom and began to pull down the blackout blind while Jake, in his pyjamas, stared out at the night sky. He said, 'The world is a very strange place, isn't it, Phyllie?'

She paused, and let the blind roll back up. She slid her arm around his shoulders. 'Most peculiar, much of the time, Jake, but I suppose we just have to keep going.' While they looked out at the rapidly darkening sky, they both heard a noise, then saw a movement in the garden. Jake whispered, 'Do you think it's a fox? There won't be more prowling round the farm, will there? I don't know if Francois knows what to do with a fox.'

Joe Bartlett stepped out of the shadows at the corner of the house and headed for the back door. Both Phyllie and Jake waited, then Jake whispered, 'Do you think he's come calling? You know, how men do, or that's what Mrs Williams used to say about the lady down the road who had all those men? You know, she'd put that voice on, and squeeze her lips, and say she was no better than she ought to be with all these callers. That lady was young, though. Do old people have callers?'

Phyllie put her finger to her lips. 'Hush.'

They saw now that Joe held three pheasants on a string. Jake whispered, 'D'you reckon they're the black market? You know, the market they talk about in the posters?'

'Certainly not,' Phyllie murmured. 'Pheasants are off ration. Into bed, and I'll tuck you in.'

Jake shrugged. 'I'm not a baby.'

She pulled down the blind again, and smiled. 'I know, but tonight I need someone to tuck in, so be kind.'

Jake grinned and hopped into bed. Phyllie risked a kiss on his forehead. He let her, and as she stood up, he said, 'I hope Francois is all right.'

'I'm sure he is.' She wasn't but what else could she say?

When she got to the door he murmured, 'So, when are you going to marry Sammy, Phyllie?'

She laughed quietly. 'Oh, that was just fun. You know what Sammy's like.'

Jake raised himself up on his elbow. 'Oh, I don't

68

think it was, nor does Melanie, or Dan. We talked about it, and we think Sammy's eyes looked serious, after he'd kissed you. Didn't you notice?'

She said, 'Off to sleep now. I'll leave the door ajar in case you need me in the night.'

He whispered then, 'Pheasants are off ration, but sugar is on it. There was such a lot, and it's a secret cupboard, isn't it? Is that the black market?'

'Certainly not,' Phyllie repeated, 'and we mustn't talk about it to anyone. Now off to sleep.'

Once in her own bed across the landing she thought of the sugar. It must be for jam, but why not come out and say it? Surely Miss Featherstone couldn't be the equivalent of a spiv, not when men were dying to bring the rationed produce across the seas? She ached with tiredness, and a creeping sense of disappointment.

Forcing her mind away from ration books, policemen and cheats, she thought of the hay-making, the children, Francois – his long tongue lolling, his eyes almost smiling. Finally, as she drifted, off, she allowed herself to think of Sammy. Was Jake right: had Sammy meant it? Could she ask him? But how, when she didn't know where he was, or the name of his new submarine so she could trace him through the Navy? But even if she could find him, and she asked him, and he was still just a friend, she ran the risk of losing him entirely, and she couldn't think of a world without Sammy being in her life. She knew her thoughts were just going round and round but here, in bed, she had no work, no children, to stop them. Until sleep finally claimed her.

In the morning she woke feeling stiff and cold, but this time she knew where she was. She was in Miss Featherstone's kitchen again with Francois, who had arrived at the back door in the early hours, having chewed through his tether. She turned, and there was Jake asleep on the sofa with Francois on the floor by him. She stared at them both. It wasn't going to work, here at Miss Featherstone's.

She'd just have to try to find a cottage to rent after all, because this boy needed the dog, and clearly Francois needed him, and that was that. The door creaked open, and Miss Featherstone entered, wearing her dressing gown, carrying a similar tartan blanket over her arm. She looked from Phyllie to Jake, who was still asleep, and came to sit at the head of the table. 'This can't go on,' she whispered.

Phyllie nodded, and she too spoke in a whisper. 'I know, and I understand, so I'll find somewhere. Perhaps in the local town, though I noticed that there's a little cottage near St James's Church that looks empty. Do you think I could rent it? I know the windows are broken, and the garden derelict, but I could patch it up. I can't separate them again, especially with Ron and Bryan...' She ground to a halt. Miss Featherstone was holding up her hand as though Phyllie was a runaway bus.

'My turn, Phyllie. One thing a headmistress, or indeed a WI president, should learn is to know when she's beaten. We will keep Francois. He will sleep in the boxroom on this blanket, but not on the bed.'

There was a noise behind Phyllie. It was Jake running at Miss Featherstone, throwing his arms

70

around her. 'Thank you, from Francois too. She's kind, isn't she, Phyllie, really kind?'

Phyllie grinned. 'Indeed she is, and I think perhaps you're rather good at acting fast asleep.'

Miss Featherstone patted Jake's back, and rested her head on his, just for a moment. 'Now, I think that's quite enough of that, young man. Breakfast and then church.' She stopped. 'Though perhaps you don't go to church, Jake?'

Jake shook his head, easing himself back towards Phyllie. 'No. I don't go to synagogue either, not until my mum is back. I just sort of can't.'

Phyllie put her arm around him. 'Let's go for a walk instead and thank God for the sky above us all.' That sounded rather dramatic. She waited for the reprimand but it didn't come, Miss Featherstone merely nodded, and smiled.

'Indeed. A similar sentiment got me through the last war, too. One has to hang on to something, hasn't one.' It wasn't a question.

Later Phyllie, Jake and Francois walked along the lanes, breathing in the soft air. Jake threw sticks for Francois to bring back, which he did sometimes, but just as often he chewed them to bits. They came to a pond, or was it a lake? It was huge with the right-hand corner fenced off. She saw that the wire was tied to trees, either side, top and bottom. Ducks and moorhens dithered about amongst the reeds. Yellow irises grew all around the edge. They passed a sign. *Mitherton Pond*. Ah, so a pond it was.

They stood and stared into the water. Minnows dodged. Phyllie told Jake how she and Sammy used to catch them with bent pins, in the slow-running stream at the bottom of the allotments. They'd put them in jam jars, to release them at the end of the day, and as she said it she could picture Sammy's face as he peered into the jam jar. The water would run into his rolled-up shirtsleeves, just as it ran into the sleeve of her dress. Now she saw his face, close to hers as he wiped some dirt from her cheek that hot summer of 1932 just before her father died. 'Your mum will fuss,' he'd said, then ripped off his socks and waded in.

'Come in, Phyllie,' he'd called. She hadn't because her mother wouldn't have liked it. Instead, she'd watched as the water swirled around his legs. He'd always loved the water. He could swim like a fish. Oh God. Bring him back. Bring both of them back.

Francois barked, again and again. They swung round, and saw Andy Bartlett walking along the lane, holding the bridles of two shire horses in his one good hand. 'Hold Francois very tightly,' Phyllie said as Andy looked up and saw them.

He glowered and yelled, 'Survived then, the mutt? Dad said he'd come hightailing it back to you so we didn't come looking.'

Jake gripped Francois' rope with two hands. 'You'd have shot him, if he had, I spect. So you just keep away from him, from us. Miss Featherstone said he can stay, so there.' Phyllie was astonished at Jake's bravery, then pleased, because now this appalling young man would see how strong Jake could be.

Andy was alongside them now. He glared at Jake, and said, 'Maybe I should have shot him when I had the chance.'

Well, that was just too much. Phyllie stepped forward. 'You need to watch your tongue, or grow up. You may be in pain, but if it makes you a bully, stay inside because when you're well, you'll be embarrassed at the harm you've done. I know you were injured, and we're grateful to you, and others like–'

'Shut up until you know what you're talking about,' Andy interrupted. He pulled the horses on. Phyllie and Jake set off back to the village, neither speaking because Andy was right, she knew nothing about how it must have been.

Phyllie spent most of the afternoon sitting in the garden knitting khaki socks with Miss Featherstone, Miss Harvey, Mrs Speedie and Miss Deacon. Melanie stayed with the women, but Jake, Dan and Tony, who was staying with Mrs Speedie, headed off to the skittle alley behind the pub. After an hour, as the talk circulated, Phyllie made tea from the mint that Miss Featherstone asked her to pick from the herb bed. As she passed the cupboard with the sugar she opened the door. The sugar had gone.

She returned with a tea tray, on which were homemade biscuits made with honey. Mrs Speedie was speaking of her husband who was a prisoner of war and Miss Deacon told of her eldest nephew who was at Catterick now that he was back from Dunkirk.

Mrs Speedie then said, 'That Andy's not much better, tongue like an axe, but not to be wondered at–'

Miss Featherstone sliced across her friend, mid-sentence, 'The strawberries are what we should be discussing. Up at five tomorrow to pick them from the allotments, if you please.'

The air was thick with tension, momentarily, but then Miss Harvey placed her drained cup onto the garden table and picked up her needles again. 'Such a relief that Joe's kitchen is now officially designated the area's Preservation Centre. We must keep a close eye out for wasps in the jam as the season progresses; I hooked two out of yesterday's batch.'

Mrs Speedie slapped the arm of her chair. 'Wasps, the very idea. You must have a little chat with yesterday's team, as you're the one who's been on the course.'

The afternoon drew on, the shadows lengthened and for this moment of time it was almost as though the war did not exist and all was well with the world. Phyllie sneaked a look at Miss Featherstone. Joe Bartlett's son had said she knew nothing about anything and Mrs Speedie had been shut up very smartly.

Chapter Five

Monday 24 June 1940, Submarine Base in Scotland

Dawn came early this far north in the summer and later, much later, in the winter. Scottish weather was not a million miles different from the conditions in the Norwegian sector, but Sammy didn't want to think of that bastard area. He and Isaac strode along the quay towards their submarine, their small canvas bags slung over their shoulders. Behind them they heard a dock-yard train clanking along rails. A crane loomed over the dry dock. The 1st lieutenant, Lieutenant Roges, who had travelled from Canada when war was declared, strode ahead of them onto the gangway, and then onto the casing. The crew was disappearing down the forward hatch as Isaac said, 'We're not late until we're behind the captain and he's way back.'

Sammy followed Isaac onto the gangway, feeling it spring slightly with each step. Once on the casing he stared up at the sky, and breathed in several times, deep into his lungs. He loved the smell of the salt-laden wind, the slurp of the sea around the boat, the feel of HMS *Vigorous* moving beneath him. It was a moment he would never hurry, not even with the captain, Old Tom, heading down the quay, hot on his heels. Isaac stopped at the hatch, his foot on the ladder. 'Sammy, get down here, enough with the breathing. You'll fill your lungs again, of course you will.' He disappeared into the bowels.

Sammy moved, now, heading along the casement, throwing his small bag before him into the darkness, and sliding through the hatch and down the ladder into the smell and the semi-darkness. Old Tom wasn't ancient – he was twenty-seven, which was on a par with most of the captains and he wasn't a captain either, but a lieutenant. But a year in the Norwegian waters made old men of those in charge of a submarine.

It was an area that cursed the submarines with virtually twenty-four hours of daylight in summer – insufficient darkness in which to surface reasonably safely to recharge the batteries. There was no place to hide in the translucent seas as planes patrolled and gave directions to hunters. Losses were absurdly high. The winters froze the bollocks but gave the gift of darkness.

Add to that, no sleep, just constant stress and danger, and was it any wonder many captains had to be posted ashore, their nerves shot? Old Tom wasn't too far from that, especially since his brother had been shot down and paralysed just before they came in for repairs.

Sammy's eyes grew accustomed to the low electric lighting far more quickly these days, and his ears to the noise of men shouting and rushing along the passage on floor plates. Beneath these, the provisions had been stored and as the patrol continued and the food was eaten, the floor plates would lower. As well as this was the rumble as the engine-room artificer, John Halford, whom everyone called chief, played silly buggers with the engines. The boat smelled like home, so what did that say about his life, for God's sake?

Sammy followed Isaac who was shouldering his way along the narrow passageway, where pipes, wires, dials, cupboards and hammocks holding bread delighted the eye. They swung themselves through hatches, all of which could be locked tight against gushing water, should they be hit at the fore-end, or aft-end, and God help all buggers if they were caught amidships.

They squeezed past others heading in the opposite direction, grinning at the curses hurled at them, and cursing in return. It was a zoo, or the underground at rush hour. 'It Don't Mean a Thing if it Ain't Got That Swing' was playing over the speakers, too bloody loud. 'You need to tell young Davy to keep it down,' Sammy grunted to Isaac. 'You're the radio leading seaman, for God's sake.'

'He's been told. He will be told again. It's Old Tom's favourite, as you know, so it's young Davy's homage, or so he says. I'll speak to him yet again when I make it my business to head to the radio shack. Calm, my friend.' They reached their billets in their mess, which was merely a widening of the passageway.

Sammy started to shove his bag into a cupboard near his excuse for a bunk, which stood three inches off the floor, but there was already a large bag in there, taking up most of the room. He pulled it out, and slung it to the floor, saying, 'I don't care what you say, Isaac, Old Tom doesn't like it so loud. You know that and we need to take care of the bugger.' He shoved his bag in. 'Who the hell put this bloody great trunk in here, anyway? Where did he leave his brains?'

He straightened, and looked around. All there was space for on board was a toothbrush, a book or two, pencil and paper, a few pants, socks, plimsolls and top clothes, all of which stank of diesel, sweat and filth, in spite of being boiled senseless. These were kept for boat use only. In the washroom there was water for teeth and face, or they could do battle with the seawater faucet and end up sticky with salt, and still smelly. Once they'd left dock they'd change into this slop order. Sammy grimaced. 'Can't be seen to let the side down ashore, can we, Isaac? Got to look smart and pretty. Reminds me of Ma Saunders.'

Isaac grinned. 'You'll never do pretty my fine friend.'

Coxswain Peters was swinging himself through the passage hatch and stopped beside Sammy, rubbing his hands together. 'Got a youngster for you, Sammy; he's taking Frank's place. It's his first patrol and green he most certainly is. Hot bunking with you, Sammy, ain't you, boy?' A child in a pristine uniform clambered through the hatch after him.

'For God's sake, he's twelve.' Sammy shook his head at Peters.

Peters grinned. 'Eighteen if he's a day, and done the Asdic training – ain't you, boy? – so he's your responsibility, as leading seaman, Sammy, my lad. Stand behind him on first watch, then you take the second. Be a good lad, now, Adrian. Don't pick your nose, Sammy won't like it.'

Adrian was looking at the bag tossed onto the bunk. 'That's mine.'

'It's too big. You only need a couple of changes. I know Mum'll be cross when that smart little outfit gets creased after you've rammed it into that bag, but that's the way it is. I'll find room somehow, but not again.' Sammy felt his stomach twist. Eighteen was too young. The minute they left harbour they were in danger, and not just from the enemy, but from themselves and their mistakes, and from the sea, and its storms, and... For God's sake, how were they going to keep these little buggers safe?

He moved closer to the coxswain, asking, 'How's Frank doing, then?'

'Getting there. He'll not be sent back to sea, that's for sure.' Peters nodded and moved forward to the bow. All the time men had been easing past, some with bags, some with provisions, and 'It Don't Mean a Thing if it Ain't Got That Swing' was still playing its guts out. Why the hell did Old Tom like Ellington's music so much?

'Frank?' the boy asked Sammy.

'Got ill,' Sammy said, exchanging a look with Isaac who was sitting on the edge of his bunk, the one above Sammy's, his back bent to avoid the one above him, and his legs tucked in to keep clear of the passage. There was no room to turn over in the bunks so they could only be used as perches, even when it was chow time.

Frank had found the last depth charging too much, seven bloody hours of terror, noise, chaos and injuries as they were tossed like a load of rag dolls by the percussion, only to be drenched on top of that by the water bursting through seals. The whole bloody performance had given the chief hours of fun as he and his crew tightened, tightened, tightened throughout the old girl. Old Tom had dived deeper and deeper, trying to escape. The boat had creaked and groaned all the while as the water pressure threatened to squeeze and squash them. Finally, and not for the first time, it had come to a choice between imploding or rising.

Old Tom brought her up, steady, steady, a peg or two, then more, with the charges rocketing about the damned place, and Sammy had watched as the captain checked the dials as though his life depended on it. It did, all their lives did. God bless him, he found a thermal, a layer of water that was a different temperature to the one they were in, a layer that acted as a protective ceiling and bounced away the enemy's Asdic signal so the skimmer – which is what they called the surface ships – couldn't detect them.

He had judged it just right, and stopped the boat, trimmed – or stabilised – it, by using the men, moving them barefoot for silence, from one end to the other until *Vigorous* was balanced and stable. He had waited, and then suddenly engaged the electric engines, moving to the west, silent running with no speaking, no noise, no movement, all the time keeping under the ceiling. It was then that Frank's screaming had started. Coxswain Peters was many things to many men on board, and also a medic. He gave Frank morphine and tied him to the bunk as they headed home for repairs. It left them all wanting a bloody large drink at the first

80

pub they saw.

Sammy hoped to God Frank recovered, as some did, though some didn't. He grinned at Isaac but it was a mask. 'Reckon I prefer Ellington's music to Frank's dulcet tones.'

Isaac's eyes were as sombre as Sammy felt. 'I know I do. Your name again, young man?'

'Smart, Adrian.'

Sammy was stowing Adrian's bag, and when he stood he said, 'Well, Adrian Smart, let's hope you are smart. We share this bunk. When I go on watch you come off, and into my pit.'

Adrian nodded. 'I've done a training patrol. I did hot bunks then, too.'

'Good, then that's one thing we can cross off the list. Watch your back.' A rating passed with a smoked ham on his shoulder, heading for the galley. Ellington's band stopped abruptly. Instead, 'Captain on board' boomed out from the speakers. The music was muted, for just about a minute more before it ceased. Old Tom would be smiling.

'Now the captain's on board, we'll power off, so let's get to where we should be. You're taking first watch but I'll be there, all the time, just to settle you in.'

The Asdic shack was just by the control room, amidships, though it wasn't a shack, it was just an open-fronted cubbyhole. Isaac's radio shack, just along from Sammy's, was similar. Word came that the torpedoes were loaded, the ammunition stowed, and the stores. The second coxswain, Roddy Goad, came round with next-of-kin forms, which had been late reaching the depot ship and had finally caught up with them here. Old Tom was staring at the dials, his face rigid with fury; they should have cast off by now. Sammy filled out his form and grabbed a sheet of paper on which he usually jotted any Asdic notes for the log. On this he scribbled a will, which Adrian and Isaac witnessed without reading it. He shrugged at Isaac's curious look. 'I know I've already done one, but that's cancelled. I need to know she's provided for.'

Roddy Goad rushed all the forms to a sailor who was waiting at the head of the gangway – he would lodge them with the appropriate officer at base. Old Tom followed Goad up to the bridge, taking up position as they left harbour. The conning-tower hatch was open, and the breeze was sweet as the boat manoeuvred out of port. Coxswain Peters was at the helm. 'Half ahead both' was telegraphed and repeated in the motor room.

Sammy stood behind Adrian. Isaac was on his way to deliver signals to the captain, and said quietly as he passed, 'It's the kiss that did it. Does she feel the same?' Around them more orders were given by Old Tom.

Sammy murmured to Adrian, 'Don't forget, lad, once at sea, keep your headphones on, and continuously sweep for the sound of vessels approaching or depth charging, however distant. Remember, *continuously*, got it? Even if we're on the surface. Sometimes you can pick up something the lookouts up top can't. If you pick up a signal, an engine, anything, tell the control room, and hone in on it. Be alert to the captain's questions at all times.' Isaac moved on.

Sammy thought it was easier to issue advice than to answer Isaac. How the hell did he know Phyllie's feelings, when he hadn't even realised his own? It had been like a damn great depth charge going off in his heart and head. How he'd dragged himself away from her he had no idea.

He looked up. He could tell from the rocking that they were out at sea. It was a relief to be here, doing what he did, because he'd be too busy to think. It was a relief that she was there, wherever *there* was, in safety. He didn't want to think about Isaac's question because what if she didn't feel the same? He thought she did, because she had kissed him back, and her eyes... The boat was dipping and rising. They were obviously gutting through a long groundswell. They rolled. The wind was up. Old Tom was back in the control room, his hair wet, his face red from the wind. Lieutenant Walters had taken his place on the bridge, keeping an eye on the lookouts.

Old Tom stood full-square. 'Good few days in Gosport, Sammy?'

'Yes, sir. Did you have a good leave?' He turned. Old Tom was standing at the chart table, next to Sub Lieutenant Gerrard, reading the signals that Isaac had brought him. The captain's hands were shaking and Sammy exchanged a look with Isaac who was on his way back to the shack. Tom Beer was on the edge, too tired, too shot, and grief was in the slump of his shoulders.

'My leave?' He looked up. His hair had gone grey over the last year, and his pallor almost matched his roll-neck sweater. When had he taken off his jacket? Probably while Sammy was nagging Adrian.

'So so. So so.' Old Tom walked across to Adrian. 'Young Adrian, how does it feel to be on your first proper patrol? Beware; it's a zoo here, but a friendly one. Just a few interruptions from time to time, bloody loud ones at that.'

Adrian remained sitting; he slipped back one of his earpieces. 'It feels fine, thank you, sir.'

Old Tom moved back to the chart table, nodding to his number one, Lieutenant Roges, or the Jimmy, as the number one was called. Roges was in control for now and said, 'They're younger and younger, or am I just getting older, sir?'

Old Tom grinned, as a swell rolled and twisted the boat. 'Bit of both. Hey ho. On we go.' Old Tom swayed easily with the motion. 'Keep listening,' he called back to Adrian. 'That's your job, young man. Listen for trouble, listen to our Sammy; he knows exactly what's what, don't you, Sammy?'

Sammy smiled. 'Sometimes, sir.' Again he thought of Phyllie, the touch of her lips, the surprise of it all, and feared he knew a great fat nothing and didn't want to push it, for they could never go back to being friends if it was a damn great no.

As the hours wore on they continued to run on the surface, ploughing through seas whipped up by a north-easterly. Sammy left Adrian to it for the last part of the boy's watch, and Old Tom gave him permission to take some air.

He donned oilskins, and dashed up the ladder and through the hatch to the conning tower, then up again to the bridge. Looking down he saw the waves rolling and surging over the bulging saddle

84

tanks. He always felt fond of the saddles, filled with the air that was keeping them afloat. The four lookouts were leaning their elbows on the rail of the bridge, binoculars to their eyes, sweeping, always sweeping, even when visibility was wretched, like today. They were seeking enemy ships, periscopes, planes, and friendlies too because collisions and friendly fire happened. Old Tom should, however, have left harbour with an idea of who was where, and each submarine was supposed to operate in its own area of grid.

Stoker Stan Brewer was having a smoke, crouched down out of the wind. Lieutenant Walters was keeping an eye on the lookouts as the waves broke over the casing, the conning tower and the bridge. The water ran down all their oilskins, coursing inside their collars and draining out at the bottom. Sammy loved the water but though it was June his hands were numb, his face too, and the elements were wiping out most thoughts of her, of his friend, his love; but only most. Sometimes a huge rolling sea crashed down on the tower, and they hung on, up to their waists in water. The language was ripe, but snatched away by the wind.

Before the watch changed, Sammy slid down the ladder, stripping off at the base of the tower, and drying off in the cacophony and heat of the engine room before joining Adrian at the Asdic desk. 'Off you go, get your head down. Come back on watch in four hours.' The lad was green. He staggered to his feet as the boat rolled and churned. 'Go and see Coxswain Peters,' Sammy added. 'He's got a cure for seasickness. Works a treat. Then get your head down.'

All around the control room the men were grinning at one another at the thought of the coxswain's cure. Sub Lieutenant Gerrard was tapping jazz on the chart table, 1st Lieutenant Roges was scanning the dials. The captain was in his cubbyhole, just off the passageway. He'd be writing up his log.

Sammy watched Adrian go. It would work, it always did, but how the hell a piece of bacon tied onto a piece of string, and swallowed, only for the coxswain to pull it back up, could work, heaven only knew. Yes, you vomited fit to die for half an hour, and then it was over, you were as bright as a bleeding button for the rest of the patrol.

At dawn Sammy was in his bunk, lying flat on his back, listening to the sounds of the boat being battered by the elements, feeling it too, knowing that likely as not his breakfast was going to be tipped into his lap, along with the plate. He slid sideways from the bunk, onto the floor, then traipsed to the heads, taking care to press the pedals in the right order, or it would all come back on him. Then into the washroom to wash hands and face and clean his teeth. At least he didn't have to change from pyjamas to clothes. On board they never changed to night attire – that was a luxury too far.

In the control room Old Tom was talking quietly with the Jimmy and the engine-room chief. Sammy caught that the chief thought one of the propellers was sounding rough.

The chief added, 'Bit bent, I reckon. They said

in refit they'd sorted it but it'll be all right for now. They'll have to get it a hundred per cent when we get back, though.'

'Ready, then, are we?' Old Tom asked.

Sammy saw Roges and the chief nod. It was what he expected and had been waiting for. Now Sammy reckoned they'd dive. Not only would that test the behaviour of the boat after its repairs, it would combine it with an exercise that Isaac had warned him was on the cards, judging from the signals as they were leaving harbour. He hurried to his shack, putting his hand on Adrian's shoulder, keeping him in his seat. 'Don't go off watch yet, this'll be good for you.'

Adrian looked up at him, preoccupied. Good, he was listening hard to the things he should be concentrating on. The movement of the boat was easing, along with the wind. At bloody last. June should be a time of sweet thoughts and gentle seas. He half laughed to himself. Who the hell was he kidding? He could hear Old Tom talking to Gerrard who'd come down from the bridge a second before. They'd be checking the expected position of all friendlies in the vicinity.

'Should be all clear,' Gerrard confirmed.

Within two minutes the alarm klaxon resounded round the boat. Feet pounded, shouts and orders ricocheted. 'Diving, diving.' Walters and the look-outs shot down from the conning tower, the last one slamming the hatch shut, sliding into the control room, ripping off their oilskins, throwing them down, and rushing, dripping and soaked, to their posts.

Sammy heard the engines stop. The main vents

would be opening, the prow should be going down, but it wasn't. The boat seemed glued to the surface. Surely it usually moved quicker than this? Sammy watched Adrian to make sure he kept listening, and then swung back to the control room, and after that, the dials. Old Tom's eyes were on the depth gauge. He ordered the men forward. There was a rush through the control room to make the boat bow heavy. At last *Vigorous* shifted her arse and dived. Sammy checked his watch. It had only been thirty seconds, about right, but it had seemed, an eternity.

Men were working their way back up the incline to their posts, finding handholds on either side. There was no tight terror on their faces, because although only those in the control room actually knew this was an exercise, the rumour would have flashed around by now. Any concern would be centred on the boat's performance.

'Proceed to one hundred and fifty feet,' Old Tom ordered, standing with his hands in his pockets, cap shoved to the back of his head. Everyone was watching the dials and listening for leaks: the telltale hiss, the call that would resound around the boat and culminate in the chief's frantic tightening of seals. Eighty feet. Ninety feet. One hundred feet. Sammy was aware that he was holding his breath. Did he think it would help?

One hundred and ten. One hundred and twenty. Still all right. God damn it. One hundred and thirty. One hundred and forty. One hundred and fifty. At last. The dive ceased. The boat was trimmed. The quiet was a relief after the heavy seas up top, the stability too, as Old Tom looked

88

at Adrian and muttered, 'Anything?'

'No, sir.'

The chief's team worked their way through the boat, checking for leaks; the coxswain was doing what he did; Adrian practised searches. Then Old Tom practised a stop trim, moving the men around, balancing the boat for what seemed like hours. Walters gave the order to surface slowly, nodding at his captain. 'Periscope depth?'

'That's the one.'

Old Tom shot another look at Adrian as they reached seventy feet. 'Anything?'

Adrian's sweat was rolling down his face as he listened. Old Tom called again, his hand up to Walters. Adrian shook his head, 'I don't think so.'

Old Tom shot Sammy a questioning look. The boat was still rising. Adrian looked like a rabbit caught in the headlights. His hands were shaking on the wheel of the hydrophone – shaking but not moving.

Sammy wanted to wrench the headphones from him but what would that do to the boy's confidence? 'Wait one, sir. Give us more time. Come on, Adrian, turn the wheel, now. Scan continuously, like I told you.'

The boat was still rising. Old Tom was standing by the periscope and didn't respond. 'Fifty feet, Captain,' Walters reported.

'Wait one, sir,' Sammy said again.

Adrian was scanning, and now swung round, his mouth working. Sammy snatched at the headphones, they caught on Adrian's neck.

'Thirty-five feet, Captain,' Barry Walters called. The Jimmy was staring at Sammy, Gerrard had swung round at the chart table. Sammy hauled the headphones free. Old Tom was bending his knees, his hands ready. 'Up periscope.' He gripped the handles as the stoker in charge of the hydraulics obeyed. Old Tom thrust his head forward, swinging the periscope around, searching.

Sammy heard propellers, and an engine in the headphones. 'Sir,' he shouted at the same time that Old Tom called, 'Christ,' horror in his voice.

'Dive. Dive. Full ahead, flood Q. Keep fifty feet.' He slapped shut the periscope handles, as Sammy shoved Adrian out of the seat, taking over. He could hear the engines, the thudding, thudding of the propellers; they all bloody could now, because it was almost overhead.

The roar of the engines almost blew Sammy's head away as the skimmer reached them. *Vigorous* was gaining depth, but too late, too slow. The rampaging roar of the engines filled the boat, clear for everyone to hear.

'It's one of ours, the skimmer's one of ours,' Old Tom said, despair in his voice as the ship took the periscopes with a rumbling and crashing. *Vigorous* shuddered, everyone grabbed for something. *How much damage? Was this it?* Adrian skidded to the floor. Sammy held his headphones tight against his ears, freeing his mind of all images, listening instead.

The engines above faded in the control room. 'Sammy?' Old Tom almost whispered.

'Astern, decreasing, sir.' Sammy's voice was measured and steady.

'Barry, go to periscope depth,' Old Tom said, panting as though he'd run a race. It was like a damned yo-yo. Up they went. The periscopes could not be moved. 'Hold it steady at thirty feet,' Walters said. 'The bugger shouldn't have been there.'

Old Tom said, 'Sammy?'

'Astern, still decreasing, sir.'

'Or perhaps we shouldn't have been where we were, or I shouldn't have been, Barry. Patience is a virtue, my old gran used to say. Our information could have been flawed, but now's not the time.'

Old Tom shot a look at Sammy, who said, 'Astern, decreasing.'

Old Tom smiled at him. 'Stay on the headphones for a while, Sammy. Let Seaman Smart catch his breath. Up you get, lad; no bones broken, eh? Pesky little buggers, these headphones, when you're new to the game. No blame. Not for you, anyway.'

Old Tom called, 'Any leaks, any injuries?' The answers came back negative. They stayed near the surface and fired smoke candles to warn of their presence should a friendly still be there, or the enemy, come to that. They were blind without periscopes and Sammy strained every fibre of his being to catch any sound as they continued to surface. Walters did as ordered, and dashed up to the tower with four lookouts, desperately sweeping with binoculars, while Sammy continued with the hydrophone, his palms sweating and slipping on the wheel.

'All clear,' he said repeatedly, knowing that at the moment he was only the backup eyes and ears, but would be far more if they had to dive without periscopes.

Old Tom ordered *Vigorous* off patrol and back to harbour, though they were unable to radio their report for fear of giving away their position to the enemy. Sammy made Adrian stay in the shack for his watch and take the headphones, but he remained alongside, saying, 'You need to get back on the horse when you fall off the bloody thing.'

Though his voice was strong, inside Sammy was shaking fit to burst. Isaac, too; everyone would be, in fact. They had survived, but only just. Adrian would need to hang onto every bit of mental strength to come back from this because he should have heard. What's more, he should have swept continuously, and bloody Samuel Williams should have made sure that he did. Yes, Old Tom should have waited, but they should have been better too.

It was then that Old Tom came to them. 'My responsibility, lads. I should have waited, given you a chance to sweep properly. You warned me, Sammy. Bloody stupid.'

In that moment, Sammy loved Old Tom because he was bestowing on the two ratings the gift of exoneration.

Old Tom seemed fine at first, but he spoke less and less; his shaking grew steadily worse. Roges, Walters and Gerrard watched him closely, as did everyone else in the control room, but they all knew he had lasted longer than most. Bastard, bastard war.

As they neared Scotland they relaxed just a bit, because attack so close to shore was unusual. Isaac radioed their situation. Old Tom now sat at the chart table, immobile, unspeaking. He was shaking so violently that he couldn't stand. Sammy never left the hydrophone, though Adrian took his time off. He must or he'd crack after the debacle, but how could Sammy leave, when the captain he had served for over two years, and whom he thought the world of, was crumbling before his eyes? Isaac had stayed on the radio, but Davy Weale, Isaac's assistant, remained as well. He also wanted to honour guard his captain. Once they were just outside the harbour the Jimmy requested Isaac to radio for medical assistance.

As they came into harbour the word went round, quietly and surreptitiously, but the men had already changed into their uniforms, all of them. Spruce and clean and tidy. They tied up, and Isaac gave the latest radio message to Lieutenants Roges, Walters and Gerrard over by the radio shack, whispering, 'The medics are waiting at the end of the gangway. We just need to get him onto the casement. We need him to march off, sir, under his own steam. We must do that for him. The men are on the casement already, waiting.'

They nodded grimly, and Barry Walters said, 'You think we don't know that, Isaac? But thank you anyway. He just doesn't seem to hear.' He and Roges were twenty-four, and very tired. None of the officers had slept either, as they would not leave their captain alone.

Roges called quietly for the chief to come to the control room. He came, smart in a way that he never usually was, with his hair combed, his face clean and shaved, and his uniform pulled straight. Together the old friends stood by their captain, the chief and Roges, taking his arms, heaving him to his feet. Walters and Gerrard were just behind. Sammy heard the chief say, 'Come on, sir, one last time, for the good of the crew. Up and standing. Then up the ladder, on your own. It will give them heart, just as you have given them heart for two years. How about it, old lad?'

It was then that Sammy slipped across to Isaac. 'Put on bloody Ellington, for God's sake. It might reach him, one last time.'

Davy found the record and handed it to Isaac as though it was the most fragile Limoges. Isaac put it on the turntable, dropped the needle arm and 'It Don't Mean a Thing if it Ain't Got That Swing' burst into life.

The officers swung round, but Old Tom didn't. After a moment he stepped forward, his hand up to prevent any help. He lifted his head, gripped his hands into fists. Swallowing, he said, 'Straighten my jacket, old man.' Roges did so. They could see Old Tom's legs shaking, the muscles in his jaw working. 'Just the bloody ladder, now. Out of my way, if you would be so kind.'

He climbed the ladder painfully slowly, the officers followed, and the crew left in the control room double backed to the aft hatch, and tore up to the casing to join their fellows who were standing to attention as Coxswain Peters piped the captain ashore for the very last time. At the head of the gangway, Lieutenant Tom Beer turned and looked to left and right, smiling at them, his face drawn like an old man's.

As one, the men straightened more than they thought they could and saluted their captain, their officers at their head. Old Tom saluted in return, his shoulders back. He turned, and walked down the gangway as though he was off to a tea party, but oh so slowly, and Sammy admired him more than he had ever admired him before and wouldn't look when he reached the quay and collapsed, like a rag doll, into the arms of the medics with such a howl of anguish that it chilled the blood. He had a child of two, and a lovely wife. He would need them.

On 5 July, as German bombers continued their attack on allied shipping in the Channel, Mrs Frances Saunders answered the phone that had been ringing off the hook at the presbytery. 'Father Francis's housekeeper.' Through the open window of the study she could hear the sound of the docks as ships unloaded, and the chatter of a group of women on their way to find some queue or other to join outside a shop, any shop. Would the bombers come here? Her mouth went dry. 'Mrs Saunders?'

She'd know that voice anywhere. 'It is,' she said. A ship's hooter sounded. One had arrived safely carrying wood just that morning, having run the blockade, or so her son had reported when he came back for a sparse lunch. The RAF had downed several of the Luftwaffe bombers and fighters.

'It's Sammy Williams.'

'Oh.'

'How are you settling in with Frankie? Lots to do, I would think.'

'He's known as Father Francis,' she snapped.

95

There was a pause. 'Sorry about that, I've been a bit … well, busy. I wondered if you'd heard from Phyllie? I'd like to drop her a line. She doesn't know where I am, and I don't know where she is, so it's hard to figure out a way to keep in touch.'

'No. No, I've heard nothing yet. She's obviously busy, and so am I. I'll let you know if you give me your details.'

Sammy said, 'I don't know where I'll be but she could find me through the Service Post Office. Isaac hadn't heard from Jake either or the authorities as to where he was, when I last saw him. He's on a different submarine and on patrol at the moment, and I'm off again any minute, so I won't know if he hears. Sorry, this is … well, muddled.'

'I'm sorry but I can't help, so I'll let you get on.' Frances Saunders replaced the telephone on the receiver, thinking how strange Sammy sounded, as though he was crying, the big baby.

Her son said from the door, 'Who was that, Mother?'

She resumed her dusting of the bookshelves. 'Not someone to concern you; just one of Phyllis's old colleagues she didn't particularly like wanting her address.'

'Well, we ought to write and tell Phyllie, surely. She can then make up her own mind. Did you take this colleague's address? I don't think we should tell outright lies, Mother.'

She rubbed hard at a brass candlestick on the writing bureau. 'Very well, I'll mention it when I reply to her note.' She wouldn't, of course. She picked up the photograph of her husband, Cyril, and flicked the duster over him. She liked him to look pristine, though he never had in life, any more than that Sammy. Yes, he'd phone again, and if she answered, she'd say the same thing again, and in time Phyllis would find a more suitable friend. If the war did nothing else it would put some distance between the two of them.

Mr and Mrs Williams were a nice couple, and she missed them now they'd evacuated, but that son of theirs had the cheek of the devil – always had, and always would. Not the type of person any grown-up daughter of hers should have as a friend, or anything more. Picked up by the police at that Cable Street riot, along with a load of godless communists. How dare they behave so badly to that handsome Mr Mosley, who was always so smart in that black uniform? She slapped the photograph of Cyril down, and shuddered at the very thought.

Chapter Six

Monday 26 August 1940, Little Mitherton

It was Monday, and Phyllie had phoned her mother early that morning, suddenly frightened and homesick for her old life and family, because the war had come too close. She looked around the classroom at the children. Though it was holiday time the children had come in to school for the day. Miss Featherstone thought it the best thing, and Phyllie agreed. She looked at the clock

97

on the back wall of the classroom. It was almost 'going home time' but there was no excitement in the high Victorian classroom, no sighing, no wriggling. There were just fearful glances out of the window, up at the blue sky, and startled jumps if someone dropped even a pencil.

Nor was there any eagerness to rush to the stream when school was over to catch minnows with bent pins, or to dash off in every direction with their friends. Instead, they wanted to stay together. Nothing was as usual; even in her classroom, which was crowded with seven-year-olds, as well as her eleven-year-olds. Elderly Mrs Whitehead, who taught the seven-year-olds, had gone home to Swanwick with a malaise of the spirit, or so said Miss Featherstone, her own grief palpable. Once more Phyllie began to take the two classes through the three times table, because there had been an error the first time.

'Come along, children, concentrate; this is a valuable chance to refresh your memories for when school term really begins. Once three is three, two threes are...'

They all groaned, and looked at one another. Well, that was normal at least.

The children had written compositions for the first hour of the day, then they had painted until lunch break, which was taken in the playground in an effort to show that here, in Little Mitherton, they were safe. The children, though, said that the asphalt was too hot to play on, and asked to return to the classroom. It wasn't too hot. They had all picked up brushes and resumed painting, even the eleven-year-old boys, their

Cowboys and Indians forgotten.

Phyllie strolled around as she listened to them now, breathing in the smell of powder paint, seeing the paintings produced on the back of the wall-paper Miss Deacon had found in her loft. Miss Deacon who would now become WI treasurer, now that Miss Harvey... No, enough of that. The paintings were laid out on the trestle table at the back of the classroom, beneath the clock. Phyllie leaned over to look at Marjorie's view of the village street. There were other paintings of the village; the fields around it, the stream, the ducks on Mitherton Pond, and the sky. There were planes, some dropping what looked like large balls. There were splashes of yellow and red as they hit the ground. There was a little girl in one, lying down with an older lady.

The chanting had stopped. She forced a smile. 'Once more, you stumbled over three times six. Ah, you thought I hadn't noticed, but I did.'

They groaned but it was only a token. They began again.

The clearing up session after painting had been unusually quiet. There had been much washing of hands, faces and arms at the outside toilet and washrooms. There had been no splashing, or throwing of water, not even from Ron, who now lived with Mrs Campion and her two little girls. Bryan had behaved too, though now that he and Ron were members of Eddie's gang, it was prob-ably just a short reprieve. For the most part, though, the gang spent their time at Great Mither-ton, which at least went some way to keeping Ron away from Jake.

She dragged her thoughts back to the present, moving to the front of the class, conducting them. 'Seven threes are...' There would have been an empty seat in Class B. Dear, dear little Melanie Adams, who, with Miss Harvey, had been killed on the evening of Saturday 24 August in London. If only they hadn't gone at that time, on that day, to meet Melanie's mother, who had decided to go to Scotland to live with relatives. Miss Harvey had volunteered to meet her at the Lyons Corner House in Oxford Street. She felt it would make it easier for Mrs Adams, and it could serve as a proper farewell to Melanie. It was reported that all three had been walking along window shopping after their tea when London suffered its first bombing raid. The only saving grace was that, as the bombs rained down, Melanie had died in the company of two women who loved her.

Phyllie gazed out at the children, here in this room. They were all so small, so vulnerable, so dear to her, even bloody Ron. 'Eleven threes are...'

The war, which they watched as the summer progressed, made white vapour trails in the sky. Yes, they knew RAF fighter pilots were punching above their weight, taking on the enemy in air battles that spread miles from the Channel and their airfields. But it hadn't been real, somehow, more like a game.

'The four times now: once four is four... That's right, Tommy. Nice and loud now.' Thomas had sat next to Melanie in class. He had barely spoken since the news had reached them very late on Sunday. Miss Harvey's handbag had been found in the ruins. It contained Miss Featherstone's telephone number.

'Four times four is....'

Of course, the children knew that Mrs Symes, who grew the best strawberries, had a pilot husband who had died, and Mr Burley, who ran the Dun Cow – the village pub with the skittle alley – had lost his son. Bobby Burley had been in one of the ships that Hitler's bombers targeted in the waters around Britain. The children had felt Bobby Burley's death but really only because, for that week, there had been no skittles. Phyllie could still hear the cheer as they trounced Great Mitherton two weeks later, and things, for them, were back to normal.

'Eight times four is...' The seven-year-olds were having to think, but the eleven-year-olds were bored, so she grinned, at them, whispering, 'Come along, you had to learn too.'

The children had felt vaguely sorry for Martin Smith, from Ealing Broadway, who had left them in July for Wales. His mother had moved to the Blaenavon area to be with her parents. His father was a submariner but news had come that he would never again see the sky. It had made both Jake and Phyllie shudder for Isaac and Sammy.

'Eleven times four are...' she conducted, keeping them in time. The clock on the rear wall said five minutes past three. The old Victorian windows were half open, their ropes swinging in the breeze. The window monitor would close them at the end of the day. At three thirty, half of them would go to Joe Bartlett's wheatfields, and half to Sonny Jim's, as James Toogood at Great Mitherton was known.

101

Their task, it had been decided, was to glean the wheat dropped after harvesting. The farmers had used the horses to pull the harvester, having given up waiting for the tractor and harvester promised for August by the War Agricultural Executive Committee. The horses and carts would be there already, waiting to transport the filled sacks to the barn.

The children's war so far had been that of 'playing their part'. The older children, in Class A, would rush from school to salvage scrap metal in teams, with the Boy Scouts leading the boys, and Girl Guides the girls. They would pick up prams and bike carts from their respective sheds and gardens, and then tour the villages. Householders said they were almost on the point of hiding their pans and cutlery. The salvage was then collected by an old boy with an equally old lorry and taken heaven knew where. The children were convinced, as they watched the dog fights over to the east, that one of the Spitfires would be 'theirs': built from the fruit of their labours. It had kept them busy, quickly making a team of the village and evacuee children.

'Five times table now, children.' Phyllie smiled as they swung into this one because the five times was easy-peasy. 'Once five is...'

It was the children, who, with the WI ladies, now including Phyllie, had risen early every morning to collect the fruit to be bottled and preserved. They universally hated the fiddly red- and black-currants, which they picked by sitting on small stools to save their backs. Joe had contributed two milking stools against Andy's wishes, but what

102

wasn't. They picked blackcurrants, strawberries, raspberries, too, many of which had found their way into the mouths of the vacees. It was astonishing how many of those children had not, until then, understood the connection between the earth and the fruit.

The WI only used fruit from gardens, allotments, hedgerows and wherever else they could find it, leaving the professional growers to supply the commercial manufacturers. Phyllie had never realised how beautiful it was at 5 o'clock on a summer morning, even with Jake's grumbles, as he and Francois plodded alongside. Earlier this month they had gathered elderberries and late plums and these, like all the others, had been put into pails and transported in carts and prams to the Preservation Centre at Joe Bartlett's farm.

'How about the six times table...?' She ignored the groans. 'Once six is six, two...'

Miss Harvey and Mrs Symes had supervised the jam making. Poor Mrs Symes – first her husband, now her fellow 'Madam Bossyness'. Phyllie shut her mind, it was the only way to get through today, and then tomorrow, and so on...

'Six sixes are...' She walked up and down between the desks. She stroked Marjorie's hair. Marjorie, who had started by being mean to Melanie, but had eventually become her best friend. She patted Tommy's shoulder and that of anyone else who seemed lost and frightened. But that meant all of them.

'Ten sixes are...' The clock hand jerked and another fraction of time passed.

The WI jam making was made possible by the

extra sugar... Phyllie shut her mind, again. She didn't want to think of the sugar at Miss Featherstone's. She looked across at the children and moved on. Yes, here the children were safer... She gritted her teeth and set off up the aisle between the desks again. Her mother had been sad for the child; her tone had been softer than usual. It was a surprise, and had helped. Perhaps the war would bring the two of them together? 'Seven times table now. We're doing well. Once seven is...'

The WI had the freedom to sell their vegetable and fruit produce at market or wherever they chose. Here, in Little Mitherton, it had been agreed that a percentage of their profits could be put into a kitty to help support their country's war effort. So far the Mitherton WI had bought some knitting wool, new glass jars, and donated to Red Cross parcels for British prisoners of war. Not all the jars and bottles were bought, though. In July she, Miss Featherstone and Miss Harvey had scavenged for bottles in the town tip, returning smelling to high heaven, but triumphant. They had each hoped never again to meet the seagulls who flew miles inland just for the pleasure of rooting about in the rubbish. Nevertheless, they had been back there just two weeks later, to see if they could recover more jars.

'Seven sevens are...'

Miss Featherstone had told Phyllie that being pooped on by a gull was lucky. 'Stop making a fuss and make a wish instead.' She did so, but had still received no letter from Sammy, not a sign or a sound. Would she even be told if he was dead? His parents did not have her address and she didn't have theirs so she had written and asked her mother if Sammy had contacted her, but she said he had not. She had asked if she had his parents' address as she would like to contact them. She had not.

She wanted to write to the Services Post Office with just his name and rank but what would she say to him? She had to write, though, come what may, because if she found Sammy she would find Isaac. Why on earth had there been no letter for Jake? The authorities, when questioned, had written that Jake's details had been sent to his father. She must contact them again, for none of this was good enough any more. People were dying. Perhaps even Sammy and Isaac. No, the thought was too much.

'Eight times table now, and then I think it will be time.' It was nearly three thirty. 'Once eight is eight, two eights are...' She arrived back at the front of the class, and perched on the edge of her desk, with the blackboard behind her. On it was written a message: *We are sorry you are gone, Melanie.* It was written in Marjorie's best handwriting. She had had to stand on Phyllie's chair to do it. Both classes had signed their names. When they knew where to send a letter, they would write to Melanie Adams' father, though what could they really say, except they were so sorry?

Perhaps they could tell him that it was Melanie who had suggested that some of the WI produce kitty could go towards a Christmas party for all the children, one to which the evacuees' parents could be invited.

Miss Featherstone had taken a vote at the last WI

meeting and there had been unanimous agreement. A separate kitty had been set up, and donations had begun topping up the produce amount. The evening before she left for London, Melanie had said, 'Perhaps my mummy will come down for it.'

They wouldn't tell Mr Adams that.

The eight times table was complete. Phyllie turned to the blackboard, fisting her hands tightly as she struggled for control. Miss Featherstone entered then. 'The vicar would like to talk to us all in the hall, as a way of saying goodbye to our friend Melanie. So up you come, into a crocodile. Each seven-year-old will take the hand of an eleven-year-old; quick march now.'

Even Ron held a seven-year-old's hand without a fuss, and Bryan too, as they passed Phyllie, who was smiling, somehow, just as Miss Featherstone was. Except for her landlady's pallor you would not know that Catherine Harvey, her dearest friend, was dead.

After dear Jack Thompson had talked to the children about everlasting life, in his usual everlasting way, and during which they had grown restless and bored, Phyllie led her classes into the playground. They stood to one side as the Home Guard, which the Local Defence League was now called, marched in to take over the school hall. They had been turfed out of the village hall a week ago, when it was given over to a first-aid lessons for Scouts and Guides, and all manner of other things. Phyllie wondered what on earth everyone had done with their time, and their premises, before the war.

Soon the Home Guard would be back out, marching along their patrol routes, their old muskets, shotguns, and even broom handles, on their shoulders, scanning the skies for parachutists. No one knew what was going to happen, no one knew if the RAF was going to beat back 'the buggers' and stop them, from bombing. All they knew was that London had been bombed and it would surely get worse so perhaps her mother and brother would leave the city. It didn't matter where they went, as long as they were safe.

Miss Featherstone and the vicar took the seven-year-olds on up to the playing fields where the vicar had devised a French cricket match, with tea afterwards. No doubt Marmite sandwiches would be on the agenda, made by his wife Sylvia. She got completely up Phyllie's nose because she seemed so perfect, but Phyllie suspected she was also a lovely person.

The older children changed into old shorts and shirts, or frocks, in the school cloakroom, and stuffed the remains of their lunchtime sandwiches in their pockets, as so few had eaten then. Miss Deacon and Mrs Speedie then took half the older children to Great Mitherton and it was Phyllie's task to take the others to the harvest field. Francois stayed in the staff-room during the day, and so he accompanied them now, walking on his rope, sticking closely to Jake's side. Everyone would return home grubby and hopefully too tired to do anything but sleep, having been reassured by a perfectly normal non-threatening day. Their grief was another matter. It would take time.

The wheatfield looked as though it had been shaved, she thought, as she stood by the open gate, waving the children through. 'Head towards Mr Bartlett please,' she called out. Andy and Joe were standing by the cart. Joe had his usual cigarette behind his ear. It was always so bent that Phyllie could never understand why the tobacco didn't fall out. Once all the children were through the gateway she headed after them. A stack of sacks was piled beside Joe. Andy had moved and was stroking Doris's head, talking quietly to the horse. He frowned at the sight of Francois. Joe nodded and smiled at her, but Andy did not.

His bandages were off, she saw, and replaced by a sort of leather sock, and he had discarded the sling. Rooks were scattered all over the field, pecking, and soon there would be little hands at it too. The air was full of wheat dust, the sky was clear, though a few white clouds fluffed above the woods. There were still some stooks that hadn't been gathered in, and a couple that had burst from their string. Perhaps they'd be carted today?

Joe gathered the children around him. 'You have nimble fingers, not like my great mitts,' he said. 'We need to glean the fields, pick up as many of them grains that's 'ad the ruddy nerve to drop from the harvester, and pick 'em up before them damned birds get 'em. We all got to do our bit, ain't we? Even you, young Francois.'

The children nodded. Andy muttered, 'For pity's sake, bringing a bloody dog?'

Joe hadn't finished. 'You see, we're here and your little friend Melanie ain't, so we got to do our best to make sure we feed ourselves until we get that bugger Hitler on the run.'

Phyllie along with everyone else had learned to ignore Andy, and she merely wondered how many of the children would return home with a whole new vocabulary, courtesy of Joe. She started to smile, then stopped. Would they return home? What the hell was going to happen? Where would the bombers go next? Would Hitler come? She found herself checking the skies, then shook her head slightly, and returned her attention to the children. As she did so she saw Andy quartering the sky too, and for once she felt glad he was amongst them, acting as though he was on guard.

She walked with Joe and the children along the bottom of the field, dropping two off at the end of each shaved row. One was to hold the sack while the other stooped and gleaned, and then they would change places. They worked hard, because Miss Featherstone had half a bar of chocolate she had secreted from before the war, and offered it as a prize to the duo who collected the most. When the children were about a quarter of the way up their rows, Joe and Andy replaced their half-full sacks with empty ones. They then hoisted the grain onto their shoulders, and headed for the cart, while Phyllie kept score, noticing that Andy was managing quite well with one hand. He saw her looking, and scowled.

As he drew near she said, 'If the wind changes, you'll stay like that.'

She carried more sacks to the children. The rooks were flying, squawking, ahead of the gleaners, many of whom were straightening their backs, their hands on their hips. Joe and Andy brought round a water bucket. They dipped in an enamel mug and handed it to the children in turn who gulped it, then bent to the task again.

'Who's winning, miss?' Ron called.

She told them it was a close-run thing, but actually Ron and Bryan were in the lead, just. It was then she saw vapour trails as several planes whirled and dived way over to the east, perhaps near Bournemouth – or was it Weymouth? Wherever it was it was just another dogfight. Were the Luftwaffe protecting bombers heading for London again or perhaps a port, an air base, even Bristol? Who knew what they would do next? How could you get used to something like this, but one did. It was extraordinary.

She answered Ron, who wanted to do a pee. 'Go to the hedge, no one will look.'

Rosemary Linton, who sat near Jake in class, and was working close to Phyllie said, 'Life's not fair, miss. I get stung when I do a tiddle and he just has to waggle it about.'

'As you say, life's not fair, but it was ever thus.' It was what Miss Featherstone said about a great many things, a great many times. Phyllie laughed, and dragged her hand through her hair. She had forgotten her sunhat, yet again.

One of the planes was trailing smoke and she couldn't bear to look, so she walked back towards the cart to collect another sack for Bryan who was further along their furrow than the rest. At the cart she checked the sky again and it had cleared. They'd be there one minute, and gone the next, perhaps because they were flying so fast. Hang on, there was another one, or no, it was two; one was damaged, and hurtling towards the ground, way over to the south, on a line with them. A parachute floated from the damaged plane; it was just a speck. The plane crashed. Smoke rose.

'Let him land safely,' she murmured. 'Theirs or ours, it doesn't matter. They're all young men.' She followed the canopy speck as it floated to the ground, then she heard a sound, an engine roaring, far distant, but roaring. She peered through the shimmering heat of the late afternoon, and there it was, the sun flashing off a dot that was hurtling low over the distant fields, skimming the woods way over to the east near Dorchester, heading towards them. Did he think he was still being chased? Why didn't he turn round and look behind him? Or was he trying to land? But he was too fast. She saw the sun flash across the black cross, and stepped back against the cart, frozen.

Andy shouted, 'Luftwaffe. Run to the cart.' He was racing as fast as his gammy leg would allow towards the children. 'Run to the cart, now. Now.' The children hesitated, turned to one another. 'Now,' Andy bawled. They dropped the sacks, and took off, heading to Phyllie and the cart. 'Come on,' she shouted, running towards them, pushing them on, snatching a look. It was closer, casting a speeding shadow on the gentle hill in its path. Jake screamed, 'Francois.'

Francois was chasing round in hysterical circles. Joe was at the horses' heads, calming them, 'Come on, Doris. Keep quiet now; you too, Destiny.'

Jake was trying to catch Francois. Andy rushed and grabbed him, swinging him in the direction

111

of the cart, yelling, 'I'll get him, get under the cart, or into the ditch the other side of it. Run. Run. Kids, run like the bloody clappers.'

There was a rattle of machine-gun fire, someone screamed. The children were almost at the cart, Phyllie following, Andy was somewhere behind. 'Quick,' she screamed, grabbing Rosemary and shoving her under the cart. Ron? Where was he? He'd been doing a pee. She spun round, and there he was, running towards her from the left. She ran to him, grabbing his hand, 'Come on.'

Andy roared, 'Hurry up, you stupid bloody woman; he's much faster than you, so let him go.' She did. Ron roared on, and dived beneath the cart. The breath was heaving in her chest, her gumboots were rubbing and she almost fell as she leapt a furrow, and all the time there was the noise of the engine, louder, louder. Another burst of gunfire. Andy was approaching from the other direction, dragging Francois at the end of the rope. He stumbled, recovered, kept going.

The horses were panicked, Andy reached them, thrusting Francois' lead at his father, taking the bridles. 'Get under, Dad.' His mouth was moving, but Phyllie couldn't hear what else he said over the noise. She turned, and threw herself beneath the cart with the children, her heart pounding so hard it hurt. She watched the spurts of earth as the bullets hit the ground in a long trail, the fast-moving shadow of the plane skimming the stubble. But the pilot was firing on a line a good hundred yards from the cart. The children were silent, sweaty, dust-covered. She held the nearest to her. Some lay on others. She saw that her arm was round Ron. She said, 'It'll be fine. He's not firing at us. He's just in a paddy, that's all, or showing off.'

He grinned at her, fear and excitement visibly vying with one another. 'Got a big bloody temper then, ain't he, miss?'

She laughed, but it was high-pitched. The plane flew on, and away. It was over almost as soon as it had begun.

Andy called, 'You can come out now. Wasn't trying to hit us, just be a bloody nuisance.'

Bryan sniggered. 'Need a cuddle do you, Ron?'

The grin vanished from Ron's face, and he shrugged away from Phyllie's arm. 'Leave off, I'm not a bloody baby like the Yid,' he said.

They crawled out from the cart, the dry earth catching in their throat. As they dusted themselves off, most of them were shaking. Suddenly, though, the children burst into laughter, and talked, slapping one another on the back. Joe nodded at her. 'You all right, lass?' No, she bloody wasn't, and she could have burst into tears.

Then Andy yelled, 'Kids, come with me. Bring a sack each. He's set the straw alight.'

All over the field, in the path of the bullets, were small smouldering fires, and some of the stooks were ablaze. The horses were prancing again as the wind got up and carried the smoke to them. Andy shouted at her, as she grabbed a sack. 'Stay with the horses; do something useful, can't you? Jake, keep that damn dog under control, don't let him free again.' She saw that Francois was straining at the lead and yelping at the fires.

She ran to the horses, reached up, and tried to

113

grab Doris's bridle. The mare tossed free, and bared her teeth, the harness jangling, her great hooves pawing the ground. Phyllie froze. The horses were huge, and she'd never had anything to do with them. Now Destiny was tossing her great head up and down, and both were pulling forward, dragging the creaking cart. Then Jake was with her, Francois by his side.

He handed her the lead, and murmured to the horses, holding up a piece of bread in the fore-finger and thumb of each of his hands; crusts from his sandwiches. 'Quietly now, it's only Phyllie. You'll like her. She's everyone's mum. She can be your mum, too. This is for the sparrows really, but you can have it, if you're good girls.'

'They'll bite your fingers,' Phyllie said. 'You should use the flat of your hand.'

He laughed. 'Did you hear that, Doris? And what about you, Destiny? You won't hurt me, will you, girls? I can't reach with the flat of my hand unless you put your heads right down.' The horses reached down now, nuzzling his flat hand. On and on he talked, fearlessly standing between their heads, stroking their necks as they ate the bread.

Andy yelled, 'Give us a hand here, Phyllie – as you're next to useless there.'

He was holding out a sack, but was he smiling? She ran forwards, stumbling over the clods of earth, righting herself, snatching the sack. Yes, he was. He said, 'That lad's got a way with him. He'll make a horseman.'

'Like you?' she replied, smiling in return.

'Like I was.' His scowl was back.

'You still can be. You're alive, aren't you?' She

swung. on her heel. At least he was alive, so could create a way forward.

The Home Guard was hurrying into the field now, broom handles and ancient guns at the ready. They'd just been warned by telephone that the Focke Wulf had shot down a Spitfire, and was heading their way. 'Our pilot's safe,' the sergeant called to the children. 'Don't worry now, the Home Guard's here. Stay alert, men.' The children cheered.

It's a damned circus, Phyllie thought, as Joe shouted, 'Just get your arses over here and put out these fires. I've another field of wheat over yonder and I don't want it being burned off. Strange the bugger didn't fire into that.'

Phyllie looked into the distance, over to where the first plane had gone down. Smoke still stained the air. Perhaps the German pilot really had just been showing off after all, because he clearly had no intention of killing children or burning off a field. War was such a strange thing.

Joe and Andy made the children finish the gleaning, and it was good discipline and in a way showed that though it hadn't been a strictly normal day, in a way it was. Their job was to soldier on.

Later, after tea laid on trestle tables in the farmyard, Joe awarded Ron and Bryan the half bar of chocolate. The other children clapped half-heartedly and the two boys split it down the middle and scoffed it there and then. Well, Phyllie supposed, most of them would have done that, or would they? Perhaps some would have shared? They walked back as the day cooled into evening, and she dropped them off at their various houses, making a point of saying to Ron, 'Well done. You did a good job today.'

He and Bryan exchanged a look, and shrugged. She left them at Ron's gateway because Bryan had said his brother was picking him up from Mrs Campion's. As she did so she thought she heard Bryan mutter, 'You see, I said them great clods we put in would make all the difference.' But she couldn't be sure.

Late that evening she, Miss Featherstone and Jake pottered in the kitchen. Phyllie and Jake smelled of smoke, and were dirty and dishevelled but none of them was able to settle. The events of the last few days came back, again and again. What's more, the doormat had been empty of letters when they trooped in, and Jake and Phyllie had exchanged a look. Now she said, 'Letters must be difficult to sort with so many servicemen sending them.'

Jake said, 'That's what you always say.'

'The authorities *have* written to your dad, remember, saying where you are. But it will take a while to track him down.'

'You say that too.'

'I will chase them again.'

'You haven't said that before.'

While Jake had a bath, the women made cocoa, and Jake returned to the kitchen to drink it. Then Miss Featherstone chased them both upstairs. Phyllie had her lukewarm bath quickly as the two inches they had decided on didn't exactly encourage a good soak. She called goodnight to Miss Featherstone and looked in on Jake, who was almost asleep. She kissed his hair. Tomorrow she would wash it, to rid it of the lingering smoke, and she would find the name of someone higher up in the educational system who she could write to.

He said, 'No letter.'

'Don't dwell on it. Perhaps it will come tomorrow. It will be all right, I'm sure.'

'No you're not,' he said.

'Yes, I am,' she insisted. 'Because whatever happens we have one another until your dad comes back, and anyway, one day your Uncle Otto will get here. That will be exciting. Remember, way back, after your mum went, your dad said that Otto had reached Holland, and would be trying to make his escape from there, with your Aunt Rosa. One day he will come, and your mother, we hope.'

'But they might not, any of them. People do die, Phyllie. Look at Melanie and Miss Harvey. Think of that parachute today. He could have died.' He sounded so grown up, and Phyllie knew that the time for platitudes was over.

She said, 'Even if that happens, we will go on, together, with Francois, like we did today, like Mr Churchill has said.'

He smiled, and touched her face. 'Goodnight, Phyllie. I think Francois remembered Dunkirk and the bombs today, and Mr Andy saved him. Perhaps inside he's nice.'

She kissed his forehead and left, standing on the landing. It was then she heard the sobbing from Miss Featherstone's room. Phyllie waited, unsure. She knocked, and entered. Miss Featherstone was sitting on her bed, the photograph of her and Miss Harvey as young teachers on her

117

lap. Miss Featherstone looked up.

'She was my dearest friend. We taught together. We knew one another's fiancés; we were together when we each in our turn heard of the news of their deaths in the Somme. We drove ambulances together, then, in France. My heart is breaking.' She was sobbing all the while.

Phyllie sat beside her and took her in her arms, saying, 'Oh, Miss Featherstone, I'm so very sorry.'

She stayed with her until all was quiet, and then she tiptoed to the door. Miss Featherstone called, 'For goodness' sake, girl, call me Miss F, as all my friends do.'

Phyllie headed to her own bed. She felt she wouldn't sleep because her heart was too heavy, but she did.

Chapter Seven

Tuesday 10 September 1940, Little Mitherton

Phyllie stretched in bed, shoving the feather pillow back against the oak headboard and staring at the rustic beams. She must remove the cobwebs, but not today. She glanced at the clock on the bedside table: it was 6 a.m. Their neighbour's cockerel was crowing to greet the dawn. All normal here, then; but far from normal in London.

For the last three evenings she and Miss F had listened to the news on the wireless, hearing of

118

the bombing of the city. Each night she had dreamed of Frankie and her mother, and woken in a sweat, rushing to the phone, which had not been answered until last evening. They were safe. She had told her mother that she must evacuate and join her. Her brother had taken over. 'Yes, she should, Phyllie. But she won't. I've even suggested Wales. Please come, and try to persuade her.' The line had crackled. He had said, 'We must go to the shelter.' And then he had hung up.

The RAF were doing their glorious best against this appalling tide, but bombers continued to sweep across in waves, hour after hour, targeting the docks, and whatever and whomever else they chose. Today she must go and try to persuade her mother to leave the dock mission and return with her to Little Mitherton, as Frankie wished. Miss F and Jake had agreed. Miss F had said they could resurrect the attic room. She rolled over, staring out of the window at the lightening sky, visible because she always lifted the blackout once she'd doused the oil lamp before sleep.

She liked to see the stars, to breathe fresh air, and hear the sounds of the village as people came home from the pub, or walked their yelping dogs. It was grounding, and summed up this village and its people, who stoically bore the losses in their lives and the never-ending work. Even in September the mornings were fresh, as summer cooled into early autumn. She stretched. Before she walked to the station she would have time to go with Jake to the apple trees that grew around the edge of the allotments. While he exercised Francois along the lane, she and Mrs Carruthers from the WI would pick the apples.

She smiled now, pleased with her first attempt at providing a speaker for the WI, for such was her role since Miss Deacon had become treasurer, and left a vacancy two weeks ago. She had booked Sandy Morris when the original speaker, a train enthusiast, broke his ankle. Sandy had taken over the running of the commercial orchard at Great Mitherton and had told them the whys and wherefores for good picking and good storage.

She rolled over. All this paled into insignificance beside the letter that had arrived yesterday. She slid her hand under, the pillow. There it was: Sammy's letter. She really should get up, but not yet. She eased herself up on the pillows, checked the clock. Six thirty. She read it again.

Dear Phyllie

I haven't written before. Well, I have, but I had nowhere to send it until now. You see, at last Isaac has received notification of Jake's whereabouts, so I am sending this to Miss Featherstone's address as I know you won't be far from him. Jake should have a letter soon too, if not at the same time.

It's been fun and games here. Isaac and I were transferred to different submarines after there was a bit of a hitch with the last boat. I can't say which one, or the others I've been on, but you know that. We're back together again now, which is better. The authorities sent notification of Jake's whereabouts to my mum in Ealing, because they lost the letter telling them to send information through the Royal Navy. I gather you wrote again to remind them. Miracle worker, you. Finally they sent it through the Navy. It's been in-

120

teresting, for Isaac and me, I think you could say. I get a bit tired from time to time, but otherwise, all is well.

I've tried to reach you. I don't want you to think I haven't. I wrote to my mum, who wrote to yours, but I expect the letter didn't arrive because she never heard back. I rang the mission several times, but not even the sainted Mrs Saunders knew where you were. It's a crazy postal service and I expect you don't have phones in small villages to telephone her? Anyway, I will give you my service number and you know my rank, and there's the Services Post Office and if you ever feel like replying, it will find me. I wanted to talk to you about what happened at the station. I hope you didn't mind, but I love Jake, and didn't want him upset. You keep an eye on that Ron. His dad's a bad 'un.

Well, Phyllie. I would like to hear from you. Sometimes we come to Portland. I was there last month, embarking mines. Been a few times over the last few months. Not sure if that little snippet will get through the censor. I reckon if you have a phone, I could ring you and you could bring Jake to see his dad. We could have a talk too. I'd like that. I really really would, you see, well, I'd just like to talk, and perhaps you would too. Well, that's it for now.

Your friend, Sammy

She pushed the letter back under the pillow. He wanted to talk to her. She'd read the last few lines many times, and knew them by heart. He'd been to Portland. They could have met if he'd known she was here. He'd phoned her mother. The fury was rising as it had done the first time she read the letter

To damp it down, she leapt from bed, walked

across creaking floorboards to the bathroom, hearing Miss F downstairs in the kitchen. The kettle would be on, and perhaps there'd be an egg for Jake if Mr Milford's chickens were still laying well. She washed in cold water as they always did in the morning. Jake met her on the landing.

'It's not safe, you know, not in London. You be quick. They arrive at night, so come home before then.'

'Into the bathroom with you.' Through his open bedroom door she could see Francois scratching himself on the old tartan blanket. On Jake's bedside table was the letter from his father, propped up so he could see it all the time.

The train stopped so many times that it was four thirty in the afternoon before they limped into Waterloo. People were restless by then, staring through the windows and up at the sky. Few talked. Even before the train had stopped, the doors were opening and people were jumping onto the platform and pouring along the concourse, heading for the buses and the tube, fighting their way through those hurrying against them, eager to be on their homebound trains, and out of this death trap of a city.

'Really, Mum. Why on earth don't you do as your son wants and go to Wales?' Phyllie seethed, anxious for her mother to be safe, but wanting her in Wales, not Little Mitherton. How dare she not relay her contact details to Sammy? She held her basket to her, knocking the gas mask hanging over her shoulder. In her basket was 'sugarless' jam made with honey and just a quarter of the

122

usual sugar, which the WI made for their own use. They wished to use the extra sugar only for the war effort. It was, after all, the government's intention. She had also brought some eggs and honey from the hives at Great Mitherton. She had covered it all with an old piece of tarpaulin because she feared the basket would be grabbed from her if anyone knew its contents.

She reached the bus stop and realised she must have been talking aloud, because the old man in front turned round, and then shuffled forward, leaving a space between them.

The queue was long. The noise of the city was loud and strange after all this time. What on earth must it be like with sirens screaming and bombers droning overhead? Well, at this rate, she'd damn well find out. She checked her watch and shuffled along towards the bus that had drawn up, making sure to keep the space between her and the old man. Hurry, hurry, she urged silently, because Jake would worry, and Miss F would pretend that she wasn't giving it a thought. The bus squeezed in the old boy, but was then declared full. The clippie – bus conductress – tinged the bell, and the driver pulled away, but not before Phyllie had seen the relief on the old man's face. Was it because he had left her behind or because he'd reach home, or a shelter, before the bombers?

She laughed, but to herself this time, and waited, glancing back at the queue. No one complained, or showed concern, some read newspapers or books, but the rigid high set of their shoulders told the lie. Another bus drew up heading Woolwich way. It would do, and this one she was able to board, paying the clippie, taking the ticket, smiling as the older woman nodded at her basket and quipped, 'Up from the country for the fresh air and fun of London, are we?'

As they drove she felt cramped by the buildings, with their windows criss-crossed with tape as protection against blasts, and sandbags everywhere. Over to the left, as they trundled along, was an air raid shelter, piled high with more sandbags around the entrance, and grim crowds queuing to enter, some with children. Why on earth hadn't they been evacuated?

The bus powered on, eastwards towards the docks, and now people were shifting in their seats and staring out of the windows. She heard them then, the droning and drumming of the planes, the *thwak thwack* of the ack-ack. She twisted her head in the direction of the sound. Searchlights probed the dusky skies. There were sirens in the distance, but so far, no bombs. The bus pulled up at a stop. Several alighted, hurrying along the streets. Two passengers waited to board. The clippie stopped them, holding up her hand as she talked to the driver, an elderly man who wore his cap on one side. She nodded, waving the passengers on. 'We'll keep going for a bit. They're tracking the Thames, probably heading for the Bite. Or the Royal Docks again, p'haps?'

Around her people exchanged glances, and talked about nothing. The two new passengers made their way down the bus and the clippie followed, taking their money, issuing tickets. Phyllie's knuckles whitened as she gripped the handle of her basket. The mission was near the Bite. The

124

searchlights stabbed the dusk and found the bombers. The bus swung round a corner and everyone fell silent as they heard the *thump, thump* of bombs. The sky seemed to burst with light, again and again, as though giant fireworks were exploding.

A woman just behind her said, 'Gawd, I 'ope my mum turned the oven off before she went to the shelter, or the bleedin' house'll burn down.'

A man at the back yelled, 'Might not be the ruddy oven that burns it down.' Everyone was laughing as the bus roared past a bus stop at which no passengers stood. The drone of planes had become a roar, and Phyllie craned, searching through the window. High above, flying in from the south, were squadrons of bombers, with fighters, like gnats buzzing above, through and at them.

Ours? she wondered.

Some were diving down at more fighters. Theirs? The *thump, thump* was closer, the continuous burst and crack of flames louder. Phyllie wanted to crouch down, but no one else did. Much louder, much clearer, a house seemed to burst a short way off to their right. Debris flew up into the air, and dust – so much dust – rose dark against the flare of flames. It seemed as though the earth lurched, the bus shuddered and swerved. Even over the noise of the revving of the bus, and the squeal of the tyres, they heard the splintering of glass, the crash of buildings collapsing like dominoes. Bricks cascaded, drowning the roar of planes, but only for a moment.

She heard a sort of whistle, then a bomb fell to

the right, again. In the light of the flames she could actually see other bombs falling. They seemed to be chasing them, dropping through the air, just dropping, like so many sticks. Bang, bang, bang. Closer. The bus slewed to the kerb, with another squeal of brakes. The clippie rang the bell repeatedly, yelling, 'Come on, everyone out. Get to that shelter, over to the left.'

The passengers began pouring off the bus. Phyllie struggled down the aisle, her basket and gas mask holding her up. She stopped on the platform by the clippie, yelling to be heard above the noise: 'Come on, then.'

The clippie nodded at the driver. 'He won't leave the bus, so I should stay.'

The driver was gesticulating, waving her off. 'Take her with you, miss,' he yelled. 'I'll be there in a minute. Need to lock it up.' A man shoved past Phyllie, roaring, 'Get out the bloody way, I want to get under cover.'

Phyllie dragged the clippie off the bus onto the pavement as the man rushed off. They ducked as another blast tore into the buildings somewhere to the left. The pavement rocked as an explosion blew apart a house. Not on the street, but close, and the air was even more full of dust; no, it was cinders. Phyllie coughed, again, then again. She started to run, the clippie was faster, but knocked Phyllie's basket, almost tumbling her to the ground. The clippie didn't notice and ran on to the shelter, in the wake of the man.

The bombs were all around; the ground was lurching, moving. Phyllie tried to restore her balance but staggered, the basket slipping to the

126

pavement. Waves of heat and sound smothered her, she stooped, groping for the basket handle. She could barely see through the dust, so rubbed her eyes. They stung. She saw the clippie ahead of her, turning, shouting to her, 'This way, come on. Leave your bloody basket.'

She wouldn't. It had part of the countryside in it; it was sanity. She gripped the handle, lifted it. There was a whoof, a great wind, a huge noise. The shops on the other side of the street burst open, bricks flew up into the air, glass splinters tinkled near her. How could they tinkle when they were weapons that killed? She felt the hand that shoved her, but it wasn't a hand, it was a wave, and it hurled her to the ground, bricks rained, and debris, and burning wood. The pavement tipped, broke, the kerb reared up and crashed back down. There were screams.

She curled up on the ground, her arms over her head, waiting, breathing, listening, and her ears hurt from the pressure. She sobbed with the fear. Something hot hit her hand. She pulled away, sucked it. The ground was like a bucking horse. Did Destiny buck? There was a pain, and another noise, a sort of pattering of rain, but it wasn't rain. Of course it bloody wasn't. She opened her eyes. The lamppost was hanging at an angle. It was the glass that had showered in tiny shards. There must be so much broken glass in London. There was another whoof. She felt the draught. The sky was alight. Everywhere was alight.

She moved her arms, looking ahead. More shops were bursting, flames were roaring, reflected in the street. How? Then she saw the water. Had the

127

mains gone? Was that it? What about gas? Her gas mask dug into her side. Had that woman's mother left on the oven? Had their house burned? The bombs were moving away. It was like the strafing. They were bombing in a line, like a ruler, that's what it was. Bloody Germans, so neat. Get up. She tried. Pieces of brick fell from her. She couldn't, and lay there, her face grinding on the pavement, the grit digging in. All the time she sobbed.

It became quieter, in time. She groped for her basket. It was there. She felt for the tarpaulin. It was still on top, beneath debris. She eased herself onto all fours. There were more sirens now, fire engines. Hoses snaked across the road. A warden yelled, 'Get out the bloody way, and into a shelter, you stupid bloody woman.'

She tried, but failed. Her leg hurt, the burn on her hand too. 'Didn't you hear me?' She tried again and this time made it, snatching up her basket as he blew his whistle at her. 'Get out of the bloody way, you fool.' It was as though she was hearing him through water.

Phyllie croaked, her throat sore, wiping her face free of the tears, only for them to fall again, but then a great anger took over. 'Don't you dare speak to me like that, you jumped-up little Hitler. Swallow your bloody whistle, why don't you? It'll bloody kill you with a bit of luck. What's the matter with everyone, with the world?'

He heard, she knew he did, from the way he strutted away. Behind him she saw the remains of the bus, the driver half in and half out, motionless. A fireman was walking away, shaking his head. She felt her knees tremble, and reached for the wall. Don't you dare, she told herself, don't you dare. Stand straight. She did and breathed in deeply, then coughed. Not a good idea. Shallow breaths, eyes half closed, let the cinders settle, and no more crying.

Screams were still coming from the burning ruins. Had Miss Harvey screamed too? No, not that. She gripped the handle of the basket so tightly that the burn ached, and stumbled along, finding her way easily between and over the bricks, because it was like daylight. She should have worn her gloves, as her mother insisted. Then she wouldn't have this huge burn. She heard the warden call, 'Put that bloody cigarette out, mate. D'you want the planes to spot it?'

The absurdity of it made her laugh as she staggered and stumbled to the shelter, and then she couldn't stop. She stood just inside the entrance laughing until the clippie saw her, and slapped her hard across the face. Phyllie jerked away. 'That hurt.'

The clippie nodded. 'It was meant to. Hysterics don't help anyone, country girl. Neither does yelling at the warden. He doesn't come in to safety. He just tries to make sure we do. You should find him and apologise.'

Phyllie stared at her. She was right. She turned and headed for the pavement, but was dragged down the stairs into what was clearly a cellar. 'Not now, girl, but I'll give you his address and you can do it tomorrow, before you go home. That's where you should make for, if you've got any sense.'

Phyllie nodded. 'I'll make time, but it's too late for the bus driver. The bomb got him.' She was

129

shaking all over now. The moment she said it she wanted to cut out her tongue as the clippie stared, then paled, tears streaming down her face.

'That's me dad. He came back from retirement. That's me dad.' It was Phyllie who held her back now, dropping her basket to the ground as people sitting on benches looked on.

By 8.30 p.m. the raid was over, but another wave would come, or so a woman said, the one wearing a felt hat and flowery overall who was now looking after the clippie. Phyllie stuffed the address of the warden into her pocket, saying, 'Thank you, and I'm sorry. I'm so sorry. I must go, my mum, you see, she's waiting.'

'You're one lucky cow, you know,' the clippie said, her voice dead and numb, 'seeing your mum, and then going back to the country.'

Phyllie set off for the mission. It was light enough from the fires for her to see her way, though she walked through smoke that was more like a fog, coughing into her handkerchief, just like others she passed. She didn't need to call on the air raid warden because he was directing someone to the shelter. She caught his arm, interrupting. His eyes were red from the smoke, his face drawn with exhaustion.

'I was rude to you. I'm sorry. You were trying to help me.'

He didn't know what she was talking about and said, 'Got to get on. They'll be back. Get yourself to where you're going, miss, quickly.'

She didn't arrive at her mother's that evening, because the bombers were indeed back, and this time, when the air raid siren whined, she dived

130

down into the nearest tube station with all the others. She sat on the cold platform all night, as the trains continued to run, disgorging passengers, and taking on others. People talked, babies cried, and children ran over those who were sleeping.

She laid her head on her arms, which she rested on the handle of her basket, and thought back to Sandy Morris's talk to the WI about the correct way to pick and store fruit. She felt the weight of the apple she had twisted from the spur only this morning. She heard Jake's laughter as he exercised Francois, the idle chat of her WI friends as they also twisted the apples, the guffaw of Mrs Carruthers after she had related a saucy piece of gossip. They had all placed their apples carefully into the bucket, which they had lined with hay. They had taken them to Miss F's apple loft, on the back of the house. The apples might store well all winter, but would be checked regularly. With every week that passed they would become sweeter.

She watched as another train came in, and now her thoughts were different, harsh, unforgiving. So, apple picking was the extent of her war effort? She was disgusted with herself and couldn't sleep.

When morning came she moved on as others did, toiling along the pavements, and stepping into the roads when her way was blocked. All the time there was the smell of death, charred wood, debris. She picked pieces of glass and brick from the tarpaulin on her basket, dropping it anywhere. What would a little more on the pavement matter? She clung to her basket, because she would leave it with her brother for his charges,

131

and would really try to make her mother join her. Her fury had gone, only guilt and the remnants of terror remained.

She followed the route that she remembered from her visits to her brother's mission, passing people who were on their way to work, carrying handbags, shopping bags. One man held his briefcase in both arms as though it would protect him. There was a naked body by a pile of bricks, untouched it seemed, but lifeless. Was it the blast? Smoke was still pouring up into the sky the closer she drew to the docks. She turned left, then again. There was rubble to the left-hand side of these streets. The warehouses still crackled and burned alongside the river over to the south. The smell of molasses was carried on the breeze; a mass of sugar had gone up.

She thought of the mystery of Miss F's disappearing sugar and now her fury was for the complacent villagers, and for people who gained from black marketeering. She rubbed her forehead. The mission must be here somewhere. She had arrived at a crossroads and there, on the far corner, was where the mission had been. It was gone, there was just smoking rubble, but now she saw her mother, on her knees, scrubbing the remains of the tiled doorstep. Again and again she scrubbed.

Phyllie crossed the road. 'Let me help, Mum.' She knelt with her, trying to take the brush, but her mother struggled, until, with one heave she pulled it from Phyllie. 'I am the housekeeper now Mrs McBride has gone to her God. It is my job. And why are you here? It's important than one of

132

us stays safe. Do think sensibly, Phyllis. One of us–'

She stopped and began to brush again, smearing the dirt, dipping it into the bucket of filthy water at the end of the step. She brushed again, nudging the rubble from one side to the other. There was the screeching sound of chalk on a blackboard, or debris beneath a scrubbing brush. Phyllie sat back on her heels, her stockings already torn beyond repair.

She heard her brother's voice: 'Phyllie, you came.' He lifted her up, and hugged her. She rested her head against his shoulder and the dusty black of his cassock. 'I brought produce for your people. I'll swap them for Mum.' She smiled and felt the dust cracking on her face as she did. She lifted her head to look into her brother's red-rimmed eyes.

Her mother stood then. 'Have you found us another house, Francis?' she asked, ignoring Phyllie.

Her brother nodded. 'It's the old clinic on Westbury Street, but I told you that I wanted Phyllie to take you to the country, today. I thought it would be a good idea, Mum.'

Their mother shook her scrubbing brush. Grit and brick debris dropped from it, and filthy water. She stared at the step, and then chucked the brush onto the rubble. 'Well, you thought wrong. Here I am, and here I stay. You, Phyllis, can run yourself back to where I expect you're still sharing with that Isaac's son, the–'

'Mother,' warned Frankie as Phyllie tensed.

Her mother wiped her mouth. 'We need clothes, toys, books. Provisions. Send them up. That's all

133

we need. Then, I ask as your mother for you to stay where you have a chance to survive. Look at you, you could have been killed. Are you hurt?'

Phyllie shook her head. 'Just a burn.'

'Your brother should never have suggested you come.' She began to kick the bricks to one side.

Frankie took Phyllie's arm. 'She's in shock, determined to be strong. Ultimately immovable, I'm afraid. I sometimes think that if she lets go for one moment she would collapse. Perhaps that is her fear too? And you? You look as though you've been in the wars? Are you all right?'

'Yes. I found a shelter. But you two, night after night? Come away.'

Her mother had knelt, reclaimed the scrubbing brush and was working on the front step to the nonexistent presbytery again. It was madness. It was horror. Phyllie felt the wracking sobs begin, and gritted her teeth. *Not now, not ever.*

For a moment she and Frankie watched their mother, then he said, 'Now, how is Sammy? Safe, I trust, and Isaac?'

'Yes, I heard from him. He found where I was and wrote.' She looked at her mother, who had turned, and now held her gaze. She dropped the scrubbing brush into the bucket and rose, dusting off her skirt, making it even worse.

'So, he found you after all, did he? What happens now?'

Phyllie looked away from her mother, gazing instead across the desolation of the East End. What was the point of even raising the phone calls, or of being angry? She said, 'I don't know. I hope we meet, I hope we talk. I hope a lot of things.' She was aware that she had stuck out her chin.

Her mother was walking away, shouting, 'Love is not all there is. Respectability, and responsibility, that's what's important, and someone who can afford to care for you. That boy aspires to nothing. He will become nothing. Life is not a game. I want you in a nice house, with a nice teacher, or a doctor.'

Phyllie started after her, calling, 'Oh, Mother, how can you? Sammy's fighting for us. He will care for me, if... Well, he will.' Her mother kept on walking.

Frankie put his arm around Phyllie. 'Mother's wrong; you must follow your heart as I have. Love is everything and you remember that. Now, I must go after her, you know what she's like. She could barge into an unexploded bomb and expect it to get out of her way. Thank you for coming. It was worth a try. Phyllie, she loves you. She can just never find the words. All I do know is she wants you to be safe, and to be proud of you.'

With that, he was gone, swishing in his cassock, which was filthy at the hem, but she supposed the very sight of it gave succour to his flock, if there were any left. She still had the basket and a great sense of loneliness. Her mother and Frankie had always been an inclusive little gang, one that left her father and Phyllie hovering outside, peering in. Her father had once told her that her mother loved her, but that she had difficulty with emotion, and life. That people disappointed her easily, and appearances gave her a sense of security.

She stood for a moment longer, watching them

grow smaller, the dust and smoke blurring their outline, realising that her brother had fulfilled her mother's hopes. Phyllie, however, had not, and probably never would. Just as her father never had. She nodded to herself as she called after them: 'Goodbye, good luck, I love you both.'

They didn't look back. Perhaps they hadn't heard.

The train journey was much quicker on the way home, and as congested towns gave way to silver birches growing on scorched embankments, and these became freshly ploughed fields, she felt such relief, and then, again, disgust. The train drew in to Little Mitherton at three thirty. She clambered down, with her basket still full, her stockings still a disgrace, her skirt filthy, and her hair like a bird's nest.

Jake stood on the platform, in his shorts, his socks around his ankles, with Francois on his rope. Mr Hill, the station master, had his hand on the boy's shoulder as Jake scanned those alighting from the train. He spotted her and ran, hurling himself up into her arms, while Francois sat beside her, pawing her leg. Jake buried his head into her shoulder. 'I thought you'd stayed. I thought you might be dead. Your mum isn't with you. Are you sad? Is she dead?'

He was sobbing, his face sweaty and hot. She held him close, the basket scratched his leg. 'No, she's fine. She wants to stay and help my brother's congregation.'

He struggled free, while Francois whined at her for a stroke. Jake took her hand, and dragged her along the platform. Mr Hill shook his head and waved away her attempt to give him her ticket.

'You should have phoned,' Mr Hill said.

'There were such queues at the public telephone boxes, and an impatient train.'

'Still, you should have phoned. People were very worried and thought the worst. No mother? All well there, I hope?'

She nodded. Jake talked all the way home, starting with the man the Agricultural Advisory Committee had sent to advise on sowing kale. 'Mr Joe said he was wet behind the ears, but Dan and I couldn't see it. Mr Andy said the man was talking bloody nonsense and stormed off, but we didn't take any notice. It must hurt, after all, we've decided, for a very long time when you have your hand cut off. It's bad enough when you bang your knee. We just watched the man from the committee as he stood at the field and told Mr Joe to plough shallow first, as though he doesn't know. Mr Joe swore a lot, and loudly, but he always swears so that's normal too. Anyway, it's mild enough here to overwinter kale, Mr Joe said, so we'll all be helping to sow it next week. Tiny seeds, they are, Phyllie.'

As they passed the pond, the ducks flurried up into the air and Jake pulled at her hand, making her stop. 'We think there're a few more drakes, Phyllie.' Francois barked. Jake continued, 'Miss F let me stay all day at the station. She gave me sandwiches. Tomatoes, and just a little bit of cheese, that's all.' He pulled a face. 'She said that I wouldn't settle until you came home. You really should have phoned. But like you said, there were

137

queues. I expect there were some that were bombed as well. We listened to the news. It was the bombs that made me frightened. Anyway, Miss F said I might as well take my wriggly bum and put it on Mr Hill's bench and keep it there while I watched for you, and she stayed by the phone. She tried to phone your mother, but she said the line was dead. I didn't like the word dead.'

He stopped to draw breath as they stared across the pond, to the fields beyond. To Phyllie it seemed so quiet, so open, but then Jake was once again in full flood. 'Miss F said Francois and I were to be home by seven, if you didn't come. But I thought you would. I think I did, anyway. Miss F was sure. She's sure about most things. She gave me a note for Mr Hill, with her orders. Or that's what he said. "Orders is orders," he said.'

Phyllie smiled and hugged him closer, realising how much she'd missed him.

They walked on, 'The country needs kale, the man with the wet ears said. You need a bath, Phyllie. I know it's rude to say, but you're dirty and you've got cinders in your hair, and you smell of smoke, and a bit of sweat. But I don't know what I would have done if you hadn't come back, like Mum, or if you had died.' He slipped his hand into hers, and gripped it tightly until they came to the edge of the village. Francois walked close to his heel.

As they rounded the corner, Phyllie saw the children, village and evacuees, milling about, even Ron. The girls were skipping, with Miss F counting how many they managed to do without getting tangled up. Some boys were playing catch, and others squatted, playing jacks, with off-centre bounces as the balls caught edges of the hardened surface earth. The moment the children saw Phyllie they rushed at her. 'Where were you?' 'Why didn't you come back last night?' 'Miss Featherstone said there might have been a raid, so we thought you were dead.'

The younger ones were hugging her legs and waist. The older ones were standing as though they didn't really care, but sneaking looks at her, and grinning. Ron said, 'That daft mutt has been waiting at the station all day, with Jake. They wouldn't come to school. The station master phoned Miss Featherstone to tell her you had come. She came to the school hall where we were waiting, just in case. Like we waited yesterday.' There was a challenge in his voice now, and anger, but he hadn't called Jake 'the Yid', and he had waited too. It mattered, but not as much as it should, because her self-disgust was still so strong.

Miss Featherstone clapped her hands. 'As a surprise, the WI has released a little ham from the Pig Club, so there is ham salad, with Mrs Speedie's tomatoes. Then, and only then, will our ration of jelly be served, along with stewed plums and honey. Remember, children, you must save some for our dear Miss Saunders, the returning waif and stray.' She grinned at Phyllie. 'Let's feed you, and then you should wash, shouldn't she, children?'

They laughed, and ran ahead. Miss F and Phyllie followed. Miss F said, 'I tried not to worry.' She took the basket.

Phyllie said, 'The presbytery was bombed. All

that exists is the front step. My mother and Frankie are safe. They are continuing their work. I need to move to London and do something useful, even drive a bus. I can't hide here a moment longer. I am disgusted with myself.'

Miss F slipped her arm through Phyllie's and said nothing for a moment, but only a moment. 'In war, we need to make sacrifices. Yes, it would be suitably noble and dramatic to battle the Blitz, and rush around doing good works, and possibly dying in the process. There are others, however, doing that. Your place is with these evacuated children who need you. *You* are the bridge between here and home. *You* are their constant. You came with them, you know them from before, and you know their lives and their parents. When you left yesterday they were insecure, frightened, on edge; surely you can see their need by the reception they have given you?'

She had stopped now, by the village pump outside Mainspring Cottage. The pump still worked, and was often used. The stones at its foot were stained green. 'Our job isn't glamorous, Phyllie, or exciting, but who knows what's going to happen? Those brave fliers are doing their best but one wonders if, at any moment, we could be invaded.

'We could be experiencing more strafing from planes, fighting in our fields, have brutes strutting in their jackboots through our lanes. If you're dead beneath rubble in London, who is to be the children's source of strength then? Besides, while the war exists we need to educate these little monsters, or they will be short-changed. Their lives are disrupted enough; at least let's provide them with the means to *think* properly, and to know right from wrong. They'll need that if we're invaded, or if we're not, come to that.'

She took the basket, and swung it as they arrived at the playground where the children were playing noisily. Mrs Symes waved from her garden. Old Mr Walker was digging his front garden, getting ready for kale perhaps?

Phyllie sighed. 'A clippie said I was running away. My brother and mother remain. Look at this lovely place.' She swung her arm around. 'I am, you know, running away, and the thing is, I want to stay, so what does that say about me?'

Miss F smiled. 'Oh, Phyllie, there's a ghastly war on and guilt will be our companion for much of it, and for ages after. Trust me, I know from the last lot. So many ifs and buts. Look at me: should I have taken little Melanie to London instead of Catherine Harvey? Should I be driving an ambulance somewhere, as I did in the last war? If we let guilt take hold, we go mad or become foul like young Andy. We go where we're needed, and that's the end of it. Children are our future, there is nothing more precious. It's so important to love them, to teach them the values we hold dear, because if we are conquered, we need them to hold fast to those values for as long as they live.'

They crossed the playground, and waited at the double doors into the school as the children lined up. 'Tell you what, why don't we do something for your mother that might that make a difference? What does she need?'

'The people they help need clothes now winter

is coming, and produce that's off ration, books, anything really. When a house is bombed, everything is gone. Frankie could come to Waterloo to collect all we manage to send.'

They opened the doors and the children filed in, and continued on into the school hall, with Phyllie and Miss F bringing up the rear. The smell of chalk and children said she was home. But was it enough?

She could still see the smoke from the sugar warehouse, smell the molasses, see the damaged ships in the docks. And, for all Miss F's fine words there was still that business with the bags of sugar that had gone missing from the corner cupboard. Was this the source of some of the headmistress's guilt, her ifs and buts? And why ever should Andy feel guilty about being injured?

Francois was in the staffroom, and barked. Miss F nudged her. 'Time we stopped studying our navels, and putting the world to rights, and helped get the food ready. It's so boring so much of the time, and that's why they're excited – nothing to do with their beloved Miss Saunders safely home from the city, naturally.'

Chapter Eight

September to November 1940, Little Mitherton

The kale, grown for fodder, had been sown by the middle of September, and the children marvelled at the small seeds that would grow to such large plants. In the same month Miss F took to serving corncobs for tea. Jake protested the first time. 'Mr Joe gives these to his beasts.'

Miss F tapped him on the head as she passed. 'Mr Bartlett to you, young man. I ate them in Africa in 1930 and we will eat them now. Rationing is really biting now, and life needs lifting.'

'We're not in Africa now, and Mr Joe said we were to call him Mr Joe, not Mr Bartlett because it made him feel old,' he muttered, ramming a fork into either end of the corn as she had told him. Phyllie smothered a grin. Jake was so much stronger now, so much more alive, and perhaps it was because Ron was busy with Bryan and Eddie most evenings, though she had no idea what they were up to. Whatever it was, it hadn't reached their teachers' ears, so it was hopefully innocuous. Whatever, it left Jake in peace to play with Dan, and help out Joe when he needed it. It helped, also, having regular letters from his father, just as it helped her to have another from Sammy.

Miss F joined them at the table. 'I heard that

muttering, Jake Kaplan.'

He said nothing, just ate like a mouse, nibbling from one end, and by the time he reached the other, he decided he liked it, though bits caught in his teeth. Miss F said, 'It's good roughage for the bowels.' Phyllie and Jake grimaced at one another.

As September became October and the leaves began to change colour, the fruit season ended, and the women of the village took to digging in the allotments and spare ground. With the close of the jam season, Joe's big kitchen fell silent, except for pickle making, which was an altogether tamer affair, with smaller shifts. Phyllie dug up Miss F's front and back garden so the frost could break it up over winter. She also sowed kale, which Miss F swore by as a leaf vegetable for humans as well as animals. Phyllie and Jake exchanged groans, quickly muffled as she shot them one of her 'not amused' glares.

In October Phyllie also spoke to the WI at their monthly meeting about collecting any outgrown clothing for her brother's work in London. Once a week she and Jake, with a small team of vacees, collected what people could spare. Young Lily Prince gave them all her husband's clothes, because he had been killed on his merchant ship. They actually gave some of these clothes to the family who had escaped from the Channel Islands just after the Germans arrived and who were now living in Great Mitherton. The grandfather was grateful, though there was no father with them, because he was serving in the Royal Navy. Phyllie thought, as she often did, that no family was un-scathed, and for a moment her anxiety about

Sammy and Isaac rose to the surface.

By November the German bombs were exploding on cities like Birmingham, Liverpool and Coventry as well as London, and a few more evacuees arrived, though most settled in Great Mitherton or Swanwick. Every evening, Phyllie and Miss F sat by the wireless, listening to the news on the Home Service, and all the time there was the grinding sense of fear and uncertainty. At night, in bed, Phyllie reread the letters she had received from Sammy, particularly the last one, which had arrived on 3 November. He thought they'd be coming to Portland. He would phone Miss F's number. They must talk, they really must, he had written. But that was all. He never actually said what they must talk about, and neither did she, but, in spite of her mother, oh, how she hoped.

On 4 November, before school, she arrived at the allotments and discovered that their sprouts had been picked off the stalk, the plants uprooted and scattered over the cabbages. Numbed, she cleared up the remains and put them onto the compost heap. It was then she saw the small footprints in the mud. Children, but who? Why? Perhaps to sell? There had been numerous incidents recently in Great Mitherton, and in response the allotmenteers there had formed a patrol. It had clearly encouraged the budding businessmen to move on to another area.

First it had been old Mr Milford's allotment, and now hers. Was it the new evacuees? Then Phyllie caught herself. She was as bad as the villagers had been when Jake was revealed as a Jew with strange eating habits. The new evacuees

145

would settle into country ways, just as all the others had done. It could be anyone, she made herself accept.

Instead of sprouts Phyllie picked cabbage. They used every bit of the vegetables they possibly could these days, chopping the outer leaves finely to minimise the coarseness of the stalks. She also pulled one or two parsnips. In fact, the WI was thinking of making parsnip jam because it was sweet in itself, and they did have some allotted sugar left. She carried her booty home, kicking off her boots in the front porch, because the mud on the side path was ankle deep. She padded along the runner to the kitchen and dumped the cabbage in the sink, checked the time on the wall, and then saw both Miss F and Jake standing together by the Aga grinning.

'What?' she asked. 'There's nothing to smile about; some little devil, or many little devils, have not only taken the sprouts, but yanked up the–'

'They're going to come to Dorchester on Saturday,' Jake interrupted. 'Dad and Sammy. They're coming, and the vicar needs to see someone there, so he's using his petrol coupons and will take us. They can only stay for an hour, but it's an hour, Phyllie. You'll know if he really wants to marry you, and Francois can meet Dad, and it means, for now, they're safe.'

That evening she sat darning Jake's socks and listening to the newsreader telling of the Greeks who were pushing back the Italians. His voice dropped as he moved on to Petain who wanted the French to collaborate with the Germans in Vichy, in order to maintain unity within the new

146

European order. She exchanged a look with Miss F, who had been shaking her head over some paperwork at the kitchen table.

'"European order" sounds frightening,' Phyllie said, hearing Francois bark in Jake's bedroom.

'It's all ruddy frightening.' Miss F sighed, leaning back in her chair and running her fingers through her hair. 'Parsnip jam is a good idea. I'll need to go to Joe tomorrow. He's hiding the WI allot—' She stopped. 'Ah, I shouldn't have said that. The fewer people who know, the better.'

Phyllie began to move chess pieces around in her mind as she inserted the wooden mushroom into the heel of another of Jake's socks. She continued to darn in silence for a moment, and then said, 'So that's where it went? From the cupboard to Joe's? I wondered.'

Miss F looked hard at her. 'What on earth did you think? Oh, that I'd sold the lot, you daft child? Perhaps it was me who nicked your sprouts too?' She was laughing.

Phyllie concentrated on the sock, finding it less embarrassing. 'Well, it was strange, and you said it was a secret, and... Oh, I don't know.'

Miss F came to sit next to her on the sofa. 'We have to keep the sugar safe. We buy what we need for the year from our Women's Institute HQ in London. They have, in their turn, bought it with a grant from the government. We do not receive a penny for our work in the Centre, it is just our duty to do what we can to keep the nation fed. People who supply the fruit can sell it to the Preservation Centre, but no one does. We give it because we feel it is a privilege, though I have no

147

idea what other WIs do. Once the jam is made, it is delivered to a central wholesale depot. Of course, some fruit is taken to market by those with plants, bushes and trees, who make their own, usually virtually sugarless, to be sold there. We sell our vegetables too, for our own pockets, so we're not completely goody-two-shoes.'

She stopped, and pointed to the kitchen table. 'You can see how crucial it is that we take good care, not just of our paperwork, but of our sugar. With rationing and shortages it's a most valuable commodity so if any goes missing it looks as if the WI is abusing its allotment.'

Phyllie said, 'I'm so sorry to have thought...'

Miss F continued, well into her stride, 'Catherine Harvey kept the figures, and now it's up to me. We must account for every bag of sugar. The day you arrived I had a delivery, and I kept it in that cupboard temporarily until it could be taken to a place of safety. It went, overnight. So, now I will tell you that it's in Joe's store cupboard at the end of the milking parlour, which is where he keeps the dry animal food. It's right at the back on the right-hand shelves. Well hidden. The store is locked. The dogs and geese will give warning if any strangers approach. Just in case anything happens to Joe and me, now, you will know.' She touched her nose. 'We women think of everything.'

The vicar left Phyllie and Jake in the ancient Dorchester town centre, just across the road from St Peter's Church, which was almost halfway down the hill. It was where Sammy had said they should meet. Francois was on his rope, looking confused as people bustled past. They waited, looking up the hill, and then down it, then up again. Jake was pale and anxious. Phyllie felt the same, though she wore a little rouge and lipstick. She straightened her mackintosh and wished it had been warm enough to wear her grey jacket. She adjusted Jake's scarf. He looked past her, then up the hill again.

'They're not coming, are they?' he muttered.

'Of course they are. We're early. They said two.' She snatched a look at her watch. It was five minutes past two, so Sammy and Isaac were in fact late. She swallowed. Every minute they searched the pavements, and at last just four minutes later there was a flurry of activity further down the hill, on the other side of the road. They were running, dodging between buses, small canvas bags hanging off their shoulders.

'They're here,' Jake whispered. Then he shouted, 'They're here.'

Sammy and Isaac had reached the pavement now and Jake flew towards his father, with Francois leaping and barking alongside. Sammy tore past him, then hesitated, swung round and ruffled Jake's hair, before powering on again, his eyes never leaving Phyllie's. At last he stood in front of her. His cap had HMS but no name. So much secrecy, thought Phyllie as he took her hands, and so much danger; but for this moment he was here. Neither of them spoke. He smelled of diesel. She longed to be held by him, kissed again, but what did *he* want?

People were knocking into them as they blocked the pavement. Sammy laughed suddenly, pulling her to the side. They stood against the shop window of a grocer's. A queue stretched the other side of the doorway, up the hill, for ten yards. He said, 'Let's walk, or they'll think we're starting another queue in competition and we'll be attacked. We've only got less than an hour, no time for altercations. So sorry we were late, it's the trains.'

They walked side by side, downhill, leaving the queue behind and the church where they would meet Jack Thompson, the vicar. Jake and Isaac walked behind for a few paces, and then peeled off down a side road, waving to them as they went. Phyllie felt Sammy's hand glancing off hers. Then his fingers interlocked with hers. It was wonderful. She felt safe, then embarrassed. This was so new. Did she dare to hope? She said, 'Is your war bad, Sammy?'

'Fun and games, fun and games. I just–' He stopped, then looked straight ahead.

Down they went, heading for ... well, where? Just down to the bottom of the hill. It must be a bit like his submarine, heading downwards. Say something, Sammy, my head is going round, thinking rubbish. Speak to me. He had always done this. He started something, then trailed off as though it was of no importance, driving her demented with impatience.

They crossed the road at the bottom of the hill and started back up again, and still he had said nothing, but his fingers were still linked with hers, and it felt extraordinarily marvellous and she wanted everyone to see, now all embarrassment was gone. His arm was against hers, his shoes were polished, and matching her strike. How often had he done that, matching her stride so they crossed the line together if there was a race on the common? 'Stick with me, Phyllie,' he had always shouted. 'I'll look after you.'

He stopped now, well past St Peters, pulling her back to stand next to the wall of a shop that was boarded up. 'Phyllie, I need to know–' He stopped. 'On the platform, I was just mucking about–' He stopped again, and her heart sank. 'For Jake, you know. But, Phyllie, how did you feel?'

His face was close to her, his eyes on hers. She shook her head, No, tell me how *you* feel, she wanted to shout. He stepped back, and looked away up the hill, and then over at an army jeep that was roaring past. 'Forget it, yes, I was just mucking about.'

He laughed, and started to walk on. She ran after him, dodging round two women with shopping baskets, their headscarves tied under their chins, grabbing his sleeve, and turning him back. 'Don't do this to me, don't you dare. *You* must tell *me,* don't you see? I need to know, Sammy.'

He looked at her hand on his arm, then at her. 'But you shook your head?'

'Don't be so silly. You need to tell me,' she shouted, so loud that the two women they'd just passed looked back. 'You're just so bloody annoying, Sammy.'

He grabbed her then, pulling her close. 'I love you, is that enough? I love you, though you're the annoying one. You always have been, pinching my shoes and filling them with mud. You see, I knew it was you, way back then, but I didn't know this, until I kissed you. Then it all fell into place. I've

151

been lonely. I didn't know why. I've missed you...'
She kissed him then, in the middle of the street.
The women tutted. She didn't give a damn. His
mouth opened under hers, and he held her, so
tightly that it felt as though he would never let her
go.

They walked back up the hill, their arms
around one another's waist, talking of the tree
they had climbed, of their love, of her mother,
but they both decided that could wait for another
day. They reached the top of the hill and clung
together. The wind was cold. She said against his
mouth, 'We should get out of the wind. You'll
catch your death.'

He held her face between his hands, staring at
her as though he'd never seen her before, then
kissed her forehead, her hair, saying, 'I like to feel
the weather. We don't get a lot of that in the boat.
But I'll think of this moment, you and me, here,
and it will bring in the oxygen. Just look at that
sky, Phyllie.'

Together they scanned the racing clouds, the
patches of blue, the glory of it all. It was then he
said, 'Well, will you? You know, marry me? Like I
asked on the platform?'

At last. She leaned into his arms, tight against
him, trying somehow to become so close that
they could never again be separated, so close she
could feel, and remember, the beating of his
heart. 'Of course, and we'll be together for the
rest of our lives. Oh, Sammy, ever since you asked
me, I've thought about it, and hoped.'

They stayed like that for what seemed like
hours, but it was only minutes. It would have to

be enough, for now, but she knew, really knew, so the waiting would be bearable. Wherever he was, and she was, they would belong together.

Finally, she checked her watch. The time was nearly up. 'We'll be late. I'll upset the vicar, you'll upset Isaac.' They were laughing as they ran down the hill, slowing down outside St Peter's, where Jake stood with his arms out wide, to stop them. Isaac was crouching, stroking Francois, whose tongue lolled as though he was smiling.

Beside her Sammy was struggling to pull something from his canvas bag. It was a small box. He winked at Jake and opened the lid. Inside was a ring, with a small sapphire. 'I've asked her, again. She said yes. So, shall I see if she'll wear this?' Jake nodded, his grin as wide as she'd ever seen it.

Isaac stood up, pulling his son to him, still stroking Francois, who leaned against his leg as Sammy tried to put the ring on her finger. It was just too small. Sammy's face was a picture. She kissed him. 'I'll have it enlarged. It's quite beautiful.'

He said, 'Isaac and I must go. We need to catch that train.' He was leaving her, just like that, and she couldn't bear it. Isaac hugged his son, telling Francois to look after this most precious being, and then handed an envelope to Phyllie. 'Please, read and think.' She promised she would and together she and Jake watched as they ran in the direction of the station. They turned at the corner, waved, and were gone.

Phyllie and Jake were silent on the journey home. Sitting in the back of the vicar's rackety car, Phyllie read Isaac's letter. He asked if she would be prepared to act legally in loco parentis while he and his wife were absent, and if she would assume guardianship if the worst happened to both Rachel and he, and to his brother Otto? If so, would she sign the following form in front of witnesses and return it to the solicitor, which would protect her position, and write a letter confirming her agreement? He would take it from there. There was a stamped addressed envelope included with a ps at the bottom of the letter: *Think carefully, dearest Phyllie, though I can't think of anyone I would rather ask to take on this role.*

She didn't have to think. If Isaac didn't return, it would mean that neither would Sammy so of course she would do it. Why? Because they would return; they must. If they didn't, she and Jake would need one another, for the rest of their lives.

Chapter Nine

Wednesday 4 December 1940, HMS *Vehement*, out of Harwich

Most of the old team was back, though with different officers, and all were under a new captain who stormed aboard, seething with energy. He was younger than Old Tom, who would recover – that had been the consensus – and would be given a shore posting.

Lieutenant Diddy Davis, as he was called, because he was not the tallest bloke on the block, boomed through the loudspeaker as the boat rolled and surged on the surface on the way towards the seas off Norway. '*Vehement* is the best boat in the flotilla, indeed, in the whole fucking war. Why's that? Because you're the best team, or if you aren't, you will be by the time we return. And we will return, you mark my words. D'you hear that? But that's if, and I mean if, we stay alert, concentrate, and mistakes are not made – and if they are, they are reported before they bloody happen. That way we'll live.'

Adrian was back on the hydrophones, more experienced and confident now, scanning even though they were on the surface. Who knew what the hydrophones would hear that the eye couldn't see in this bastard of a weather front? Sammy was in oilskins and sou'wester on the bridge, taking a breather, giving the boy space, letting him ease back in. Some of the crew felt doubtful about his skills, thinking he'd made a balls of it last time, but from the way he was handling the hydrophones, and the men, they'd pretty soon see that all was well.

Vehement travelled on the surface towards the Norwegian waters, shrugging off the harsh gusts of wind and sleet. Sammy had heard they were to evade contact and continue surveillance of the Nazi chicken-run into and out of the ice-free port of Narvik, not for the first time. Intelligence was part of the game in a war, and they weren't the silent service for bloody nothing. Last time they'd been rumbled on their way to pick up an operative out of Norway and had ended up sinking two German corvettes and a merchant ship.

Sammy looked around, his sou'wester pulled down as icy spray burst over the bulwark. Isaac was on the bridge with him, taking a break, as the look-outs kept the bins to their eyes, and the officer of the watch made damned sure they did it well. Isaac had left Davy Weale to man the radio. Occasionally Sammy could see *Vigilant* over to the east, or was it just a shadow? Who knew? Isaac smoked a cigarette but only for a second, then the spray from the heightening seas doused it. Sammy had wrapped a towel around his neck but the rain and seawater still gushed out of the bottom of his oilskins. He loved it, even though it was cold, because he could breathe fresh air and see the sky. Isaac tossed away the cigarette, which came straight back on the wind, to disintegrate over Sammy. They laughed, balancing against the rail as *Vehement* was buffeted by waves. They were making slow headway but that was par for the course in this area at this time of year.

Sammy shouted in Isaac's ear, 'Wonder if she's had the ring enlarged?'

Isaac shrugged. 'Wonder if Otto and Rosa have reached Sweden?'

The leading seaman on watch next to them, scanning to the east, yelled, 'Too many questions, not enough answers? Wonder if the missis has had the baby yet?'

The sun was rising astern. 'Keep your eyes on the horizon, if you would, now the sun's getting his hat on. I know the visibility's poor but needs must,' shouted Lieutenant Stanning. 'I doubt any bugger will be doing anything but trying to keep his course, so I'd be surprised if we got a fish up our arse for a while yet.'

Vehement ploughed into a huge swell, lifting with it, then diving too sharply. The men grabbed the rail as the wave flushed them off their feet, and almost over. Sammy was airborne. Shit, he was going over. Isaac jammed against him, and they both tore into Lieutenant Stanning. Then the prow came up, and all three of them slumped one on top of the other, onto the plates of the bridge as the water gushed away. The seaman on the western sector, Able Seaman 'Naughty' Nicholls, swore, 'Bloody binoculars whacked me gob.'

'Broke the lens, then?' Sammy called, from beneath Isaac.

Lieutenant Stanning shoved at Sammy with his elbow, shouting in his ear, 'Personal space, if you don't mind, Leading Seaman Williams. I like you, but not this much.' Sammy laughed and he and Isaac heaved themselves to their feet, allowing Stanning to stand. Straight away he resumed his watch duties, and the lookouts theirs: scanning the seas.

Naughty Nicholls was swearing again. 'Never mind the bloody bins, what about me gob?' He scanned, his elbows resting on the rail.

'Just keep 'em up to your eyes, Nicholls,' Stanning yelled. 'And keep watching.'

'I am, sir. Bloody hero, I am.'

Stanning laughed, and shouted, without turning, 'Sammy, time you let someone else take in the non-existent view. Bugger off now.' His voice was shaking with the cold.

Sammy and Isaac did as they were told, gripping the ladder tight as the waves threatened, and sliding down the conning tower, water cascading after them, and into the control room. They stripped off their oils at the base of the ladder and handed them straight to the two stokers who were waiting, in search of a fag, not fresh air.

Sammy lurched his way to the engine room as the boat pitched, tossed and rolled, with Isaac on his tail. Here it was bloody noisy but warm and their sweaters steamed as they started to dry. The watch keepers were either end, checking dials, and always there was the chief, a filthy oil cloth in his hand, even more dirty than the stokers, if that was possible. No sweaters, just grubby vests. God, he thought he smelled when he came off the bloody boat, but they must stink.

He looked at Isaac and grinned. There was no point in trying to talk against the engine noise. Those buggers who'd obviously just come off their watch and gone up top would freeze after this heat. They stayed for twenty minutes or so, until dry, and then pitched into their bunks, fully dressed as always, hearing the battering of the waves through the casing. Sammy was dozing when the boat heaved, almost over it seemed, paused, and then righted. How was Adrian doing? Would the chief have to do the bacon on a string trick again? God he hoped not, the heads were bad enough as it was in this weather.

He heard the captain call 'Prepare to dive' as he was on the point of sleep again, seeing Phyllie smiling at him, feeling her lips, her body against his and he felt utterly complete. She loved him. *She* loved *him*. All these years they'd been friends, best friends, and now they were something else as well. Something wonderful.

Isaac called, 'About time we dived, eh, Sammy? Our Adrian will have a better chance of picking up enemy engines and propellers now, not to mention keeping his food down. Better than all that peering through curtains of rain.'

Sammy didn't answer. He preferred for those off watch to think he slept when Phyllie was in his head, as she usually was these days. Phyllie, the love of his life, as she always had been – he could see that now – and always would be. Diddy had better be right and bring 'em home, because now he had a real life to live, and soon a wife and children to come home to. Soon, yes, soon he'd marry her. They were diving deeper now. He slid in his bunk, just a bit, but the boat was calm, the tumult of the waves was gone. He slept.

He woke for his watch, he and Isaac together. Coxswain Peters stopped in the passage. 'You awake?'

'Always,' Isaac muttered, easing himself sideways out of the bunk above Sammy's. All around the men were going on watch, coming off watch, talking, belching, complaining. Sammy took over from Adrian, who was green, but not that bad. 'You all right, lad?'

Adrian nodded. 'Better now we're deep. Don't mention bacon. Do not, under any circumstances whatsoever, say that word, and definitely do not say string. I'm getting my head down. Kept the bunk warm for me, have you?' Behind him Sammy could see Diddy and the Jimmy, 1st Lieutenant Michael Dorian, laughing.

Sammy slipped into the Asdic booth. 'You'll

love it, lad. Better than a hot water bottle any day, but not nearly as nice as a good woman.'

The boat had been running for about an hour into Sammy's watch, making better time than they had done on the surface, when Sammy heard it. But what? He held up his hand to the captain, shut his eyes to hear better, scanning, coming back to the direction. What? What? Diddy was next to him now.

'Anything?'

Sammy nodded. There it was again. He swung to the left, then back a fraction, no, just half an inch more, slowly. He wasn't breathing: there. 'Sound bearing zero six zero – but weak. Really weak.'

Diddy leaned close, taking one of the earpieces, holding it to his ear. Sammy kept his eyes shut, reporting, 'Depth charges. Scattering? Not sure. No question, though, they're raking 'em.'

Diddy straightened, returned the earpiece. Sammy pressed it to his ear. Diddy said, 'Good call, Sammy. Where now?'

'Zero six five, sir. Moving astern. Way off.'

The Jimmy said quietly, 'That's *Venture's* sector, damn it to hell.'

Diddy was nodding. 'Time to gulp down some air; let's see how the weather's doing.' He reached for the loudspeaker. 'Lookouts – get ready, and up that ladder before we've even bloody surfaced, if you please.'

The Jimmy was officer of the watch and headed for the oilskins and ladder before Diddy had stopped speaking. The lookouts were hot on his heels.

The captain ordered, 'Course zero three zero.

Prepare to surface.' He flung a look over his shoulder. 'Note for the log, Navigator. In spite of weather conditions, decided to proceed on surface in search of convoy.' Sammy knew it was also to recharge the boat's air and batteries, in case *Vehement* was the next one that had to hit the depths, and stay there until the predators moved off.

The prow was rising, Sammy was listening, but there was nothing closer. The captain was at the periscope, scanning three six zero degrees continuously, although the waves would be breaking over the lens. Diddy ordered the periscope down, and the boat broke surface, heeling over and back in response to the force of the waves. Sammy almost fell from his perch, his pencil falling to the plates, below which he could hear the slurping of water in the bilges. The storm had obviously increased. He grinned at the thought of bacon on a string. Poor bugger. Isaac looked across as though he had picked up the thought. He laughed, mouthing: 'Bacon?'

Sammy stayed glued to the hydrophone in case he picked up sounds that evaded the lookouts. He looked back at Isaac who was twiddling some dials. Strange, how when you lived and worked with someone, you often didn't have to speak. It had been like that with Phyllie when they were kids, and would be again, when they were married. He imagined waking up with her, then he thought of going to bed with her, and felt the heat rising, and listened hard, anything to keep his mind off that.

Water poured through the conning-tower hatch. He shut his eyes, and kept listening. On and on

161

Vehement went, grinding through the weather, the lookouts changing, Sammy listening, the captain at the chart table with Sub Lieutenant Norton, so young he looked as though he should still be at school. Adrian came for his watch but Sammy waved him back; he stank of the sick that stained his top. 'Get your head down. I've got it for now.'

Diddy passed on his way to his cubbyhole. He might be doing paperwork, or getting his head down while Lieutenant Dorian ran the control room, but he'd also have both ears pricked, too bloody right he would. An hour passed and by then there was a smell of food from the apology for a galley. Sammy could slaughter a plate of chips, an egg too. Adrian came through. 'Grub's up. You have yours. I'll cover you.' He looked better. Sammy raised an eyebrow. Adrian's grin was weak. 'Yes, bacon and string and Coxswain Peters promises it will work this time. Says he's never had to do it more than once, so I'm a bloody champion if it goes to a third round.'

Sammy handed the headphones to the lad, who put them straight on, taking his seat, his hands already on the scanning wheel. Sammy was making his way out of the control room when the call came from the bridge.

'Masthead off the starboard bow.'

Sammy spun round; Adrian shook his head. Sammy hurried over, bent and listened in the earpiece Adrian offered. No, nothing. Silently Diddy appeared beside them. Both Sammy and Adrian shook their heads. Diddy spun off, heading for the ladder, tearing up, his bins round his neck, and no oilskin. It was then Adrian vomited, off to the side, onto Sammy's boots.

Sammy sighed and nodded. Adrian left the shack and Sammy took his place. No one could listen properly when they were upchucking. 'Mop up, then get your head down. Come back when you can.'

Adrian grabbed a mop from the bucket, swished it around Sammy's boots, and left.

Isaac was waiting expectantly because it was up to him to report the information gleaned by Diddy, if it couldn't wait until harbour, though it stood a good chance of giving away their position at this distance. The call came from the bridge. 'Hard to starboard, steer one six zero.'

A long wait, then they heard Diddy, who was sliding down the ladder into the control room again, say, 'Fuck a duck, destroyer bearing towards us, maybe others from the convoy will join the party. Could be coincidence, or could be the skimmer's seen us.' He grabbed a pencil, wrote the details of his observations. Young Norton took them to Isaac, who knew to wait until the order to transmit was given, for they needed to be well clear of all contacts, unless they were hit on the surface and beyond help. Then it would be the last thing *Vehement* did.

The alarm was given, though. The watch rushed down through the hatch, which was being slammed shut, the dive commenced. Sammy stayed glued to the hydrophone. Around him they'd be opening the vents to flood the tanks. He heard the coxswain's orders, then spare bodies clattered to the prow; any extra weight would help the dive. Any. The bloody destroyer must still be

163

on a bearing heading straight for them, from what Diddy and the Jimmy were saying. Shit.

Vehement was prow down, the mop slid across the floor. He forced himself to concentrate and listen, scanning. Nothing, but at least the rolling had stopped as the boat's engines ran hard. Diddy called, 'Depth?'

'Thirty feet, sir,' reported the coxswain. Yes, Sammy had found the enemy engine noise now. He lifted his hand. Diddy came. Took an earpiece. Listened. 'Distance?'

Sammy stared. For God's sake, the bugger wasn't going to attack? *Vehement*'s job on this patrol was to report and, later, to collect an agent from the Norwegian shores, again.

'Report,' barked Diddy.

Sammy checked. 'Port bow, increasing.'

They waited. The captain ordered water pumped from the forward trim tank towards the stern. They were now horizontal, at periscope depth when they should be diving. Diddy was back at the periscope, scanning, sweat beading his face, just as the condensation was beading the internal casing. It was then that Sammy's doubts were pushed aside. The bugger was observing as he should, double checking he'd copped the convoy right. His heart was pounding as the engine noise drew closer, but he was sure there was only the one. He told Diddy who replied, his eyes alive, his mind already plotting, 'For now, young Sammy. Keep reporting.'

Sammy's neck ached with tension as he scanned. 'One skimmer, still.' He listened, tracked the noise, 'Skimmer contact fast approaching, sir, getting louder...'

Diddy gripped the periscope handles, bent his legs, scanned again, stopped, fixed in one position, then slapped the handles up, the periscope descended. Sammy breathed a sigh of relief as would everyone else in the control room. The periscope would leave a wake, which any sharp-eyed lookout on the skimmer could see if he did see it, then it'd pinpoint *Vehement*'s position, and that would lead to a damned loud bollocking. If the Germans had Asdic as well, God help *Vehement*, because then they'd be like butterflies pinned on a collector's board.

Sammy gave the update: 'Contact closing quickly, sir.' While what he wanted to scream was: dive, for God's sake, dive.

It came then: 'Dive to two hundred feet. Quick as you can.' Diddy's voice was calm, not the scream that had been in Sammy's mind.

The captain called, 'Thirty degrees down, full ahead. Flood Q. Peter, note in the log: one destroyer in pursuit. Convoy consists of further twelve merchants, four corvettes. Did you get that, Isaac? Make a note for transmission later. Add the position and time, both of you. Quietly, everyone.'

'Sir.' Sub Lieutenant Norton started writing as he stood at the chart table, struggling to keep his feet. Lieutenant Stanning was studying the dials, the hydroplanes were hard down, the control room tilting. Isaac wrote. Sammy scanned. Men were rushing through the control room from astern. One slipped as the tilt increased, cursed as he crashed into some pipes. Was Adrian at his battle station? Probably, but that wasn't his business, his was to listen. 'Passing sixty feet,' said Lieutenant Stanning.

'Slow ahead both. Blow Q,' ordered Diddy. 'Sammy?' he called softly, his voice as calm as the pond Phyllie wrote about at Little Mitherton.

Sammy told him, 'Louder on a line to port, sir.'

'Well, that's something,' breathed Diddy.

Dorian, Stanning and the captain shared a look, one of tempered relief. The Germans didn't know exactly where they were, then Sammy, quietly, 'Still on a line to port, sir.'

Sammy breathed easier. 'Fading on a line to port, sir,' he said.

Isaac snatched a look at him. Sammy suspected they were both thinking Diddy had cut that a bit too fine. Sammy could see the hams swinging in the passageway, and the bread, too, in their nets. Was it mouldy yet? The coxswain murmured the depth, anything to help them hide. Sammy whispered the distance and Diddy read his lips. Sammy could see in his mind's eye the destroyer carving its path, closer, closer in distance but still off to port, but not by much. It was bloody tight, and would they drop ashcans and if they did, would they guess the range?

Diddy was by the chart table. Sub Lieutenant Norton was marking the chart. His hands were shaking. Poor little bugger, thought Sammy.

'Two hundred feet.' They were levelling out and as they did so Sammy heard the depth charges hit the water through his headphones, but they were off to port. Well, obviously. He raised his hand, whispering. 'Sir, ashcans.'

Diddy nodded. Crump, crump, crump, to port,

but closer than he'd thought. The boat shuddered as sledgehammers pounded the water around them. There were roars, the usual bloody roars outside, beating at them, making the boat shudder. Sammy clung to his table. His ears felt as though they were bursting with the headphones' resonance, and he shoved them back, just for a minute. Young Norton looked stunned, and called softly, 'What the hell's that noise?'

Diddy spoke, his voice casual, but little more than a whisper. 'Just think about it, Peter; if you remove water with an explosion, then more will come in. Think bath. It's just like a bloody forceful tap. It roars. They've not got us pinpointed, they're scattering their toys from the pram, so it's all right. Pass the word, again, Coxswain. Silent running. Silent. Socks only, when you move them to trim the boat, Stanning. Can't have any motors when they're close. Don't want their big ears picking us up.'

Actually, it isn't bloody all right, Sammy ground out to himself. I want to get back, to Phyllie. I really really do. So, no, it's not bloody all right.

Crump, crump, and then he caught another blip on the scanner, tuned in, heard another engine, distant. Shit. It had to be a corvette. He whispered the contact to Diddy. His captain raised an eyebrow, that was all. Two ships looking specifically for them, or were they just fishing, thinking they might have seen us? Whatever it was, the skimmers would be criss-crossing the grid, having a fine old time as they tried to flush them out.

Crump, crump, closer now, and *Vehement* didn't like it, shaking herself like a doxy being given a

167

shower. The engine noise was loud in his ear-phones, when it wasn't smothered by the mayhem of the depth charges. Crump. Shudder. Roar. They were bloody close and *Vehement* was still being chucked. Another huge crump.

Norton staggered, gripped the chart table. Sammy fell back and knocked his headphones to one side, and it damned well hurt. Diddy hadn't moved, but the sweat was no longer beaded, it was running down his face. Sammy checked the condensation on the inside casing. It had gone, been shaken loose, the floor was damp.

Another crump: an explosion louder than all the rest, right on top of them. The other skimmer was approaching from starboard. The boat jerked and jumped, the casing seemed to flex, the lights went, and the darkness was total. Naughty Nicholls shouted, 'Auxiliary lighting out.'

Diddy murmured, 'Somewhat superfluous loud report, one feels.'

Coxswain called, as quietly as he could, 'Damage report?' Torches were stabbing the darkness; the other skimmer was approaching, ashcans were dropping. All this Sammy relayed, but they'd all know soon enough.

Sammy lifted his right earpiece, just for a moment, to ease the noise, and thought he could hear water in the control room. His mouth was dry.

Reports were pouring through. 'Main motor room in order.' The chief's voice came through next: 'Engine room in order.' Another report: 'No leakage, sir.' They waited as Sammy reported on the approach of the hunters, because he was the

168

only eyes they had and his head, back and shoulders ached with the tension of it all. Dorian was moving some men about, trimming the boat. It must stay level, and they daren't use the engines or the noise could help the buggers up top locate them, exactly. It was just guesswork at the moment. Pretty good guesswork.

The next explosions were deeper, the floor plates jumped. Beneath them were the stores. Well, they'd all had this before but in Old Tom's time and then it was sardines that had burst their tins and soaked into the sugar. Disgusting, worse than bacon on a string. He knew he was very frightened because his thoughts were jagged. He heard the engines, louder. Much louder. 'Increasing, sir. Smaller skimmer.'

He was still whispering as everyone was but why bother, when the pounding above was so damned loud? Was Diddy a lucky captain or not? Would he find a layer to hide in or would he be able to break and run? When would he make that break or that find? Because he'd bloody well have to, unless the skimmers lost their marbles and pottered off back to the convoy, their fun over for the day. Or was it night? What the hell did it matter, they were still here, stuck in the path of a load of rubbish.

Diddy flashed his torch at Sammy who reported: 'Both decreasing, one astern, one to port.' Sammy scanned, feeling terror at the thought that the other convoy skimmers might join in the hunt. If they did, it would be over. 'Still only two, sir.'

Diddy shot him a smile, and murmured, 'You read my mind, Sammy. Take her down further.

Keep two hundred and fifty feet. Not a sound from the rest of you. Still silent running, if you please. Remember, not a bloody word from anyone, shoes off if you move.' Stanning's men had been gliding about, trimming silently with their weight, for what seemed like forever so they weren't about to put clogs on, were they?

Sammy listened hard. They all waited, as the sounds decreased, and waited again, but then he heard it. 'Destroyer is closing again, sir. From astern, sir, maybe trying for a better line. Corvette coming in from port.' If he *was* trying for a better line, it could mean he'd guessed they were here.

Diddy nodded again. The ashcans were dropped, by both, but not as close. Ah, so they were still scattering, thank God. They crumped and again, and again, growing louder, louder, and closer – too close.

Sammy mouthed to Diddy, 'Destroyer almost above, sir.' But he'd know that, if he had the sense of a bloody gnat, because the propellers were so loud. *Vehement* waited, the skimmer moved over them, the engine noise decreased slightly, then the ashcans were hurled again, and this time the boat seemed to implode and then expand. Sammy looked over his shoulder, and saw, by the light of the torches, Diddy standing at the control panel, his eyes closed. He willed his captain to get it right because they all knew that he was calculating their course, the enemy's course, ways of escape, how deep to go, when to break and run.

The coxswain was levelling at two hundred and fifty feet. Stanning moved the men backwards and forwards because the last thing any of them

170

wanted was for the boat to lose stability and slip, arse down, into the depths and finish the Germans' job for them. Dorian was at the control panel, alongside Diddy. The torchlights stabbed the darkness.

'One moving away, but slowly, sir,' Sammy said, listening to the crump, crump, tracking both engines, repeating their positions to Diddy.

Suddenly there was a different crash, within the boat. Everyone froze. 'Plates in the galley,' the coxswain whispered.

'I'll give him bloody plates,' Diddy seethed. 'Send Cookie to see me, if you please, Coxswain, when we've sorted this little problem, or would he like to send up a flag to show them just where we damn well are?'

Sammy pressed the earpieces, crump, crump, decreasing. He reported on both, and then eased an earpiece. Somewhere he could hear the hiss of water. Senior Rate Ted Simpson came into the control room from the engine room, in socks, his torch bobbing. 'Tightening some valves, sir; superficial, sir.' His socks were soaked, his voice was little more than a breath.

Sammy was counting the circling corvette's ashcan explosions. He looked up, they were all counting, but he was the only one able to visualise the surface. He had a talent for it, Old Tom had said, and he had. He could see what was happening, and who was doing what, though sometimes he wished he couldn't. Cookie should bloody well have slung the plates into a hod, daft bugger.

The destroyer was running in again, on a better line, for him, but not for *Vehement*. Diddy was at

171

his elbow.

One explosion seemed to catch them under the keel, their soft underbelly. Dear God, where there were bloody millions of flanges and plugs. The corvette was widening his circle, but the big bugger of a destroyer was ploughing overhead, clearly audible. Well, he would be big if he was a destroyer, so shut up, Sammy, he told himself. Diddy was back with Dorian, but watching Sammy who gestured. Diddy nodded. Isaac's hands must be sweating, because his pencil slipped from his grasp. It rolled to the edge. He caught it before it dropped.

Depth charges don't have to hit a submarine, they just need to explode within the lethal radius. If a water pressure wave hits a boat it rips it apart at the seams. Sammy wished he didn't retain these facts. He was listening, scanning. The destroyer was overhead, but then it was steadily decreasing, taking its ashcans with it; crump, crump, getting fainter. Sammy was scanning, working from one to the other, and the corvette was narrowing the circle, sniffing like a bloodhound, closer to them, too bloody close. He couldn't have heard the plates. It was just luck. Had he got them cornered? Hang on. He put his hand up to his captain, who crept across.

'Corvette circling, but more than slightly astern, sir.'

Diddy nodded, standing by him now. 'Perhaps we shouldn't be here,' he murmured. 'I've a mind to shift our arses when they next draw away.'

Sammy nodded, still tracking one, then the other. 'Might be an idea, sir.' But then he caught

Diddy's sleeve. 'Destroyer's come about, sir. Bearing two nine zero. Closing rapidly.'

Diddy's lips thinned, but that was all. They all waited, the trimmers moved about to Stanning's signals. There were four explosions in quick succession, but slightly astern, then another cluster, the plates leapt, one very close. Norton, the young navigator, was making a note by torchlight for the log. Sammy hoped someone would be left to bloody read it.

Coxswain came to Diddy's side. They were back by the controls. 'Lights fixed, sir.'

Diddy shook his head. 'Only essentials, if you please. Who knows how long we'll need to stay down, so let's be kind to the batteries.'

Sammy said, 'Corvette decreasing.' Everyone was watching him. 'Destroyer close circling.' He scanned for the corvette. Bugger. 'Corvette increasing, closing.' He could see them, up there, getting their act together.

They came again. Crump, crump, bloody crump, getting louder and louder, but they were still scattering, so still not sure they were even here, or if they were, not sure where exactly. One dropped much too close, the boat bucked, and tossed, then another exploded, far too bloody close. The lights flickered, but stayed on. Distantly someone screamed, Sammy cursed, whacking his head against the compartment wall, his headphones were ripped from his head. Isaac was thrown from his post to skid into the pipes. One of the trimmers flew into the hatch, and cursed with pain.

Diddy grabbed the chart table, everyone

173

grabbed something, more water hissed, Norton also grabbed for the chart table, missed and was hurled into the periscope. They all heard the crack. The lad crumpled unconscious, blood poured from his nose, across the deck plates. Stanning hissed, 'Nicholls. Medic, immediately.' Dorian and Diddy trimmed the boat with those who had recovered their feet.

Crump, crump, so many were being dropped, from both ships. Naughty Nicholls hurried off, grabbing the pipes for support as the boat shuddered again and again under the barrage. Sammy groped for his headphones, the back of his head hurt. He felt it. Blood.

Diddy found his way to Sammy. 'They might be thinking they've got us. I need to know the moment they move off, this is getting tiresome. The moment, Sammy.' He moved back to the nerve centre.

Sammy listened, and pictured the surface; the corvette was overhead, crump, crump, then another, exploding too close, within the lethal radius. Again they were tossed and knocked. Isaac had clambered back onto his perch, and was clinging to his table. Sammy's head hurt, he felt sick, but no, he needed to listen. Where was the destroyer? He scanned. Got it. Another close one lifted him from his seat, his breathing stopped, he lifted his earpieces away from his head, the noise too loud, but he was scanning, always scanning, because even if they were torn apart, that was what he must do.

Davy, Isaac's assistant, was beside Isaac now, in case he was needed, but Isaac sent him back to his

174

action station. Perhaps he was a trimmer? Sammy didn't know, hadn't noticed, all he knew right this bloody minute was that his head hurt and he was bathed in sweat, cold sweat. He dropped his earpieces back to where they should be, and scanned. Hang on, the corvette was moving off to port, but still scattering. Where was the bloody destroyer? Ah, he'd got it.

'Both decreasing, sir.'

Diddy swung round, nodded to Stanning, 'Hard a-starboard. Now. Quick.'

'Still decreasing in sound, sir,' Sammy said.

'Full ahead.'

It seemed that they were all holding their breath as they ploughed on, trying to make their escape. God damn it, Sammy picked up the skimmers again. Increasing. Damn and bloody blast. Increasing. But then suddenly, both were faint. Sammy pressed the earpieces. Yes, suddenly faint. It could be a layer, or the start of a layer at least? Sammy told Diddy, his voice not even a whisper. Diddy grinned at Sammy. Then they were back, louder, closer. If it had been a layer, it was only a teaser.

'Another fifty-foot dive, if you will.' Diddy ordered. They dived. They stopped, levelled. 'Stop engines, let's wait awhile, again. Quiet as you like,' Diddy ordered. Norton groaned, loudly, as the medic, young Simons, worked on him. 'Silence.' Diddy sliced through the air with his hand. The medic put a hand over the lad's mouth to stifle the moan.

Crump, crump, crump, overhead, the Germans had got the depth wrong, but no, there was one too close, again, the casing flexed, water spurted from a seal, shooting in a loud jet across the control room, it was bloody freezing, and too damn close to Sammy. Then another seal gave way, another jet of water, loud. Sammy worked the scanner, and listened. God, did he listen. 'Both decreasing again, sir. To port and starboard.' The chief entered, tightened the seals, the water died to a trickle. The noise stopped.

'Full ahead, both engines,' Diddy ordered.

This time it took longer for the destroyer to come around, and he was now too far to starboard, and the corvette too. They fell silent again when they drew close, and while they did the medic suddenly straightened, snatching away his hand from Peter Norton's mouth, as though he'd been stung. 'Jesus.' It was the medic who groaned now, a groan he snapped off as Diddy swung round. Peter Norton's head lolled to one side. It was only then that the control room realised young Peter was dead, for how could you breathe when your nose was crushed, and your mouth covered? You couldn't. You were being smothered. You died.

Sammy turned back, and continued to scan, continued to report. They were decreasing, the explosions were quieter, and now they had a cat in hell's chance of getting out of this bloody mess alive. Sammy snatched a look at young Norton, but there was work to do. The medic was sent to action stations because it was best he had something to focus on. As he went the tears were pouring down his face, bloody pouring. He must have been the same age as the man he had just killed and Sammy was relieved that he was stuck with the hydrophones.

Within half an hour they were running free, and Isaac could send his report from the surface before they resumed their patrol, but only after they had buried young Norton, at sea. Before that, Diddy had called the medic to his tiny cabin. The coxswain, Peters, had helped clean Peter Norton as best he could, because he insisted the lad deserved the works. Diddy told the medic quietly, though they all heard in the control room, that the coxswain had reported Sub Lieutenant Peter Norton's forehead was like a broken eggshell, and that was why he had died. Nothing more. Nothing less.

The coxswain had seen Sammy watching, and shrugged. 'Well, you can't let a lad go through life thinking he'd killed like that. Even though he had.'

Before Sammy went to his pit after coming off watch, he climbed up onto the bridge to look up into the sky. It was night again, but that was the time to surface. It was clear; the stars seemed so low he felt he could touch them. Diddy came up too, talking quietly to the lookouts, then coming to Sammy. There was a moderate wind after the storm. He lit up a cigarette and offered one to Sammy, who took one, though he didn't smoke. His hand was shaking.

Diddy said, 'You did well, Sammy. You should think of taking a commission. Let's see how you do this patrol, but I reckon you should have a go, especially as I hear you could be a family man soon.'

Sammy coughed on the smoke, and tossed the cigarette over the bulwark. It was taken by the wind. 'Not sure if marriage is fair on the women, you know, sir.'

Diddly leaned his arms on the rail. 'Nothing and nobody's sure of anything these days. You have to take happiness where you find it, Sammy. If you don't marry her, then you'll break her heart. If you die, then you'll break it too. Maybe you should think of making one another happy while you can. My wife says she takes it one day at a time, and is thankful for each one. God in heaven, Sammy, you could get run over by a bloody bus crossing Oxford Street so don't hold back. I told you I'd bring you all home, and I will. God willing.'

He had said 'God, willing' very quietly. They both looked up at the sky while the four on watch stayed glued to their sectors, under Stanning's watchful eye. Sammy thought about a commission. Well, it would shut up the future mother-in-law. He laughed quietly as Diddy returned to the control room, and Isaac took his place up top. Together the two friends let the wind blow in their faces, knowing that today they had nearly died. So what was new? They'd lost count of the times that had happened.

Chapter Ten

Sunday 8 December 1940, Little Mitherton

It was barely light, with a heavy ground frost and a harsh wind beginning to build, when Phyllie attached the wooden cart to Maeve, Miss F's bicycle. She set off to collect compost that the villagers in Little Mitherton and Great Mitherton left at the designated collection points. Phyllie grinned to herself, pulling her woolly hat well down, before ringing her bell at chickens in the road. Honestly, if these WI women were set the task of planning the whole war at one committee meeting, it would be over before you knew where you were. She looked up at the grey sky.

'Hello, darling Sammy,' she whispered. 'I love you so much. I can't wait until I see you in January.' For that is what he had promised in his letter.

She picked up the pails, labelled with their owners' names, and rode back towards the allotment. While she did this, Miss F and Jake would be walking Francois to the pond, checking on the ducks, and throwing bread. Ice had formed at the edges yesterday, black and sinister somehow. When it froze over completely the ducks just 'shoved off' to the hide in the fenced-off area, Miss F had told her.

Phyllie bumped over the ruts leading to the allotment. Ice filled the hollows and cracked as

179

she skidded over them. To the left she could hear hedging and ditching. Clearly there was no point in going to see Joe about the new scheme she and Miss F had devised until darkness fell.

She swore as she fiddled with the padlock on the wooden allotment gate because the metal was so cold, but no one was prepared to make it easy for the vegetable thieves. She pushed the bike with its cargo along the frosted grass track leading to the compost heaps. She was racing against the clock, and lifted the old carpet off the first of them, feeling the warmth, seeing the steam. She lowered the back of the cart, slinging the contents onto the heap, before replacing the pails and the carpet. She checked the lists that had been wrapped round the handles of the pails, then set to, digging up parsnips, leeks, the odd cabbage from the various plots. She felt that hacking concrete would have been easier. Back she rode, delivering the contents to the drop-off points.

The cold had bitten deep, but she wore extra socks and the gumboots, which were a size too big, had been warm enough. While she was doing this, Mrs Speedie would have collected up the scraps from the pails marked 'Pig Club'. It used to be done by young Alice Martin but she had joined the WAAF. The WI had thrown a farewell party and Phyllie, single and young, had felt momentarily isolated as they'd all raised their glasses to her. As the villagers flung themselves into the Gay Gordons, however, and she had whirled with the oldest of them, she felt truly proud to be amongst them.

She still felt that, day after day, as these women

looked after children, foster children, visiting parents, while all the time making preserves, chutneys, and baking something out of nothing. You would never know they tucked away telegrams bearing bad news of their sons and husbands, and smiled. They were completely wonderful.

Once the pails and their contents were returned, she replaced her load with that of the metal salvage the WI had helped the Scouts to collect on Saturday afternoon. She cycled it to Mrs Symes's back gate and now they both trundled to the town collection area in her old Morris, its boot filled.

On their return it was time for morning service and while the vicar said prayers for those who had embarked on the first major British land offensive against the Italians in the Western Desert, she and Jake walked. They headed for the pond and she thought of the bombs falling on so many provincial cities, including Bristol. She remembered that day and night in London, and was amazed that anyone had survived, and *was* surviving the bombing of Britain's cities. She phoned the new presbytery from time to time, and Frankie always said that her mother would be pleased to hear her news on her return, but was off out – busy, busy.

While she mulled, Jake made notes for the nature journal he was preparing for his mother and father, and for the school. Miss F and the vicar had suggested he kept a diary of God's work during wartime, together with the occasional drawing. They didn't say 'just in case', but why not? It might be something to cherish if the Germans came: Britain how it once was.

He was drawing the old man's beard, growing in

and over the as yet uncut hedges, as they reached the pond. He had shown a talent for art as the months had passed, which was hardly surprising, because his mother had designed wallpaper in Berlin, he had told Phyllie. Francois leapt over the ice and in after a duck. 'Out of there,' she and Jake shouted together, fearful that Andy Bartlett would come to hear of it.

Jake said, 'We should whisper it, you know. It's a dead giveaway, yelling like that. Mr Andy's all right sometimes, but you still never know, do you? He's very up and down.'

Francois was out by then, shaking himself all over them. He was shouted at again. They laughed together. Jake pointed to the horse chestnut on the edge of the woods. 'Race you to the tree, Phyllie.' He took off and she followed, and it was easy to let him win, because her oversized gumboots slopped and flopped and it was like wading through treacle. She snatched off her hat and threw it at him when she arrived. He laughed. He laughed a lot now.

They collected ivy and the old man's beard that was growing within the wood and once they reached the centre, half a mile from the pond, they risked life and limb to yank down some mistletoe. They would store it, then use it for Christmas decorations. They noted exactly where the best holly trees were.

'The birds might take the berries before then,' Phyllie said, 'but at least they'll have full stomachs, and the branches will look good anyway. We could make paper-chains by cutting paper strips, then colouring them. We can then make paste out of flour to stick them together. Perhaps write that down too.' He did.

In late afternoon, all three of them were in the kitchen listening to the wireless while Miss F did the WI sugar accounts, Jake made paper-chains, and Phyllie cooked. She was preparing a pie for supper from a couple of rashers of streaky bacon, parsnips and carrots, with sage and thyme they had dried in late summer, when the telephone rang. Phyllie looked helplessly at her pastry-covered hands. Francois barked, while Jake grimaced and waved his paste-covered fingers, to which a strip of paper had stuck.

'Paper-chain making,' he said.

Miss F looked up. 'Well, all right, I think I've got the message. I'll go, shall I?' She called from the hall, 'Phyllie, it's your brother for you.'

Jake swung round, his fingers seemed to be stuck together. 'You're not going to London? They still bomb it. Say you're not going?'

Phyllie washed her hands, wiping them on her apron as she hurried into the hall, calling, 'Just wait. We know nothing.'

The hall was freezing. Miss F was holding the receiver as though it might explode at any moment, which Phyllie suspected was pretty much her expectation of this new-fangled thing.

'He seems agitated.' Miss F's whisper would reach the end of the village. She thrust the receiver at Phyllie and hurried into the warmth of the kitchen.

Phyllie said, 'Hello, Frankie. Is everything all right? Mother?'

Her brother's voice was strained as he said, 'Miss Featherstone is correct, I am rather agitated, and I wonder if it wouldn't be a good idea for Mother to visit the countryside for a few days. Perhaps over Christmas, if that is possible?'

'Here?' Phyllie, said, and now it was she who felt strained.

He muttered, 'Well, you're in the countryside, Phyllie. Must you be so obtuse?'

Phyllie spoke before she thought. 'I'm not aware I'm being obtuse, Frankie, but *here* is the last place Mother would want to be, and you know that very well. In spite of bombs raining down, she sees her place as beside you, especially at Christmastime, like a good Catholic, I would think. Certainly not here, with a heathen like Jake, and, indeed, me.' She was surprised at her bitterness, and felt ashamed.

There was a pause. 'Phyllie, dear Phyllie. It's as much of a burden to be the favourite, you know. She's exhausted, and needs some noiseless nights, and the company of her daughter, though I know she finds it difficult to say this. What's more, I am not a saint, and I could do with a bloody break.'

Phyllie stared into the mirror, and tucked a strand of hair behind her ear in the glow of the electric light. They were only electrified downstairs. Upstairs she had grown to like the smell of the oil lamps. She knew she was being manipulated but it was her own mother they were discussing. 'Heavens, Frankie, you do sound stressed.' She half laughed. 'Is it Mother or the bombing?'

'A bit of both, my dear. She can be remarkably

difficult, but I don't need to tell you that.'

Phyllie laughed; at least her brother was feeling the heat for a change. 'Of course, put her on the train and I will meet her. She may come on the twenty-fourth, Christmas Eve, and if she is unkind just once to Jake, I will put her on the first train back. She may stay for a week. Don't hang up. I need to confirm first with Jake, and Miss F, not forgetting Francois.'

Frankie said, 'Francois? You have some French evacuees too?'

'We have a dog evacuated from Dunkirk.'

'Oh, for heaven's sake, how can a dog object?'

She laughed again. 'You'd be surprised. Wait a moment. I'll be back.'

The warmth and light of the kitchen was welcome. She explained. Jake and Miss F exchanged a look. Francois appeared concerned at the sudden tension in the room. Miss F smiled suddenly. 'Of course. Perhaps she could have your bedroom, Phyllie, if you can manage with the sofa? It could be a blessing; she might come to accept the things she should.'

Jake stood up. 'She can have my boxroom. I can go on the sofa with Francois. He'll settle by the fire.'

'You're very kind, both of you. We can sort out the details.' Phyllie headed back into the hall.

Miss F followed her and now her voice really was a whisper. 'We don't want any of her nonsense about Jake killing Christ. I won't have it, not in this village now everyone loves the boy and understands his culture and is mortified at their previous reservations. Well, I say everyone, but it seems to me Ron is building the bullying again, which I'm sure is because his mother might not be coming for Christmas. Why that ghastly woman can't commit as the other mums have done, I do not know. It's making the lad so... Well, so angry.'

Phyllie nodded, but she needed to finish the telephone call. She picked up the receiver, the line was crackling, and there was the sound of bangs. 'A raid?' she asked.

Frankie laughed. 'The Nativity in the hall being put together.'

She said, 'Mum will be welcome, as long as we have no nonsense about Jews and Christ, is this quite clear?'

She could almost see her brother nodding, with a finger in his ear, as the banging heightened. 'I'll have a word, and I will telephone you once we've sorted times. She can get the first train in the morning, or perhaps a little later?'

Phyllie murmured. 'It would be excellent if she could be in time for the carol service, after which is the children's party. In addition there's to be an adults' knees-up. God bless the WI for contributing the costs, and organising both beanos.'

'Sounds like fun. The WI seem a formidable bunch.' He sounded relieved, but exhausted.

She thought that indeed they were, and if any bunch of people could contain her mother, it would be them.

Once the pie was ready and supper eaten, Phyllie set out once again, with a note for Joe from Miss F, and her own begging words carefully rehearsed in front of both the others. As she cycled, Jake's warning that Joe might say she needed to talk to

186

Andy about it rang in her ears.

The moon was bright, so there was no need for the minuscule amount of light the bicycle lamp was allowed. She pedalled off, through the blacked-out village. She wore the gumboots again, and felt sure she'd be left with permanent welts on her calves from the slapping. Owls hooted, and the breeze stirred the bare branches as she took the left-hand turn to the farm. Yet again she wondered why she had opened her mouth, and even Sammy had said when he telephoned from Harwich, 'Well, the one that suggests it has to carry it through, daft glorious girl.'

Tonight, if he rang, she would tell him that the jeweller had promised that her ring would be ready for collection by Christmas and now the smile faded. Would she have the courage to wear it in front of her mother? The farmyard was in darkness too, but from the milking shed came the clanking of pails, and the mooing of the cows, as she leaned the bicycle against the stone wall of the yard. It would be Joe and Old Stan because Andy left that to the two-handed brigade, or so he had snapped at her when she was last here.

He had added, 'I'm left with the accounts, the cooking, and things like ditching or driving the horses. I'm safe to do that. What a bloody life.'

The geese came flapping, but knew her so it was only a token gesture. 'Just which of you will be here after Christmas?' she murmured. The dogs waited patiently for a stroke. There was a duck quacking somewhere. She banged loudly on the milking-parlour door. Joe opened it at crack, slipping through, and shutting it quickly so that darkness resumed. He dragged his cigarette from his ear, and lit it.

She explained to Joe that in summer there was plenty of room outside for children to play, and they'd been managing with the school hall and the village hall in the cold of winter. 'But now, the Home Guard need the village hall more and more, and the Scouts and Guides need the school hall and it's not big enough anyway, for all our children, especially with the new evacuees from the cities. I am thinking of your old barn for a sort of indoor play area. I know the roof is damaged at the far end, but I wondered whether we could all come and tidy it up, draping a tarpaulin...'

She faded to a halt as Joe put up a hand, dragged on his cigarette, looking not at her, but over to the house. 'Not sure our boy would like that, but it might be an idea to ask. I'm sick of trying with t'lad. He used to be a goer, but the going's gone out of him. It might stir something.'

She thrust the letter from Miss F at him. 'Miss F has thoughts about the wood burner. Perhaps it could be brought out of the stable store, where it's doing nothing. We could incorporate it into the barn, safely, because Mrs Speedie knows someone who can rig a flue. The straw could be cleared, with just a few bales for seats, and one, of us will be on duty all the time.'

Joe read the note from the light of another match. He tucked it in his pocket, smiling slightly. It was the smile he kept for Miss F. She had her own in reply. Not for the first time Phyllie wondered why they didn't just get on with it?

The match spluttered and died as he tossed it

onto the muck of the yard. He noticed her boots. 'Big enough, are they? Setting yourself up as the woman who lived in a shoe, and had so many children...' He was laughing.

'Never mind my boots, Joe, let's just concern ourselves with the children.' She was smiling. 'What do you think? These children are far from home – the evacuees, anyway – and *all* of them seem to have a member of the family away on active service, which means they worry. They're vulnerable.'

He waved her down, and drew on his cigarette. 'I read the note, got me orders, but it's not me you need to convince, lass. We need to get him pushing himself. It's no good hiding away when you think you've done something wrong. You have to face it.'

She stared at him. 'How can it be wrong to be wounded? That's absurd.'

'That's not quite the ruddy story, lass. Time you knew, like the rest of the village. On occasion Miss F can hold her tongue, you know. She'll have left it to me to decide a good and proper moment to fill you in. You see, he was driving a lorry, a damned dog ran across t'road, he swerved to miss the bugger, went arse over tit the bloody lorry did and into a ditch. Two of his mates died, 'e togged along for help, though he was injured right badly. He thinks he ran away, on top of killing 'em. Don't like dogs now, he don't. Don't like much, he don't. He never even got to the war, you see.'

He dropped his cigarette. It spluttered and died. He dug into his pocket and offered her one from his pack. She shook her head but at this moment she wished she smoked. How sad war was.

As he lit up again, Joe said, 'We need to get him out and about. He used to be a nice lad. He's not now. He be a bugger.'

'He's feeling guilty.' She knew how he felt. Well, not to that extent. 'Poor man.'

'Aye, stands to reason, we all know that, but it's not going to get any better sitting nursing it like a bleeding 'obgoblin, and 'e's paid his price. He's lost his bloody hand, and has a buggered leg. They're healing but 'is head's a bit behind his body, if you get my drift. Seen it with me beasts. The head takes longer to mend, it does.'

Old Stan called through the door: 'These danged udders ain't going to milk themselves, boss. But we're nearly done. Just need an 'and on the home straight.'

Joe shrugged, patting the pocket that held Miss F's letter, looking around the yard, then stroking the dogs' heads. 'Look, it's all right by me. We'll just shut our lugs to complaints from the lad, and I'll give you an 'and with the tarpaulin. You and me, Phyllie, with our Miss F at the bottom of t'ladders, darting from one to t'other and giving us the benefit of her advice.'

She grinned. 'Not a happy thought.' She was eyeing the farmhouse as he made to open the milking-parlour door. 'He's in your kitchen, is he? Maybe best that I go and ask. Bit rude otherwise.'

Joe grunted. 'If you're looking for an early death, lass.'

She felt her way across the yard, as a cloud went over the moon. It cleared. She was at the porch.

The dogs licked her hands, and returned to their kennels. She knocked. There was no reply. She entered, and shut the door behind her quickly to keep the blackout. Andy sat at the table, reading the paper, one edge of which was propped up between two empty beer bottles. There was an oil lamp set in the centre of the pine table. He looked up. 'What the hell...?'

She yanked off her boots and tiptoed across the cold flagstones. She left damp patches. Her feet probably smelled, but you wouldn't notice in this mess of unwashed dishes piled high in the sink. Rubbish overflowed the bin. The range was exuding heat, so that was one good thing. The old sofa, to the right of the range, was covered with dirty – or were they clean? – clothes. Certainly unironed, anyway. Oil lamps lit the rest of the room. She pulled out one of the kitchen chairs and sat opposite him, uninvited.

He returned to the *Daily Mail*. She said, 'If it's all right with you, Miss F and I would like to use the old barn as a play area for the children after school. It just needs a tarpaulin slung over the bad end. Your dad said we could drag out the old wood burner, and we're sure we can find someone to sort out a flue. Thought I'd just check with you that you are agreeable to having us all after school and at weekends.'

He put the paper down, shaking his head. 'No, it's not going to happen. We can't have kids messing around here. They'll get into everything, hurt themselves, and you had no bloody right to set this up with Dad without talking to me first.'

'I haven't really set it up, just sorted things out

a bit. Here I am, running it past you. I'll be here
to stop them getting into mischief, or one of the
others will be, all the time.'

He stared at her, his grey eyes as cold as the
sea. Oh, Sammy, if only it was you. You'd get that
tarpaulin up in no time. She shook her head, and
concentrated.

He said, 'Why would you think that having you
or one of the others here makes it any better? We
have enough WI women fluttering about being
busy. I repeat, you didn't bloody ask me before
you launched into action.'

She shook her head. 'You know very well the
women have stopped preserving and pickling for
the winter now. Which means they have more time
to keep a check on the children.' She went into the
speech she had practised for him. 'We need help,
you see, Andy. These children are vulnerable,
scared and living away from their families. They
need somewhere to play, somewhere to spend
time, safely. The Home Guard, Scouts and Guides
are so busy for the war effort, we thought you
might consider that it could be part of the farm's
war effort.'

He said, 'We have morons from the ministry
telling us how, where and what to farm, and what's
more, we work our fingers–' His laugh was harsh.
'Well, some of my fingers to the bone, and that's
enough of a war effort. Bloody cheek of you to
suggest we have children on top of that. You've
talked to Dad, and now you've talked to me. I've
answered no.' He was looking down at the newspaper.

She stood up. 'Well, that's not good enough. I

repeat, there's a war on, they're far from home. We need somewhere safe for them to play, so I'll take that as a yes.'

He stood up too, thrusting back the chair. It teetered and fell.

She insisted, 'I'll be back early tomorrow to work on the roof. I'm sure you have a tarpaulin, and I'm sure I can manage with Joe's help to put it up. Miss F will take the bottom of the ladders. See you then.' She tiptoed to the door, and shoved her feet into her boots. The socks had gathered into uncomfortable folds but she wasn't going to undermine her exit by faffing about. She left, almost bumping into Joe in the porch. He was grinning, and gripped her shoulder so hard it hurt. 'Thank you, lass. Feisty little thing, ain't you? Let's see what 'appens.'

She rode away, her feet hurting as the socks bunched even more. Owls hooted as she wondered how anyone could not get feisty, when there was a war on. For goodness' sake, the child she lived with was making a notebook about the nation's culture in case it was destroyed. Feisty? Why not?

Miss F and Phyllie arrived at seven in the morning, with a cart full of brushes and pails. They had not brought Jake or Francois, who were being looked after by Mrs Symes, in case there was a scene. The first thing that they saw and heard was the tarpaulin almost fixed, with Joe and Andy working together.

Andy shouted, 'That's about it, Dad.' He clambered down the ladder, saw Phyllie, and grunted,

'One day this war will be over and you'll go home and take your bossy mouth with you. You just make sure those children are careful of the pond as they walk to us, and no fannying about on farm property; the stables, the milking parlour, even the fields are out of bounds. Can you get that through your head?'

He didn't wait for her to reply, but strode to the stables, where Destiny waited, already harnessed into the cart. He began to load his ditching gear into the wagon while his father helped Old Stan with the milking. The whole village worked hard on the barn all week, and by the next Saturday it was functional. It was here that the Christmas carol concert rehearsals started after school on the Monday. If only Sammy and Isaac could be here for it, but some never saw their men at all, so rare was leave, so there was no cause for complaint.

As the children arrived they saw that a table tennis table had been set up. Joe appeared with four bats, and some balls. He winked at Phyllie. 'A certain person remembered there was one up in the attic, so thanks, lass, and pass that on to our own ganglin' Hitler, will you? I think we're on the mend, don't you?'

She hoped so, and then life would be easier for absolutely everyone, but somehow she doubted it. Things weren't mended that quickly, but she didn't share that with Joe.

As they walked home after the first rehearsal – Mrs F bringing up the rear and Phyllie leading at the front – the children started to sing 'Tipperary'. As she listened Phyllie heard one voice rise steadily above the rest. It was pure and true. She turned around, astonished. She hadn't heard anyone singing like that in rehearsals. At the back of the column Miss F was pointing to Ron, who walked just in front of her with Bryan. Phyllie turned back, even more astonished, and continued on into the village, dropping off the children at their homes. Ron and Bryan, of course, had been playing table tennis, uninterested in stupid carols.

As they reached Mrs Campion's house, three-year-old Rosie Campion banged at the front-room window, and then waved. Phyllie said, 'That singing was lovely, Ron.' He coloured.

Bryan hooted. 'Only big girl's blouses sing carols, you daft idiot. You want to be one of 'em, do you?'

Phyllie snapped. 'Bryan, what about the singers who are entertaining the troops, or singing on the radio? They're not big girl's blouses, are they?'

Bryan kicked out at Ron. 'But he ain't good, he's just loud.'

Phyllie could have kicked him back, only harder, as Ron sloped into the house, head down, shoulders hunched, with Rosie still banging on the window. Miss F said, 'I'll take this young man home, Phyllie. You have some sneaky thinking to do, my girl, if you want that particular soloist.'

She and Miss F discussed it later while Jake put the finishing touches to a paper-chain. As he tested its sticking strength, holding it up, tugging it slightly, he said, 'If my mum could come I'd want her to be proud of me, and see me doing something special. I've been thinking – what if Ron's mum isn't coming for Christmas because she hasn't got the money for a ticket?' He dug in his pocket. 'I've got sixpence from my pocket money that Dad sent for you to put into a post office savings account, Phyllie. Mrs Cummins can have that. If she comes it might stop Ron being so angry.'

The sixpence sat in the palm of his hand. The two women looked at it.

'Out of the mouths of babes and sucklings,' said Miss F.

Phyllie said, 'Pop that back in your pocket. I will sort this out, and if we need your money, I'll ask you. How about that? Mrs Cummins could stay at the vicarage with the other mothers. The attic rooms are almost ready.'

The next day Phyllie talked to Ron when he took a break from playing table tennis. 'Is your mother coming for Christmas?' she asked. 'I'm sure she'd like to. Have you even mentioned it in your letters?'

He shrugged. 'Where'd she get the money for the train? So no, course I ain't asked her.' Phyllie felt pure anger at herself. She had suggested that the parents should be invited, and had organised accommodation, but not for a moment had she thought through the practicalities. It was amazing Jake who had done that.

Andy entered the barn, coming towards the table. He had a few more ping-pong balls cupped in his hand. 'I thought I might show your hooligans the finer points of the game.' The children who were playing stopped. She thanked him, surprised. Bryan said, 'I'll play you.'

Andy shook his head. 'No, I think I'll use Ron,

if that's all right.'

Ron coloured again. Phyllie left them to it, pleased, incredibly pleased, at Andy's efforts. That evening she wrote to Mrs Cummins, enclosing the train fare, which Miss F knew by heart, saying, 'It's just like railway timetables; I always remember them. Queer, isn't it?'

Jake nodded until Phyllie kicked him under the table.

Within days she heard the postie, Willie Carslake, who nipped in for a quick cuppa as usual, slurping it as she tore the envelope open. It had been addressed in an untutored hand. It was from Mrs Cummins, wanting more money, to buy a present for the lad. Also, she said, the fare had gone up. She wrote, *But once I have this extra, miss, nothing will keep me from my boy.*

Phyllie replied, giving details of the train to catch to be in time for the concert. Ron would be singing a solo, she explained, because his voice was so glorious. She enclosed the extra money. If that didn't persuade Mrs Cummins she didn't know what would. She also explained that other mothers would be on the train, and that she would have her own room at the vicarage, on the top floor, with a fire in the grate. She felt it best not to mention that the attic rooms had been servants' quarters.

She carried the good news to Ron at break time, suggesting he might like to surprise his mother, by taking part in the carol service as a soloist. He shoved his hands in his pockets as Bryan nudged him. 'Oh, what a little angel, singing in the choir.'

'Step away, Bryan, let Ron make up his own mind. He's big enough and old enough to do what he wants, and perhaps he wants to please his mother,' Phyllie insisted. The children were playing tag all around them, while the sky threatened snow. Would it be a white Christmas? And where would Sammy be?

Ron looked at her. 'How do you know she's coming?'

'She wrote to me asking the time of the concert, because she doesn't want to miss it.'

Ron looked up at the sky too. Phyllie could almost see the cogs moving in his mind, and then up came the question, to be answered as she had rehearsed. 'How did she know where to write?'

'All the parents have the address of the headmistress of the school so she knew it would find me.'

On Christmas Eve the train arrived with its full complement, bar one. Mrs Cummins was not amongst the disembarking passengers, though Phyllie's mother was. Phyllie directed everyone to Joe's cart, and then ran up and down the platform checking the carriages. No. She ran out and checked with the other mothers, some of whom were sitting in the cart, on straw bales. Others would walk alongside. No. They had not seen Mrs Cummins at the station.

Phyllie's mother was standing by the cart, tapping her foot. Not a good sign, Phyllie thought. 'Mum, so sorry to keep you waiting. How lovely to see you. Merry Christmas!'

Her mother allowed herself to be held, and pecked her daughter's cheek. She wore her usual lavender water, but looked exhausted and had lost weight. Phyllie smiled encouragingly. 'Let's get home. There's room on the cart or we can walk. It's not far.' She could see her own breath as she spoke. 'We must hurry, Joe. The children are in the church, getting ready. I'll drop Mother at home, where there's a cup of tea on the go. Oh, looks like we're walking.'

She ran to catch up with her mother, who was walking quickly ahead of her. 'The government's extra Christmas ration of tea and sugar for us all has made it special, hasn't it, Mum?' Phyllie took her case.

'That's twice you used the word "home",' her mother said. 'You have a perfectly good home in Ealing. It's upsetting to your family if you forget your roots, Phyllis.'

They plodded on in silence, keeping to the edge as the cart overtook them. They were not alone, other mothers followed, chattering excitedly amongst themselves. Each of them held presents for their children.

Phyllie took her mother's arm. 'I never forget about you, Mum,' she said. 'I ring a lot, don't I? Miss F's at the church, with the carol singers. If you'd prefer, you can come up there with me, but a cuppa is waiting...' She paused. 'Waiting at the house, where there's an Aga so you can warm up. There are some scones, too, with honey. Joe Bartlett has given us a small pat of butter for you. You need to rest, Mum. You look very tired.'

'Extra butter? Good heavens, we don't get that in London.'

Finally they reached her mother's choice: the house. Phyllie opened the back door, which was unlocked, as usual. Her mother sat down at the kitchen table, her hat and coat still on, and her gloves, refusing all food, but agreeing to a cup of tea. Phyllie drew a deep breath. 'I have to go and check on the children at the church, and then nip off to the station to meet someone who missed that train. She'll be on the next, I'm sure.' She wasn't sure at all. 'The concert starts in an hour. I'll pick you up, or send someone. Afterwards we're having a party at the children's barn. It's a bit of a walk in the dark but we're all used to the dark, aren't we? I'm so glad you're here. You must have something to eat at the party; you will feel restored.'

Her mother smiled as she lifted her teacup. 'It is good to be here, and to have some quiet.'

Phyllie grinned with relief, and said, 'Enjoy your tea.' With that, she was gone.

At the church the children were having their costumes adjusted by competent Mrs Symes, and fingers-and-thumbs Miss F. The children were restless. Tea towels and old sheets had been cut up to make shepherd outfits. Ron was to sing, a solo of 'Silent Night' and his eyes were fixed on Phyllie. 'Is she here yet?'

'I'm going to the station to meet her. She wrote and promised, didn't she? She's been saving, for this.' For this is what Mrs Cummins had promised to say when she arrived.

'So you said.'

Phyllie checked her watch. She'd have to run to meet the train.

By the time she arrived at the station the train was drawing out. Phyllie rushed onto the platform, but there was no one waiting. Mr Hill, the station master, shook his head. 'I checked the carriages, Phyllie,' he said. 'She bain't come.'

Phyllie stood, feeling desperate, because it wouldn't be *her* heart that broke, and she'd thought she'd been so damned clever. Mr Hill patted her shoulder. 'If she comes in on the next one I'll tell her where to meet you. If she comes after the concert, I'll phone Joe. He don't like using the phone but farmers need one. He'll come from the farm for her, but you'd best get back up there and flannel the lad with some tale or other, and besides, you don't want to miss the concert.'

She ran all the way back to the church, and slipped in. She'd worn her best dress, which wasn't saying much, and with all the running about the seams of her stockings were probably all over the place. Her court shoes had rubbed her heels, and her feet were frozen. The church was full, and the candles flickered in the windows, all of which had been fixed with blackout material. The children's choir stood on the altar step, clustered around a manger, singing 'Away in a Manger'.

Even from here, Ron's voice rose like the angel he wasn't, but perhaps could be. Phyllie felt such anger, such shame, because she had tricked him. She hadn't meant to, but she had. She saw him looking at her, and then beyond, searching. She nodded, knowing it was a lie, and hating herself. But this boy had a right to shine, he damn well had.

She could barely see through the mist in her eyes.

The applause at the end of the concert was prolonged and the parents came to hug their children. Ron wove his way towards her, searching, always searching. Taking hold of his shoulders, she said, 'She missed that train, but she'll be here for the party. Mr Hill is phoning Joe when she comes in.'

The church was emptying past them, mothers from London, a few fathers, all clutching their children's hands as though they'd never let them go, their faces full of happiness and relief. Dan's parents had both come, and they walked with Dan and Jake, Dan's father, in his Royal Navy padre's uniform, was holding Jake's hand, and Dan's mother was holding her son's. Francois was at Jake's heels.

Phyllie gripped Ron tighter, turned him, and walked with him, seeing the braced shoulders, the jutting chin, and she felt something other than irritation for this lad. Perhaps it was admiration, or maybe just pity? They walked together, in the long column, with Jake and Francois way ahead, but not the Andertons, because Bryan had not sung. Mrs Anderton had said they might meet them at the party, which they probably would, Phyllie thought, as there was free food and tea.

She and Ron didn't talk, they just walked, but as they entered the freshly swept farmyard, she said, 'A friend of mine said to look up at the sky and when we're not with the people we love, we know they're under the same sky, so distance doesn't matter.'

He looked up. 'The stars are bright, ain't they, miss? But she'll be here, any minute, won't she, like she said she would?' Then he saw Bryan with his parents and said, 'And like *you* bloody said she would.' He slouched across. The old Ron was back, but Rome wasn't built in a day.

The party began with fiddlers from both villages playing. Some children ran amok, some danced with their mothers. All the children, village and evacuee, looked unnaturally smart and tidy. The Girl Guides had earned their badges by sewing dresses for the girls from old skirts provided by the women of the village. Mrs Thomas, who had five daughters in the WAAF, had dug out summer skirts from a trunk in the attic. In the far corner of the barn lay the children's discarded costumes.

Discarded? It was then Phyllie nearly died, because she'd forgotten all about her mother, and it was as though the invasion had begun, such was her panic: Miss F waved at her from the wood burner, with her mother safely beside her. 'Thank you, God,' Phyllie murmured. 'And you too, Miss F.'

A voice behind her said, 'Talking to yourself now, Miss Saunders? Whatever next?'

It was Andy, in a suit, as were some of the other men, most of them elderly, and their suits even older. He stood beside her, his cuff hiding his stump. 'Has it ever occurred to you that we are almost the only young single people left in the world, or in this world anyway?' There was not a touch of bitterness in his voice, only amusement. She kept her eyes front to hide her surprise. She said, 'Always. Always it occurs to me, but that's just the way it is, isn't it? And besides, we're too busy to notice, or I am.'

She stopped. Oh Lord, he'd think she was having a dig. She said, 'So are you, of course. I didn't mean…' She petered into silence. He was looking at the dancers, and then at Francois, sitting by Miss F who had linked arms with Phyllie's mother. They were chatting to the vicar.

He said, 'Oh, so this is one thing the amazing Francois can't do, then? I see he's sitting it out.'

She laughed, and realised he was too. Had he been drinking? His father's elderberry wine was terribly strong.

The fiddlers were playing some sort of a waltz now. He said, 'Should we keep the youngsters end up, and strut about a bit?' He moved to stand in front of her, his hand out. She took it. It was rough from his farm work. Yes, he must have had a snifter of wine, surely?

'What dance is it?' she queried as she moved with him into the fray of adults and twirling children.

He laughed, his head thrown back, his mousy hair freshly washed. 'Who knows? We must just keep moving or we'll be mown down.' She assumed the waltz position but didn't know how to hold his non-existent hand. 'I'd rest it on top of the end of my arm, if I were you. It's better than staring at it as though it's a puzzle that would stump the whole world.'

Stump? Had he said it deliberately? She looked at his face then. He was grinning. 'What are you made of, then, Miss Saunders? Can you summon up a quickstep? I took lessons at grammar school and can lead.'

They were off, carving a path through the melee. She felt the tension in his body, and knew that beneath the repartee he was as nervous as hell. Over by the fiddlers Joe was watching, as tense as his son. She smiled, because this young man was trying, and that was a damn sight more than he'd done for a while. Joe smiled back now, and nodded. The fiddlers somehow settled into a rhythm and soon others were finding their way to a quickstep. Even Joe dragged Miss F onto the floor, by which time the children were heading to the table tennis end of the room, under the watchful eye of Mrs Speedie and Miss Deacon.

Phyllie said, above the music, 'Thank you for making this barn work as a play area.'

He replied, 'You'd have come after me with a chopper, wouldn't you, if I hadn't?'

She shook her head. 'No, a saw.'

He laughed again, and she joined in, but her feet were sore from all the running and her eyes were continually on the door, but why? The last train from London had arrived a good hour ago. False hope was better than none, she supposed. Andy said, 'Dad phoned Hill at the station before he came here. Ron's mother wasn't on the train. I should have said. I forgot.'

Around they spun, and it was so strange to be in a man's arms and suddenly she longed, absolutely longed, for Sammy with a physical pain. She remembered the ring then. It was still at the jeweller's. How could she have forgotten it? But on the other hand, how could she have remembered with all that was going on? Sammy wouldn't mind, and at least she wouldn't have to face her mother with the news, because if there was tight-lipped disapproval she might well have responded.

The music drew to a close and the dancers

wandered from the floor towards the homemade wine being served along the rear wall. Her mother caught up with them, standing between them and the bar. This woman knew all about tactics, Phyllie thought. 'Phyllie, dear, introduce me to your friend.'

Phyllie did so. Andy shook hands. Mrs Saunders said, 'Miss Featherstone said you and your father run the farm, this farm. It seems very large?'

Andy nodded. 'Well, yes, it is, or at least it's middle of the road really. Mixed farming.'

Mrs Saunders was smiling. 'You own it, or are you tenant farmers?'

Phyllie sighed, wondering why her mother didn't just put up a sign declaring that she was interviewing for a son-in-law of status and means. Jake interrupted then, with Francois at his heels. 'You do dance well, Phyllie. I bet Sammy does too, because he does everything well, doesn't he? She's got a ring now, Mrs Saunders, haven't you, Phyllie? It's being enlarged so it will fit. They're getting married.'

The smile on Mrs Saunders face changed to a rictus grimace. Andy was staring at Phyllie. 'I didn't know. I'm sorry. I didn't guess.'

He looked from Phyllie to her mother, and then Jake, after which he blundered away through the crowds. Her mother said, 'You're a fool, Phyllis. How could you, after all I've said? You could have been secure, looked after.' She turned on her heel, but hissed over her shoulder, 'There is one train home tomorrow, Christmas Day, at dawn. I will be on it.'

Jake had run back to the table tennis, unaware

of the displeasure he had caused. Phyllie weaved her way outside, and stood in the cold. Snow was falling. Andy was standing there.

'Don't be sorry,' she said. 'We were dancing. I thought perhaps we were becoming friends, two against the tide of marrieds and elderly.'

He stared over at the farmhouse, the snow settling on the roof, and on his hair and eyelashes, and the shoulders of his suit. 'He's serving?'

'A submariner.'

'Ah.' He shrugged. 'You've nabbed yourself a hero. How very sensible.' He limped away to the house, went inside and slammed the door.

She rubbed her arms, her lacy cardigan hopelessly inadequate, but there was to be no escape. The barn door whacked open and Ron slouched out. He stood before her, his lips a tight line. 'You said she'd be here. It was a trick, to make me sing in your poxy bloody choir.' Bryan was beside him now. Their breath smelled of alcohol.

'What have you been drinking?' she almost shouted, looking back towards the barn.

Bryan sneered. 'Never mind that. You lied, tricked him. Course she can't come, she's got no money. She never said she was coming, did she?'

Phyllie waited for a moment. How could she say that his mother had taken the money, asked for more, and still not come? She said slowly, 'I think we should contact your mother. I have the number at the local pub. I think perhaps there's been a raid and—'

'We did ring the pub. It's the one she always uses so I know the number,' Ron burst out. 'We sneaked in and used the Bartletts' telephone, and she said she didn't know nothing about it, and if she had she'd have done everything she could to be here.' Phyllie stared at this boy, his fierce scowl, his vivid blue eyes full of tears, his lips that were pressed hard together, his hands gripped into fists. How do you tell a son his mother would take money, and spend it on, well, what? How do you let him think that she'd do that, rather than come to hear his glorious, wonderful voice, and see her son at Christmas?'

She just shook her head. 'I'm so sorry, Ron. You're right, I did so want you to shine tonight, to show people your amazing talent, and the boy you are. I'm just so–'

The door was opening again. 'That's not true.' Jake stood there, behind Bryan, the door ajar. Snow was falling heavily.

She tried to reach him. 'No, Jake.'

He sidestepped her. 'It's not true. She sent your mum money – twice – and your mum promised she'd come. It's in her letter. I saw it.'

Bryan hit him so hard he fell, then he reached down, gripping Jake's shirt, his fist up to strike again. 'Typical Yid, all you know is how to lie.'

The barn door opened fully and Francois was out, barking. Phyllie was reaching for Bryan as Joe roared out next, along with a burst of music from the fiddlers. Francois leapt at Bryan. Phyllie dragged the dog off, Joe pulling Bryan away from Jake. Ron just stood there, staring at Phyllie, tears streaming down his face. 'Bryan's right,' he shouted. 'He's a bloody liar, just like you.' He was pointing to Jake, then at Phyllie.

Miss F was out next, shutting the door behind

208

her. 'It's a pantomime, isn't it? A complete pantomime on Christmas Eve; how delightful.' She
came to stand beside Ron. 'There's obviously been
a grave misunderstanding, and of course your
mother would have come if she could. You were
the star of the evening, and you must remember
that, my dear Ron. Now your Mrs Campion is
bringing the younger children away from the jelly;
they've had too much anyway, and she will be
taking you home, after the vicar has praised you
publicly. She's had the most marvellous time,
listening to her foster child taking centre stage.'

Joe was holding Bryan in an arm lock. The boy
whinged, 'Let me go.'

'Certainly not, Bryan,' Miss F continued. 'I
haven't finished speaking to Ron. We'd like you to
stay on at the party, Ron. Our star should, because there's still lots of food to eat, and like I
said, the vicar so wanted to praise.'

She turned to Bryan, as Ron stood as though un-
decided. 'You, however, Bryan, have a mother who
is to take you home because you have struck another person. This I will never allow. Mrs Symes is
right this minute suggesting, nay insisting, that
Eddie trots on home with you both. Jake, up you
get, no need to make a meal of the shiner you'll
have for Christmas Day, but first you three will all
shake hands. This will then be forgotten. I insist.'

They did shake hands, but Ron leaned forward.
'I'll get you, Jake. See if I don't. My mother
wouldn't lie, and she's not a thief, so I'll get you.
Not yet, but one day.'

Phyllie watched the Andertons leave, and Miss
F escort Ron back into the old barn. Jake leaned

209

against her, crying quietly, his nose was bleeding and his lip was split and already swelling. 'I'm sorry, Phyllie. I made it worse.'

She held his head against her, her reply fierce. 'You never, ever make anything worse, lovely boy. You are my sunshine, you and Francois. We are a team. One that is waiting for our men to come home, and we will be strong while we wait, won't we? We'll also go on doing what we think is right.'

He stopped crying then, and whispered, 'Your mother is going home early.' His smile was mischievous. Phyllie crouched down next to him, stroking Francois. 'I know. I don't think she really wanted to come. I think she's just tired, and worried, and she doesn't really know what to say or think.'

He put his arms round her neck. 'I do love you, Phyllie.'

She wouldn't cry, but her voice shook as she said, 'Oh, Jakub Kaplan, I love you, and Francois too, both of you, so much. Now, we have a party to join again.'

Phyllie had never felt less like tripping the light fantastic but needs must; though as midnight came around she drew the line at dancing the can-can. Mrs Speedie and Miss Deacon called her a spoilsport and linked arms with her as the music began. She was about to break free when she saw her mother's face, pinched in disapproval, then looked at her friends. What on earth was the harm? She remained in the WI line-up, and even the pinching of her shoes and the blisters on her heels didn't spoil the fun.

The party closed with 'Jerusalem', and the words

filled her with emotion, just as they did at the opening of each WI monthly meeting. She sang loudly, hoping their combined voices would soar to the heavens, and that Sammy could somehow hear them. I love you, my darling love, my friend, my everything, were her thoughts: I will not cease from mental fight, Nor shall my sword sleep in my hand: Till we have built Jerusalem, In England's green and pleasant land.

Would Ron ever sing for them again? She had to make sure that he did. And would Britain remain unconquered? They must all fight on, whatever the cost, as Churchill said. Just as long as that cost wasn't Sammy. But everyone must say that. She looked across at Mrs Symes, who had lost her pilot husband, and saw that though she smiled, the smile did not meet her eyes. She looked at her mother, and her heart ached at the tiredness in her face, the slumped shoulders, but somehow there was no way to reach her.

Chapter Eleven

Saturday 25 January 1941, Little Mitherton

In Miss F's kitchen Jake grinned as Francois nudged him. 'No, you can't come, not when I'm going to the horses, you know that, silly boy.' He snatched up his old mackintosh from the back door, glad that Miss F and Phyllie had put hooks there when the real cold snap came. It meant it would be warm on this freezing-cold morning. His gumboots were on the doormat, brought in from the back porch to warm up by Phyllie, when she went out to feed the hens. He wore two pairs of socks anyway.

They'd called the new hen, which had arrived on Wednesday, Tobruk, because the British and Australians had taken Tobruk from the Italians. It made Jake happy because it meant the war might be over soon. If it was, his dad would come home, and maybe his mother, and the bombing in London would finish. Mrs Saunders and Father Francis were all right, though, and Jake didn't quite know how he felt about that. Of course he didn't want them dead, but he didn't want that horrid old lady back here either, because she had whispered that there was no point in wishing him a merry Christmas just before she left, and worse, she had told Phyllie that she must never let herself down in public again because that's not how she had brought her up. She had kissed her cheek, though, and patted her shoulder. It had made Phyllie cry.

Or at least, she had cried after Mrs Saunders caught the first train on Christmas Day morning, in her bedroom. She had been crying again when her brother had telephoned to say their mother had reached home safely. Jake had answered the telephone, and Father Francis had been kind and embarrassed and said that his mother sometimes said things she didn't mean, and then wished she hadn't. People did that when they were worried and very tired, he said, and were stuck in a habit. He didn't say what the habit was, though.

Jake had not known what to reply so he had passed the receiver over to Phyllie who had come downstairs. He wanted to tell Father Francis that Phyllie had been crying, but he expected that Phyllie wouldn't want him to sneak. But if her brother knew he could say a prayer or something to cheer her up. It was frightening when grown-ups cried, even if they thought you couldn't hear. His mother had cried before she'd gone back to Poland.

He heaved on the mackintosh, and concentrated on that, because he didn't want to think about his mother. He thought about the hen instead. It was a plump fluffy one, though when you picked it up it felt as bony as they all did. They had taken it in because the evacuated mother and her two little girls who had come in November to escape the bombing in London had gone to Cumbria when their daddy was hurt in the desert. But he didn't want to think of that either.

Miss F had found the old mackintosh in her attic after Christmas. It was one that had been found in a school cupboard years ago. At the Christmas party Joe had said he could help with Destiny and Doris, after Andy said he thought he had a gift. They needed someone to clean the tack, too, and to groom them and if he did that well, he could do more. Miss F seemed to have lots of things up there in the attic and had said she collected them 'in case'. He'd asked, 'In case of what?'

She'd said, 'In case of a wretched little hooligan in need of one. And here are some trousers. Shorts are not suitable for cold weather.' She'd rubbed his hair and kissed the top of his head. He quite liked it, though he wouldn't if she did it outside the house.

The doormat prickled through his socks as he did up the buttons of the mackintosh. There was no belt, but it made him feel like a real horseman to have a piece of string round his waist, like Joe. He tied it in a tight bow. Tim Morton came to the stables too. He was fifteen and had come from the Channel Islands before the Germans got there, or was it after? Jake couldn't remember. Anyway, he'd got out, and lived in Great Mitherton in Mrs Fuller's house. Mrs Fuller had taken in some other evacuees from Bristol and London just before Christmas. Now, though, Great Mitherton was as bunged full as Little Mitherton, Miss F said, so evacuees were being sent to the other villages.

Tim had told Jake, as they had mixed the bran mash one freezing morning in early January, that it hadn't been exciting, it was just horrible, and his pony and his mum and dad were still there. Or he thought they were.

Jake patted his pockets, checking for his gloves. When she found the mackintosh, Miss F had also found two pairs of long baggy trousers. He didn't like to wear them, though he did. She had found gloves on elastic, too, which she tried to persuade him to thread through his sleeves and wear. They were for little kids, he'd protested, and for once he had refused. Phyllie had laughed, and cut the elastic, but put it into the sewing box, 'just in case'.

He pulled on his boots, tucking in his trousers, while Francois whined and pawed at them as

Miss F came from the scullery. Jake hushed him, 'No, you have to stay here, by the Aga. Don't be daft. You don't want to be mashed up beneath Destiny's hooves, does he, Miss F? Go to your rug.'

Francois, head down, made his way to the ancient wool rug in front of the Aga. Phyllie opened the back door now, banging it into Jake and shoving him off the doormat. 'Sorry.' She stood there, her boots dripping, the open door letting in the cold.

Miss F shooed her out. 'In the back porch with you, Phyllie Saunders, if you please, as you very well know.'

Phyllie did as she was told, raising her eyebrows at Jake as he passed her on his way out. 'Remember, do not go on the pond.'

Jake pulled his balaclava over his head. 'I won't forget. Anyway, you tell us every day at school.'

'Andy will clip your ears if he finds you on it.'

'I told you I won't, so I won't.'

Behind him, Phyllie started to close the door and he heard Miss F's bark of laughter. 'He's right you know, you do go on, and on, and on. Your brother phoned again, to thank us for the provisions and clothes and to hope that you are feeling less upset about your mother.'

Mums shouldn't make you cry, Jake thought. Not unless they walloped you for doing something bad. Then they expected you to. The snow crunched under his feet as he walked through the village. There was no point in setting off any earlier because it was too dark. In the spring and summer he would have to, because farmwork wasn't ruled by the clock, but by the daylight, Joe had said. Andy hadn't said anything because he was back to being really grumpy after the party. He didn't come and play table tennis in the old barn any more, and he'd said that if Jake brought the damned dog, he'd shoot it. Jake wasn't sure if he really truly would, but he wasn't going to risk it.

Smoke was trailing from the chimneys of the houses in the village. Dan lived next to the post office with Miss Deacon and usually he and Jake did everything together, but horses brought his friend up in hives. Jake slapped his arms to keep warm; his breath billowed in clouds before his face. He didn't like balaclavas because they made him itch, but it was better than freezing. Did his dad's breath freeze in the submarine? When would he see him again? He was busy, all the men were busy, but he would get leave at some stage, his dad had said. He had thought it would be in January, but it wasn't going to be now. His dad said this happened in a war.

He slipped and slid on the road. It was icy beneath the snow, but Joe's tractor had been along, and the tyre ridges gave him some grip. It was cold in Poland, really cold. His mum would have a fire, though, in his grandma's house. Surely she would. It wasn't as though she was outside, working in this, like Joe.

He turned left, and headed up the lane towards the farm. He loved the horses: the smell of them, the feel of their coats, their strength and their huffs. Yes, the huffs were special, and their lips were soft and fluttery on his hand, and their eyes were kind. He often wondered why he liked them

216

so much and that's why, or he thought it was. But it was something else as well.

Over to the left he could hear the neighing of one of them, carried on the wind. He recognised it as Destiny, and smiled. It meant that Mr Andy had already started on the ditching around Haydock Field, where the wheat had been last year, and which this year grew kale. Joe said you had to grow different things to stop the soil getting sick. Jake liked farming. It was interesting, and sensible, and magical. You put in a seed and then something really different grew. He was near the pond now and could hear the wind in the rushes – the few that grew this side – and see them moving. It had become light, but then it did in the time it took to reach this point. The ducks were in the hide, and Joe fed them every day, because they were his babies, Miss F said.

He carried on along the lane, the ice still slippery under the snow and his nose almost numb. He saw shadowy movement on the ice and shook his head. Bryan and Ron, it had to be. Everyone else had more sense. He wouldn't look because Ron had been worse after the Christmas party. Jake dug his hands further and further into his pockets, and kept his head well down. He grew almost hot from the shame, remembering his words. He shouldn't have said it, but it had all come out before he could stop. It must be horrid to know your mother didn't want to come. It wasn't like his own mum...

He concentrated on the way the snow was squeaking beneath his boots when he walked, and prayed that the two of them wouldn't see him. It didn't work. As he came abreast of the pond Ron called, 'Well, if it isn't little Mr Yid. And how are you today as you sneak away to your horses? Farmer Bartlett's little favourite, aren't you?'

Jake snatched a look. He'd been almost right, but it was only Ron, skidding about on the ice, which was the same colour as the grey-white sky. Why didn't he listen? Phyllie and Miss F had said people went through into the water. For a moment he thought of the future if Ron plunged right through the ice. Then he'd be gone. There'd be no more...

'Come on then, little Master Perfect, do yourself a good turn and break a few rules. It feels good. Look at this.' Jake sneaked a look as Ron flung his arms in the air and half ran, half slid towards the centre of the ice, his knees bent, his arms in the air. 'Whee,' he yelled, sliding to a stop. He ran and slid back, jumped, turned, ran and slid again, getting right down on his knees, then again, and again.

They both heard the crack at the same time; but it wasn't a crack, it was a sort of long tired sigh. Ron slid to a stop, and straightened slowly. He was looking at his feet and there was a black line, a funny jagged one, growing, and then others.

Jake stared too, and then they looked at one another, frightened. Ron shouted, 'Help me.' He had a scarf on. It was Bryan's so why was Ron wearing it? 'Help me, I said.' Ron was almost screaming now. The ducks flew up from behind the fence. Jake couldn't move his feet. He couldn't move at all, he just watched the lines, spreading out, creaking. 'I said, help me. I can't swim.'

Jake didn't want to help him, he really didn't,

218

but he must. He eased himself down the slope to the pond, slipping and sliding, gripping the long snow-crusted grass to slow himself but his hands slipped. He slid on, and on. The snow had gathered in great clumps on his woollen gloves, which were now wet and freezing. He was at the bottom of the slope. 'Stand still,' he called, because Ron was walking towards him, the ice cracking more and more.

Ron yelled, 'Get a move on, then.'

Jake made himself ease out onto the ice, slowly, slowly. He held his breath. It helped him hear. The ice cracked. He didn't know what to do, so he leapt the crack, landed, crashed through, into freezing water almost up to his knees, but not over the top of his boots. He was stuck in the mud, and fell forward, onto the unbroken ice. He worked his way upright, then dragged one boot free, and knelt on the ice. He pulled up the other and went a yard on all fours. It cracked again, and down he went, through into the water, all of him. He swallowed some. It was cold and horrid. He floundered, coughing, then straightened, standing still, the water up to his thighs, his clothes much heavier now they were wet, and very cold. 'It's no good, I'll get Mr Andy. He's ditching. He'll have a rope. Stay still.'

He dragged himself back through the water, breaking the ice as he went. It floated in jagged slabs. Ron shrieked, 'Don't leave me, you bastard. Don't leave me.'

Jake was on the bank now, his boots full of water. 'I've got to get help.' He could hardly talk, he was so cold. He ran down the lane, the water sloshing in his gumboots. He slipped, whacked to the ground, clambered up, took to the verge where the snow was deeper, the going tougher, but not as slippery. He was freezing, he couldn't feel his legs.

He reached the entrance to Haydock Field and halfway along the ditch he could see Mr Andy slashing at the brambles that choked it. The cart was piled high with soggy weeds, roots and more brambles. Rooks were wheeling. A few gulls were clustered in the snow-covered furrows. The young winter-sown kale showed through. He called, 'Mr Andy. Help, Mr Andy.'

He struggled along the edge of the field, shouting, 'Mr Andy, please. Please. Listen.' He wanted to cry but he mustn't. His lips felt funny, sort of heavy and they didn't work properly. His whole body was shivering but he couldn't feel his feet, or his legs, or his hands and arms.

Destiny neighed. Mr Andy, turned, clambered from the ditch, irritation showing as be yelled, 'What – the hell's up with you?'

Jake stopped. 'It's the ice. Ron. It's breaking. I couldn't... Please.'

Mr Andy grabbed the rope he kept beneath the seat. It was always there, just in case... Just like Miss F's just in case but Jake'd never asked him what *his* just in case was because no grown-up ever replied.

Mr Andy was running now, waving him back. 'Go back to him, I'm following, but I'm slow, my leg. Keep him calm.'

Jake turned, and ran as fast as he could, but Mr Andy overtook him after all, so he wasn't that slow. At the edge of the pond he waved Ron down, 'Keep still, you ruddy idiot.'

He saw the broken ice. 'What's this, then?'

'I tried...' Jake began.

Ron yelled, 'He took off, and left me; he did, Mr Andy. We was here together and he ran for it, went through just there.'

Mr Andy swung round. 'For God's sake, what's the matter with you bloody kids? Why in hell don't you do as you're told? And you, Jake, you help your mates, you don't run away, that's cowardly. Come here.' He was panting, and cursing as he pulled Jake close, bending down, their faces inches apart. 'You're going to have to go back on the ice; I'm too heavy. You need to take the rope with you. Slide on your belly to distribute the weight. You've got to do it, lad, or you'll never forgive yourself if he drowns.'

Jake stared into those grey eyes, the colour of the sky, and the ice, and there was such rage in them, but he hadn't really been on the ice. He had left Ron, though. Yes he had left him, and he'd been thinking about if Ron went through...

Mr Andy was tying the rope around his middle, knotting it with his right hand and his teeth. 'Now, get on there quick, and grab the silly little sod. I'll pull you both back across the ice. Go in where it's broken, because it's no thicker anywhere else and you're wet already.'

Jake waded out through the water, feeling it surging back into his gumboots, and washing up against and round him. He reached the edge of the unbroken ice, and bent over, lying down. Somehow he pulled himself forwards until his legs were on the ice too, but not his boots. They were stuck in the mud. It was so cold, and the ice cut his hands and tore his trousers and hurt his knees. He kept Ron in sight; crawling and sliding closer and closer. Ron was crying, his nose was running. He was wiping it with the scarf, which was revolting. Besides, Jake wished he'd stay still because the ice was creaking. Mr Andy shouted, 'Just keep still, Ron; do you want to drown?'

Ron stopped moving, at last. Jake was almost there, but he wanted to cry too, because he was so cold, and his knees really hurt, even though he thought he couldn't feel anything. Well, he could and he was really frightened. The ice was creaking, badly, and then he felt it move, sort of sag, and there was one huge crash, and the ice split, and he slid into the cold dark water. His head went under, but one arm was still on the ice. He lifted his head and hung on, coughing. There was nothing under his feet, and his arm was sliding, he was going to drown.

He heard Mr Andy yelling. 'Grab Jake, Ron; just grab him, for God's sake, what's the matter with you? Get him, and I'll pull you both just a bit to the left of where you are now. Jake, kick your legs in the water, and try to get up onto the ice.'

Jake felt Ron's hands on his arm. He was kneeling, pulling him, and suddenly it was easier. He kicked, got his other arm up. He felt Ron take that hand. It hurt. There was blood dripping on the ice. Ron pulled, hard. The edge of the ice dug into Jake's stomach, caught on the string around his raincoat but then he slipped past, kicking, and throwing his weight forward. He shook off Ron's hands, and used his elbows and nails to claw his way out, until he lay full length. Beneath him the ice was creaking badly. Ron was still kneeling, his long trousers stained wet from the ice. 'Lie down,' Jake croaked, shivering so much he could hardly speak.

Mr Andy called from the edge. 'Jake, keep facing Ron, ease yourself onto the rope. Then I can pull you back in a straight line. Ron, do as Jake says. Lie down, grab Jake's hands, I'm going to pull you both in now. If the ice goes, hold onto one another and I'll continue pulling. You will be safe. So keep calm, both of you!' They gripped hands, lying down, facing one another. 'I'm pulling you now.'

How? Jake wondered. How can he pull, he's only got one hand? But his back was to the shore, he was facing Ron, their hands were clenched, he couldn't turn to look. He asked, 'How's he pulling?'

Ron said, shivering, 'The rope's round his waist and he's sort of pulling with his hand, and he's squeezing the rope between his elbow and his body. Pull, squeeze, that's how.' They were moving. Their eyes met, and then fell away. Jake stared across the ice. Ron's eyes were the colour of summer, so bright, so blue. He couldn't remember what summer was like. The ducks were circling and landing. They'd be warm in the hide. Jake couldn't think what it was like to be warm.

Mr Andy shouted, 'Nearly there, but you'll have to go in the water now. The ice is in bits.'

He slid backwards into the water. Ron clung to

his hands and followed. Their feet sank into the mud. 'It's not deep,' Jake said. 'You can let go, now.' He dragged himself round, and began to wade through the water. The bank looked funny, it was jiggling, but perhaps it was because he was shivering so much his cheeks hurt. He felt and heard his teeth banging together. He could hardly struggle to the bank but Mr Andy got in the water and pulled, and then he was unknotting the rope from around Jake with his teeth and one hand. He was saying, 'I told that damned teacher of yours to tell you to stay off the ice. What the hell's the matter with her?'

Jake wrenched free of him, and almost fell. 'She did tell us, again and again she told us, and don't you swear about her. Don't you dare.'

Ron was standing there now, shaking. 'Jake said it would be all right, he said it would.'

'I never did. You liar.' He launched himself at Ron, his arms flailing, but he slipped and fell. Ron laughed.

'Shut up, the pair of you.' Mr Andy was coiling the rope. He threw it down. 'I suppose I have to get you both home, but we'll have to walk. The cart's full and we can't mess about. You need to get warm.'

Jake's teeth were chattering, his balaclava was wet, everything was wet, and he felt like an icicle. 'Will Destiny be all right alone?'

'You should have thought about that earlier, instead of causing trouble.' Mr Andy was striding down the lane, and the boys hurried along after him, Jake in socks but his feet didn't hurt because he really couldn't feel anything, not his feet, not his cut knees, not his cut hand. But he walked like a robot, all a bit funny and wobbly. His blood was bright on the snow.

Mr Andy stopped and looked back. He stared at the trail of blood. 'You can't walk like that.' He went back, and swung Jake up and over his shoulder, like a sack of coal. They walked on in silence now, and Jake's knees were rubbing on Mr Andy's old mac, but they weren't sore, they weren't anything. He said, 'I'm sorry, Mr Andy. Your mac will be dirty.'

'Typical...' Ron started to say something, but now Mr Andy roared, 'I don't want to hear another bloody word from you, boy. Just shut it.'

As they walked, Jake felt the breath jog in his chest. Mr Andy's arm was strong around him, and he began to feel warm across the back of his thighs where he was held. They dropped Ron at his house. Mrs Campion took one look at him, and yanked him in. 'Thanks, Andy. I don't know how many times he's been told. That Miss Saunders even sent a letter round.'

'I told you not to swear at her,' Jake said, as Mr Andy left the house, still carrying him, but perhaps he didn't say it aloud, because Mr Andy didn't reply. They continued down the snow-covered road. Jake felt very sleepy. His eyes were closing, they just wouldn't do as he wanted and stay open. He couldn't stop shivering. He bit his tongue. That hurt because it wasn't numb, and he could taste the blood but it kept his eyes open. He knew they'd stopped at Myrtle Cottage when Mr Andy opened the gate, and walked up the path. Mr Andy knocked, and waited. Then at last he heard her voice, his Phyllie, saying, 'Oh my God.'

Mr Andy swung him down, and steadied him. Phyllie lifted him up. 'Oh my God,' she repeated. 'His feet, his knees, his mouth, and he's bleeding. He's so cold.'

Mr Andy said, 'You need to keep these bloody boys under control. They were on the pond. I don't want him near the horses again until I know he can be trusted. Water can kill, you know, Jake Kaplan. It drowns people but you townies don't have the sense you were born with.'

Phyllie carried Jake into the house, through the cold hall, and up the stairs, calling to Miss F, but then she remembered she was out at Mrs Symes's. She wrapped him in a towel, and ran the bath, urging him out of his clothes, shouting at him when he said, his voice shaking with cold, 'I don't want you to see me.'

'Don't be ridiculous, I must get you warm.'

She stripped him, tested the water and lifted him in because his legs wouldn't work. The blood from his knees and feet coloured the water, she bathed his hands, and that blood darkened the water further. She felt a thickening of her throat, as she ran more and more hot water. He cried out, 'It hurts, Phyllie.'

Downstairs in the kitchen Francois was barking, and clawing at the door into the hallway.

'It will hurt as the circulation gets going again, and it will hurt a damn sight more when I tan your backside. How dare you go on the ice? How many–'

'I didn't,' he wailed. 'I was walking past, and Ron was on it, and it started to crack. He told Mr Andy I had been on it with him and had run away. I wouldn't go on the ice with someone who hates me. Why would I? I went on to help and the ice broke. Then I went for help because I heard Mr Andy doing the ditch in Haydock Field.'

Phyllie turned off the taps and wiped his face with her wet hands. 'Shh, it will be all right. I'm sorry, of course you weren't. I don't know what I was thinking. Lie down, let's get that noddle of yours under the lovely hot water.'

'I'm not a baby, Phyllie.'

'To me, you are, just for this moment.' She didn't know how to show this boy how much she loved him, how much she worried.

She dressed him in two pairs of pants, the second baggy pair of trousers. She made him wear two pairs of socks, and two vests, a sweater, and covered him with two blankets on the sofa. She remembered that Sammy had said that if one of them fell in the water, their mate would bunk in with him, to give him warmth. She let Francois lie with him, while she boiled the kettle to heat him up from the inside.

She rattled about in the pantry, looking for something special to go with the pot of tea she was making. He could have her ration of sugar. When she returned to the fireplace he was gone, so were his school shoes, and his new school mackintosh, and Francois.

She made herself think. Where? Where? She rushed upstairs. No. Not there. She tore down again, and saw the front door was ajar. She flew

227

into the kitchen, hauled on her boots, mackintosh, scarf and woollen hat, ran down the hall, and out to the gate. She looked to the left and the right. She thought she saw him, disappearing towards the pond. It was certainly a shape, a small one.

She ran but slipped and fell. She scrambled to her feet and half skated, half walked because, of course, he had returned to the pond, where else would he go if not to face his demons? 'Get back on the horse,' she and Miss F told the children. The wind was like a knife, the sky was heavy with snow. If it fell now it would be a blizzard.

There he was, ahead of her, standing at the pond's edge, staring out over the damaged ice, and at the black dull water. It looked like a scar. Francois was sitting beside him, licking his hand. She ran on, her gumboots slopping, and finally stood next to him. Without speaking he slipped his hand in hers. 'Mr Andy said I couldn't be trusted, and until I could be I couldn't go to the horses. I don't know how to show him, Phyllie. I was in the water, you see. I can't swim and I had to get help, because I couldn't do anything on my own. Mrs Campion told him you had sent a letter to everyone.'

She squatted down beside him, her arm around him. 'Tell me exactly what happened.' He did, even telling her that he had been thinking what would happen if Ron went through, explaining that for a moment he thought how nice it would be without him. On and on he went, and then he said, 'Water kills. He said it drowns people, but I knew that. But I didn't *really* know it until today. It's so cold and dark when you are in all that water, Phyllie, and you can't help yourself. My daddy's down there; Sammy is, too. They're in something like this water but much worse, much deeper. There's no one to help if it goes wrong, only Germans wanting to hurt them. They drop bombs on them, but they don't call them bombs. I can't remember what the name is.'

Phyllie hugged him. 'Nothing will go wrong.'

He pulled away. 'We can't know that. War kills, water kills, and it's horrid and it's frightening, and...' He trailed to a stop.

She shook her head. 'Submariners know what to do when those people come to find them. They do, truly they do.' She was trying to convince herself, as much as him.

She stood up, held out her hand, and together, with Francois, they returned home, into the warmth of the kitchen, and Miss F.

That evening she walked to the farm. She could hear Joe in the milking parlour, so she carried on to the house, tapping on the door and entering. Andy was at the table, doing what looked like accounts in the dim light of the oil lamp. He stared at her. She came to the table, not stopping to remove her boots. 'Thank you for saving the boys.'

He shrugged. 'They shouldn't have been on the ice in the first place.'

At that, she leaned forward, brought her arm back, and slapped him so hard across the face that her hand stung and he was knocked back in his chair. He put his hand to his cheek, his shock visible. He rose, thrusting back his chair. She didn't give him a moment to respond, for she was rushing round the table, leaving clods of snow and mud on the flagstones, and she didn't give a damn, let this bully clean them up.

'You utter bastard,' she shouted. 'You know perfectly well I told them, even Mrs Campion told you that. What's more, you know my boy well, so how dare you say he's not to be trusted? Ron lied, my Jake did not go on the ice with him, he knows better.' She was beating at his chest now, and his arms were up, shielding himself. She hit his stump, he cursed, grabbing for her hands but it was an uneven contest when you only had one.

She kept on hitting him. 'You know what a troubled boy Ron is and how much he takes it out on Jake. How could you? Yes, you have problems; yes, you killed your friends; yes, you think you ran away, but you didn't. You did the right thing and went for help, like Jake. So get over it.' She was tiring, but still hitting and now he was letting her.

'These things happen, and you can blame yourself, but not a little boy whose father is down under the sea. I hate you, Andrew Bartlett. For a moment, at Christmas, I thought you had a heart, but now I know better. You're weak and cruel, and as much of a bully as Ron, but with nothing like the excuse. I have had enough of people like you.' She stopped talking and hitting, quite suddenly. Instead she backed away, her voice hoarse, wanting to burst into tears, but she bloody well would not. She turned and left, slamming the door behind her, hurrying across the yard and back to her home.

Chapter Twelve

March 1941, HMS *Vehement* on patrol off Norway

Sammy and Isaac grinned at one another, then looked back at the sky, the grey lolling seas, enjoying the taste of brine, the sense of space, before they took up their posts.

'Same old, same old,' Isaac said and yawned.

The light was clear, the sky streaked with white cloud. It was spring. The days were becoming longer and soon it would be summer. Sammy's shoulders tensed. Everlasting light was the enemy of submarines, so even now, at three thirty in the morning, the lookouts ceaselessly scanned the sea and sky, 'just in case'. Anyone else taking a break must do the same. German success meant the bastards could over-fly an increasing number of spotter planes from conquered Europe. These could discover their hidey-holes deep down in the clear springtime ocean depths and report their position. Recharging was a bugger too, because the nights were getting so short that it couldn't be completed in the dark.

'T-t-time up, lads,' Lieutenant Stanning muttered, sweeping the horizon, along with the lookouts.

Sammy and Isaac slid down the ladder. Sammy presumed *Vehement*'s orders were still the same.

Observe, report, discharge torpedoes only when necessary. On their last patrol a destroyer had come straight at them, but Diddy had fired one, two, three, four, and more torpedoes. They'd sunk it, and left the skimmer's lifeboats alone to make for Norway, though they'd picked up oil-soaked stragglers.

There was no room or reason to keep them as prisoners. They had, instead, been dried, warmed, fed, and then rowed in *Vehement*'s inflatables under cover of darkness to the coast of Norway. It had been tense, with everyone praying that they didn't meet any of the mines that had been laid months before. Once there, they'd been tipped out into the surf and safety.

Sammy reached his post and tapped Adrian on the shoulder. 'Off you go, little 'un. Bed all warm and sweaty for you.'

Adrian eased his shoulders, and grimaced. 'No dancing girls?'

Sammy laughed, and called to Isaac who was taking over from Davy. 'These youngsters; enough is never enough, is it?'

Diddy called across from the chart table where he was using dividers, while conferring with Sub Lieutenant Roddy Rogers. 'Old man you, Sammy – ready for the pension?'

'That's it; twenty-five last month, sir.'

The Jimmy, Lieutenant Michael Dorian, laughed.

They'd had days of inaction, days of boredom, of tension, wondering when it would break, but at least Adrian, who was handing him the head-phones, had not been seasick again.

232

Sammy scanned. It might be light up top, but, as always, sometimes the hydrophones picked up what others couldn't. He ached for Phyllie, because he hadn't seen her in January as he had hoped. Instead, he had travelled to the village near Cardiff, desperate, because his father who was his pal, his idol, had suffered a heart attack. The sight of his son's ugly mug had boosted his recovery, his dad had said.

Sammy had to make do with telephoning Phyllie from Harwich just before embarkation, thanking God that she lived with a headmistress who had to have a telephone. They'd talked for half an hour, he freezing off his bollocks in a public booth, with a queue of people waiting. Finally a stoker had threatened to stuff the receiver where the sun didn't shine if he didn't get out 'right bloody now'. He'd heard Phyllie's laugh.

'Anything, Sammy?' Diddy called, leaning back on the chart table.

'Nothing, sir.'

Diddy scooted up the ladder onto the bridge. Sammy scanned. He'd talked to his dad and mum about Phyllie. They'd been unsurprised. His mother said, 'Of course you're getting married. You've been joined at the hip since you could walk and you've loved one another all your lives, daft boyo.'

He scanned ceaselessly. Their boredom had been broken by a skimmer three days ago. It must have spotted the periscope wake. Sammy hadn't heard them; it was just one of those things, Diddy said later. Diddy had got off a couple of fish but they were both misses, and they'd dived pretty damn sharp. As the depth charges began they'd levelled off at two hundred and fifty feet. They'd silent run for three hours with batteries that had been fully charged so it had been no problem. No planes had come to spot them. They had survived.

He didn't know why that one had got to Stanning as it had but since then he'd stammered. Lack of sleep? Perhaps. He felt a touch on his shoulder. It was Diddy again. 'Anything?'

'Nothing, sir.' Diddy grinned but it didn't reach his eyes. It used to, when he first took over. He'd talked more to Sammy about moving on up in the Navy, and maybe he would. It would be good for the family because Sammy would like three children. He'd talk to Phyllie about it, but they'd have what she decided, because all he wanted was to make her happy.

Diddy moved off, round the control room, checking this and that. He went to his cabin, but he wasn't sleeping. By the end, Old Tom hadn't slept, but bloody hell, Sammy wouldn't sleep if he had to think of everything, take chances, calculate, calculate. So did he really want more responsibility? What if he had to decide whether to attack, dive, run... He shrugged. The war wouldn't go on for ever, he just had to survive it and the peacetime Navy would be different. But why stay in?

He and Isaac had trained in firing the 4-inch gun on their lay-off and so had Adrian and Davy. It was all part of being able to do what was necessary but how necessary was it in peacetime? Maybe operating hydrophones was more transferable? The problem was, he didn't think he could bear to be away from Phyllie when it

234

wasn't absolutely necessary.

He smiled – he always did when he thought of her – then grew serious. She'd written about Andy and little Jake, but she'd said he was not to tell Isaac, for what could he do from a submarine? She'd also told him about Andy, how he'd been nice, and then changed at the party when Jake had mentioned the ring and she'd said Sammy was a submariner. How he'd mocked Sammy for being a hero. *Well, you are,* she'd written; and it must be hard for him, stuck at home.

Sammy wondered if Andy had thought Phyllie was available. If so, he'd punch his bloody lights out. His hand tightened on the scanning wheel, but then relaxed. No, there'd be no need because she'd said that she'd always loved him, and always would. It was just that sitting here, twiddling, listening, playing cards off duty, scratching your arse, talking of life, women, sport, women, things got to you.

He sighed. His catarrh was bad this trip. Seawater had got into the batteries in the last storm and there'd been some chlorine gas seepage which always set it off.

Diddy was back, pacing, then he went to the bridge. The captain was never officially on watch, but he might as well be. The boat was tossing and rolling now. The batteries were fully charged, must have been a few hours ago, but they made more speed on the surface; speed to where, though? Sammy knew his thoughts were chasing one another around. Diddy was back again. What did he know that they didn't? Orders were in sealed envelopes, seen by his eyes only. Were they picking someone up again? Sammy glanced towards Isaac who was listening intently. He was pressing his earpiece hard against his head.

Diddy saw. 'What?' Dorian and Stanning swung round.

Isaac said, 'Far distant, sir. One of ours stating position and situation.'

'B-b-reaking radio silence?' Stanning said, his tone telling the story. Surrendering or the end? Diddy was at Isaac's elbow. He bent down, shared the earpiece. *'Vanguard?'*

Isaac nodded. *'Variant* is nearest.'

Stanning was checking all the dials.

'We remain on sector,' Diddy said. He checked his watch, looked up, nodded at Stanning. 'Prepare to dive,' came the order. Stanning was unsurprised. It was therefore an exercise. The lookouts slid down into the control room, the hatch was secured, the prow dropped, all hands knew what to do and where to do it. 'Periscope depth, if you please.'

They stopped at thirty feet. The Jimmy took the periscope. First a quick all-round look for ships, and across the sky for aircraft. Now a slower look, carefully scrutinising every sector. Sammy listened, and waited for the periscope to lower. It, and its wake, must not be seen. They ran just beneath the surface for half an hour. Every five minutes the periscope was raised, the area was searched, they were blind except for that eye, and Sammy's ears. The stoker in charge of the periscope hydraulics and Diddy seemed to have an almost telepathic understanding. The problem with boredom, Sammy thought, as he rolled his pencil between his fingers, was complacency. You forgot to stay alert, and this is why Diddy was geeing them up.

Stanning was with the new sub lieutenant, Roddy Rogers, examining one of the aides-memoires piled by the chart table. The officers needed to know their ships in order to calculate the performance and armament of their foe. Diddy, knees bent, hands flopped over the brass handles, was swinging the periscope round when he stopped, retraced, froze.

'Sammy?' he called.

'Nothing,' Sammy answered, concentrating. 'Nothing.'

Stanning was on the scope now. Diddy and Dorian stood quite calmly beside him, which meant Diddy knew damn well what he'd seen, and it was something nasty. Stanning, looking through the search periscope, was adjusting the range finder. Not just observing, then? Is that what had been in orders? Sammy listened hard. He glanced towards Isaac, who was also concentrating, his hand to his earpiece.

Stanning nodded at Diddy, and stepped away. Diddy snatched a look through the scope. He stood. 'Action stations, if you please.'

The leading seaman read off the range marker to Rogers, the torpedo officer. 'Range is eighteen hundred yards.'

Sammy heard propeller noises now. *Vehement* was capable of nine knots submerged but only for a short time. If it was a pack of torpedo boats escorting a cruiser, well, they could do thirty knots. Shit. Sammy preferred boredom, if he was asked. In fact, he'd like to put in a request.

'All tubes to the ready.' The torpedo men would be letting water into the tubes from within the boat so the weight forward wouldn't change.

'Begin the attack.' Diddy was at the periscope again. Sammy listened, they were closing on the skimmers. Rogers was plotting the relative positions between *Vehement* and the enemy. Dorian watched the controls, Stanning supervised the trim, Diddy was working out the range and bearing of the target, Rogers waited, and Sammy prayed he'd calculated correctly just how far ahead to fire the torpedo, or they'd miss and have a bloody lot of skimmers after them.

The control room was silent, the motors at slow ahead, using the attack periscope so the wake was minimal. Once again the bearing and range were read off. Diddy lowered the periscope.

The order was given and the torpedo men readied all ten forward-firing torpedoes, opening the bow caps.

Diddy signalled the stoker. Diddy scanned. A leading seaman reported, 'Twenty-two hundred yards, bearing zero two zero.'

'Shit and double shit; still doable, though. Fire a dispersed salvo, if you please, Mr Rogers.'

Mr Rogers pleased, the boat shuddered every six seconds as the torpedoes were released. Sammy confirmed they were running. As the water flooded in to balance the weight Stanning lost control of the trim, and the boat became bow heavy, diving below periscope depth. They were blind except for Sammy. Dorian and his men struggled to gain stability, and now the prow was rising, but, bloody hell, they must not break surface.

Diddy strolled slowly between his officers, waiting for Stanning to regain control but probably wanting to snatch the bloody boat into his own hands. The boat regained stability. Sammy picked up no explosion. The second hand on his watch ticked by. Then there was the sound of rending metal. Sammy nodded. Diddy shared the headphones. There was a second, then a third.

Diddy flicked his hand, the stoker sent up the periscope, Diddy peered. 'Gotcha,' he said. 'Time we were away, gentlemen. The torpedo boats will be hot on our trail.'

He gave them the course. His eyes met Sammy's, who nodded. He'd scan for his life now as they dived deep, engines full ahead moving them to the west, and then the south. After five minutes, engines were ordered to slow ahead, and silent running. The torpedo boats were hunting, all three of them, but the exploding ashcans were quite a way off. As a precaution they made way during the explosions, but lay stopped and silent when they ceased.

In time, as the hours passed, the air thickened and depth charges continued to explode all around – closer, but not on. When they stopped, Stanning trimmed the boat, using the crew much as if they were running up and down the length of a seesaw. The watch changed, Adrian took over the hydrophone, and Davy the radio while Isaac and Sammy sat on the mess deck plates, playing cards, or moving to prow or stern on orders, talking only in whispers, planning their futures

239

when Rachel was back and Phyllie was Sammy's wife. A plan began to form, as though they'd both made a decision during the last few hours, and ideas tumbled out. They would live near one another; they would never leave their families, so they would need civilian jobs.

Eventually, when they were sleepy from lack of oxygen, they chose Phyllie and Jake's village. Why not? Another hour passed, there had been no ashcans for a while. Isaac slept, his head lolling, his cards scattered on the floor but now it was time to change the watch. Sammy kicked Isaac awake.

They hurried to the control room. Davy and Adrian left, relief clear on their faces. Sammy and Isaac took their positions as they rose to periscope depth. Diddy checked with Sammy. 'Nothing, sir.'

The speed was reduced to minimise the wake, the stoker worked the hydraulics, and Diddy gave the honour of scanning for the enemy to Stanning, whose trimming had been exemplary. Dorian and Diddy exchanged a look. All eyes in the control room were fixed on Stanning as he assumed nonchalance, slapping down the brass handles, bending his knees and taking up the periscope, scanning round as quickly as it had ever been done, then again, more slowly. They all saw the lowering of his shoulders, and their own dropped. 'All clear, sir.'

The stammer was gone.

Diddy nodded. 'Very good, let's take her up, and get Cookie on the food stakes. I'm bloody starving. I'll be in my cabin, writing up my log.'

Once they were on the surface and the watch was in the control tower Sammy and Isaac were allowed to take their turn at the heads, desperate by this time, because of course they could not be used when they were being hunted: the bubbles would give away their position. As Sammy returned from the heads, he promised himself he'd set about devising a bathroom for the house he was planning. It would be the best money could buy. In fact, he'd start his own plumbing business. Yes, that's what he'd do, then he'd never have to queue for a bog ever again.

Chapter Thirteen

March 1941, Little Mitherton

January and February had been their usual harsh selves, with snow, ice and wind. The Home Guard had taken up lookout positions in the belfry rather than slip and slide in the lanes on exercise and on patrol, ending up with broken bones. The vicar had been heard to mutter as he cleared the snow from the path leading to the church, 'Anyone parachuting down in this weather deserves a cup of tea, not a pitchfork up the bum.'

During these months the school children had gone straight home after school, not to the old barn at Joe's farm. It had been at Phyllie's suggestion, citing the dark evenings and the intemperate weather, and Miss F had agreed, after a

241

prolonged pause.

Towards the end of March, Miss F, sitting in the old armchair to the left of the Aga, the one with a seat that sagged 'just right', dropped a stitch when they heard the presenter announce that the government was to freeze food prices. 'At last. That Mr Samson in the town is profiteering, you know. The price of his pickle is disgraceful, and I'm sure it's some the WI sent to the wholesaler.' She fiddled with her knitting, caught the stitch and rectified the situation. Jake and Phyllie, sitting together on the sofa opposite, shared a grin.

Jake said, 'Mr Joe's opening the old barn again, Phyllie. Mr Andy's been working on the roof since the wind lifted the tarpaulin and Mrs Whitehead came in and pinned a notice about it on the board. The one in the school corridor by the pegs. She and Mrs Otis were chatting over a cup of tea in the staff room, with the door open. Mrs Otis wished he'd come and work on her roof. Mrs Whitehead laughed, then sort of coughed because Mrs Otis has bought Miss Harvey's house, and I think Mrs Whitehead is still upset about Miss Harvey dying. Anyway, we can go back to the barn now it's spring, can't we, and the roof is done?'

Francois stirred on the rug. Phyllie checked the clock. 'Good grief, is that the time? You should have been in bed half an hour ago.'

'But, Phyllie—'

'No buts. Up you go.' Jake put the Airfix aeroplane he was building on an old tray up onto the shelf above the pan cupboard, and slouched out of the door, with not a goodnight, or by your leave,

242

and even Francois' tail was between his legs as he followed.

Miss F said, counting her stitches, her finger flying along the needle, 'Spring is coming; it really is time the children got back to the old barn, you know. There's been no ice on the pond for weeks, if that's what's been worrying you, or is it Andy and his rudeness? Joe says he's improving, and after all he's been working on the roof, for goodness' sake.'

Phyllie held up the skirt she was hemming for a new evacuee from London who had very few clothes. She said, 'I'm wondering if Fanny Mc-Travers, who works a few hours behind the bar at the pub, could cope with Ron? It's too much for Mrs Campion, and not good for the little children.'

Miss F just looked at her. 'Ah, so we're not going to discuss the old barn, then? Yes, I have been thinking of Ron, and you're right, Fanny's used to dealing with all sorts as a barmaid. She might be just the sort of lass who could cope with him. Her aunt lives with her, and can mind him when Fanny's working. We've simply got to get him away from that ghastly Anderton gang. They're up to all sorts at Great Mitherton. The public telephone was broken into last week.'

'Goodnight, anyway, I suppose,' Jake called from the top of the stairs.

Phyllie laid the dress on the arm of the sofa, and stood, raising her eyebrows at Miss F, who whispered, 'He is a dear. He actually wants to pummel you for sending him up without answering him.'

'Coming,' Phyllie called. Pummel? Was this a dig

at her for her behaviour towards Andy? Had Andy told Joe? Had Joe told Miss F at one of the quiz evenings at the pub? He had taken Miss Harvey's place on the team and had been a surprising fount of knowledge. Well, he should confine his chatting to that, not her behaviour towards his son. She felt herself flushing as she left the room.

The stairs creaked less this week. It was strange how the cold had made them worse. Yes, the weather had lifted, spring was coming, and there was no earthly reason not to resume the after-school activities at the barn. But how could she ever go near the farm again? Shame drenched her, as it did every time she remembered slapping and hitting Andy.

Jake was standing at the window, the oil lamp unlit, the blind up, Francois sitting beside him. She loved that dog, his devotion, his energy, the way he still played as though a puppy, but who was to say how old he was? Together they would look up at the sky, the same sky above his father and her Sammy. She stood next to him, Francois in between them. She turned the ring on her finger. Wonderful Sammy. She dropped her hand, and stroked Francois.

Frankie had telephoned last week. The days were as busy but the nights were much quieter and their mother was getting more rest. They were grateful for the pickle, and the clothes, he had added before, surprisingly, her mother had taken the receiver from him and thanked her for the wool for the knitting circle she had created. They needed more, she added, her voice crisp.

'Perhaps I can find some. This was from the

Bartletts' attic. Mrs Bartlett knitted,' Phyllie had said calmly. 'I'm pleased you are getting more sleep. Take care, Mother.'

'It's a bomber's moon,' Jake whispered now.

She replied, 'It's so bright. One day we'll call it a hunter's moon again.'

Which city would be targeted tonight? Perhaps, with the Luftwaffe expected in North Africa, there would be fewer aircraft flying towards Britain? But that would mean British troops would get it. She stopped the thoughts by counting stars because it was all so impossibly difficult and Britain's efforts seemed to be getting them nowhere. Yes, the invasion by the Germans, which seemed so probable last year, hadn't happened, but it still could.

She laid her hand on Jake's shoulder, half expecting him to shrug her off. He didn't. She said, 'It will be wonderful when your dad and Sammy get the plumbing business up and running, won't it?'

He grinned up at her now. 'Dad said they'll have to train, but then they'll live here or in the town. That'd be good, wouldn't it, Phyllie? We won't have to leave Miss F, and Mum will like it, and probably my grandparents. I haven't met them, so I can only guess. Ron will be gone then, back to London, so he won't be mean to them because they're bloody Yids, but Bryan will, and Eddie and the gang...' His enthusiasm faded. 'I hope the Germans are being kind in Poland.'

She gripped his shoulder. 'I expect they are. They're not fighting any more, are they? Try not to worry.'

He said, without turning, 'The Germans said

they don't like Jews, before the war, though. They hurt Mum's cousin in Germany.'

'Well, Krakow isn't Germany, and people say a lot of things, don't they? Jake, you and your family are not bloody Yids. I do wish you'd stop saying that.'

'I think that's what Mr Andy thinks I am, but he doesn't say it. I think that Mr Samson thinks it too, but he doesn't say it either, he just looks and takes ages to serve me, and so does Mrs Wellington when I go with Miss F to her café, with the pickle she'd ordered. Mr Joe's nice, though, and I've missed him and the barn, and the horses. Farms don't do much, do they, over the winter, but he'll need all of us children again now the spring is coming.'

Phyllie pulled him to her, Francois pressed against them both. She kissed Jake's head, fiercely. 'Yes, he is nice, and I'm sure that's not why Andy is as he is. After all, he's grumpy to everyone, and we haven't seen him much at all over the winter, and only then at a distance, so he might be feeling better. I mean, why would he sort out the roof if he was grumpy?'

'He did before, and then went grumpy again.'

'Oh, Jake, sometimes we have to be hopeful. When you think about it, it must hurt to lose your hand, and if that happens, perhaps we lose something else, something inside ourselves. And I think he's cross because he's trying to find it. I think in some sort of way, that's happened to Ron too.'

He pulled away from her. 'I can't breathe when you do that, Phyllie.' His face was red.

246

She laughed. 'Say goodnight to your dad and mum.' He returned to the window, looked up at the sky, and his face said everything.

She tucked him in and kissed his forehead, 'Sleep well,' she murmured. The floorboards creaked a little on the landing and the stairs, the cold of the hall flagstones seeped through her thick socks, and she sidestepped to the runner. Her slippers had gone the way of all flesh, and there were none to be had in the shops. In the kitchen, the wireless was still muttering, and Miss F was still knitting. There was, however, a mug of chamomile tea steaming on the table beside the sofa.

Last year they had picked the chamomile that grew in the troughs at the end of the long thin garden and dried it in bunches. They had hung it from the airer that was suspended from the ceiling in front of the Aga. It usually helped her to sleep, but had been failing recently.

Miss F laid down her knitting and took up her own mug. The steam furred her spectacles as it always did. She tutted and removed them, then blew on the liquid and said, 'It won't do, it simply won't. You have avoided the farm as though it contains the plague, and what's more, you have denied the children the pleasure of it. I remind you that there's a notice at school, basically an invitation from Joe and Andy–'

'From Joe, not Andy,' Phyllie shouted. Even she was appalled at her tone of voice.

Miss F banged her mug down on her side table and sat upright, replacing her spectacles. 'I beg your pardon, young madam.'

The women stared at one another. They had never had a disagreement before and Phyllie felt like a naughty schoolgirl. Well, perhaps she was. Miss F pointed her finger, emphasising each word. 'I want to know exactly what has happened. You said Andy was unkind to Jake over the pond incident, that's all. Now, the rest, at once.'

It tumbled out: Ron's accusations, Andy's cruel words, and how she had gone to the farm, how she had hit him, again and again. She ended, 'I hit his stump. Not deliberately, or I don't think so, but... Jake's just said he thinks Andy doesn't like him because he's a Yid.'

Miss F sat back, her hands in her lap. The only sound was the Aga crackling and the clock ticking. Above them, in the bedroom, Francois yelped, probably in his sleep. At last, the headmistress said, 'Let me get this straight. Andy was ditching. He saved the boys, he carried the bootless Jake home, he gave them a rollicking, and you too.'

'He believed Ron,' Phyllie cried, her hands fisted in her lap. 'He said Jake couldn't be trusted and denied him the horses.'

'So you went and hit him, many times.'

Phyllie dropped her head, unable to meet Miss F's eyes. Miss F said, 'Well, I think perhaps there's a bit of guilt swishing around here, don't you? Your guilt.'

It was what Phyllie knew only too well to be the truth, and it was what Sammy had written to her too. *Get it over with,* he'd written. *The bloke saved the little idiots – well, the one idiot was Ron. Perhaps Andy was scared for them, or it touched something he was scared of, who knows? We say things we don't mean when we're scared. You need to go and see him.*

Miss F said, 'I suspect that the incident struck a nerve in Andy, who used to be such a nice boy. Jake did what he did: he left the scene, seeking help. Perhaps he was angry all over again, but at himself, or perhaps he wanted to prevent Jake from feeling that same anger and guilt? Who knows? I expect he doesn't. I doubt he'd put his feelings into words, but he might put it into a roof. I thought our Joe was being a bit quiet on the subject, and I can see why now. It's not every day one's son gets metaphorically put over a little slip of a girl's knee. If Joe even knows, of course; it's not something Andy would shout about, is it?'

There was silence. Both women looked at the Aga, Phyllie drawn by, its warmth and familiarity. Miss F continued, 'One thing of which I am absolutely certain is that there is no prejudice in either of the Bartlett men.'

Again there was silence. 'Drink your chamomile, my dearest Phyllie. I think, don't you, that we both love that little boy to distraction, and therefore we are inclined to tear anyone who hurts him limb from limb. We have to assess the situation object-ively, however, and you must put aside your own embarrassment and guilt. Further, we must, above all, remember Jake is not ours, he's on loan. He will go back into the care of his parents, God willing, and we must celebrate that fact, and, until then, do what is best for him.'

To her horror Phyllie saw Miss F's lips trem-bling, and her eyes fill with tears, and she felt frightened, much as a child did, when a parent became upset. It wasn't just Jake she had come to

249

love, she realised. Perhaps that was why she was able to detach from her own mother, and was interested, but not affected, by her. This woman had taken her mother's place.

She shared with Miss F the plans the men had of moving to Dorset once the war was over. 'As long as Rachel agrees, so we won't lose him entirely.'

She reached for her chamomile tea, sipped it. 'You drink yours, Miss F,' she said gently.

They talked into the small hours, and at last Phyllie headed up the stairs, accepting that Sammy and Miss F were right, it was high time she faced Andy. It was also time Jake realised that life isn't necessarily fair and anger is about many things, not just prejudice. Most of all, that love could heal many hurts.

Chapter Fourteen

The following Saturday morning, at ten o'clock, she led the school along the lane, keeping 'eyes front' as they passed the pond. They were singing, 'This Old Man'. Jake was walking with Dan, deep in conversation about the model Hurricane they were working on and the table tennis league that Mrs Otis was mapping out. Ron was just behind her with Bryan, keeping their voices low. Skulduggery in the offing, no doubt, Phyllie thought, glad to have that to concentrate on, rather than the thought of what she must do. Miss F was bringing up the rear, and Mrs Otis held the mid-line position.

They were going to see the lambs that had just been born, and which were kept in the new barn, opposite the old barn. They were corralled with their mothers, or so Joe had said in his phone call. There were some older ones in the field to the left of the lane, chomping their way through the turnip tops. Temporary fencing had been erected, which would be moved back progressively as the tops were cleared, leaving the turnips to be dug up later.

They entered the yard, and Phyllie's nervousness increased, but Andy was nowhere in sight. It was Joe who waited for them, his trousers tied below the knee to prevent the rats roaring up and taking his goolies, as he delighted in telling anyone who cared to ask. He had his mac tied around his waist with string. She caught Jake's glance. He straightened, bracing his shoulders, proud of his own 'working' mackintosh, which had been washed after the pond episode and was none the worse for it. It, too, was held together with string.

The school children were sorted into groups, and the first went into the new barn, while those that waited went into the old barn to sweep the floor and dust the table tennis table. In the new barn Joe leaned against an upright, while the children gathered at the pens, laughing and pointing at the lambs. He fingered his cigarette, pulled it from behind his ear and began the lambing chat he had promised. 'You see them tiddlins having a good old go at their mother's tits. Well, you did too when you was tiddlins, but you won't remember that. Mayhap you'd need to talk to your teachers about that.'

He looked up at Phyllie and Miss F. Phyllie murmured, 'Well, thanks so much.'

'Quite,' whispered Miss F, but as always, her whisper was clearly audible. The children looked round puzzled, then back at Joe who was laughing quietly as he continued to roll his cigarette between his fingers. Little Clive, from Mrs Otis's class of seven-year-olds, and before that Spitalfields, called, 'You smoke that and you'll set the whole bloody lot alight, then we'll be having roast lamb.'

Joe pointed. 'That'd be right, young 'un. You can fiddle with the little rascal, but never more'n that. Never ever light a match near a barn. You got that, all on yer?'

The children had long ago come to terms with the language that floated around willy-nilly, and barely noticed it, just as Phyllie did not. They were nodding their heads, including Ron. Bryan also looked thoughtful, though he always worked hard at being uninterested. Joe pointed to the older lambs. 'Them lot of tiddlins need more'n milk, so we give this clover hay that we chaff to short pieces.' He reached into a bucket and brought out a handful, letting it drop back. 'That'll go into that there trough at feeding time. We'll creep the fencing forward to keep the tiddlins on one side, and their mums t'other. They're not like our mums, giving us the best and going without themselves, but'll shove 'emselves forward and guzzle the lot. Survival of the fittest, you might say, eh,

Miss F? Reckon we even give 'em a nibble of the linseed cake as a treat. We all like treats, don't we? I spect we've got the ladies from the WI in the big kitchen right now, putting together something to titillate your tiddlin taste buds.'

Miss F nodded, as the children swung round to look at her. 'But there's someone else in t'other kitchen I'd like you to meet,' Joe added. Phyllie and Jake snatched a look at one another. Just then, little Sally Taylor from Miss Otis's class, who had lived in the village since she was born, pointed to a lamb huddled in the corner, with something tied round it. 'Excuse us, Mr Bartlett, why's the tiddlin wearing that?'

'Ah, young Sally, thought you'd a known that. You see, you vacees, you're helping our own children learn things.' The evacuees amongst the children grinned at one another, clearly feeling important, and Phyllie could have kissed the man.

Joe said, 'Now where was I? Ah yes, that tiddlin's a little orphan Annie, that she is.' Joe had moved to the corner of the pens, and was pointing. 'You see, she lost her mum to a fox, or maybe a pack of dogs who don't know how to behave.'

Jake shot round to Joe. 'It wasn't Francois, honest. He's not allowed out on his own, is he, Phyllie? Is he, Miss F? So you don't need to shoot him, you don't.' She heard the terror in his voice.

She felt a familiar anger stir, because that was down to bloody Andy. Joe leaned forward, and tousled Jake's dark hair. 'Course it weren't, and we all know that, don't fret. Now, that tiddlin 'asn't a mum, and that big lump of a lady sheep standing

253

near him, looking as though she's about to make a decision, has lost her lamb. So we skinned the dead 'un, and put it round the orphan, and we 'ope the mother thinks it's her own tiddlin, and lets her suckle. P'rhaps a bit like you lot. Well, you don't wear skins, but these good ladies in the villages look after you until your own mums can, don't they?'

The children were silent, watching, barely breathing, as the sheep moved nearer to the lamb who was bleating, his little legs fragile and unsteady, his tail going nineteen to the dozen as he made his way towards her. The sheep sniffed, and then butted him away. The children groaned, as did the two women. Joe hushed them. 'Patience. Give her a chance. Nothing 'appens overnight, do it?'

Twice more the lamb was rebuffed, and now they were all holding their breath. The fourth time the sheep let the lamb come close. She sniffed the coat for a long time, and at last the orphan was allowed to suckle. The relief in the barn was palpable, and even Joe was rubbing his hands, though he ruined his cigarette by doing so, with flakes of tobacco falling into the straw.

Ron looked from the lamb to Joe. 'What happens when the sheep won't let it near? Does he, you know, the little chap, does he die?' His voice was anxious. Joe rubbed his chin, nodding a little. Oh surely not. Phyllie groaned. 'Well, you see young Ron, we take them into our kitchen, put them into a cardboard box by the Aga to keep 'em warm, and feed them with a bottle every few hours.'

The relief on Ron's face was obvious. Phyllie

thought of his mother. Did he fear he could be, or even had been, abandoned? That damned mother had never been to see him, but she had written once or twice, so there was hope. When Joe led them across the yard she manoeuvred herself to Ron's side. 'Mothers always love their lambs, or children. It's interesting, like Mr Joe said, that if something goes wrong, then there is always someone who will care.'

Ron turned. 'D'you reckon so, miss?'

Bryan knocked him now. 'Yes, they'll fatten the little bugger up and eat it, that's how much they care. That's how much they care about children, too.'

'Bryan,' Phyllie's tone was sharp, 'don't be so ridiculous. Of course human beings care. Look at the way mothers in the villages have taken so many children in. Your mother did for a while.'

'Yeah, for the money.'

'It isn't just for the money.' They were at the kitchen door.

'Boots off,' Miss F ordered. 'And you, Bryan Anderton, stop showing your ignorance. Money doesn't come into it.' But Phyllie feared the damage had been done, as Ron kicked off his boots, dug his hands deep into his pockets and slouched.

There were two cardboard boxes near the Aga, and each contained a tiddlin, both of whom were trying to clamber out, bleating fit to burst, their little pink mouths wide open. There, too, was Andy, holding two baby bottles. He looked up and smiled at them all, his gaze sliding past Phyllie. She found she was holding her breath.

She said, 'I hope we're not disturbing you?'

255

'We knew you were coming, so you're obviously not.' His voice was neutral, and he looked not at her but at little Clive, who was reaching up for the bottle. 'Can I do it, mister?'

Jake was easing his way to the back of the group, but now Andy called, 'Jake, you can start with number one. You take number two, Clive. You're next for number one, Ron. Teachers, what we need are some children to commit to coming regularly, to feed them. It will be, I repeat, a commitment, for the teachers too, as you'll need to stay with them. But the children will probably be here anyway, at the old barn, so it shouldn't be beyond your capabilities.' There it was, the challenge in his voice.

Miss F laughed. 'We can do it with one hand tied behind our back, young fellow my lad.' Phyllie closed her eyes. One hand, for goodness' sake? Andy laughed, abruptly, but then it was gone. It had been a laugh, though. Miss F was colouring in her turn.

'One hand is good enough,' Andy said.

Phyllie felt glad she wasn't in the firing line, but was it that? He wasn't scowling but then again, he wasn't smiling.

Jake was working his way to the front, reaching out to take the bottle, keeping his eyes on that; not on Andy. Little Clive was already gripping his tiddlin, fighting it and forcing the teat into its mouth. In time the tiddlin was guzzling, and dribbling the milk, his tail shaking fit to burst. Jake, meanwhile, knelt and stroked his lamb, then let him come to the teat and guzzle. It was an altogether gentler, slower affair. After five minutes, they changed to the next person. Ron did as Jake had done. Phyllie watched closely, then nodded. She had felt at the carol service that there was a decent child underneath all his bluster, and now she was even more convinced. They simply must move him from Bryan and Eddie's sphere, somehow. Finally the bottles were finished.

Andy stood by the kitchen table, and checked his watch. 'Tea should be ready. Off you go, and don't forget the rota, teachers.' He took the bottles to the sink and eased off the teats. Miss F opened the back door, but before the children filed out she said, 'What have you to say to Mr Andy, children?'

'Thank you, Mr Andy,' they chanted.

Andy called over his shoulder, 'Well done, you lot. You fed them well, particularly Jake and Ron. Gentle is good.' He looked long and hard at Phyllie, and it was her turn to colour.

The children filed out, with Miss F leading. Phyllie turned at the door. 'I'm sorry, Andy. I shouldn't have hit you, especially your... Well, your wrist.'

He was using a brush to clean the innards of the bottles. 'I think you mean my stump. Apology accepted, reluctantly. Now it must be time for you to scamper off to help Dad with the other groups.'

She wanted to slam the door, but didn't. She wanted to take him back to the moments he had been so foul to Jake, but didn't, for what was the point? All that mattered was that he was good to them now.

Later that evening, Miss F left with Mrs Symes, for the farm. It was time to stock-take the sugar, stashed in large tins, hidden behind the sacks of seed, in preparation for a new delivery. The jam season was almost upon them. Miss F cycled, her gas mask and her old music case hanging off the handlebars. It was in this case that she carried the record of the sugar stocks. They unlocked the storeroom, or so she told Phyllie on her return, moved the sacks, lifted down the tins, huffing and puffing, as they were so heavy, but not as heavy as they had thought. They checked the stocks against the records. They were twenty pounds short.

They had checked three times. Mrs Symes brought Joe to the store and checked it again, with him watching at Miss F's insistence.

When she returned home, she told Phyllie the bad news, adding, 'The problem is that Mrs Symes, Joe, Andy and you are the only others who knew where it was, though I wonder if Jake heard us talking of it that evening in the kitchen. You see, I found one of his pencils in the store, his name clearly scored near the top.' She looked old, suddenly, and tired.

Phyllie stared. His pencil? How on earth...? No, not Jake. 'There's got to be another reason,' Phyllie insisted.

Miss F sat at the table, her head resting on her hand. 'Of course I know that, but... We can't obtain more than our designated amount. And if we have a shortfall of produce because of this it will be advertising the loss outside the five of us. This could lead others, including the WI ladies, to think that we have actually used it ourselves. We have to keep it quiet, and make sugarless jam. I will tell the others that it's an experiment, and I do know that the government is thinking of reducing the amount we get anyway, as a result of the convoys being bashed to bits. Dear God, this is a nightmare.' She paused for a moment. 'Hang on, Mrs Otis was also in the know, but surely not...?'

'As you say, a nightmare,' Phyllie echoed.

'We say nothing, nothing at all. It's our secret, just you, me, Mrs Symes, Mrs Otis and the Bartletts.'

Chapter Fifteen

Mid-June 1941, sheep washing, Little Mitherton

Joe stood on the bank of the stream. 'Late shearing, we bloody are, late. But that's the war for you, and all down to the ministry lad who's so wet behind the ears he leaves a splash wherever he goes, and who came when we *should* be washing before shearing...' He took a breath. 'Came with his bleedin' orders to plant late oats, and so off we went, faffing about with the ploughing again, and here we are having to dam the stream to wash the little buggers, late.' He scratched the back of his head, knocking his cap forward.

I think we got that, Joe, thought Phyllie but knew better than to say it. They were surrounded by her class of eleven- and twelve-year-olds, for Ron was now twelve, and Bryan, Sylvia and

Prudence too.

They'd all been given parties; a card had not been sent by Mrs Cummins, and in the absence of a present, one had surreptitiously been provided. Fanny McTravers and her auntie had packaged up a pullover for Ron and talked the post office into delivering the package, with its fabricated franking marks. The handwriting had been more difficult, but Phyllie did her best, copying from the letter she had received at Christmas, asking for more money for the fare. The pullover was sleeveless, and knitted late in the evening by Miss F, with the armholes finished by Fanny, as they were a step too far for either Phyllie or Miss F. No one but these few knew the truth, not even Jake. Ron wore it constantly, even today, here by the stream, with the sun beating down.

It had been nearly a year since they arrived and so much had happened, but so little too. The war was still grinding on, they were still just holding their own. The raid on London a month ago had been terrible, though. Phyllie had phoned Frankie, and they were safe, but so many others weren't. 'But it's war, Phyllie, so what else do you expect?' Her brother had sounded exasperated. She'd replied, 'There's no need to take that tone, not everyone can be a hero, some of us just have to get on with what we have to do.'

There had been a long silence. Finally he'd said, 'Thank God that is still possible, Phyllie. I'm sorry.' It transpired that her mother was too busy to talk, and she probably was. She heard the laughter of the children around her. Joe must have said something. She smiled. The village, the seasons and the children were a reminder of normality, of hope.

On the bank Joe, his two sheepdogs at his feet, was now conferring with Andy who had arrived with the cart, talking quietly to Destiny and Doris as he slapped the reins gently on their great flanks. He had drawn up nearer the stream, the cart laden with railway sleepers and sawn trunks of coppiced trees. She stroked Francois who sat beside her. The children, in their grey physical education shorts, were chatting to the Guides and Scouts.

All winter the WI and Guides had been busy sewing dungarees for the school children, to equip them to help Mr Bartlett sow plants and seeds. Today, though, they'd get wet, so shorts were the thing. The dungarees could wait for tomorrow, for not a day went by without some farm chore being scheduled. In fact, there was a farming calendar on the school noticeboard with dates blocked off for 'essential war work'.

The children's letters home chatted about their chores, their table tennis, even the two land girls who had arrived, but departed the same day. 'Surplus to requirements,' Joe had roared to the official who had strutted up in the wake of their departure. 'I'll be letting you know if I need 'em back, you 'ear me. Until then, I have me boy and Old Stan, and the tiddlins, and it be good for them. So be on your way.'

Soon it would be time to hoe between the potatoes with both the Scouts and Guides. This would not be enjoyed as much as the dawn strawberry picking that they would be doing the next day, but would nonetheless be done. At the thought of the jam making, Phyllie stared down at her plimsolls, the anxiety that was constantly gnawing at her rising to the surface. A twenty-pound loss couldn't be hidden for ever but Miss F was still trying to find a solution.

'Miss, miss, look at this.'

Phyllie looked up and saw Sylvia holding a buttercup under Dan's chin, and then Jake's. 'They like butter, miss. Miss, d'you know what's been happening at the pond yet? We've all tried to find out and them Bartletts won't say.'

Phyllie shook her head. 'No, I don't. Mr Joe said that nothing good comes to nosy parkers and to pull my trunk in and wait. So wait we'll have to. It looks like some stakes have been driven from the bank into the middle, doesn't it, with a walkway on top. I saw some Scouts helping, but they didn't know what it was, or said they didn't. Perhaps it's something for the ducks? You know how fond Joe is of them.' She had drummed up the courage to ask Andy, and he had also told her to mind her own business. So she had.

On the bank of the stream Joe was clapping his son on his back before turning to his helpers. 'Less mucking about, more doing, you sorry-looking lot. What we're about is fencing a channel for 'em sheep to funnel down into the water, and we're making a temporary dam, an' all. We need the bigger lads for that.' He thumbed towards the older Scouts, who had congregated by the cart, and included Peter, Miss Deacon's younger nephew, who had evacuated from the Midlands a month before. 'You tiddlins might well be needed to give 'em a shove.'

Work began, the logs being offloaded from the cart, in the shafts of which the horses stood, tossing their heads as flies pestered. The Scouts then dragged the logs to the bank while the children pushed at the other end, sliding them down the slope into the stream. The water was only a foot deep now but soon it would stack up.

'There'll be seepage,' Andy called, 'but don't worry, the sheep only need to be run through to get the worst of the grease and debris from the fleece. The shearers arrive any day now.'

Phyllie moved further back, Francois following. They watched Dan and Jake being directed by two Scouts who chanted as they pulled a log towards the stream: 'Push, boys, push.' The Scouts went backwards, as Jake and Dan shoved. All were bare-foot, the plimsolls were piled up together, hope-fully tied by the laces into pairs, or it would be bedlam when it came to which belonged to whom.

The log was in the water now, where it floated, all four boys guiding it to the dam as per Joe's instructions. Jake was laughing at Dan, their teeth flashing white against their tans. They all looked so well; and now the London evacuees were in-distinguishable from the natives, as Sammy had called them in his last letter. She laughed along with Jake, not knowing what was so funny for him, but Sammy was coming on leave, and happiness coursed through her.

Just one more month and he'd finally be here. It might just be for two days, or one day, or a week, but it didn't matter. All that mattered was that he'd be here, and she'd feel his arms around

263

her and know that she was loved. The boat was coming into Portland. He and Isaac were taking rooms in a guesthouse in the nearby market town, Bestminster, which served Little Mitherton and all the surrounding villages.

Francois tugged on his lead and she stroked his head. 'You could do with a bath too, you dear old thing,' she said. It was still the old rope lead, but why not, everything was in short supply and it belonged to the soldier who had saved him, so was precious.

Joe had dotted the orphaned lambs the children had fed in March with red dye, so the children could identify them as they walked past the field on their nature walks. These lambs would be amongst those herded down the channel that was being built by more Scouts, Guides and children, under Andy's eagle eye.

Phyllie and Andy now spoke, but he remained distant and still Jake had not been invited to help with the horses and had felt crushed when Thomas Healey, just arrived from London, had been taken on. Thomas, though, had told Miss F that there was too much to do, and he needed help or would have to leave, like Tim Morton, who had helped before he came. Phyllie had pleaded with Joe to let Jake back. Joe had shaken his head, and said that the horses were Andy's province and therefore it was his decision. Jake had forbidden her to ask Andy. 'I don't want any favours,' he had insisted.

The sheep were bleating in the field behind and around her, and Andy called across from the bank, standing firm in his gumboots, 'Miss Saunders, move that dog now. I'll be working mine in a moment to get the sheep into the river, or had you forgotten?'

'No, I haven't forgotten,' she replied. 'I was waiting for your signal as your father arranged. You will notice that Francois hasn't moved a muscle. Jake has been training him, and we trust Francois implicitly.' She led Francois across to the stone-built shelter at the entrance to the field, shut the door behind him, and locked it with the huge rusty key. 'Don't you dare make a fuss,' she breathed. It had been Joe's idea to bring him, to show Andy how trustworthy both Jake and Francois were. He yelped. 'Quiet, all this is for Jake. So be quiet,' she said. He stopped.

She walked back to the sheep run, listening for the dog's bark over the bleating of the sheep, which were being rounded up by the sheepdogs. Nothing. Thank heavens. She gave Jake a thumbs-up. The Scouts, with a couple of Guides, were standing on the dam, holding long paddles. The milling sheep, who had been herded to the mouth of the channel, were being harassed by the dogs – nipped, yelped at, pushed. The bleating grew louder as Joe called, 'Let 'em through.'

Old Stan moved the wicker hurdle from the entrance to the channel and the sheep and lambs seemed to pour into it, two by two. A large old girl rushed and leapt, trying to clear the stream, but she was doomed to fail, and splashed down. Joe and two of the Scouts stood in the river, shoving them under, and the Scouts and Guides on the dam did the same with the paddles. It was mayhem, a riot of splashing and cursing, not to mention bleating. And still no barks from Francois.

Andy had his back to her, standing at the head of the channel as his dogs worked. He grabbed the sheep and shoved them along, shouting, 'Go on, down, down.' Some Scouts leaned over the fencing and pulled them onwards too. One sheep milling near the entrance broke free of the dogs, heading back into the meadow. Andy whistled, and a sheepdog gathered it up. He shouted across to Phyllie, '*That's* a well-trained dog for you.'

'Francois is silent, haven't you noticed?' she countered.

Andy shrugged and grabbed another sheep. Joe called, pointing, 'It's that old white-faced cardy trying for a break, Andy lad, get the old devil in, she'll tear off if she can.'

The sheep were scrambling out on the far side, shaking the water from their fleeces, and Phyllie could have sworn that they glared defiance before scampering off, still shaking.

They were there for three hours in total, because once the sheep had been washed, the dam had to be dismantled, and the logs heaved up onto the cart. Each time it seemed the Scouts and Guides took an inordinate time checking one another's hands for splinters, and whispering sweet nothings. Destiny and Doris shifted from leg to leg, and all the time Jake sneaked glances. Phyllie knew he longed to slide off and run his hands along their flanks. She also knew that nothing on earth would make him do so.

She collected Francois, who strained on the lead initially to get to Jake, but walked to heel on command. He would only go if Jake called him.

Basically, the dog deserved a medal and she crouched next to him, pulling his ears, whispering, 'A marrow bone for you, if only we had one. Now, what shall we do this afternoon, a walk? We'll take the lot of Class A, shall we? Then their mothers can continue with jam making and they can run off even more energy.'

Joe was calling all the children to him now, as the sheep grazed the meadow on the other side of the stream.

'You've all been mighty nosy about the goings-on at the pond, ain't you?' The children nodded... 'Any ideas?' Joe asked. A cluster of hands shot up.

'We asked, you wouldn't say.'

'Something for the ducks? They're your babies, Miss F says.'

'A sort of fence?'

'It looks like a path.'

Joe held up his hand. The chatter died out. 'Mr Andy has something to tell you.'

Andy stepped forward, the dogs at his heel. Phyllie was interested, because he had turned against them after his accident. He did seem to be healing in every way. He said, 'What I want you to do is to go back to your homes and change into your swimmers. I know you all have them because I put in a secret request to the Guides, who got going on them during the winter. After two of you went through the ice it seemed it was high time you all learned to swim. The "pathway" is a boardwalk. It's not for the ducks, as your teacher suggested, unless they choose to share it with you, but it's a sort of jetty to walk along. It is from this that you will enter the water, either down the ladder or by jumping in from it. You will not enter via the bank, which will ruin it.' He looked across at Phyllie, his face unreadable.

The children were grinning at one another. Andy continued, 'We village children all learned in the pond. We have done for years and years until, in fact, the jetty collapsed five years ago. Some of the Scouts and Guides can swim, some can't. Those that can will be in the water, helping. Those that can't will also be in the water, like you, learning. You see, what you have to understand is that water can kill, but it can also be fun, be a great form of exercise, it can just be ... well, nice.'

He was looking at her again. 'Off you go now, get those costumes. You too, Miss Saunders. Miss F says you have one. We need all hands to the pump.'

Phyllie stood, aghast. She didn't enjoy swimming, and would like it even less in front of everyone. The water looked cold. How dare Miss F...? Andy turned his attention to Ron and Jake. 'The most important thing to learn, though, is that if someone says that you must not do something, there is usually a good reason. I will see you in fifteen minutes.'

When they all returned, they had their costumes on under their clothes. Phyllie removed her skirt and blouse, self-conscious and embarrassed to be so exposed in front of this man. Andy gathered them all together. He was in his trunks too, and it was only now they all realised the extent of his wounds: deep welts, burns, a chunk out of his upper arm, one out of his thigh. Phyllie felt a surge of guilt and compassion, but only until he bawled at her to get along the jetty with the youngest children, and into the water, rather than stand like a stuffed dummy.

She did so, clambering down the wooden ladder the Scouts had built on the end of the jetty, gasping at the cold, but trying to look as though she was enjoying every second. She managed half an hour before, shivering, she led the seven- and eight-year-olds out.

'Leaving us so soon, Miss Saunders?' Andy called as she dripped her way along the jetty, herding the children and shuddering with cold.

'I rather feel I am, Mr Andy,' she retorted through chattering teeth. 'The children have had quite enough. I will come back to help from the jetty once I've restored some feeling to my body, if you don't mind.'

'Children have had enough, my Aunt Fanny,' she heard him hoot. 'You're a really good swimmer, and teacher. You did well.' She grabbed her towel from the pile, and dried herself, hearing his laugh, and not minding suddenly. Indeed, she was laughing in reply and feeling young for the first time in a long while.

She helped the children to dry themselves, listening to their excited chatter as they talked of floating and of allowing their faces to go into the water. She heard their boasts of how they had used their arms and legs to propel themselves along.

As they ran about playing tag, she watched the swimming lessons from the bank. Some children seemed to sink like stones, while others took to it effortlessly. It seemed connected to confidence as much as anything else. Bryan was ducking and diving immediately, clearly already a swimmer, Jake was pretty much middle of the road, while Ron clung to one of the uprights of the jetty. Within fifteen minutes he was clambering back onto the boardwalk refusing to return, slouching off, dressing, searching for his plimsolls in the pile, then picking up another pair by their laces, and throwing them high up in the air, and into the pond. 'Here's your plimsolls, Jakey boy,' he yelled.

Phyllie was stunned. He ran past, calling to Bryan that he was going back to the McTravers dump, he'd had enough of fannying about like a bloody two-year-old. Phyllie started after him, calling, 'Ron, come back this minute.' He didn't even bother to turn around and she couldn't leave the children to chase after him. She returned to see Bryan heaving himself up on the jetty. It was at that point that Andy looked across at Phyllie. He was nodding, grimly, then returned to his teaching. Bryan dragged on his clothes, but this time Phyllie guarded the plimsolls. Bryan just looked at her and laughed, as he followed Ron.

The swimming lessons continued for another hour, during which time Andy remained in the water and Phyllie allowed herself to be aware of his strength, and his patience. She heard him laugh again and again, as he cheered the children on to greater efforts. When each session ended she moved amongst the children helping until finally the last of the swimmers was out. They were talking and laughing, and wondering when they could come again. 'Please, miss, when?' She didn't know, but would find out.

It was then she saw Jake shivering on the jetty,

still in his trunks, about to jump in. She called, 'What on earth are you doing?'

'I need my plimsolls,' he said. 'I think I can dive for them.'

Robert, one of the Scouts, shouted, 'No need, tiddlin. Andy's already on the case.'

Phyllie saw Andy swimming towards the point where Jake's plimsolls had sunk. She watched as he dived until he found them, swishing them in the water until they were mud free. He tossed them onto the jetty, where Jake was waiting, dressed now, but barefoot.

'Thank you, Mr Andy,' Jake called, untying the wet laces, dragging on his plimsolls, his head down because although there had been much laughter, Jake had taken care to stay well away from this man.

When his laces were tied, he stood by Phyllie's side, reaching for her hand, squeezing it, just once, and whispering, 'That was kind, and it was for me.' He said nothing about Ron's behaviour, and seemed these days to accept it with something close to pity. Dan joined them, and the two boys talked of how cold the water seemed when you first got in.

Soon even the Guides and Scouts were dry, and Andy was dragging on his trousers. The children began to line up in front of Phyllie. She did a head count and realised she was missing one. It was Jake. She spun round. Francois stood up, catching her concern, but Jake was back at the jetty. Andy was now squatting at his side, talking intently. Jake stepped back, half shaking his head, and then he pointed to Phyllie. Andy stood up,

271

nodding at him.

Jake took off around the pond, full of suppressed excitement, pulling her to one side, whispering, 'He's asked me to help with the horses because Doris and Destiny have missed me. He said Thomas can't manage, really he can't. He said that I'm clearly totally trustworthy.'

Phyllie looked down into his face, whispering in her turn, 'Did he apologise?'

He grinned. 'I think perhaps he did. He said he wished it hadn't happened, that perhaps he'd been a bit quick to judge. What do you think, Phyllie?'

The children were restless in the line-up. She waved them to order. 'What do you want to do?'

He laughed. 'You know what I want, and it's just the most perfect thing, because I can tell Dad I'm working with the horses, and I can tell him that water isn't scary, and that will help him feel safer, won't it? It's not always dark and frightening, is it?'

'Off you go then, but hurry. This lot are champing at the bit to get home for their tea.'

He ran back to Andy, who was waiting, looking out over the sheep in the meadow, and soon there could be cows in the corn, she thought. Jake was right, it all was the most perfect thing.

In July, on the first Friday, as the wheat was beginning to ripen and the blackcurrants, redcurrants and gooseberries were still going strong, she and Jake caught the first bus after school. They were going into Bestminster, to meet their men. They ran to the guesthouse where Isaac and Sammy would be waiting, if their train had been on time.

There they were, at the gate, in their uniforms, looking like two peas in a pod but so tired and old. Jake streaked ahead of Phyllie who for a moment felt shy, hesitant and frightened by the change. Then Sammy smiled at her, and it was the same wonderful smile, and she was running again, into his arms, into the smell of the submarine, the diesel, the ... well, everything. He was kissing her face, her neck and then her lips, his hands on either side of her face, his eyes open. 'You are so lovely,' he breathed.

Jake was dragging at Isaac. 'Come on, Miss F is waiting with supper.'

Isaac laughed at Phyllie. 'Hello, and let's get going I think is the greeting.'

The men tossed the usual small canvas bags over their shoulders. Sammy put his arm around Phyllie's waist, hugging her to him. She said, 'Miss F hasn't room for you to stay, I'm sorry, I thought you realised, so perhaps you should leave the bags at the guesthouse.'

He bent and kissed her lips, 'What a worry guts you still are. I know that. We've just got a few things for you.'

They caught the bus back to the village, where Miss F had pheasant pie ready but before they sat, Isaac and Jake took Francois out for a run, or the dog would never have settled. As he went Isaac grinned at Sammy and nodded at his bag. 'Don't take all the credit, all the lads leaned on Cookie, remember. They were all prepared to do without, including the captain.'

Sammy laughed. 'As if I would. Go and stretch

the mutt's legs.'

'He's not a mutt, Sammy,' Jake yelled through the back door. 'He's *un chien*.'

His father laughed. 'Show off; come on, you.'

Isaac was shutting the door behind them, when Phyllie heard Jake ask, 'Have you heard from Mum or Uncle Otto?'

Phyllie didn't hear the answer, and Sammy was no help, as he dug around in his bag, coming up with packet after packet of sugar. 'Twenty-five pounds of sugar for the use of, well, jam. With the compliments of all aboard *Vehement*, but I need to take some jam back with me. Phyllie says you've made "sugarless" in the Aga. As well as honey, and a bit of sugar, I think that needs salt, Cookie says. Well, there's some salt here, too. So, we'll have a few jars out of your pantry, and you can slip this into your new hiding place, Miss F. It will make up the shortfall. How's that for a fair exchange?'

Miss F kissed him on the cheek. 'Christmas has come early, and, my dear Sammy, you and Mr Kaplan will make simply splendid plumbers. I will stack up the jobs in readiness.' Phyllie gripped his hand, and wondered how she could possibly love this man more than she already did, but he had just shown her that it was possible.

After tea and as evening came it was hard to say farewell, and so they didn't. Isaac slept on cushions in Jake's room, which, he said in the morning, Francois had thought a wonderful idea, and had crept under the blanket with him. Sammy slept on the sofa in the kitchen and Phyllie lay awake upstairs, wishing the war was over, and that they were in their own house, with a child in the boxroom. Then they would lie together, their arms around one another, listening to the birds singing, and she would feel his lips on hers... All that day, as the village went to church, they had held hands, or hugged, even when watching Jake swimming in the pond with Isaac. As the afternoon wore on, she led Sammy off into the woods, where she showed him the tree where she and Jake had found the mistletoe. He kissed her as though it was still there.

She and Jake led them to the school, where the Home Guard marched in the playground, with a great clatter of boots, none of them in time, before walking to the Preservation Centre at the farm. Although they were quick to shut the door behind them, Mrs Speedie and Miss Deacon flapped tea towels, shouting, 'Wasps!' Mrs Speedie's hair was escaping from the other tea towel she had tied around her hair, the air was full of the sweet smell of jam, and was as hot as a brothel in Egypt, Sammy whispered to Phyllie when they left. She slapped him, asking when he'd been in such a place. He'd pretended to be hurt, but was laughing so much he could hardly speak. Isaac raised his eyebrows at Jake and said, 'There are some strange people in this world.'

Jake dragged his dad into the old barn, where many of the children were playing. 'This is Dan, and Dan, this is my dad.' He was so proud as Isaac joined Dan and four others, who were playing darts, while Phyllie and Sammy chatted their way around the room until they reached the table tennis area. Ron and Bryan were playing, and

Sammy said, 'I'm rusty, who's going to get me back into the swing of it.'

The two boys looked at one another. Bryan said, 'I'd wipe the floor with you. Ron, why don't you give him a whirl?' He sat on one of the bales of straw that Joe had brought in to demarcate the areas, lounging back as though he owned the place. Ron and Sammy played, and some of Sammy's shots were wild. He kept asking Ron to show him how to get it right, and slowly he improved, until they had a decent game. By this time lots of the children were watching and Sammy was only narrowly beaten.

He shook Ron's hand. 'You're a good player; a good teacher too, isn't he, Miss Saunders?' She agreed, loving this man more than life itself, and what's more, clearly he'd be the most wonderful father, if this short time with Ron was anything to go by. Ron grinned, wiping his hands down his pullover.

Sammy said, 'I'd like one of those pullovers. Bet your mum got it for you.'

Ron's grin grew even broader. Sammy tossed the ping-pong ball at Bryan, who dropped it. The others laughed. Bryan scowled.

'Better luck next time,' Sammy said. 'You can't have too much practice, you know.'

They all walked along the lane, and Jake pointed out Mr Joe and Mr Andy in the potato field way beyond the allotments. They were leading the hoeing teams between the furrows. Some of the WI members were in the allotments, sitting on small stools and picking redcurrants. 'It's been a bad year; uncertain weather has led to poor soft fruit. We're hoping for better things next year,' Phyllie explained.

Jake ran ahead with Francois, and waited for them to catch up. 'We use milking stools to pick the currants for the jam, or it kills your back. Phyllie makes a fuss because she says she's taller than we children and has more back to ache.'

She chased him, hand in hand with Sammy, and they stopped, panting, by the gate to the potato field. They all leaned on it, resting their elbows, watching the line of Scouts, Guides and children hoeing. She wanted to be closer to Sammy, squeezed up against him, so that there was no space between them, and never ever would be.

Jake said, 'The WI jam makers have to do a course – sort of going back to school – because it has to be good. Some of the ladies were cross because they said their jam was already good but Mrs Symes has done the course, so she tells everyone what's what, and now there are no wasps or hairs. I think they look funny in their tea towels, but they flick your legs with one if you laugh. It stings.'

'Bit like our captain,' Isaac murmured, winking at Phyllie.

'Is it really? Really, Dad?'

'You should see him,' Sammy joined in. 'But Cookie's the worst. Anyone gets in his way and then he comes and flicks us all.'

Jake was laughing so hard he couldn't breathe. He took a deep breath, and said, out of nowhere, 'How do you escape when a ship is hunting you, Dad?'

Isaac looked at Sammy, and then said, 'We've a

great captain, haven't we, Sammy? He gets us out of lots of fun and games because he knows all the tricks.'

They were walking along again, Jake holding his father's hand. 'What tricks?'

'Ah,' Sammy said, tapping the side of his nose. 'That would be telling.'

'But tell me then,' Jake insisted.

'One thing that he's good at, or lucky at, is finding the layers. You see water isn't just water, it forms layers like rock does. The salt content and the temperature differ, and it disturbs what their hydrophones hear. All we have to do is to find a different layer and it's like being in a cave. We still have to be quiet, but their Asdic, which is coming down like signals, gets bounced off at a different angle.'

Jake and Phyllie were listening carefully, and Jake said, 'So he's lucky, your captain?'

Isaac said, stooping to pick a buttercup, holding it beneath his son's chin. 'Very lucky, so we're lucky too. Look, Jake, Sammy and I are like everyone else, we're all doing our bit, like the village, and the WI, and you children. You've been brave and lucky, because you've moved from your houses and ended up in a different, but happy place. And what's more, I can tell you like butter.'

Phyllie watched Jake. He had the same shaped face as his father, with fine cheekbones and full lips, and the same habit of frowning so that two lines dug deep between his eyebrows. He was doing so now, and said, 'It's not brave but it is lucky because I feel as though I'm at home, with Phyllie and Miss F. Francois does too, and he's in a strange place, stranger than for all of us really. Yes, I do like butter, but we don't get much with rationing because Mr Joe is very strict, and we don't have "any bloody favours".'

Francois had leapt up in the air at the sound of his name, and was now chasing his tail. Isaac picked up a stick and threw it, and all five of them chased it. So it went on, and they had one more day, but she wanted to be alone with Sammy on that last day, so she could remember every moment, and add it to the memories of all the years they'd had together, and would have again. She must believe that.

The next day, as the morning went on, Miss F gave each of the men a hamper. 'Take this off, and go your separate ways. Spend some time with your son, Mr Kaplan. Sammy, if I may call you that, concentrate on your fiancée; she loves you so very much.'

Sammy kissed Miss F, and she flapped him away. 'Off, off, the lot of you. I have church to attend. You will know, Mr Kaplan, that Phyllie takes Jake to commune with nature as there isn't a synagogue nearby. Or should that be the temple, I never do know. I know that this walk should take place on Saturday, your Sabbath, but somehow–'

'Miss F, he can go wherever he pleases. If he wishes to go to church, then of course he can. There's only one God, I suppose.' If indeed there is such a thing, his voice implied, though he didn't speak the words.

While Jake and Isaac went to the stream, Phyllie and Sammy made their way back to the woods, looking up at the canopy of trees, as the birds fluttered up and off at their approach. A deer bounded across the path. Phyllie said, 'If Joe was here, that would be shot and cooked.'

'Quite right too.' Sammy swung her hand as they walked. 'I gather from Isaac that Jake and Andy have made their peace?'

Phyllie pointed to a squirrel scrambling up the trunk of the horse chestnut. 'Pests they are. Yes, Andy saw Ron throw Jake's plimsolls into the water. He also saw that Jake responded calmly, without rancour. Ron is a problem, especially hooked into Bryan and Eddie's gang. As long as he "belongs" there, no penalty seems to make any difference. Miss F and I think all he needs to know is that his mother cares, that he "belongs" in her gang. We tried just the other week to encourage her to come down again – I telephoned the pub and offered her the train fare. She said she was too busy. We suggested we arrange a time for Ron to call her at the pub. She said she had more to do than keep tabs on the "little bleeder". As for his father, well, we know all about him but Ron, in his ignorance, is proud to think he's away fighting for king and country. I suppose, his behaviour towards Jake emulates his father's behaviour in support of Mosley.'

When they reached the oak Sammy dropped the hamper, and took Phyllie in his arms. 'I don't want to go back,' he said, into her hair. 'I want to stay here for ever and ever and ever, with you. Together we could sort the lad out.'

She kissed him. 'We have all afternoon and then the rest of our lives, just as we've had all the years together, growing up. We're so lucky, Sammy. I can't remember a time without you – looking after me, driving me mad, showing me things, making me feel as though I belong. Frankie said to choose love, always.'

'I expect that Mrs S doesn't quite see it that way.' Sammy laughed. 'I doubt plumbing will be good enough, but just you wait until her lav blocks, and then we'll see. But she's bound to change once the children come. She'll love 'em if they look like her or Frankie. All is lost if they look like me.'

They were both laughing now, and they kissed, and kissed, and sank to their knees and it wasn't enough, it would never be enough, because though they talked of the future, she wasn't sure she believed there was one any more.

Later, they lay quietly, their arms around one another, looking up through the leaves to the blue sky beyond. She had never known such happiness, and knew no shame, as she supposed she should. It was war and all they had was this moment and to lie with him, to feel him on her, in her, was what she had wanted. She wished that the vicar would not leave the village today, and drive this man to Portland, as he had promised, out of the kindness of his very big heart.

Sammy said, 'It's so beautiful here. I will think of it when I'm on board. It's heaven; the woods, the leaves against the sky, Jake, Francois, and always you. I love you so much, darling Phyllie. Whatever happens, never doubt that.'

Chapter Sixteen

Mid-August 1941, Little Mitherton

The school holidays were halfway through, and though it had been an indifferent year weather-wise, the children had taken full advantage of the good days. They had rushed through the early-morning chores of soft fruit picking in July, and now the apple picking of August. In the afternoons, they disappeared in groups into the woods, meadows or lanes, taking sandwiches, playing Cowboys and Indians, or careering on bikes, girls and boys together. Miss F wanted fresh air in the lungs of every child, she had said.

'I don't want a lot of silly sitting about inside playing with dolls when the sun is shining,' she had ordered, even when parents had come down to stay in the vicarage attic. No parent had voiced dissent. One didn't, with Miss F; besides, they agreed with her. On days that rained the children holed up in the old barn, playing table tennis, or just playing, under the eagle eye of whoever was on duty.

Miss Deacon monitored the table-tennis league, which, as well as their own village, included Great Mitherton and Swanwick. The vicar was referee, and there was something about a dog collar that stopped any querying of the decision. Little Mitherton was climbing up in the league, and so too was Ron's skill. Phyllie knew that Sammy would be so pleased, and mentioned this in her latest letter, which was long and loving, because at last she had received one from him.

It had arrived today, in a creased envelope, with a note, scribbled in pencil on the back. It was an apology from his depot shipmate, saying that he should have posted it weeks ago, when Sammy asked him, before he went on patrol, but he had forgotten. She had read it in the hall, tearing the envelope open, unable to wait, because there had been such silence from Sammy since he had left.

She had feared that he had thought she was cheap, and just a good-time girl. Each day her panic and pain had been overwhelming, and it was all because this silly clot had forgotten to post the letter. Daft beggar. She scanned Sammy's writing, his beautiful writing, leaning against the hall wall. He had written words of love, asking her to talk to the vicar about marrying them on his next leave, hating every minute away from her, loving her more than life itself, longing for the war to be over so they need never be apart again.

She posted her reply on her way to the milking parlour after breakfast, at the crack of dawn, walking along with Jake and Francois, but wanting to dance in the light early-morning warmth. They were to marry. *They* were to marry. They were to *marry*.

'You're in a good mood, miss.' Sandra was striding just ahead, her plaits swinging, her dungarees a little baggy. One strap had slipped off her shoulder. Evie's were immaculate as she walked at her side, taking neat steps, her parting straight. 'Do

283

cows bite?' Sandra added, shouting over her shoulder, and yanking up her strap.

Jake laughed, 'Don't be daft.'

Phyllie tapped him on the shoulder. 'That's quite enough of that. You wouldn't have known when you first arrived. Stop showing off.'

Jake huffed, and ran forward with Francois at his heel. Andy allowed the dog to come with Jake to the farm now, which had endeared him to the inhabitants of Myrtle Cottage like nothing else would have done, Miss F declared.

Phyllie grinned to herself as her own dungaree strap slipped off her shoulder. Everything was improving, and soon she would be Mrs Williams. Swallows were soaring into the sky, the pheasants flapped out of the oats. At that, Francois broke ranks and bounded forward, yelping. This Jake allowed, because he was on a hopeless quest along the lane, and he knew better than to dart off into a field. What's more, he would come back when called. Far over, the fields of wheat were being harvested, with the Scouts busy following Andy as he drove the Fordson and the reaper, gathering up the straw into stooks.

The cows were in the milking parlour when they arrived, and Jake turned right for the stables, while the girls turned left. The milking parlour was dark, the air full of the scent of hay and cow pats. The girls stopped, and Phyllie urged them on towards the cows lined up in their stalls, tearing hay from the nets. Joe and Old Stan waved, and it was Phyllie who showed the girls where to wash their hands, and then she squatted on the short milking stool, with a pail between her legs and another with warm water and a clean cloth at her side to wash their udders. 'The thing is, not to be frightened.'

At that moment Daisy shifted on her feet and swiped with her tail. It caught Phyllie across the face. The little girls laughed. Phyllie removed a hair from her mouth. 'It's her way of saying hello.'

She washed and dried the udder and teats, and settled to milk. 'Now, don't tug, just squeeze and stroke downwards, see?' The teats were warm, the squirt of milk made a high-pitched sound as it hit the side of the pail. By the end of milking it would be full of frothing goodness. Sometimes Phyllie thought she'd like to draw or paint the patterns of a mixed farm: the milking, the harvesting, the sowing. She must suggest to Jake that a day in the milking shed might enhance his nature journal, for they still spent their Sunday mornings notating the natural world. She leaned her head against Daisy's flank, and smiled. Would she marry Sammy in St James's?

Of course, where else? Would her mother come? Her smile faded but she wouldn't dwell on that.

'Can I 'ave a go, miss?' Sandra asked, dragging Phyllie back to the present. She rose, and the girls took their turns. Sandra took to it like a duck to water, but the whole thing seemed a step too far for Evie who couldn't bear the feel of the teats and refused to do more than tinker. This annoyed Daisy, who whacked her tail sideways, startling Evie who leapt off her stool, spilling the milk. It ran down the slope and into the gutter.

Evie's face crumpled and tears were a step away

285

as Phyllie rescued the rolling pail. Sandra slipped in, righted the stool, and set to again. Evie clutched at Phyllie's hand and whimpered, 'I'm sorry, miss.'

'Hey,' she said, 'we all have to learn.'

'But we should waste not, want not. Milk's on the coupon.'

Joe came up behind them, and laughed. 'That's about a teaspoonful, in the scheme of things, lass, but well done, all of you.' They watched Sandra going at it like a child possessed, while Daisy stood still and chewed the cud. Joe murmured, 'D'you reckon America will come in, now them blasted Germans be turned on Russia? Them fighting on two fronts will give us a chance, anyway, eh, lass?'

She nodded, thinking how strange it was that they were all becoming experts; but how could they not? What on earth had they all thought about before the war? She couldn't really remember.

As they returned, the three of them sang the village version of 'The White Cliffs of Dover' – *over the shingle beach of Weymouth*. It made them laugh. Phyllie left them at their respective houses, before heading towards home. Later, she'd be harvesting along with the others, but before that she had to make an appointment with the vicar. She ran down the road towards Myrtle Cottage, waving to Mrs Speedie who was clipping her privet hedge. 'I'm getting married soon. Very soon.'

Mollie laughed. 'Am I to sound surprised?'

She ran on, her gumboots slapping some of the mud and straw off into the road, round the side of the house and then she burst into the kitchen, 'I'm off to the vicar in a minute, Miss F.'

Miss F was sitting at the table, her head in her hands. Phyllie rushed to her, her gumboots shedding small clumps of mud and straw. 'What's the matter?'

On the table was a note from Mrs Symes, which Miss F handed to her, straightening up. 'Read it.'

Miss F, I don't understand this. I went for sugar and I'm sure there is some missing. Not a lot, but about ten pounds. Is there an explanation? Perhaps you'd double-check the figures.

Below there were the amounts as per the stock book, and the amount that actually existed. 'But who knew where it was? Only the usual ones,' Phyllie almost wailed.

Miss F said, 'I'm going to talk to Bryan and that ghastly older brother, Eddie, because, as you and I both know, they are the most devious little thieving toerags the world has ever seen. I'll find Ron, too, because he's still spending far too much time with them and I don't trust the whole bag of them further than I can throw them.' Miss F paused and stood up, thrusting back the chair, which grated on the flagstones. 'I might be some time, and when I return, I will have some notches in my belt, you mark my words. I will require a gin. How sad we have none. I will make do with Joe's elderberry poison.'

Rather than hang about worrying, Phyllie took herself off to the vicarage. There was no answer from the front door, but she heard laughter from the back garden; she slipped round the side of the house and stood on the terrace. Jack Thompson was standing on a ladder picking plums, while Sylvia stood on the grass holding up a wicker basket into which her husband threw the unblemished fruit.

'You should place them carefully, Jack,' Phyllie called. 'They'll bruise, for heaven's sake. Then Mrs Symes will have your guts for garters.'

Sylvia turned, laughing. 'Phyllie, how lovely to see you, and that's just what I've been telling the idiot, but he has a hotline to God and so knows everything.' Their new baby, Melanie, slept in her pram, but not close enough to attract the attention of the wasps. She had been named for Melanie Adams, and it had warmed the village.

'Come on over, Phyllie, if you promise to stop nagging,' Jack called. 'I can have a break if you'd only say you'd like a cuppa.'

'I'd better not; it's business: wedding business.' The chamomile and low-growing thyme, which grew amongst the crazy paving, oozed scent as she hurried along the path to join them. The wasps were busy doing what they do to fallen rotting fruit. She took a full basket of fruit from Jack and replaced it with an empty one from a nearby pile, while Sylvia looked at her impatiently.

'Oh, come on, Phyllie.' Sylvia shook her arm. 'You say something about a wedding, and then leave it hanging. It must be Sammy. Oh, how utterly divine. What with that and Germany turning on Russia, it's such a good day. Now, are you going to cycle over later with the cart and collect our baskets of fruit for the Preservation Centre?

I'd be so grateful.'

The plum that Jack threw missed the basket. He groaned, dusting off his hands. 'Well, that's that, I need a cuppa, even if you two don't. Sit with me, Phyllie, and fill me in, and let's get it all sorted out, and leave the war to itself just for a moment.' He started down the ladder.

Sylvia walked back to the house to make the tea. Phyllie watched, and in the pause, the sugar came to mind, again. Jack said, 'Come on, then, tell me all.'

They sat in the heat of the sun at the pale green wooden table, while the breeze stirred the plum trees. Sylvia brought tea. Phyllie wished the table was in the shade as she'd been feeling a bit sick and dizzy from the heat recently, so she had a cup after all. It was mint, as was common all over the village now, and, what's more, was supposed to settle stomachs. Jack and Sylvia listened, smiling, and Jack then explained that as Phyllie was resident at Little Mitherton, which her ration book could prove, there would be no problem. 'We could call the banns, and then when he's next on leave we can do the deed.'

There were a few more formalities but in no time at all it was sorted. Phyllie checked her watch. 'I must go. Miss F's on a mission, and I need to catch up with it all.'

Sylvia pulled a face. 'Oh dear.' That's all anyone ever said when Miss F was on a mission, and Phyllie made herself laugh, but even though she was alive with happiness in one way, she hated the thought that Ron might have dug himself into a hole, tumbling in behind Bryan and Eddie. She had thought that his success with table tennis might woo him onto the straight and narrow, but she must not give in to doubt too easily. It could all just be a great error. She'd tell Sammy all about it this evening, when she wrote to him about the wedding. Again her heart lifted with happiness.

Miss F was waiting for her in the kitchen, a key in one hand and a glass of elderberry wine in the other. She was pacing backwards and forwards, her frown in place. She shook the key at Phyllie. 'Ron was with them. He said to look in Jake's mackintosh pocket, because he and Bryan saw Jake unlocking the door and returning the key to his pocket. It was there, where they said it would be.'

Phyllie took a moment to absorb her words. When she did, she snatched the key and examined the label. *F Store,* there it was, in Miss F's handwriting; she had used the F as a code. Her mind was racing, searching for some common sense, and at last she found it.

'Nonsense,' she muttered. 'How did the wretched little tykes know it was in Jake's pocket? They put it there, to cover themselves. It's so very clever. Don't you see? If we pursue the matter of the missing sugar, they'll say it was Jake – the proof is that you found the key in his pocket. They will say that we are covering up for Jake, by accusing them. Good grief, they should be fighting Hitler.'

She took the glass from Miss F's hand and took a large sip. It seared her throat. Miss F snatched it back, and did the same. She paced as she did so, and then stopped in front of the photo of Miss Harvey and her together in Margate. Miss

F took the photo down from the mantle over the Aga. 'Once, in this village, things were simple. Once.'

Phyllie didn't know what to say but after a moment she murmured, 'There's a war on, nothing is simple.'

Miss F sighed and replaced the photo. 'You're right; those boys are clever. If only we could direct them down legal channels they'd be very successful. We do nothing about the sugar. We try to extricate Ron. I will explain it to Mrs Symes and I dare say she can stretch it out. It is only ten pounds. They can have my ration.'

'And mine. And we need to hide the sugar well, and in several places, so that it can never happen again.' She sat down at the kitchen table, pointing to another chair. Miss F sat. They each took another sip of the wine. Miss F said, 'We shouldn't; the sun's not over the yardarm.'

Phyllie shook her head. 'We need it. What about putting it within Joe's farmhouse itself, locked up tight? Not even that little load of louts would rampage through Joe and Andy's home, would they, though they did use the phone at Christmas.'

'It's a huge house. There are so many nooks and crannies with locks, I think it's the safest bet. We can but try, and Joe and Andy will keep quiet about it all.' Miss F sipped again. 'Oh, Phyllie, the little buggers will get away with it, that's what grips my knickers. So so clever.'

'We have to get Ron out of their clutches before the situation is irrecoverable,' Phyllie said, 'but I don't know how. I'm worried they'll find another way to get at Jake, or perhaps he's just a tool. If there's no sugar, there's no need to point the finger at him?'

Miss F looked again at the photo and murmured, 'I just don't know. We stay alert and calm, my dear. We watch and we wait. I'll talk to Joe. We are to meet at Burley's pub tonight to celebrate a good harvest.'

'Are you indeed?' Phyllie smiled. 'This is becoming rather a regular occurrence, isn't it?'

'Don't be absurd,' Miss F snapped, colouring. 'If you'd let me continue I was going to say that I'll talk to Joe, and then Mrs Symes, explaining everything, so that if it is tried again, they can support us in our defence of Jake, and the past lies perpetrated by these appalling boys.'

'Do we tell Jake about this, and the previous pencil that was found?'

Miss F now finished the wine, patting her mouth with her handkerchief. 'We need to think about that. I don't want to panic him, but I want him to be aware that... Oh, I just don't know.'

The two women sat quietly now and then Phyllie remembered the wedding. How could she forget? 'Some better news,' she said. 'In Sammy's letter, the one I received this morning and which was so delayed, he asks me to arrange the wedding ready for his next leave. I've just been to the vicarage and Jack is sorting it out.'

Miss F rammed her handkerchief back in her pocket, and gripped Phyllie's hand. 'My dear, I am not totally stunned by the news, but I am inordinately thrilled.'

There was just time for Phyllie to cycle over and take what plums the Thompsons had picked to the Preservation Centre. By this time her head was spinning and she knew it had been a mistake to have the elderberry wine and the sickness was back. Heat and Joe's homemade wine were a terrible mix.

Jake walked with Phyllie to the field later that afternoon. She, the children and the Guides and Scouts followed the Fordson, which hauled the reaper loaned by the 'men from the ministry'. Andy drove. The reaper threw up dust and bits as it separated the wheat from the chaff, churning out lengths of straw. This they scooped up and tied into bundles, with Joe cursing at the 'bloody hopeless wartime string', which constantly snapped.

They wedged the bundles upright into stooks, with Jake on one lane and Phyllie on another. The heat beat down, the insects swarmed, the swallows took flight, gliding constantly to and fro, making her feel quite strange, so much so that suddenly the world swam and her legs turned to water, and the blackness threatened to drag her to the ground. Joe caught her as she sank. 'You all right, lass?'

He pushed her head down, and poured water from his flask on her neck, soaking her shirt and hair, which she had cut quite short after Sammy left. She felt desperately sick, and fought the blackness.

Jake came running across into her lane, calling, 'Phyllie, what's wrong?'

Joe squatted beside her, offering his flask to drink from. He waved Jake back to work. 'Sip it, Phyllie. It's just a mite hot, and you ain't got a hat, silly bissom.'

She sipped, and fought down the nausea. She said, 'We had a few sips of your elderberry wine, which was a real mistake. Miss F will explain why, Joe, this evening.' The water was warm, too warm. She couldn't drink any more. 'Help me up, Joe.' Her voice was a whisper. For goodness' sake, woman, pull yourself together, she told herself.

He grabbed her arm, and hauled. She stood and her head swam. She swallowed. Lord, she felt so awful.

Joe called to Peter, Miss Deacon's nephew. 'Take this lass back to her house. She needs to cool off, and Phyllie, wear a bloody hat next time. You're so busy telling the kids and look at you, a right red-faced mess.'

'So kind,' she muttered, as Peter stood awkwardly by, holding out his hand. She smiled. 'Really, I'm fine. I will go home, though, to hunt out a hat for tomorrow.'

The relief on the boy's face was palpable. She searched for Jake. He was standing in the next lane, watching her, tension in the rigid set of his shoulders. She called, 'I'm off to find a hat, so come home when the others do.' Francois was beside him, as always, but even he was hot, panting as though he'd run several miles.

Jake's smile was relieved and broad. He waved. She stumbled home, the bits of straw itching. She felt so hot she feared she would sink to the ground again, at any moment. Once home she vomited before crawling to bed, pulling down the blackout blind, and lying in the dark, until at last the nausea eased and she slept. Miss F came back from the Preservation Centre in the early evening and checked on her, but Phyllie waved her away. 'It was just too hot today, and I will never ever have elderberry wine again as long as I live. I must remember to take my hat, next time.'

Miss F said, 'I'll put mine out for you if you don't. That'll make doubly sure you remember to take your own.'

Phyllie laughed, and then slept.

The next morning, she woke early, and the nausea caught her again, as she swung herself out of bed. After an hour or so, it faded, but only a bit.

'A hangover,' she muttered, wondering how people could drink too much on a regular basis. It was the same the next morning, and then the next and it was then she remembered the sickness she had felt last week, and the light-headedness when she had hurried downstairs, having overslept.

So, it wasn't the wine or the heat and she remained quite still, thinking, and slowly things began to click into place. She reached for her diary, trying to remain calm, opening it and working her way backwards with shaking fingers. At breakfast she refused the cup of coffee essence that Miss F offered her as a special treat and a cure for lingering hangover-cum-heatstroke.

Instead, she sipped cold water and picked at her dried toast. She must look at things practically. She must not panic.

Jake and Francois had already left for their walk around the village and Jake would later head to the farm, to do whatever was on his agenda for the day. Miss F had dug out a hat for Phyllie. It was a grubby white, with a floppy brim. She tried it on, unable to bear the thought of climbing up the stairs again for her own.

Miss F looked her up and down, saying, 'My word, you're quite the colour of the hat. It's not something that would rise to a wedding but for grubbing about in a harvest field, I think it's just about the ticket. And now I must tart myself up, before heading off to overheat in the steam of the Preservation Centre. Keep your hat on, madam, or Joe will have your guts for garters and mine too when he pops round this evening with some wine. No, don't panic, don't you remember your brother felt those in London might like a slurp. Jake's chatting to Dan next door, while they find the eggs for Mr Milford. He'll be back in a minute. Go and look at yourself in the mirror, see if the hat is just too awful.' She headed for the stairs, pounding up them.

Phyllie smiled, and followed her into the hall, risking a look in the hall mirror. She saw the darkness beneath her eyes, and her pallor, which could not have occurred overnight, but which she had failed to notice. It did indeed match the floppy off-white old hat. She pressed her hand to her belly, then let it hang at her side. Oh, Sammy, hurry home.

The doorbell rang. She snatched off the hat, and opened the front door. It would be the postie, knocking, eager for his drink of mint tea. He stood on the doorstep and held out a letter in a buff envelope. He didn't smile as usual. She looked at the letter, aware that Miss F had come downstairs, and was calling, 'Don't make the doorstep untidy, Willie. Come into the kitchen, for heaven's sake.' But Willie was hurrying back along the path, and both women looked after him, confused.

He was already latching the gate behind him, when Miss F turned to Phyllie who was studying the envelope. It was for Jake, but marked for her attention, as Jake's guardian. Miss F was beside her now. The letter seemed to weigh an absolute ton, and to suck the air from this dark hallway.

'Shall I?' Miss F asked, her voice gentle suddenly. Phyllie couldn't move as she watched Miss F take the letter from the envelope and read it, silently. Phyllie watched the colour leave her face. Miss F now read it aloud. It was a letter from the Navy. Phyllie heard words, some lodged: 'Leading Seaman Kaplan ... *Vehement* ... not returned from patrol. It must be presumed ... he had died in ... of his duty ... or some such. Some bloody such. Outside the sun was still shining. How? Why? Some bloody such. No. No. If Isaac, then Sammy. She reached for Miss F, feeling her head swimming, her legs shaking. She felt Miss F's arm around her, holding her up.

'Now, now, Phyllie,' she said, dropping the letter onto the telephone table.

Oh God, Jake. He'd be back, any minute.

Phyllie pushed free and snatched up the envelope from the table, because she could see the corner of another letter. Phyllie saw sloping writing in black ink. It said that Jakub could rest assured that his father had served and died for the good of his adopted country, and in the pursuit of valuable intelligence.

She heard the awful wailing inside herself, but no, Jake would be back. Any minute. Rest assured? Rest? Assured? How could a child do that? She crunched the letters in her fists. Damn and blast and bugger the bloody war. She fought against tears.

'He'll be back soon, with Dan.' Her voice sounded strange as it squeezed past this huge lump in her throat. 'He will be back, and I must be the one to tell him, Miss F.'

Miss F wasn't looking at her, but at the path. She was so still.

'Shall I, while you telephone your mother?' Miss F said, her lips barely moving, as though they were numb.

Phyllie turned to stare at the telephone. 'Why would I telephone my mother?'

'I think that perhaps Sammy's parents might have contacted her, to pass on news to you. They don't know our telephone number and they are Sammy's next of kin, so it is they who would be informed. I'm sad to say that I'm not totally sure your mother would telephone the news to you.'

'No, Sammy will be coming home. Don't say that.'

Jake was turning into the gate now, with Francois at his heels, carrying the basket with a few eggs given by Mr Milford, as always. Dan called, as he headed for Miss Deacon's, 'See you later, Jake.'

'Don't say that, not now, Miss F,' Phyllie said. 'We need to look after the boy. We really do need to look after him. Jake, Isaac's boy, Rachel's too. We need to take care of him. Sammy will be all right. Yes. No. I don't know. It's the boy first.'

She couldn't stop herself talking, as she watched Jake practising his whistle, his lips pursed, one hand in his dungaree pockets, strolling down the path. He only looked up when Francois stopped dead, his head cocked to one side, looking at the two women; finally his tail drooped, his ears flattened. Jake hesitated, put his hand out to his dog, watching them, puzzled.

Now, Phyllie was silent as she watched the whistle die on his lips. She watched as he looked at their faces, and then the crumpled letters in Phyllie's hands. He stared for a long moment, then his face changed, and the light went from his eyes, and he looked as he had done before they came to Little Mitherton. Phyllie lifted her arms to him, her hands still in fists, the letters within them. He ran to her then, into her arms, and only now did she open her hands, and let the letters fall. His sobs were almost silent, though his body heaved, and now Francois came, and sat so close that Phyllie could hear his breathing.

That day they did not return to the wheatfield, and Miss F did not go to the Preservation Centre. 'Just for today,' she said, and for them the world stood still as they sat in the garden, beneath the flowering cherry tree. Though he was now twelve, Jake sat on Phyllie's lap and wouldn't move. He just wept until he slept. It was then Miss F took him from Phyllie and kept him on her lap while Phyllie telephoned her brother.

'Darling Phyllie,' he said, 'I'm sure we haven't heard. Mother would have said. Let me talk to her. Hold on. It might be all right. Remember that. It might be.'

He was gone for a while, but it didn't matter. Nothing really mattered any more, because there was no hope. She knew that. She heard Frankie's voice as he shouted at someone, really shouted, saying, 'All right, so you were struggling to find the words to tell her, but I could have helped. Oh, Mother. When did Mrs Williams telephone you?... But that was hours ago.'

She held the receiver against her ear, opening the front door, because she needed air, so she could breathe. She stared at herself in the hall mirror in the light that streamed in through the front door. She still existed, how extraordinary. She reached up and touched her mouth. She'd never feel his lips again, she knew. He'd never know...

Amy Jackson came up the path with Mrs Speedie, who called, 'Is Miss F coming today, Phyllie? We were worried. She's usually with us by now.'

Phyllie placed the receiver on the hall side table, and met them on the doorstep. 'She won't be able to leave the house today. Jake's father is dead.' How could she stay so calm? How could her voice sound so strange? But it still had to squeeze past this great big lump in her throat. Amy blanched, Mrs Speedie reached out, but Phyllie withdrew. No, she must stay strong.

'Sammy?' Amy asked.

'I'm trying to find out. I'm not his next of kin, you see, so why would anyone tell me?' She thought it totally reasonable. Of course it was. She was nothing to do with Sammy in anyone else's

300

eyes. But she was everything. Why didn't the world know that?

What did it matter to them that she had grown up with him, breathed the same air, done the same things, climbed the same trees, and loved him, felt him, *known* him, isn't that what they said? What did it matter that he'd gone, and was drowned, was wet, pale and lifeless? She stopped. Enough. Why would anyone tell the woman who loved him more than life itself? Why was there no pain? Why was there nothing; not the feel of the floor beneath her feet, nothing to touch her, in the whole world? She needed to die, too. That's all she needed.

Amy and Mrs Speedie were nodding, backing down the path. Mrs Speedie said, 'I'm going for Jack, dearest Phyllie. Go and sit down, do you understand? I'm going for Jack.' Why was Molly crying? It wasn't she who had lost a father. It wasn't she who would now be mother to Jake, and how could she be good enough? Now. She felt her abdomen. Sammy. She heard this scream in her head, but her mouth had not opened. It was still roaring on and over it she heard a strange tinny voice. It was near her.

She looked at the receiver on the side table. Ah yes, Frankie, Father Francis, who used to be Frankie. She held it to her ear. 'Phyllie, it's your mother. I couldn't phone you earlier. I was trying to collect myself. I didn't know how to tell you without upsetting you. Mrs Williams received a letter early this morning and rang us from a phone box. Phyllie, I'm so sorry. Francis will telegraph to Mrs Williams immediately with your telephone

301

number, because I failed to give it to her. I just couldn't think. This will pass. You will get over it, as I did when your father died. There will be someone else for–'

Phyllie didn't say goodbye, she merely put the receiver back on the hook, very carefully. Jack Thompson was running down the path now, as though there was a fire. He swept her into his arms, and she almost overbalanced. 'Oh Phyllie, dearest Phyllie.'

She wasn't anyone's dearest Phyllie any more. She had only been Sammy's. She wasn't her brother's, she had never been her mother's, her father was dead, and she wasn't Jack Thompson's. She let him lead her through to the garden, where he sat with them, as Phyllie lifted Jake from Miss F's lap and set him on her own again. She needed to look after this child. She had promised Isaac. Always, she had said. But it should be his father, or his mother, and she wasn't good enough, not any more... She shut her mind.

They sat with him all night, he in his bed, Francois on the rug at the side, and Phyllie and Miss F in chairs beside him. He cried. They let him, but each placed a hand on his back, or lay on the bed and held him in their arms and spoke words of love, but it wasn't their love he needed.

In the morning, as they drank breakfast tea, proper tea as decreed by Miss F, the telephone rang. It was Mrs Williams. She and Phyllie talked, or rather, Mrs Williams talked. Phyllie nodded, but she couldn't hear, not really. There were words, but the nausea was rising again. Miss F came and took the receiver, and spoke quietly, before hanging up. The front door bell went. Phyllie opened it. It was Ron. He stood there, his hair unbrushed, his knees grubby because he wouldn't wear dungarees, neither he nor Bryan would, because they were cissy. 'I'm sorry, miss, about your Sammy. I liked him. He was kind.'

She stared at him. 'Then why do you do such mean things, Ron?'

Ron stared at her, surprised. 'But that's different, miss. Jake's a Yid, and fair game, like me dad says.'

'Go away, Ron.' She shut the door, and leaned back against it. She couldn't cry. The pain had come, and it was too deep, and the world too bleak, and she simply didn't know what to do any more because how could anyone bring a child into this terrible world? How could she? But she must, because the child she was carrying was Sammy's, and so it was the most precious thing she would ever possess.

Her legs were turning to water, and she slipped down the door until she was sitting on the floor. The doormat was prickly, the flagstones cold. Miss F and Jake found her when she did not return to the kitchen. It was Miss F and Jake who looked after *her* all day, and as they sat under the flowering cherry tree Phyllie wondered how all the broken hearts in the world could ever be repaired.

Chapter Seventeen

Mid-September, Little Mitherton

With September came a return to school: fresh sticks of chalk, which screeched against the blackboard; assembly; the ragged voices singing the morning hymn. On the second Monday Phyllie stood at the board; the long division straggled down and down. Sammy had gone down and down.

She turned, smiling. 'You have worksheets on your desks. You'll note that they are inclined to curl, and that's because...' She paused, pointed to John, whose red hair seemed to have bleached with the summer sun. 'Because?'

He grinned. 'It's wallpaper, miss, from me mum. She says thank you for the note and call in for a cuppa.'

Everyone was being kind, including the children, but they were used to being so when someone's son, husband, brother, mother or daughter had been killed. Phyllie found its comforting that she was not the only one, that people understood and didn't avoid her when they saw her but instead chatted about the ploughing, about how Jake was, and, lastly, how she was. They would look deep into her eyes, and understood when she said, 'I will be all right, but not yet.'

The following Thursday, Mrs Symes squeezed

her hand. 'It gets easier,' she said, as they almost collided on the path leading up to the village hall. Phyllie carried milk, chamomile, mint and the WI's tin of tea. There was a little sugar and a pot of honey in a basket, Mrs Symes carried her Treasurer's kit, because the committee had changed again, though Phyllie was still the speaker gatherer. Behind them was the rest of the committee, with Miss F in full voice.

These days they arrived to set up the hall immediately after school, because earlier meetings allowed the children to go to be looked after in the old barn, and be home in time for a good night's sleep before school the next day. Phyllie greeted Mr Roberts, the speaker she had arranged, who talked of his adventures in Outer Mongolia when he was a young man. The slides were interesting, but verging on too many. Miss F caught his eye after half an hour and he responded with good grace, saying to the packed hall, 'I do rather agree with your president that it is high time I tailed off. Twenty minutes is more than long enough, after that I tend to bore myself, so you must all be catatonic.'

The laughter was genuine, the life he had lived extraordinary. Mrs Symes and Miss F countersigned his cheque during tea and honey biscuits.

Mrs Symes and Phyllie smiled as they tried to work out how many years it had been since Mr Roberts had been that young man, then they fell silent. Neither of the men in their lives would have the privilege of looking back on their youth. Mrs Symes gripped Phyllie's hand. 'I know I repeat myself, but it does get easier; somehow one gets used to it. We have to.'

At eight, Miss F and Phyllie walked to the old barn, their mackintoshes buttoned up against the chill of the evening. They helped Molly shut up the barn, and walked the children to their homes. They watched carefully as Jake walked, hands in pockets, avoiding their eyes, kicking at stones, ignoring Dan, ignoring Francois, who trailed in his wake. They longed to help, but since the news he had withdrawn into a dark, silent misery. He had become a stranger, he walked alone with his nature journal, he dug his hands into his pockets and refused to wear his dungarees because they were cissy, as Ron and Bryan always said, and to whom, inexplicably, he seemed to be drawing closer. Worse, he had stopped tending the horses. Andy seemed to understand, and said that the lad would come round, he was angry at the world, and perhaps himself. 'He's survived, you see,' Andy had said.

'Andy's right, he *is* angry,' Phyllie said as they walked along.

Miss F nodded. 'Death is the ultimate rejection.'

'But Francois?' Phyllie stroked the dog's head, and pulled his ear. 'Why? Is he frightened of caring too?'

'Probably. We must just wait it out. The village understands, so we must. Think back to that little evacuee, what was his name? He came to us from Bristol, then within two days his mother was killed in the bombing.'

'Yes,' Phyllie said. 'Wasn't it Albert someone? I'd forgotten, he was with us such a short while. He set fire to one of Joe's haystacks, and then

306

kicked Nora, his foster mother, blaming us all. I can understand. I could kick someone most days.'

Miss F nudged her. 'You keep your feet to yourself, young lady.'

Phyllie smiled. It seemed strange to find things amusing, but it was so fleeting and then the misery returned.

They walked on. The moon was bright; a bomber's moon. No, a hunter's moon is what it should be called. But was that any better? Bombers were hunters. Shut up, Phyllie told herself. Andy had ploughed the lower field today; the rolled sods glistened. So straight, they were – the furrows, that is. She was tired; her thoughts were fragmenting, the agonising ache was creeping out of its crevice and swiping her, just as it swiped Jake, and had swiped Mrs Symes, and the rest of those left behind.

She heard the owl. 'Listen,' she said to the children.

Bryan called, 'They look good stuffed.'

'That's enough of that,' Phyllie answered. They were on the outskirts of the village. Jake shouted, suddenly, 'I bet I could hit one with an air pistol.'

'You're all talk, you are, Yid,' laughed Bryan.

'And that's enough of that,' Miss F roared, barging alongside the crocodile, yanking Bryan out by his ear.

He yelled, 'Ouch.'

Jake swung round. 'I can fight my own battles, I can. It's my mum and dad's fault I'm a Yid. And I won't be one any more.'

'You be quiet, Master Jake, or I'll have you by

the ear too.' Miss F dragged Bryan to the front. 'You'll walk with me, and if I had soap, I'd wash your mouth out.' Phyllie was looking from one to the other, bewildered and aghast.

Bryan muttered, 'I'll get my brother on you.'

Miss F said, 'I'd be delighted to discuss the matter with Eddie. He has been through my hands before he changed schools, and I suspect he remembers every delightful minute.'

Phyllie felt utterly exhausted. Well, it was late, and she had a call to make in the morning, to her mother. It was what she had decided she must do, after agonising for too long, because she couldn't bear the shame of explaining her condition to all those of Little Mitherton who were being so very kind.

But on the other hand, how could she leave while Jake was sliding heaven knew where? She would take him. It would solve the problem of Ron. She half stumbled into a pothole, righted herself. Heard the owl again. Yes, that was the only answer. But... What about Miss F? How would she manage alone? When would they return? Would people be kind to the baby if they did? Would her mother have her? Sammy had said she'd soften with grandchildren, but this one was illegitimate. If it had been her father, he'd have... Oh God, her head was splitting. She couldn't think. One thing at a time, that was it. Just one thing at a time.

She waited until Jake had reluctantly taken Francois round the block before school, and Miss F was out feeding Mr Milford's hens, because he was with his sister for a while. She asked the operator for the number, swallowing down her relentless nausea. It was her mother who answered. 'St Luke's Presbytery.'

'Mum, it's me.'

'Ah, you sound well, I'm pleased. You're obviously getting over it.'

Getting over *it?* 'It's only been a month, Mum. No, I'm not quite tickety-boo.' She pressed her lips together. Shut up. She softened her voice. 'But I'm getting there.'

'Yes, you will. And as I said, there will be someone else for you. There's that nice farmer's son.'

Phyllie's hand was clammy on the receiver, clammy with rage. Cold sweat was breaking out all over her body. It beaded her forehead. She reached out a finger and traced her face in the gloom of the hall mirror, rushing out the words. 'Actually, Mum, I need your help. Sammy thought that you would like grandchildren. I hope you will. You see, I'm pregnant. It's Sammy's. Can I come to London, to be with you and Frankie, just until I've had it? I need to bring Jake, too. I'd be so grateful. I really do need help, Mum, and we seem to be getting on better, don't you think? You liked the wool, you were trying to find the words to tell me of Sammy because you didn't want to upset me. We are family, after all. I really need this, for me and Jake.'

There was a long silence. She could hear her mother breathing, almost feel the moistness, then came her voice, high-pitched and strained. 'Phyllis Saunders, you are right, I would like grandchildren, but not like this. Yes, I feel we were reaching

309

an understanding, and so you must surely see that you can't possibly come to a place of God. I mean, this is no example for a presbytery to set its faithful. Oh, I just can't think about this. It is too dreadful, and how can you conceive of working with children with this ... this disgrace about to burst upon you? Whatever will everyone think? I simply do not want to hear any more about it, do you understand, until it is sorted. I'm so deeply upset, Phyllis, and I can't think where I have gone wrong.'

In the background she heard Frankie calling, 'Everything all right, Mother? Is it for me?'

'No, it's not for you,' her mother replied.

Phyllie tried once more. 'Please, Mum, let me come to live with you, just for–'

The line buzzed in Phyllie's ear. Her mother had hung up.

Her hand shook as she replaced the receiver. Why had she thought it would be any different? Was she mad? A draught ruffled her hair. She had asked Sarah, the village hairdresser, to cut it shorter still. Why? Sarah had asked. She didn't know except that she wanted to be shorn in grief.

'Phyllie?' Jake called. There was an edge to his voice but there always was these days.

'Coming.' She straightened her blouse, shaking all over. There was no bump and though her breasts were sore, she had time, but to do what? Jake had his satchel on, and was waiting impatiently as she entered the kitchen. She collected her bag of tricks, and he swung out of the back door in front of her. She followed him to school, while he rushed on ahead, only to slope around

310

the playground, alone. She found him by the bicycle shed, with Ron and Bryan, who slouched off when she arrived. She held Jake's shoulders, then stroked his face, seeing the darkness beneath his eyes, the paleness of his skin. 'Dan is your best friend, he cares for you, and you ignore him. Friends can be a great support, Jake, and your dad liked him. Don't you remember?'

Jake stuck out his lower lip, and said, 'What do I care? Mum went off and left me, she preferred her parents to me, and I just heard you ask your mum if you can go and live with her. People leave all the time. Anyway, it doesn't matter: Ron and Bryan said they wanted to be my friend, now I don't want to be a Yid any more.'

Phyllie stared: the draught, her last words to her mother. Oh no. 'I love you, Jake. I just am not very well, I wanted to go to Mum for a while, but I wanted to take you with me. Anyway, I'm not going. I'm staying here. Of course I am.'

'But you asked her. That's what's important. You were going to leave me.'

'I was going to take you with me, I've just said.'

He stared at her. She swallowed, feeling sick, guilty, utterly desperate. He said, 'But your mother doesn't like me. So why would you make me go there?'

School gave her life a structure, a reason to 'be', she thought, as she stood in the playground at lunch break, but all the while guilt and distress tore at her. She chose to do playground duty so that she could keep an eye on Jake. Dan was playing with Bertie, a lad from Bermondsey who had evacuated down here in 1941.

After school she walked all the classes to the old barn as usual. She prepared milk on a trestle table at the end furthest from the table tennis, and a biscuit, but one each only. She stood close, keeping watch, because last week there had not been enough, though there should have been. All the while she was watching Jake, wanting to talk to him, but to say what?

Andy approached her now, smiling because Jake had just asked if he could come back and work with the horses. 'He seems eager,' Andy said. Phyllie felt a huge relief as Jake stood in the old barn entrance.

She smiled at Jake. 'Wonderful,' she called.

Jake turned and headed to the stables. He had not smiled in return. Mrs Price from the post office was on duty in the barn as well today, and halfway through the evening Phyllie left her while she crossed the yard to the stables. Joe was peering into Desmond's stall. He was new but settling in well. Phyllie called, 'May I have a word?'

She had not spoken properly to him since the news had arrived. Joe looked up, the cigarette behind his ear as usual, and she found comfort in that. 'You all right, lass?'

'Thank you, yes. But I wondered about Jake. I know it's only been an hour or so, but how is he?'

Andy was heaving a great heavy bridle up onto a peg. Dust motes danced in the air, bits of straw flew up as Doris neighed in her stall. Joe looked thoughtful as he limped to the open door of the stables and leaned against the doorpost, taking out his cigarette and fingering it. 'Oh, well, he's a mite angry, and poor old Francois is getting the brunt of it, but you know that. No mother except you to speak of, for now anyway, and who knows where poor Mrs Kaplan is? Don't 'elp that she went away willingly. Don't forget, you're deep in the "missing" too. Grown-up glums is frightening to a child. He wants to break eggs, he does, with a bleedin' mallet. Life's a trial, sometimes, but only sometimes. It perks up in between.'

Andy had finished his task, and now he joined them. He was smiling at her, his back to Desmond who was nudging him. 'Didn't ask for a sermon, did you? Reckon you just wanted to know if he'd settled back in here this evening. Yes, he has. I reckon he finds solace with the horses because they expect nothing of him except to be kept clean and tidy, and he doesn't hurt *for* them, if you know what I mean. He loves you, Phyllie, so he hurts for you, and for himself. He's chucking away things like his Jewishness because... Oh, I don't know, perhaps he thinks it hasn't done him much good being loyal. It all gets such a muddle in your head when it goes so dark. We'll keep watch on him, won't we, Dad? He's over in the tack room, giving the bridles a good polish. Let him kick himself out. The real Jake'll come back.'

Phyllie couldn't bear the kindness, it would have been better if he had been his usual gruff self. She nodded, and tried to smile, wanting to tell someone, anyone, of the mistake she had made. She turned on her heel and hurried back to the old barn, and the laughter of children. It was then it struck her that she'd been unfair. Andy was no longer unkind. Joe was right. Things 'perked up', but how could they for her? She didn't deserve it. Panic stirred the grief. She heard Joe then: 'Wait up, lass. Just wait.'

She stopped halfway across the yard, looking ahead, seeing and hearing the flapping tarpaulin, which was slung over the barn once more, as a sheet of iron further along had slipped down in the last bad storm. Soon Andy would renew all the joists, he had promised.

The dogs slunk out of the kennels, sniffing at the barn doorway for Francois, who had been allowed into their gang. But Jake had not called into Myrtle Cottage for him, and he would be curled on the rug in front of the Aga, grieving too.

Joe was lighting his cigarette at last. He drew deeply, exhaled, and the wind snatched the smoke. 'You need to tell someone about the baby, lass.'

It didn't surprise her that he knew. There'd been something in his eyes when she'd fainted at the wheatfield.

'I have,' she said. 'I told my mother who says pretty much that I am no better than I ought to be. She's quite right, of course. I'm not a nice person to know, not the sort of person to teach children. I will have this baby, Joe. I don't know how, but I will, because then Sammy will go on, and I won't have lost him completely. Besides, I want the baby for herself.'

There, if they were in the business of sermons then this was hers. She felt some of the weight lifting. She looked at him, not sure what she was expecting. He was eyeing the tarpaulin.

'Better get a few more ropes on that, I reckon.' His roll-up had burned to a stub. He looked at it and dropped it to the cobbles. It hissed. He ground it to nothing. 'Tell Miss F. She'll 'ave the answer to it all, and there'll be none of that "not a nice person" in Little Mitherton, you mark my bloody words. You were to be married. The war spoilt that. We've a lot of bossy old bags 'ere, but there are hearts of gold buried under the bustling. So, it's a girl, then? That be nice.'

She smiled. 'I'm sure of it, but I don't know why.'

That evening, after she had tucked in Jake, insisting on kissing his forehead, which he reluctantly allowed, she said, 'Another day over, and we're getting there.' It wasn't a question. She leaned down and stroked Francois. 'He's a good and faithful friend, Jake. Like Dan and Miss F. I would never leave you. Where I go, you go. You must believe me. You would, if you didn't feel so sad. I would have discussed all this with you when I had it sorted, but we're going nowhere. We're staying here. You and me, staying here.'

There was no reply. Jake just turned to the wall and pulled the blankets up over his head. 'Sleep well,' she said. Again there was no reply.

Downstairs, the evening news was beginning, and a mug of chamomile tea steamed on the side table on her end of the sofa. Miss F was pulling a face as she ate a piece of toast with a skim of butter, and a lathering of honey. 'It's the butter I miss. After the war, when we've won, I will feast on butter until I am very fat.'

Phyllie laughed somehow. 'You'll never be fat; you'll run your brogues ragged as always, and the weight will not dare to stay on those hips.'

315

The broadcaster was telling them that there had been yet another sortie over German-occupied territory in Europe. He ended by saying that Roosevelt had vowed in New York to do everything in America's power to crush Hitler and the Nazi forces.

Miss F sniffed, and turned off the wireless. 'Fine words butter no parsnips, any more than they butter my toast.'

Phyllie smiled. 'You are obsessed with butter.'

Miss F tossed her head. 'Thank heavens we have Churchill. He just stands there, a far better version of Canute, forcing the tide back, or at least, to begin to turn. There are no jackboots here yet, and I do think we'd fight on the beaches if they had the nerve to try. People told Winston it was impossible to hang on, but he's as cunning as the rest of them, and he's damned well doing it.' She was knitting something khaki.

'Another balaclava?' Phyllie asked.

Miss F held it up. 'Well, it's not socks, is it? I suppose next it will be baby bootees, for young Master or Mistress Saunders.' She looked over her knitting at Phyllie. 'Joe brought round a pheasant while you were putting Jake to bed. He thought you could do with some meat. It's his answer to everything. He told me, of course, but I already knew.' She jabbed her needles at Phyllie. 'He's not the only eagle eyes in the village. We've just been waiting for you to let us know, and it's high time you visited the doctor. It's in the face, you know, always in the face.'

She started counting her stitches.

Phyllie felt relief take her over. 'You don't mind?'

'Nothing to do with us – the whys and where-fores, that is – and as long as the wretched school board don't hear about it, we can't see the problem. The good ladies of the WI are in support. Of course, it's not ideal. A husband is a good idea on these occasions, though I gather they are next to useless most of the time. Of course, one doesn't want to encourage others to follow, willy-nilly, so I wonder if we should say that you have been married on the quiet. What do you think? Just for the children's sake. Or no. We should be honest.'

Clearly the great and the good at the WI had been chewing over the Phyllie situation, and from the great goodness of their hearts were circling the wagons to protect her. Suddenly Phyllie was crying, which was something she usually left for the darkness of her bedroom when she couldn't sleep, or woke after dreaming about him, and the water, and the fish. She had explained a gentler version of the dreams about fish that nibbled Sammy deep down in the ocean to Jake, some weeks ago, in case he was having them. She had insisted that they were normal, as Mrs Symes had said. He had shrugged her off, but there had been some vestige of relief in his eyes.

Now she told Miss F of the phone call, of Jake believing she was leaving him. Miss F grimaced. 'We can only show him every day, in every way, that though you might have gone for a little break, he could have chosen to be with you or await your return, here, with me. We must tell him of the baby, choose our moment or this could be another worry. He might think there is no room for him in your heart.'

Two days later, in the early morning, Sammy's mother phoned. 'Phyllie, cariad, your brother wrote and I have taken time to think things through, so muddled have I been and so tearful I could hardly speak. Now Bill and I have decided what is for the best, so I am telephoning you. Frankie wrote of your news, and that perhaps it is not suitable for you to come to term in the presbytery. Bill and I would like you to come to us. We will then adopt our Sammy's child, to leave you free to pursue your life, with no one the wiser.' She spoke so quickly that she was tripping over her words, and the tone was high-pitched and breathless. She waited.

Phyllie laid her forehead against the coolness of the mirror. Her breath fugged the glass. 'No.' She was shouting, she knew that, her breath fugging the mirror more and more. She straightened. 'No.' This time her voice wasn't loud, but it was low and dangerous. 'No, this is our child – Sammy's and mine. He loved me, Mrs Williams; you must know he did, and I loved him. No, not loved, but love. I still love him and I always will, and our child. We will stay here, together. I could never ever give her away. Miss F says I can stay as a teacher and therefore I can earn a living. I can't hand her over, of course not, but you will always be my family and her grandparents.'

Jake clumped down the stairs for breakfast, and now she saw him, staring at her. She waved for him to wait. He fled through the doorway into the kitchen. 'Wait, Jake,' she cried, flinging the receiver back on the hook. She ran through the hall, and into the kitchen. Miss F was staring at her, then at the back door through which Jake had rushed.

Together they followed him, in their slippers, the morning dew soaking through them. They caught him up by the hedge, grabbing his arm. Phyllie made him face her. 'Yes, I'm having a baby, but I keep telling you, I'm not going anywhere, you are still my child, until your mother comes. You are quite safe, you always will be, whatever happens. I love you, Jake, I've told you before and I'll go on telling you. You are my family, just as this child will be. I've been clumsy. I was going to choose my moment. I'm so–'

He was shaking his head. 'No,' he shouted. 'Look at the evacuees, they're not the same as the real children.'

Miss F tried then: 'But they're evacuees, as you say, and you are not like that. You are Phyllie's child, just as much as if you were born to her. She promised your father, and what's more, she wants you, and will not let you go, never, ever, unless it is to your mother. You are her life, you are mine. That's right, isn't it, Phyllie?'

Phyllie felt the nausea rising. She said, 'Absolutely. Really, absolutely.' She rushed inside to be sick. When she staggered downstairs, Jake was gone, but to the horses. Miss F had phoned and checked that he had arrived. She had told Joe the facts, all of them. He would keep a bleedin' eye, he said.

On Tuesday of the next week, Phyllie was called into Miss F's study. A man stood there, in a suit with a starched high-wing collar, his briefcase on

319

the chair reserved for visitors. He was holding his homburg.

Miss F said, 'Phyllie, would you please go home and fetch your in loco parentis letter and the guardianship documents that you and Isaac Kaplan agreed upon. Mr Grimes would like to examine them.'

Phyllie ran down the road, until she was flagged down by Miss Deacon. 'Walk don't run, for goodness' sake, girl; you'll do the babe an injury.' Phyllie walked quickly, dashed into the house, found the paperwork and hurried back. Her hands were shaking, and her breath was coming in short bursts as she handed over the papers.

Mr Grimes was sitting now, one leg crossed over the other. Alfie rested on his knee. He was about forty, with his hair greying at the temples. He pursed his lips, and read through the documents twice. He handed them back to Phyllie, saying, 'Shouldn't you be sitting down, in your condition? I must warn you both that we have had a complaint from an anonymous source who has alerted us to the fact that you, as an unmarried mother, are teaching at Little Mitherton School. It has been decided that this must stop, forthwith. It is not the example we expect from those in positions of authority. You must find other employment, within a month.'

He opened the file, and then closed it again. Miss F sat motionless, her eyes never leaving his face. Phyllie continued to stand. He looked at the file, not at either of them, as he continued. 'As for Jakub Kaplan, I can see no grounds for removing him from your care, at this precise moment,

320

especially as you live with Miss Featherstone. I was taught by her, and it was an experience without parallel.'

He rose, shook Miss F's hand, and Phyllie's. 'I'm sorry, I know that you are an exemplary teacher. What's more, young Jakub is a fortunate child.'

Phyllie shook her head. 'No, he's not. His mother is somewhere in Poland. God knows exactly where, if indeed she is still alive. We have heard nothing. His father is lost under the sea with the father of my child, and I, well, I could do better. No, he's not fortunate. Neither of us are.'

Mr Grimes couldn't meet her eyes. He made for the door, opened it, then turned back and said, 'I beg to differ. He has you, and he has Miss F. Between you, you will manage to pull the chestnuts from the fire. My deepest regrets, Miss Saunders. Truly. You will, of course, work out your notice, which will give you a little more time. Incidentally, you might let your minds stray to the older Anderton boy, nasty piece of work as I remember, with a very big mouth, who asked to remain anonymous. But then, I haven't actually given his first name.'

Miss F and Phyllie looked at one another when he left. Miss F said, 'Well, thank you, Eddie. Perhaps this is the end now. Joe has seen him a few times, sniffing around the yard and barns, clearly looking for the rest of the sugar, so the phone call could be payback. Let's hope so.'

By 3 November Phyllie was without a job. On 10 November she received a letter from her brother. Forty pounds in cash fell onto her lap. His note said that he was thinking of her. She bundled it up, and returned it, though some money would undoubtedly have helped her sleep at night. She just didn't know what to think of her family, didn't know what to think of herself.

On the following Monday she received a letter from the war office that stated: *I am directed to enclose a certified true copy of a will executed by the late No 4024511, Leading Seaman Samuel Frederick Williams of the Royal Submarine Service, in which you are named as chief beneficiary.*

The will explained that she was to inherit the property in Downley, near High Wycombe, that Sammy had in turn inherited from his godfather. In addition there were shares to the value of £1,000. The solicitor's letter explained that following probate he would be happy to expedite the sale of the house. She had also inherited half the Ealing house, the share that had been bequeathed to Leading Seaman Samuel Frederick Williams by his paternal grandfather. If she so wished, she could request Mr and Mrs Williams to, in essence, buy her out.

The decision wasn't hard. She instructed that the Ealing house situation should remain as it was, for his parents' peace of mind. In due course, on their death, she would require 50 per cent of the sale proceeds because they would bequeath their share as they wished. She also received a similar letter from the War Office for Jake. She explained to Jake that he was to receive his father's naval savings, which would be put into deposit for his future, plus the sum of £400, which was in his father's private savings account.

She posted the letter giving her instructions, and visited Dr Nicholls' surgery, thinking how Sammy's arrangement helped with the practicalities beyond measure. Having received the all-clear for moderate exercise, she cycled around collecting salvage, and then began to clear up the remains of the runner beans in the allotment. That night she slept, her heart full of love for the man who had protected her, yet again, even from beyond the grave.

By mid-December she was just over six months' pregnant, and was completing on the purchase of a small cottage close to the church in Little Mitherton for her and Jake. It had three bedrooms, and a small orchard at the bottom of the cottage garden. Jake had slouched round it, refusing to react, and then rushed off to the horses, and probably to meet Ron and Bryan. As he left he'd yelled, 'It's your house, do what you like. What do I care?'

'It's our house, Jake,' she had called after him. 'Ours.'

His time-keeping was becoming lax, Andy said, when she was on duty at the old barn later that day, wrapped up against the cold, listening to the children who missed her, so much, they said. Andy waited as they told of the new teacher, an elderly woman called Mrs Gentle. She *was* gentle, the children whispered, but rather deaf so they had to shout. They ran off, to play tag.

She turned to Andy, 'Lax time-keeping? I'm so sorry. I suspected as much, but short of sticking by his side day and night, I'm not sure what to do about it.' The baby was kicking. She straightened, torn between love for this baby, distress for Jake, and the heavy guilt of the telephone call, which had shaken his trust in her.

Andy said, dodging young Sandra who was 'it' and chasing the others, 'You're blooming, you know, Phyllie. Once we sort out Jake, things will settle down for you and you can stop whipping yourself. How are the dreams? Any better this week?'

'Yes, the dreams—' She stopped.

He said, 'I didn't mention to you, last week, that I used to think about Mum, about what was happening to her down in the ground. Bloody awful it was. Stupid really.' He had a woollen hat pulled down over his ears.

She nodded, looking at him more closely, and asked, 'And dreaming they are still alive? You had those too?'

'It stops,' he said, nodding. 'Dad said it was all part of it. I expect it happened with Miss F. She and Miss Harvey, you know, survived the first war just for her to take a dive in this. The upside is that perhaps now she's gone there's room in Miss F's life for someone else. I suppose that's how it works.'

She smiled. 'Your dad's round there with another pheasant this evening, I noticed.'

He winked. 'So I gather. Well, well.'

Phyllie thought yet again how strange it was that they seemed to be friends now. She wasn't sure how it had happened, but perhaps through a history of loss.

'Good that the German bombers are busier and busier on the Russian front,' Andy said. 'Gives the

324

cities a breathing space. Good too that the Americans are in after Pearl Harbor.' He lifted his stump. 'I'm wondering if I should get a hook? It would help to have it, but somehow it means – well, it means I haven't got a hand. I really haven't.'

Bertie was passing, 'You should, Mr Andy. You'd be like Hook in *Peter Pan*, but you'd have to get a crocodile.'

The children laughed.

Dan said, 'Get it to swallow a clock so you can hear it coming. Like Asdic.' He stopped. 'Sorry, miss.'

The boys moved away.

Andy said, 'It will get better, Phyllie.' Then he left too, to do what he had to do.

She joined the children in setting up their indoor skittles, which had been donated by the Bestminster skittle team now the grown-ups had taken over the pub skittle alley for their Christmas league.

On Christmas Day, over the tender goose and roast potatoes, Miss F said, 'I wonder if you and Jake would consider continuing to live here, with me, Phyllie. I know your dear little cottage is ready, but you could let it, and the income will mean you don't have to dip into your shares. I hear that you asked Joe if you could clean for him. You are worth more than that, isn't she, Jake?'

Jake shrugged. 'I don't know.' Last year's paperchains were looped across the ceiling and the small Christmas tree was festooned with painted baubles. Miss F and Phyllie wore paper hats. Jake did not.

Phyllie studied her sprouts, rather than Jake's face, which was full of resentment, and perhaps hate. She should eat but she suddenly had no appetite.

'Rubbish, silly boy,' Miss F snapped. 'Before you ask, no, it's Christmas Day and you are not going out with Bryan and Ron.'

'I'm not a Christian, I'm not anything, so what difference does it make to me?' He didn't look at either woman, and it was this inability to face them that made them feel that they had not lost him entirely, that he could be regained. The baby kicked then, and Phyllie smiled as she put her hand on her belly. Jake saw and stared past her, the muscles working in his jaw. She said, 'I hope you like your bicycle, Jake. It's from us both, to say we love you.'

He shrugged. 'You can afford it.'

Phyllie shook her head, avoiding Miss F's furious eyes. 'Just, but I need to keep enough money for you and the baby. Who knows what we might all need in the future? We'd love to stay with you, Miss F, if you are sure it is all right. You must tell us the moment you want your house to yourself.'

'Why on earth would I want that? I love you both, as though you were my own. In fact, daft old thing that I am, I feel that's what you are. Absolutely my own family and I wouldn't know what to do if all was peace and quiet. I love you both, quite without end, just as you, Phyllie, love our Jake.' Miss F laughed. 'Besides, I need Jake here, to keep me young.'

Phyllie reached across and held Miss F's hand. 'You know it is the same for me.' She felt almost at peace because here, in Myrtle Cottage, was unconditional love, and at last she accepted the situation with her own family, without pain.

Meanwhile Jake was poking his goose around the plate, finally flinging his knife and fork down, slumping back, his arms crossed. 'I'm bored, and I hope my mum comes back, because then I can go with her and it won't matter what you two have decided.'

'Then we'd keep in touch, because we couldn't bear not to see you,' Phyllie said. The two women exchanged a look. They were used to this, but there seemed not to be the great rage there once was, it was more like a habit, as though he was going through the motions.

In the afternoon, the two women sat in their usual places as Jake played cards. Phyllie dozed; the dreams were not so stark, and the loss not so sharp, and inside her Sammy's baby was growing, and around her were friends she had never dreamed would become so. When she woke the Aga was grumbling, and Miss F was snoring. The small baby bonnet she was knitting was in her lap and there was no sign of Jake, though Francois was sitting just inside the back door, whining quietly. Did he need to go out for a pee, or had Jake gone, when he'd been told 'no'? She checked the clock. It was three in the afternoon.

Phyllie eased herself off the sofa, pulled the dress she called a tent down over her bump, and waddled, for that's what it felt like, to the bottom of the stairs. 'Jake?' No reply. Well, so often there wasn't. She slogged up the stairs, her back aching. His room was empty and she felt the familiar worry spurt. As she eased her way back down the stairs, there was a furious banging at the front door. Miss F called from the kitchen, 'What? Er, what?'

Phyllie yelled, 'I'll get it. Jake's gone, I do hope...' She felt her way through the darkened hallway and was at the front door as the banging began again. It was Andy, his face smoke blackened, gripping Jake by his shoulder. Behind them, stood Percy Pringle, the village policeman, his helmet at a slight angle, as it always was.

Andy seethed, 'He fired the old barn, the little devil.' He pushed Jake into the hallway, and came in after him. The smell of smoke was heavy. Miss F had joined them in the hall. Percy closed the door behind him, and they all trooped through to the kitchen.

Jake was shaking, his face pale, but smudged with soot. Phyllie felt quite faint, suddenly, and sank onto a kitchen chair. 'I can't believe this. Oh, Jake, what's going on?' she murmured.

He lashed out with his fists at Andy. 'Nothing's going on; it's all just a mess.'

He was kicking and shouting. One kick landed on Phyllie's leg. Andy grabbed him, and pulled, him away from Phyllie. 'Don't you dare kick Phyllie. Don't you dare, after all she's done for you. You're not the only one who's lost a parent. Look around the village, the country, you daft selfish lad, see how many there are. And has Phyllie or Miss F given up on you for one minute, though you've been testing them for months?

Doesn't that prove anything? What do you want, the fact that they love you bawled from the heights, night and morning? You just don't know how lucky you are.'

He lifted Jake off the ground, backing away from the table, and let him flail around until he grew weaker and weaker, while Francois growled and leapt at Andy.

'Enough, Francois,' Miss F shouted. Francois backed away, confused. At last Jake stopped, and Andy let him down, keeping hold of his arm, looking anxiously across at Phyllie. 'Are you all right?'

It hurt, but nothing like as much as seeing the despair in this boy's face. Why on earth did Andy and Joe have to involve the police? 'Yes, I'm fine. How much do I owe you for the damage, Andy?' She could hear the coldness in her voice.

He waved his stump. 'Nothing. The damage wasn't great, but that's not the point; imagine if it had been the horses.'

Percy had brought out his notepad, and was licking his pencil. Jake yelled, 'But it wasn't the horses, that's the point. They wanted to, cos they couldn't find the sugar. They were angry. He'd been drinking cider. It was frightening. I was scared. I didn't know that's what they were look-ing for, I just thought they were poking about, and then they said they were going to burn down the stables. I snatched the matches and ran. They caught me in the old barn, got 'em back. They chucked matches at a straw bale, then ran away, I tried to put it out–' He stopped. Everyone focused.

329

Miss F was holding Francois' collar, and shrieked, 'It's those boys, isn't it?'

Phyllie said, 'You could have been killed. Oh, Jake, what would we have done then?'

'Those boys?' Percy boomed. 'Which boys? Oh, hang on... Cider, you say? Sugar?'

'It was no one,' Jake muttered. 'I shouldn't have said that. No one...' He tried to shrug from Andy's grip.

Andy said, 'I caught him in the old barn. There was no one else by then, but the straw was well alight. Thinking about it, he'd used his mackintosh to try to beat it out. It's ruined now.'

'Like we did in the wheatfield, when the plane came over,' Jake whispered. 'But I couldn't stop it, so I was trying to be brave enough to run in and tell you. I'm sorry, Mr Andy.'

Andy was staring at Phyllie, but clearly not seeing her. He lifted his head to Percy now. 'Just a minute, how did you know to come to the farm?'

Phyllie felt an inexplicable relief. So Andy hadn't involved the police and she didn't have to raise the energy to dislike him all over again.

Percy shrugged. 'It was an anonymous call.' He came to stand in front of Jake. 'Fine friends you have, boy. Now's I know the story, I know damn well who called, and who "those boys" are. I should've clocked it was Eddie Anderton's voice sooner, but it was you saying he had a taste for cider that made me put two and two together. He must have been talking through his snotty handkerchief. Panting he was, run all the way to the telephone box, I dare say, just to drop you in it.

My word, and you're happy to take the rap? Well, Miss Phyllie, what d'you reckon his father would think of him?'

The policeman never took his eyes off the boy. Jake sagged against Andy now, all the fight gone from him. He put his hand out to Francois. Miss F let the dog go, and Phyllie said softly, 'His dad would be proud of his son, for preventing the horses being burned. Proud, just as I am, for remembering who he is.'

'We,' said Miss F. 'Just as we are.'

Jake stroked Francois and muttered, 'I knew they were rotten, really, but Ron's not, you know. He gave me sweets that Bryan's mum made. She's got a lot of sugar, you see. He's just lonely, and cross. His mum never comes, and I thought I... Well, nothing.'

Andy looked across at Phyllie and Miss F, then asked Jake, 'Are you going to behave yourself, for a moment?'

Jake nodded dumbly, getting down on his knees and hugging the dog, tears falling now, as Francois whined his pleasure.

Andy and Percy were talking urgently. At length, the policeman tucked his notepad and pencil into his top pocket, saying, 'I'm letting you off with a warning this time, sonny. There had better not be a next time. Get to your feet and promise me that, because this is my Christmas Day you're ruining, along with everyone else's. My missis is not best pleased, let me tell you that.'

Jake jumped up, and stood almost to attention. His knees were red with cold, his shorts smut-covered. Why on earth hadn't he worn his trousers? Phyllie wondered. Ah, they were in the wash, and he had a new pair from Father Christmas still half unwrapped and thrown to one side. His gumboots were mud-covered, as was the kitchen floor. He looked exhausted, but as she stood to go to him, Miss F pushed her down, shaking her head.

Andy said, 'Jake, see Constable Pringle to the door, then come straight back, and perhaps you have something to say to these two women who care about you so much.'

Jake left the kitchen, Francois at his heel, and before he followed, Percy winked at Phyllie. 'He's not a bad 'un, and I'll be seeing the ones that are. I'll come down heavy on them. I'll be careful they know it's not come from yon lad. I'll say I've only just realised whose voice it was on the telephone. I'll ask Andy if I can say he saw them running away. I won't check for sugar at this stage. I'll leave that for later, or those two Andertons will know I've had information. Be a bit like pointing a finger right at this little devil.' He headed for the front door.

Andy took a third seat at the table, dragging his hand down his face. 'It's been brewing a long time with Jake, and something had to break. I reckon this is it. I know I'm interfering, and I know we've had our differences, Phyllie,' he was tracing the pattern of the oilcloth, 'but he's not had a burial, a service, nothing, for his dad; neither have you for Sammy.'

Phyllie nodded, they were almost whispering. 'I know. I felt I couldn't until Jake did something for his father, but he won't go to church. Miss F and I have been trying to find a synagogue, but he won't go – he's not a Jew any more, he says. Though he might well have changed his mind after this.'

Miss F was thoughtful. 'I wonder if it would be better to do something here instead, where he knows people. It could perhaps cleanse the past if his friends are with him?'

Phyllie wondered why on earth she hadn't thought of any of this. 'Yes, it can't hurt, can it? We can suggest it, so thank you, Andy.'

Jake was opening the door, and he stood just inside it, as though he didn't know if he should enter. Tentatively, Phyllie held out her hand to him. He came, with Francois sticking like glue. 'I'm sorry, Phyllie, Miss F; you too, Andy. I'm so sorry. I just don't know anything about anything any more.'

Phyllie murmured to him, 'That makes two of us, Jake.' He smiled at her, really smiled.

He was too tired for more tears, and Phyllie led him upstairs, into the bath. She waited for him in the bedroom. The smell of smoke was still in his hair, but it wouldn't do any harm for him to be reminded for a few days. She kissed his forehead, as always. This time, though, his arm came round her neck, and held her there. 'I'm sorry, Phyllie. I love you, Miss F and my daddy and mummy. I know I'm a Jew, and that's all right. Because then I'm like Mummy and Daddy.'

She sat with him until he slept. He was only a child, haunted by the dead and the missing. Poor little boy. Whatever they did, there would be no quick fix. He'd still have to battle through.

Jack Thompson contacted a rabbi he knew the next day, and it transpired that they could create closure at a place of their choosing without a rabbi, and include readings of Old Testament psalms and some Hebrew prayers, which the rabbi had offered to send. 'So I can do the job,' said Jack, continuing for some while about the beauty of the psalms, as only he could.

On 27 December practically the whole village congregated around the ice-covered pond to wait for Phyllie, Miss F, Francois and Jake. They were late, because as they left the house, Jake said, 'I want–' He didn't say what he wanted, he just ran inside, and up the stairs, then down again and out, clutching the tallit Phyllie had last seen the day they arrived at Myrtle Cottage. It seemed much more than only a year and a half ago.

They walked along the street, the four of them, with Jake wearing the tallit, his family's prayer shawl, around his shoulders. At their approach, the villagers stepped back, opening a channel through which the little group walked until they reached the bank. The channel closed, and Phyllie felt the protection of these good people. Jake gripped her hand, and she knew that he felt it too. They all sang, Eternal Father, strong to save, Whose arm hath bound the restless wave, Who bidd'st the mighty ocean deep, Its own appointed limits keep; Oh, hear us when we cry to Thee, For those in peril on the sea.

Phyllie and Jake then read, together, the twenty-third psalm, with Francois at their side: The Lord is my shepherd; I shall not want. He maketh me to lie down in green pastures: he leadeth me beside the still waters. He restoreth my soul...

They didn't throw flowers on the pond, as Jake had explained that it wasn't part of the Jewish tradition. Prayers were said, first for Sammy and then for Isaac, with Jack struggling manfully with Hebrew; and from that moment it was clear that Jake looked on him as a special person. Jack closed the prayer book. He asked Jake if he'd like to talk about his father.

Jake stepped forward, his breath visible in the air as he said, 'I love Daddy. That's all. I just love him.' Jack looked at Phyllie.

'I love Sammy. That's all. I just love him.' She echoed Jake's words, and it was enough. They held hands again. The service was over. No one moved, but stood with their thoughts, their breath visible in the cold air.

Andy had brought the horses to stand with him, at the rear. Desmond, Destiny and Doris huffed in the silence and Jack said eventually, 'Thank you all for coming. I believe there are a few eats at Mr Burley's hostelry.'

Now people moved, making their way along the main village street to the Dun Cow.

Jake spent a few minutes with the horses. They nuzzled the tallit, and he laughed. Phyllie felt Miss F's arm around her shoulder. It was the first laugh since the news had arrived. Andy took the horses to their stables but Miss F, Joe, Phyllie and Jake followed the villagers to the pub, with Dan and Miss Deacon. The Andertons had not been invited to the service, but Ron had. He had come, with

Fanny McTravers and her auntie, possibly unwill-ingly, but he was there. Even Percy Pringle came, with the missis.

Chapter Eighteen

New Year's Eve, 1941 Lower Mitherton

Jake sat next to Phyllie on the sofa, while opposite, he watched Miss F snuffle into her handkerchief. She had a streaming cold, and Phyllie had shaken her finger at her and told her she should be in bed. It had made Jake laugh. It still felt strange to laugh, really laugh. It almost creaked in him. The Aga was rattling a bit. He fed it logs. He and Mr Andy had brought the logs down a few days ago, in the cart drawn by Desmond, and he had been allowed to take the reins.

It was New Year's Eve tonight and still the Germans hadn't come marching into Britain. Perhaps they never would, now. It was much easier to believe that with America in, and the Germans chasing the Russians, just as it was easy to believe Phyllie when she said, again, that she'd never leave him. He didn't know why he had not trusted her before, because she'd never let him down.

The wireless was sort of whistling, and some music was playing. He thought it was that man Glenn Miller, who Sammy had always liked. He could think of Sammy now, but not Dad. Not yet. He could still see him, though. Sometimes just there, at the edge of his eyes, he could see him. Or when the men were coming out of the pub he thought he saw him.

He had told Miss F and Phyllie earlier today, when they had a piece of the Christmas cake they'd made, after saving up their rations. Phyllie and Miss F had put their pieces of cake down on their plates, and let their tea get cold, though it was a proper cup of tea, made with fresh tea leaves. That's when he knew again how much they loved him, because not everyone would have let tea like that get cold.

'I'm so pleased you told us that,' Phyllie said now, shuffling a bit on the settee, 'because I still see Sammy, all over the place, and sometimes I dream that everything is all right, and then I wake up and it isn't. That's horrible too.'

Her words made him feel better. Opposite Miss F was blowing her nose again. It was strange how quite a small nose could make such a loud noise, but then, Miss F made a noise even when she whispered.

'I see Miss Harvey still, sometimes,' Miss F said. She coughed into her handkerchief.

On the airer, above them, were some baby clothes drying that someone – he thought it was Mrs Eaves from the bakery – had brought round to give Phyllie for Charlie, because that's what they had decided to call the baby. Miss F had said the name Charlie would do for Charles or Charlotte until they knew. Phyllie had asked if he'd like to feel Charlie kicking, but that was disgusting.

He checked the clock. Four twenty. Phyllie looked as though she was about to fall asleep, but she had to go to the vicar for a bit of a chat, and a tiny piece of cake with Mrs Speedie and some other people for New Year's Eve. He nudged her awake, and she struggled into her coat, kissing him, closing the back door behind her.

'Don't slip on the snow,' Miss F called after her.

Miss F then went to lie down, just for a moment she said, but she'd said that yesterday and it had been hours. Dan was going to call for him at about five o'clock, and then they were going back to Miss Deacon's house. It's not that he was frightened of Ron and Bryan, or Eddie, not really, but Constable Pringle, Mr Andy, Phyllie and Miss F had said he had to have Francois with him, or if not Francois, then Dan, or whoever he was out with. Peter, Miss Deacon's nephew, would bring him home at nine in the evening.

He leaned forward and stroked Francois. Well, if he was honest, he really was a bit frightened. Actually, he was a lot frightened, because Constable Pringle had gone round to Ron, and then Bryan and Eddie's, to tick them off, and put them in his notebook. Jake knew they'd know he'd talked. Those boys seemed to know everything but he supposed that with a gang like Eddie's, there were a lot of ears and eyes bringing lots of news.

Jake picked up the pack of cards from the arm of the sofa, and the tray, which stood on its edge on the floor by the arm. He'd play Patience until Dan came, on his bike. Jake had left his own bike at the side of the house so he was ready. They'd ride back to Dan's house, leaving Francois here.

He looked up at the airer again. It was strange not to be angry. After the day at the pond, when

338

they had said the psalms, the anger had gone so quickly. Not completely, though. It still came back, sometimes, but lighter, and in between it was nice. He was still sad, dreadfully sad, but it was as though he'd been away in his head for a long time, and now he was back.

He could see things he hadn't seen, like the knitted clothes for Charlie, the patchwork quilt that had been on his bed since his father had died, which Phyllie and Miss F had made him. He sort of remembered them saying it was there, and it must have been, but now he really saw it. Yesterday Mr Joe and Mr Andy had brought round a cot for Charlie. It was really old, and had been Mr Andy's but he'd cleaned it, and he could really see the picture painted on the headboard.

It was going to be a nice late night with Dan tonight. The grown-ups would stay up until midnight, though Miss F had said that chance would be a fine thing if she did, because all she needed was a warm bed and a hot toddy with honey.

It would be the first New Year without his dad in it, but at least his dad was with Sammy.

He sighed and remembered Miss F's nose, so red from blowing. It made her look like Rudolph. He laughed as he laid out the cards. She had a lovely smile, but she was lovely anyway. She liked to make people think she was cross, but she wasn't, and everyone knew that. She had started kissing him at night now, but that was all right, he just didn't want it happening in the day. Glenn Miller was still playing on the wireless, which was acting up, and sounding like rushing water. He wondered if he'd want to swim in the summer but he knew he must, because otherwise it would be running away.

Mr Andy had talked to him about that, when he was cleaning the tack yesterday. He had told Jake how he had tried to run away from what had happened to him with the truck, and had got really empty inside, and then cross and horrid to people, but that now he felt he'd moved on. He had shown him a picture of the hook he was getting. It looked strange, but would help, because it was so difficult for him to even do up a bridle with only one hand.

He checked his cards and supposed that Mr Andy couldn't even shuffle the cards. He tried to do it with one hand. They spilled all over the floor. He bent to pick them up but then the doorbell rang. He rushed to pack them away, checking the clock. It was thirty-five minutes past four. Dan was really early. He grabbed the new mackintosh that Miss F had found in the attic, and hauled it on, then rushed towards the front door, shouting, 'Hang on, Dan; I'm coming.'

He remembered the brown paper bag into which Phyllie had put some slices of Christmas cake for Miss Deacon. 'Just a minute,' he called and returned for the bag. He didn't like the cake really, because there was no icing, but he wouldn't tell anyone that because Miss F and Phyllie had been so proud of it.

He stroked Francois. 'It's Dan. Be a good boy, I'll be back later.' He shut the kitchen door behind him, and rushed down the hall, opening the door. 'Sorry–' he began. It was Ron, not Dan, standing on the front step in the gloom of the late afternoon and he was panting, as though he'd been running. He had a black eye too. Jake stepped back in surprise.

Ron said, 'Thought you'd never come. I heard you call Dan's name, but he's at the pond, helping Mr Andy with a pram he was bringing for Miss Phyllie. The wheel's fallen off. I said I'd come to get you to help because Mr Andy said Miss Phyllie was too big to help. So can you? I know we ain't been friends, but I feel bad. I thought if I said I'd fetch you it might make it better.'

Jake felt confused and a bit nervous, trying to think if Mr Andy had said anything about a pram. He didn't think so. 'I don't know,' he said. 'I'd better ask Miss F and I should take Francois too. Why's your eye all bruised?'

Ron reached out a hand. 'I slid on the ice. Look, I'm sorry about your dad, that's why I came to the pond for the prayers. I'm lucky, mine's still alive. Come on, I'll show you where, it's only by the pond. We can do it, the four of us. You, me, Dan and Mr Andy.'

Jake hesitated, trying to decide if Ron was really being nice. Ron dropped his hand to his side and shrugged. 'I'm only trying to help, for once.'

Jake thought he looked different, sort of awkward, almost scared, not as though he was going to shove and push. And he *had* come to the pond for the service, and if he was being helpful, then it would be rude to be difficult. And what would Mr Andy think if he said no? He said, 'I need to get Francois and then I'll come.'

Ron bit his lip, then said, 'Nah, we don't need

341

'im. He'll get in the way.'

Jake insisted, half turning, 'I'll just get him.' At that, Ron grabbed him by his mackintosh collar, pulling him right up against him. 'You think you're such a clever little snot, don't you? OK, there's no pram, but we've got Dan, and we won't let him go until you come, so don't make a noise. Eddie wants to talk to you about telling tales. He thinks you've talked about the sugar, because the police saw him trying to sell some yesterday. He thinks they've been watching him. We've got your mate, so you'd better come or he gets hurt.' His breath stank of cigarettes, and something else? It was a bit like Eddie's cider, and Jake was frightened, but they had Dan. Ron said, 'Come on, if you want to help your friend. Come on, or I'll get it too, I'll really get it.' His voice really did sound scared.

Jake tried to pull free, but then he thought of Dan and in the end he let Ron drag him down the path. As he did so, Bryan stepped out from behind the buddleia bush and Jake's heart sort of stopped, and his legs felt funny, and he wanted to pee himself. Bryan grabbed his other arm. Jake tried to call out, but he couldn't find his voice. His mouth was moving, but that was all.

Bryan said against his ear, 'Not a sound, if you don't want your friend hurt. Do you think we don't know where you were going tonight? We know everything, so we got to him before he reached you.' He was dragging him out into the street and along the road. Jake tried to pull away, but Bryan twisted his arm. Jake felt his hand open, and the bag of cake dropped. The front door of

Myrtle cottage was still open, and Miss F would feel the cold and come. She'd bring Francois. He'd attack them.

Bryan hissed at Ron, 'Door's open. Go and shut it, I've got him, and don't you call anyone either, Ron.'

Jake could have cried as Ron tore back, closing the door quietly, before catching back up with them.

Bryan had put his arm around Jake's shoulders and gripped him tightly. 'One sound and Dan pays for your loudmouthed rubbish. Tell the cops, would you?' Jake was shaking his head. Bryan pulled him closer. 'Well, it must have been you, because if it'd been Ron he'd have told us after the whacking Eddie gave him. Eddie's got to go to court, he has, and that's got to be at your door. You need to be taught a lesson that everyone can see, to stop any more of this gobbing.'

Ron and Bryan pulled him along. Dan was waiting, Jake thought, and it wasn't fair to leave him with them, so he didn't shout out, instead he stumbled and slid on the snow, along with them. They passed Old Stan who peered through the half-light, and said, 'You boys had better be good tonight, don't want to start 1942 on a bad note.'

Bryan laughed. 'It'll be a good one for us.'

They hurried him, skidding a bit on the frozen snow, until they reached the pond, which was black and still, though the snow was white and threw back some light. They carried on to Haydock Field, and the stone store where Francois had been locked when they were washing the sheep. 'Where's Dan?' Jake asked, hearing the hoarseness of his own voice.

'In the shed, waiting for you,' Ron said, when poked by Bryan.

Jake knew he wasn't. He knew he'd been tricked. But even as he thought it, he wasn't sure. Perhaps Dan was in there, and couldn't speak. It was like his mother. She'd gone to help her parents, though she sort of knew the Germans would come. She must have known that she might be made to scrub pavements like her cousin, but still she went. So how could he not go in? As he stepped forward he understood why she left him, at last. It felt like the last piece of a puzzle was in place.

He entered the darkness. It smelled of damp sacks, and was empty. It was no surprise, there was just a deepening of the fear. He was pushed to the back of the store, and a torch with the blackout slit shone in his face. He couldn't see anything other than the light, but then the beam played across Ron and Bryan's faces. Then Eddie's. Crowding beside and behind him were the three other members of the gang, one of whom held the torch. Eddie gave the command in a harsh whisper and they all stood to attention and gave the fascist salute, grunting, 'PJ.'

'Is that right, then, Ron?'

Ron said, 'Yes, that's how my dad does it.' His voice sounded funny, almost as though he was trying not to cry.

Jake didn't understand what PJ meant, but he did understand the roll of tape that Bryan had dragged from his pocket. He unpeeled a length, tearing it with his teeth. He stuck it across Jake's mouth as Eddie grinned beside him. Bryan ripped more tape from the roll, tore it across, again with his teeth. Eddie grabbed Jake's shoulders and turned him round, and muttered to Ron, 'Hold his arms together then, behind his back.'

Ron said, 'Why? We're only ducking him, aren't we? He'll need his arms to swim.' His voice was shaking now.

Eddie hissed, 'Shut your noise, else someone will 'ear. They've only got to pass down from the farm, or along the road, you bloody fool. Arnold, get the Yid's arms.'

Another of the gang shoved Ron out of the way, and wrenched Jake's arms behind him, hurting his shoulders. He felt the tape wound round and round.

'But why?' Ron persisted. 'I'm telling you 'e can't swim if we push him off the jetty. That's not fair. It's not right. That Phyllie sent money to me mum, Jake told me. Yes, I was angry, but she's kind, and he's just a kid, and his dad's dead. It's not right, I'm telling you. It's all daft.'

'Hold his feet,' Eddie ordered. Another boy knelt, grabbing Jake's ankles. Jake kicked out, catching his face. Eddie punched him in the stomach. It doubled him over and took his breath. He felt sick.

'Leave him alone. What're you doing to him?' Ron was shouting now, and Eddie hit him too, and now Ron doubled over, gasping, and vomited over Eddie's boots.

Eddie whispered, 'Dirty pig. I told you to keep it down. 'E dobbed us in, and now he needs to learn a lesson, all you vacees do. You lot are nothing but trouble.'

Ron was on the ground, coughing and retching. 'If you throw him in he'll drown.' He was dribbling in the light from the torch, and Jake saw Bryan nudging his brother, and grinning. Bryan said, 'Don't be daft, we're not going to drown him. I told you, we're teaching him a lesson and you're coming along, because you'll run off, as sure as eggs is eggs, and tell them damned teachers. You're just a coward, Ron Cummins. A right floppy townee, you was never one of us, just a vacee, that's all.'

Ron scrambled, retching, to his feet, and he was grabbed, but not taped. Eddie and two others lugged Jake up, carrying him between them as though he was a log. He struggled. Eddie bent over him. 'Shut up, or I'll visit your Phyllie and she'll get it next, and that bastard she's carrying.'

Jake lay still, because Phyllie mustn't be hurt, and he wished he'd never said a word to the policeman.

They didn't need the torch outside, the moon was bright now. Jake was lifted and carried between them – and was jogged about as they walked along the edge of the pond. Snow made everything seem quiet. It was strange to be carried, to see just the sky, and the top half of these big boys. He had no idea of the time, he had no idea of anything. In front of him he could see the top half of Ron, who hadn't said another word, but was being dragged along by Eddie, who had hold of his arm. On the shoulder of one of the bigger boys was a coiled rope.

They headed for the woods, and behind him, on the other side of the hedge and the pond, he

346

heard Mr Andy leading Destiny, Desmond and Doris from their field to the stables, talking to them, as Jake talked to Francois.

He wriggled again, but Eddie whispered over his shoulder, 'You're taped, so no point in struggling.' He stopped. Ron was looking over his shoulder, in the direction of Mr Andy's voice, but he made no sound either.

As they entered the woods, Eddie said, 'We could try the big oak in the middle, or there's the other one, near the edge, but anything that's big and will take a rope.'

Ron swung round, his voice a hoarse whisper, 'You're mad.' An owl hooted, then another. Somewhere a fox screamed.

Eddie laughed quietly; the others too. He said, 'He's a Yid. It's what your dad would do. These bloody Jews caused the war, just like that Jew Churchill. The poor old King is trying to keep us safe from the Commies and the Jews, so we need to do our bit. You told us that's what he said.'

Ron said, 'Churchill's not a Jew, not really. Dad just says it.'

Bryan came alongside Ron. 'That's bollocks. You said Perish Judea like the rest of us.'

Jake was sore from the way their fingers dug in as they carried him, but at last he knew what PJ meant, and now he was really really frightened and he peed himself. It dripped onto the ground as they walked. No one saw, but they might smell it.

Something woke Miss F at five o'clock but when she listened, heaving herself up on her pillows, she heard nothing. She thought it was must have been

347

Dan banging on the door, and anyway, it was time she got up, or she wouldn't sleep later. Her head was splitting, but a cup of hot chamomile would do her good.

She dragged a shawl around her shoulders, put on her slippers, and made her way downstairs. She opened the kitchen door, and Francois almost bowled her over in his rush to get into the hall. He tore to the front door, and whined. She called, 'Oh come here, you silly dog. Dan's come for him, and you and I will have to keep one another company. You can't go everywhere with your lord and master.'

He wouldn't come and she hadn't the voice to shout, so she hurried down the hallway and dragged him into the kitchen, shutting the door and sending him to his rug in front of the Aga. She lifted the kettle from the simmer plate and put it onto the booster and while it heated she sat and stroked his head, and smiled. 'You and I are to keep one another company while the others are out having fun, though I'm not sure that tea and buns with the vicar quite meets that criterion. Perhaps cycling through the village with your best friend does.'

Chapter Nineteen

The clock on the mantelpiece chimed and Miss F jerked awake, checking the time. Nine thirty. She was still drowsy, still poorly. She tightened the scarf around her neck, and reached down to stroke Francois but he wasn't there.

She heard him then, whining, at the back door. Ah, it must be Phyllie. Perhaps she'd met Peter and Jake on their way back? She felt so thick-headed it was hard to think and it really was time she gave up on the evening and tottered up the wooden hill to her bed.

She waited, but there was no Phyllie. She topped up the kettle through the spout, wincing as the water caught an edge and sprayed her. She shook the splashes off her scarf, and placed the kettle on the booster plate. Tonight she'd have a hot water bottle, a proper one that would warm the small of her back, and keep her scarf on. At her feet she put one of the bricks they'd brought in and warmed in the oven. There, top and tailed, and tomorrow she'd feel a new woman.

She looked up at the photograph of Catherine Harvey. She reached out and touched it. 'I do miss you, but thank heavens for my little family, and now Joe. You'd raise your eyebrows, but he's a real dear, you know. I'm so glad you died with Melanie near. You know that Jack and Sylvia named their baby after her? How sweet is that?

'I'm still angry, though, my dearest Catherine, that either of you had to die at all.'

Within a few moments the kettle lid was rattling. She whipped the kettle off the hot plate before the whistle could start, and poured half onto the tea leaves in the pot, leaves that had only been used twice today. She left it to brew on the side plate. She kept talking because there were times when she didn't like a quiet house. 'Joe would like us to be ... well, more than we are. We kissed, Catherine. At our age, for goodness' sake. It was nice. We kissed again, but I have my little family here, and I feel, just at the moment at least, I'm not sure I want to move up to something else, if you know what I mean? Well, of course you do, you always did. He says to take my time, and so I shall.'

She filled her hot water bottle, and sat back in her chair, clasping it to her midriff, before slipping it behind her. The Aga was easing out heat, as it always did, but the hot water bottle was comforting. She felt she was brewing a temperature and simply hadn't the time to deal with that, what with the WI, the salvage, after-school rotas, the preparations for school, though Phyllie, bless her, helped beyond measure working on those preparations at home, unofficially and unpaid. She heard the side gate, and so did Francois, who hadn't moved from the back door. It opened, and she watched Phyllie start to enter, bringing in the cold, which clung to her mackintosh and hat. There was snow on her boots.

Miss F stood, and busied herself at the Aga, saying, 'Come by the range. I've tea in the pot, and will do cocoa for you, Jake.' She looked round, and saw only Phyllie on the doormat, her left boot half off.

'Jake? He should have been home an hour ago.'

Phyllie pulled her boot back on. Francois tried to push past her to get to the door again. She was tired, and Miss Deacon had promised. Still, it was New Year's Eve and these things happened. She said, 'It's all right, he'll have overstayed so I'll go out again and get him.' It was so cold it was the last thing she wanted to do, but at least she'd had some rather delicious sausage rolls, a miracle in these rationed times, and she blessed Sylvia's careful padding of the sausage meat from the Pig Club.

She yanked her hat back on, sent Francois to his rug, but he wouldn't stay. She shrugged and laughed at Miss F. 'I'll take him, but on his lead or he'll barge past Miss Deacon and upset her ornaments. I can't cope with that embarrassment again. He can do his business while we're out. You stay by the fire, and leave the cosy on the tea-pot. I won't be long. You keep warm, now.'

She trudged along the road, slipping from time to time, especially with Francois pulling on the lead. He wanted to go the other way – to the fields, she supposed. Her back ached, and she felt as though she should hold her belly with both hands to stop it pulling her to the ground. 'Well, Charlie,' she muttered, 'you're getting to be big, aren't you, with feet that kick soundly. Go to sleep now.'

She opened Miss Deacon's front gate. The house was just past the post box, which must be handy, as a favourite niece was in the WAAF and

351

letters could just be slipped into its gaping mouth. The path was cleared, which made things feel much safer. She knocked, and waited. There was the sound of the wireless in the front room, which Miss Deacon didn't usually use, but she supposed it 'came out' over Christmas. The blackout was drawn across the door, and parted. When she saw Phyllie she looked puzzled, then smiled. She called back, 'Douse the lights, Dan, there's a love.'

She opened the front door and slipped onto the step. 'Happy New Year to you, Phyllie, it's so nice of you to call. How is Jake now? Dan was disappointed but we thought you had other plans. He knocked and no one came to the door.'

Phyllie's breathing stopped. 'What do you mean?' Now she breathed again, but it was shallow, and rapid.

Miss Deacon said, 'Just that. He came, knocked, there was no reply, so he came home. We thought you must have forgotten and all gone out. Francois barked, but that was all. Are you all right, Phyllie?'

Phyllie was hurrying back along their path now, gasping, and holding her belly. Francois pulled on the lead, wanting to go ahead, but she hurried to Myrtle Cottage and down the side path. She slammed into the kitchen. 'Miss F, did you have a sleep?'

Miss F was in her armchair, sipping her tea. She stared, trying to catch up. 'Yes. Why? Where's Jake?' She jumped to her feet. The mug dropped to the floor, its contents soaking into the rug. She came to Phyllie. 'Oh God, why are you asking?'

Phyllie was shaking her head, as Francois

whined, straining to be out again. 'Dan came, knocked and went away again, thinking we'd forgotten. But where is he? Where's Jake? Why didn't he take Francois?' She could hear her own voice ending on some sort of ridiculous screech, as Miss F reached for the table for support.

Miss F said, 'Something woke me, I thought it was Dan collecting him, I came down at about five and Francois was here, and Jake had gone. I thought... Oh my God, Phyllie. Why would he go out without Francois?'

There was a knocking on the back door now. It was Peter, Miss Deacon's nephew. 'I was telling Auntie I saw the Great Mitherton gang in the village, with that Ron, earlier on. They were hanging about down your end. I was cycling, bit slippy but all right, and I didn't think anything of it, because they went on to towards the pond.'

'When?'

'About three or four o'clock.'

Phyllie pulled him in. He snatched off his woollen hat, and crushed it in his large hands. His nose was red, and he smelled of beer. Even underage Scouts drank, then, on New Year's Eve. 'I was at the pub, and Auntie Anne nipped in to see me, to tell me. Mr Burley said he'd get up a search party.'

Miss F was clinging to the kitchen chair for support. 'We need to think. I'm going to phone Joe, in case he's gone there.'

'Why would he go there, without Francois?' Phyllie shrieked, but Miss F was already in the hall. Three or four o'clock? But that could have been for any reason. And Jake had been here

353

when she left, so it probably meant nothing. Stupid woman, she knew it meant something. He wouldn't forget Dan. 'Where do we start? It's dark; he could be anywhere.'

Peter said, 'Sit down, Miss Phyllie. Sit.' He pulled out a chair. 'We could follow Francois. He'll know.' She looked round for Francois, but he was gone, and the back door was open. Peter said, 'I'll go out after him, he'll have left a trail.'

He ran out, just as Miss F came back into the kitchen, shaking her head. 'No, he's not with Joe and Andy, but they're coming down the track, looking. We mustn't worry, Joe said.'

Miss F was heaving herself into her mackintosh, and hauling on her gumboots. 'Come on, we've got to use Francois, Peter's right. He's gone off to try and catch up with him. Do come on, Phyllie.'

But Phyllie was already out of the back door. 'Catch me up, Miss F. You'll need your scarf.' She hurried down the side, then out of the front gate, to the right she kicked something. She picked it up. The paper bag with cake. Clever darling Jake. They must have gone this way. She hurried as fast as she dared, towards the pond, holding her belly. She was forced to slow to a fumbling walk after slipping and nearly falling. Peter was clearly visible in the moonlight cycling back from the lower end. 'No sign, no sound of the wretched dog. I'll go up to the top end now.'

'He dropped his paper bag full of cake,' she called. 'It's a clue. I'm heading towards the pond.'

She moved onto the untrampled snow at the verge, hearing Miss F blowing her nose behind her. She shouldn't be out, but they needed

354

everyone. She called back to Peter, 'Please thank Mr Burley; we need everyone, do you hear? We need absolutely everyone's help.' He was so far away that she didn't know if he could hear, but he waved without turning. She began to cry, and dragged her hand across her face. Shut up, no time now. She had reached the point where the graveyard started when she saw someone running and sliding towards her – a boy, surely.

'Jake, Jake,' she cried.

It was Ron. He was crying, his nose was bleeding and dripping onto his mackintosh. He stopped, bending over, and blood dripped onto the snow, visible in the moonlight. 'They made me get him, miss. I got away, I didn't want that, I tried to stop it. They hit me first, then sent me to find him. I made him come, because I was scared. I thought they'd duck him for gobbing on us, but they've got a rope. Two of them took me back to the stone store by the stream just as they got into the woods. They stuck that tape over my mouth, and some on me wrists, behind me back. They locked me in, but I got me hand free, I shouted but no one heard. They thought I'd get help, you see, and I wanted to. I tried but I couldn't get out. I undid a hinge with me penknife; that's what I did. They didn't know I had it.'

She shook him. 'What do you mean, they've got a rope.'

'We've got to find him. They was going to hang him in the woods, I think. Might be an old oak tree, but I don't know. He's a Yid and they said they'd teach any other gobbers and Yids a lesson. They taped me, like they taped him. But he

355

couldn't get free, there were too many. I should have fought 'em, but there was too many.'

Phyllie couldn't grasp the words. These were children. What did he mean, hang him? Gobbers? But he was pulling her back, down the road, and now Miss F was with her. 'Come on,' Ron was saying. 'We've got to follow Francois. He passed me, he'll have a scent.'

Peter was skidding to a halt beside them. 'Nothing at the top end.'

'He's in the woods,' Phyllie called. 'Francois is on the trail. Hurry the helpers.' But he was already cycling towards the pub. She hurried then, clinging to Miss F's arm, and at the turn-off to the farm Andy and Joe were waiting. Ron told them again, and Joe thrust a handkerchief at him. 'Wipe that nose, lad.'

Andy passed around torches. 'Phyllie, take Miss F home. We'll find him.' His voice was shaking, and he wouldn't look at them. 'Ron, come with us. You've done well.'

Phyllie cried out then, 'What do you mean, he's done well? He was with them, he took my boy.' She launched herself at Ron, but Andy stepped between them, his arms out. He wore a hook. It glinted. She hadn't seen it before. He held her gently against him and said, quietly but firmly, into her hair, 'Now is not the time, Phyllie. We need to find your boy, and this lad put himself in harm's way to help. We need to go, and you must head off home and look after Charlie. Can I let you go because we haven't time for this?'

Joe and Miss F were already heading to the woods, with Ron. Phyllie rested her head on

356

Andy's chest. 'I'm so sorry,' she whispered. 'I'm so sorry, and you're quite right, but I love him so much.' She pulled away. 'Come on.' She headed after the others. Andy caught her up. 'That's a no to staying at home, then?'

She didn't bother to answer, but waved him on. 'Go ahead, Andy, find him. I can't run and you can.'

She heard voices behind her, and turning, she saw what seemed like hundreds of narrow blackout beams of torchlight jogging as people ran towards her. Mr Burley passed her with ease. 'Don't worry, lass, well find him.'

She called, 'Talk to Andy, he knows about it all.'

'Right you are; go steady.' They were all running on past, puffing and panting, and there was Jack Thompson too. They would be forced to slow when they reached the woods, or stumble into trees, or over roots. The smell of cider had been like a cloud, bless them; it was New Year's Eve, they were celebrating, and now this.

Where was he? Hanged? Hanged? How could children do this to one another? How could beliefs be so corrupt? Or was it just a stupid game? Please, let it be that. Hanged? She twisted her ankle, and nearly fell. 'Where are you, Jake?'

She had left the pond behind, and the ducks they had disturbed. She could hear the distant barking, and voices shouting. At the edge of the woods, Miss F waited for her, and they were joined by Mrs Symes and Mrs Speedie. Miss Deacon was staying in with Dan, in case he took off, trying to help, and made things worse, Peter said, as he ran past them. They heard Joe and

Andy calling to Francois, who was barking in the distance, high-pitched and desperate. But where was the damned dog? How much time did they have? Had they any? Was it all too late?

The women hurried on. They could hear the men calling to one another, but there was no, 'We've got him, he's fine.' Just an increasing desperation as they searched. How could they ever find him or the dog in this darkness? She shouted then, cupping her hands round her mouth, 'Francois, here, come here, now.'

Why hadn't she done that earlier? Where were her brains? The barking stopped for a moment, and then began again but drawing closer. Miss F joined her, and together they called him, 'Francois, come here. Come here.'

He burst through the bushes then, like an arrow. Miss F brought out his rope lead from her pocket. Phyllie smiled at her. 'You think of everything.' She put the noose over his head, holding the end tightly, shouting, 'I have Francois. Find him then, find our boy.' Her voice wasn't calm, it came out as almost a scream.

She took a breath. 'Come on, boy.' Jake mustn't notice her fear if he heard her calling. Inside, though, the panic was building, brick upon brick. She stared at the noose around Francois' neck, at the way he pulled, choking as he led them. Miss F took him from her. 'We can't have you being tugged like that, Charlie might think it's time to pop out, and we have enough to do without fumbling about delivering a child in the snow.'

Her voice was a poor attempt at heartiness, and she was coughing continually. 'You should be home in bed,' Phyllie panted.

'If I'd been up, this wouldn't have happened.' Miss F's voice was broken, but then she straightened. 'But it will be all right. We're on the trail now.'

Phyllie held Miss F's hand. 'They'd have got him some time, you know what they're like.'

Miss F didn't answer, just held on grimly to the lead, calling, 'He's heading in the direction of the old oak. I think Ron mentioned it, didn't he? But it's too hard to find in the dark'

Phyllie stood still, holding her side. She had a stitch, and Charlie was headbutting. She cupped her hands again and called, 'Head for the old oak, Francois is going in that direction. He's pulling us that way. Quick, all of you, for God's sake.'

Mrs Symes took up the call, and further ahead John Myers, from the top end, echoed it. All along the line, the call was carried, as they wove under snow-heavy branches and over roots. When they were much nearer to the oak, Miss F called back to Phyllie, 'Shall I let him off? But what if that's not where he's headed?'

Phyllie was straddling a fallen log, her gumboots heavy with clumped snow, but she was over now. She stumbled, righted herself, and plodded on. 'I don't know. No, let's keep him. If he's not there, then we have to start again. Let him take us.' Francois was yelping now, trying to run. Phyllie didn't know where she was in the darkness, and blundered into branches. They hurt. Snow fell, but what did it matter?

'Where are you, Jake? Stay alive, stay calm. I'll kill those little devils. Where are you? Isaac, help him. Sammy, please be there for him. Look up at the sky, Jake, remember I'm under the same one. I'll kill them, kill them. Find him, Andy.' She was alongside Miss F, who was coughing and wheezing.

Miss F said, 'Save your breath, I'll kill them, if anyone does. It's that Eddie if it's anyone. Like his father he is.'

Mrs Symes was with them, they were almost running as Francois wrenched Miss F's arm. She said, 'He's trying to be a big gangster, stupid boy. It'll be a prank. It's got to be.'

There was shouting, a lot of it, not far ahead. 'We're here. We've got him.'

Miss F said, 'I'm letting him off; come on, Phyllie.' She let Francois go, and he was off, kicking up leaves and snow in his wake. Phyllie was really running now, with the other women, and Charlie would just have to cope. The breath was jolting in her throat. Jake, Jake.

The shouting had stopped. Instead, there was utter silence. An owl hooted, but that was all. The women ran on.

'Oh no, please no,' Miss F was crying, really crying, and the clearing was ahead. They passed banks of rhododendrons, and thinning silver birches and young beech saplings. They could see the moonlight up above, casting shadows. Joe was ahead of them, with Ron. Joe faced them, his arms held out, and John Myers was there too, stopping them. There was no noise except for the whining of Francois and Ron's crying.

Joe said, 'Wait, a minute, just for a minute. Let Andy sort it out.' But Phyllie and then Miss F burst past, tearing into the darkness beneath the oak. The men were gathered there, but parted to let them through. Andy crouched, with Jack Thompson by his side. Andy was kneeling now, on the ground, busy. Jack too. Then came the sound of Jake's voice, weak but clear. 'Thank you, Mr Andy. Thank you.'

'Let's be having you now, Jake. I expect you're numb with cold.' Phyllie watched as Andy lifted her boy up in his arms. He'd been wrapped in Andy's mackintosh. He turned, shivering in his shirtsleeves, Phyllie saw.

'Here's someone who's aged a fair bit over the last hour or so, young man. He was tied to the trunk of the tree, but he's safe and sound, ladies. Just cold. Very cold.'

Phyllie was stroking Jake's face, kissing away the tears that ran like a stream across his cheeks. Some, though, were hers. Andy laughed his relief, and said, 'The little buggers. They just meant to frighten him, I reckon. But it's too damned cold, and he could have been here all night. Just think of that, young Jake. These women would have been grey-haired by the morning. Just think how they'll be from now on, when you're late home from the pub, or from taking a girl out.'

'Oh, Mr Andy, I don't like girls.'

Joe said, 'You will lad, you will.' He patted him as Andy walked on.

Jake said, 'I expect I'm heavy, you can put me down and I'll walk, Mr Andy.'

'Light as a feather, you are, Jake,' Andy said. 'Let's keep going as we are, shall we?'

Miss F was rubbing Jake's shoulder, and bunching her scarf up round his neck. 'I'm so sorry, so sorry. I was asleep so I didn't hear them.'

Joe had hold of Ron's arm, now, as the men passed by, looking at him, then away, fury in their rigid shoulders. Ron hung his head until Jack Thompson came to him. 'You did well, young Ron. You tried to help.' He raised his voice, calling after all those who had come to search. 'Thank you all, and we do need to thank Ron. This would have happened anyway, whether he was there or not, and he stood against them, in the end, when the chips were down. Without his help, I dread to think...'

The men hesitated, then Mr Burley called, 'Right you are, Vicar, if you say so. I'll have a pint ready for you on the bar when these youngsters are in bed, where they damn well should be.' There was anger in his voice, just as there was in Phyllie's heart.

She walked beside Andy, reaching over to keep hold of Jake's hand and his grip was so tight it hurt until he seemed to sleep and released his grip. They straggled on home through the woods. Mrs Symes had taken the arm of John Myers, and Joe stuck like glue to Miss F's side. She was coughing fit to burst. Behind them trailed Ron and Jack, talking quietly.

Phyllie stayed by Andy's side. As they walked she heard the chattering of Andy's teeth, and removed her scarf, draping it round his neck. 'You'll smell of lavender,' she said, 'and have all the girls running after you.' She tucked Andy's mackintosh up around Jake's neck, and pulled up her own collar, her hands shaking, and not from

362

the cold, but from remembered terror, and continuing fear, because this child had become dreadfully cold.

Jake opened his eyes. 'Mr Andy, I really can walk if I'm too heavy.'

Andy grinned down at him. 'I've carried far heavier loads than you, lad, so it's a doddle.'

Jake closed his eyes again, and his voice was drowsy when he murmured, 'Phyllie, I looked up at the sky like you and Sammy did. I looked up and I knew you were under the same sky, and I knew you'd find me. Ron tried to help me. They were horrid to him.'

They walked on. After a moment, when Phyllie could trust her voice, she replied, 'I'll always find you, always, wherever you are.'

She thought he had fallen asleep again, but he was still talking. She bent to hear, clutching his hand. Andy listened too. 'I thought of Dad and Mum. I wanted to be brave for them. I hope Dad hasn't forgotten me, because I haven't forgotten him. Do you think he has, Phyllie? Forgotten me?'

She shook her head, trying to speak. She tried again. 'Of course he hasn't, darling boy. He will never ever forget you.'

Behind her, there was silence for a moment between Jack and Ron and then the murmuring started again, but this time it was louder. She heard Ron say, 'I took the first lot of sugar, and blamed Jake. I sent the money I got to me mum, so she'd come and see me but she didn't. Then, at Christmas, Jake said miss had sent money to me mum too. I hated him for that, for telling me.

Hated him. Then they took more sugar and thought they'd do it again and again, but they couldn't find it. Then Jake dobbed us in with the fire, and now they hate vacees. It's gone daft, it's all strange, and I don't know what to do now.'

Jack Thompson said, 'War causes problems, my dear boy. We just have to do what we think is right.'

Phyllie felt Miss F clutch her hand. 'Oh, Phyllie, it's so dreadfully awful. These are children.'

Phyllie leaned over and kissed Jake's head; Charlie kicked. She replied, 'Not everything is awful. We have Jake, that's a start, and it's a new year, that's another.'

They walked along, their little group of seven, eight with Francois, and Phyllie wondered if Ron's 'hero' father was enjoying his new year, safely tucked up in clink at his majesty's pleasure, alongside his other BUF friends. And what about Ron's mother? Was she in the pub, celebrating?

As they reached the edge of the wood, she dropped back and walked alongside Ron. She took his hand, expecting him to shrug away, but he didn't. She said, 'Thank you for saving my boy, Ron. I will never forget it. It is a precious thing to save a life, while putting your own in danger. The Jews say that those who save a life save the world entire, or something like that. Just remember you have done a good thing this evening, something to be proud of.'

'Thank you, miss.' He paused. 'Do you think *my* dad has forgotten me?'

She said, 'Of course he hasn't. Fathers never forget a child, ever. Letters are difficult when people are fighting, especially in the desert. It's probably just that he's somewhere where there's no way to get a letter home. He could be in the middle of something important.'

Ron tightened his grip on her hand. 'Thank you, miss, I thought it might be something like that.'

They held hands all the way back to Myrtle Cottage then Phyllie prised herself free, about to follow Andy down the path as Miss F hurried ahead to open the front door.

Ron said, 'I don't think Mrs Fanny will want me back. She said she didn't want to hear of me in trouble again, because it was too much for her auntie to put up with. I don't know where to go, miss.'

Jack put his arm around the boy's shoulder. 'We have a baby, but you wouldn't mind a few nights with us, I'm sure, until we get things sorted.' They walked on now, and Phyllie heard Jack saying, 'We'll just pop in and pick up a few of your things.'

'Do I have to? Her auntie will be there, while Mrs Fanny's pulling pints at the pub.'

'I rather think you do, because you need to face people. It's called consequences.'

Chapter Twenty

Dr Nicholls arrived to check Jake, bending over the sofa, huffing on his stethoscope before placing it on Jake's chest. 'Disgraceful carryings on. You'll report that Eddie, of course, and get Pringle to take him in. He needs a good dose of borstal. Father's a menace. Sons will so often follow a father's lead, and in his case, it's a road to nowhere.'

'No need for the lecture, Toby,' Miss F grumped. 'Just tell us if he's all right.'

Dr Nicholls straightened. He still had his trousers tucked in his socks because he usually cycled from Great Mitherton. The other alternative was to saddle his horse, or try to start his car, and use his precious fuel allowance. 'Course he is, nothing wrong with the lad that a good soak, a good sleep and a dose of common sense won't cure.'

Phyllie clenched her hands, relief drenching her.

He squatted down in front of Jake, his stethoscope tangling in his tweed jacket. 'Jake, this will not happen again; that is the first thing to understand. The second is that you will have learned from it, and will not go with idiots. The third is that you are surrounded by people who care, so you are quite safe now.'

He left in a flurry, calling over his shoulder to

Miss F, 'I'll be back to deal with you, too, if you don't get to bed. I can hear your chest from here.'

Miss F said, 'Over my dead body.'

Dr Nicholls popped his head back round the door, ramming on his hat, 'Don't raise my hopes, you ghastly old crone.'

Miss F waved him away. 'Sticks and stones, you old fool. Sticks and stones.'

The doctor looked at Phyllie. 'You don't need excitement like this either. So get your feet up when everyone's gone. I don't know, a houseful of bloody women and chaos reigns.' With that he was gone.

Andy carried Jake up the stairs to the bathroom, with the women following like a trail of clucking ducks. Joe called from the foot of the stairs, having nipped in for news to carry back to the pub, 'Met the doc. Says all is the usual chaos.'

Miss F said, 'You can keep quiet too, Joe Bartlett, and go away. Your pint will be getting cold.' She called to Phyllie who was ahead of her, 'There's no nonsense about a few inches in aid of the war effort tonight. A good old hot soak is what he needs.'

Andy knocked the bathroom door wide. 'Rather than talking about it, would one of you like to put in the plug and turn on the tap?'

He was pale and drawn, the bathroom was freezing, and he leaned back on the wall, Jake still in his arms.

'Let me down, Mr Andy. I need to get my clothes off.'

Andy lowered him carefully, keeping his hook clear of Jake's legs, as Phyllie said, 'I'll help you;

just let me get the water going.'

Miss F said, 'I'll get the kettle on, chamomile, and perhaps cocoa for Jake.' She left as Phyllie slid past Andy and Jake, to sort out the plug and turn on the tap. Hot water gushed and steam rose. The water would soak into Jake's bones, and it would ease his mind, or so she hoped.

Andy was whispering to Jake, who replied, 'Yes please, Mr Andy.' He clung to the man's arm, his knuckles white. He was unsteady, but of course he was.

Phyllie sat on the edge of the bath and called to Jake. 'Come here, and I'll help you undress.'

Jake looked up at Andy, who smiled at Phyllie. 'I think perhaps this is men's business, Phyllie.' His tone was gentle but firm.

Phyllie felt Charlie kick. All right, she said to the baby, I get it. She smiled, at Jake, 'Of course. Meanwhile, I'll set about doing women's work with Miss F, so when you're both ready, come down.' To Andy she said, 'If you need to leave to celebrate the New Year, I can sit in here with him while he's soaking. I promise not to look.'

Andy laughed. 'I can celebrate later at the pub while you lot are all warming up in front of the Aga, hugging your chamomile. With that pint in mind, would you please take yourself and Charlie downstairs, and let us get on.'

Andy knocked on the kitchen door half an hour later, and Jake came to sit next to Phyllie, in his pyjamas and dressing gown. Andy tucked the patchwork quilt round both Phyllie and Jake, and asked Miss F if she needed tucking in too. Her gesture was unmistakable and he left, on a tide of laughter, shouting over his shoulder, 'Dad will be back soon, I have no doubt, just to check you're all fine. If you want to be in bed beforehand, it doesn't matter. He'll just come on back to the pub. He brought down some elderberry wine this afternoon.'

The women groaned. They sipped their chamomile, and Jake his cocoa.

After a while, Jake said, 'It was strange. I could see the moon through the trees and in a way, I felt warm, because Ron tried to help. They hurt him because of that, but he went on trying. I think that is so brave, and here I am, with you two, and he hasn't really got anywhere to go. It's not fair, is it? I suppose he'll be quite happy at the vicar's but he sort of drones on, doesn't he, Phyllie? The vicar, I mean.'

That was all. Within half an hour he was in bed, with a hot water bottle, and hot bricks at the top and bottom. Phyllie carried up more hot bricks, but this time to put in Miss F's bed and her own. She then returned to sit by the Aga with her friend. Joe tapped on the door and thrust his head round. 'All well here, with the young 'uns, and the old duck too?' Miss F threw a ball of wool at him. He laughed, tipped his cap back. 'Happy times. Happy times. The tenants from your cottage have poked their 'eads in for a glass of me wine, Phyllie. Seem harmless. Old, but harmless, from Birmingham, but you know that, of course. Happy New Year.' Then he was gone.

She had forgotten all about her tenants moving in today. She had meant to visit, but there was always tomorrow. The two women stayed up until after midnight. 'Might as well see the new one in, Phyllie,' Miss F said, coughing into her handkerchief. 'It should be interesting, and I expect you're thinking, as I am, that we need to clear that attic room?'

They smiled at one another as Phyllie said, 'Well, we can't have Ron putting up with minute-by-minute sermons from the lovely Jack, bless him. Besides, like Jake, we know what the boy did to help. I believe there's something good in him, which is being smothered by pain. We can start clearing tomorrow, but you, my friend, need to hit the wooden hill. Listen to that chest.'

Phyllie bundled Miss F up the stairs, boosting her pillows while she dashed in, and then out, of the bathroom. It was icy in the bedroom but would be snug under the covers. Once Miss F was in bed Phyllie felt her forehead: she was burning. Phyllie hurried to the kitchen, and brought up water and a soaked flannel. She laid the flannel on Miss F's forehead. 'You must drink, all through the night, and call me, if you need me.'

Phyllie lay awake all night, listening to Miss F coughing, and waiting for cries from Jake, but they didn't come. Nonetheless, she was up, on and off, going from his room to Miss F's. He never stirred, but he clutched the photo of his parents to him, and Miss F smiled, and told her to bugger off, and get some sleep. Phyllie in her turn held the photo of Sammy in his uniform that was the most precious item she possessed.

The next day Jake was up before it grew light, and came down to the kitchen, where Phyllie was making porridge, with honey. 'Happy New Year,' she said.

He laughed. 'I'm glad it happened yesterday, because that was the old year. How's Miss F?' She sat opposite, eating her own porridge and he tucked into his, and within seconds it seemed he was scraping the bowl, and licking the spoon both sides. For once she didn't say 'Manners' but smiled at the resilience of children.

He saw her looking, and replaced the spoon. 'Phyllie, I was thinking of Ron. Jack and Sylvia are nice, but they're a bit boring. They've got a baby, and perhaps they won't want him for long, then he'll have to move again. What if Mr Andy and Mr Joe had him, I thought. Then I thought again, that he really needs you, and Miss F to get him right. But then I thought again that there's Charlie coming, so perhaps you wouldn't have time?'

Phyllie finished her porridge, laid her spoon back in the bowl, and leaned back. 'Goodness, with all that thinking going on, no wonder you're hungry. Interestingly, young man, last night, as Miss F and I welcomed in 1942, we wondered if it would be a good idea to have Ron here, and, don't worry, I can cope. We have the attic room; it was once a bedroom, where the maid slept, in years gone by. I know the stairs up are a bit winding, but they're sound. We would need to clear the clutter, clean the windows, and so on.'

Jake said, 'Well, we wouldn't need to tell him it was the servant's room, or he might think that's how we thought of him and get all angry again.'

Phyllie gathered up the bowls, thinking hard. 'Jake, Ron has been part of all the bullying and

371

cruelty towards you for a long time. Also, as you've just said, he gets angry, or *is* angry, deep down. I want you to really mean it about Ron living here, because it might not be easy. He won't change overnight.'

'But he's changing already. You didn't hear him. He was nearly crying, and he really believes you sent his mum the money, and he was trying to stop them. I think he feels as muddled as I have felt, but he feels it all the time, just the whole time, because his mum won't come. Not can't come, but won't come.'

She took a hot drink up to Miss F. She was sitting up on her pillows, and clearly much worse. She did not disagree when Phyllie insisted on calling Dr Nicholls again. She apologised for calling him out on New Year's. Day. 'It'll set my year up beautifully, to see her twice in two days, old trout that she is,' Dr Nicholls barked.

He was there within half an hour, cold from the cycle ride, and asking for a cup of coffee essence to clear his head, grumbling about the Scotch he'd finished last night and the headache it had produced. 'I only bloody well sipped it,' he barked. 'Must have been a bad bottle. She'll have pneumonia, of course. She shouldn't have been out, but you try telling her. I've had my stethoscope out all the way here, getting it good and cold.'

He grumbled his way upstairs while Phyllie and Jake looked at each other, trying not to laugh, but worried too. They followed and heard Miss F saying, 'You huff on that stethoscope, or you're not putting it near my chest, you hear me. You'll have made it nice and cold, you old bugger.'

They crept down again, and only in the kitchen did they laugh. 'You'd never think they are the best of friends, would you?' Phyllie said as she made the coffee.

'I wonder if Ron and I will be like that?' Jake said. 'I keep seeing him last night, in my head, fighting for me.'

Dr. Nicholls was grumbling down the stairs. The telephone rang in the hallway and Phyllie went to answer it while the doctor drank his coffee. It was Mary Nicholls: 'Do tell that little ray of sunshine, otherwise known as my husband, that he has another call. Would he cycle his little legs along to the Andertons' place? Mrs Anderton is in a tizz because her boy Eddie has been arrested again and Bryan, too, this time, and there is no bail. She called from the telephone box, insisting that he give her a sedative. He'll actually want to give her a kick up the bum, but he might manage to talk some sense into her.'

'Yes, I'll do that...' Phyllie began but Mary was in full flow.

'Hope the old battleaxe is battling on? School term starts next week, so you'll have to man up and step into her place. Unofficially, of course. I expect the old dear put in an order to up high to be ill, so there was a reason for you to return. Hope you're feeling fit enough. I know you've been helping with homework marking and schedules at home but this is a bigger thing by far. Happy New Year, keep well.'

Phyllie replaced the receiver and delivered the message about Mrs Anderton to Dr Nicholls who was finishing his coffee. 'Arrested, you say?

373

Not before time. Your young lad's been telling me about the attic. Like you, I said it needed a long think.' With that, he was out of the door, having given them some slippery elm tincture for 'her highness' and advising that wrapping her chest in goose grease and brown paper would draw the mucous.

He finished with, 'Good luck with that. I'd rather try it with a grizzly bear. Call me at any time, night or day, do you hear me?' His voice was fierce, his look even more so. 'Can't have her flouncing off to sit on a cloud and look down on us all; we'd not have a moment's peace.'

They were about to take up a few drops of tincture in water when there was another knock on the door. Phyllie shot a look at a clock. It was nine o'clock, so who was visiting, when they'd rather be in bed nursing a hangover? She wasn't surprised to see Joe stick his head round the door. 'I'm not coming in, just checking on the lad, and the old 'un. Coughing like an old steam train, I spect.'

'I think you could say that.'

'And you? Bit like Piccadilly Circus for you. Tired?' He was inching through the door, and stood on the mat in his boots. They were muddy, but he came no further.

'Pleased to have Jake back, in all senses of the word, and worried about Miss F. I couldn't bear it if anything happened to her.'

Joe smiled. 'She's a tough old bat, and you and me, Phyllie, won't let anything happen to her. Never you fear, I'll sit with her in the day, cos you'll need to be back at school until she's well.

You all right to do that? Or you too tired with the bump an' all? I'm sure the ladies of the WI will arrange a rota for the nights.'

Phyllie just nodded. She'd never be too tired ever again. She had Jake back, and Miss F would recover, or she'd want to know the reason why. She'd rebuild the school, if it would make the woman better. She took up the medicine and a couple of aspirin and floated the idea of a chest poultice. It was sunk almost the moment it had left Phyllie's lips. Miss F scowled at the aspirin, downed them, and handed back the glass to Phyllie. 'It's the school that's the problem.'

Phyllie shook her head. 'I have enough people telling me it's not, and I agree. I'll go in.' She felt the smile that played on Miss F's lips had more than a satisfied edge to it. She'd been played, and she knew it, but actually Miss F was really poorly. That night she sat with her as she grew worse, and Jake did too, bundled up in the quilt. Dr Nicholls came the next day, and every day for almost a week. Phyllie barely left her side.

Joe slipped in every day, tiptoeing up the stairs in socks that needed darning. 'You need a good woman,' Phyllie whispered as they stood together at the end of Miss F's bed, watching her battle for breath.

'I don't know any,' Joe replied. They both laughed, feeling the frost on the air because Miss F insisted that the window should be open to let the germs escape. Joe stayed on, while Phyllie slept for two hours every afternoon.

A few days before the start of term, Miss F allowed Phyllie to wrap her chest in brown paper, comfrey, mustard and goose grease. 'Damned nonsense but worth a bash,' she had muttered before falling into a fretful sleep.

There was no obvious improvement in the morning, but she was not worse, and that was, in itself, a cause for relief. As Phyllie sat by the bed, preparing lessons for school, she heard Joe on the stairs. He entered, and took the wicker chair beside her. They heard a scraping above them. Joe raised his eyebrows, 'Still at it, is 'e?'

Phyllie smiled. 'Yes, he's determined. He's had no nightmares, no after effects, just a determination to make life better, and today, Dan is helping, so I've left them to it. It was a good idea of Percy Pringle's to give Ron work on the farm as a punishment for his involvement. It means Jake's had to work alongside him in the stables and there have been no grumbles. What's more, Jake seems to have wangled himself into Andy's good books and got him to heave the big stuff around or out of the attic. I'm sending some of it to my brother. He might find it useful for those who've been bombed.'

She kept her eyes on Miss F, and Joe did the same. 'You heard from your mother, have you?'

'No, but Jake's setting me a good example, Joe. I realised a while ago that my family is here, not there, not any more, and I have learned to understand and accept that.'

'And Sammy?'

'Ah, Sammy; I'll always love him, always. He's part of me, especially now.' She patted Charlie. 'But everyone is right. It's become a little easier, the sun comes out more often, I even laugh.

Sometimes I think I shouldn't, because I miss him so much, but I live, go on, am grateful that Jake is safe, and Miss F is improving. That is the greatest gift.'

There was a crash from above. Dan called, 'Ouch, that was my foot.'

Joe muttered, 'If you're all agreed, I reckon that Ron should help 'em up there. If you haven't agreed, really agreed, then put a stop to it, because Ron's life ain't a game.' He leaned on the bedstead, fingering his cigarette, his cap on the back of his head. 'You'll have your hands full, lass, with Charlie, and maybe teaching too, and the two lads, especially if this old lass pops her clogs.'

He grinned, winked at Phyllie and they both waited. Miss F piped up, 'I'm not dead and I'm not deaf, and I'm agreed, and will help Phyllie, of course I will. A child's life is precious and should be nurtured. She might want to marry, and who'd want someone with three children, that's what she needs to think about. But I'll keep Ron on if there's a problem. He's got a good core.'

She fell asleep again, her mouth open, her chest rattling.

Married? Phyllie thought. I was to marry Sammy, no one else. She walked round the bed and felt Miss F's forehead with the back of her hand. Hot, but not roaring. She pulled a face. 'She's turned the corner, I reckon,' she whispered to Joe. *Married indeed.* She looked at Joe's face as he reached forward and held Miss F's hand. Phyllie watched as Miss F's fingers tightened around his. Married? Any day now, she reckoned, but not her. She half laughed, and left.

Over lunch she talked to Jake, and Dan, who was staying for the day. 'So, we've reached the decision point. Jake, you really need to think very seriously if Ron is to live with us. You would have to share the friendship you have with Dan. You never know what will happen in London, Mrs Cummins could be killed; and Ron would be with us for ever...'

Dan was poking the sprouts that Phyllie had picked this morning, from the bottom of the garden. He tucked them neatly beneath his knife and fork, saying, 'Yes, he could. Think of the six in our class who have gone to live with their aunties, after their mums were killed by bombs. Or his dad could be killed. He's in the desert and the Germans are doing well there, aren't they, Miss Phyllie?'

She and Jake exchanged a glance. Phyllie nodded gravely, and Jake smiled approval as she said, 'Indeed, Mr Cummins is away fighting. War is a messy business, Dan, as are uneaten sprouts, which poke out either side of a knife. Eat two of them, and I'll let you off the rest. But I still haven't had your answer, Jake. You have an opt-out, because Jack Thompson has found a family in Swanwick who would take Ron.'

Jake watched aghast as Dan stuffed both sprouts into his mouth and chewed, almost retching. Absorbed in the sight, he muttered, 'Yes, yes, I keep saying he should come. The horses like him, Phyllie, and they only like good people so something in him has changed. He lets me show him how to do things, and he never would have before.

378

Francois doesn't growl any more either.' He reached down and stroked his dog. Phyllie hid her grin. It seemed that animals were to be the arbiters of Ron's fate.

'Very well.' Phyllie was watching as Dan's bulging cheeks slowly resumed their normal shape, and with a final swallow, he was back to normal.

'I don't like sprouts,' he muttered.

'I think we gathered that. I will bear it in mind for the next time you're here, but not tomorrow, because you will be in church, and we'll be on our ramble.'

Jake was playing with the salt and pepper, and he shrugged. 'No, I think I'll go to morning service. Mr Jack tells me he always reads a psalm, and they're Old Testament, and the church is a nice place, and Ron is doing a solo in the choir. He told me Mr Jack said he could have a decent pair of gumboots if he joined, so he did. I'll see him with that white frilly thing round his neck and it'll make me laugh.'

School opened on the Tuesday, and as the children sang the hymn 'God Speed the Plough', which was traditionally sung to celebrate winter farm work, Phyllie stood in Miss F's place and felt yet again that she truly was home. There was no money with which to pay her, of course, or her cover would be blown. It didn't matter, she had the interest from the shares, and the rent from the cottage, and felt truly blessed in the man she had loved and who had provided for her and their child. As the children ended the hymn she realised just what she had thought. *Had* loved? No, still loved, and always would.

At lunch break she slipped home, with Jake, to check on Miss F. The WI did the mornings, and prepared lunch, while Joe babysat in the afternoon. They hurried upstairs, hearing voices. Sitting around the bed were Andy, Joe and Mrs Symes, and of course, Francois, who had taken root on the rug by her bed. Miss F was picking at a bacon and egg pie. She looked pale.

Andy leapt to his feet. 'We only came ten minutes ago.' He looked like a naughty schoolboy.

Joe held up his hand. 'Brought the invalid some extra milk, put hairs on her chest, it will, underneath the poultice.'

Miss F said, 'That is a vision I'd rather not contemplate. They're just leaving; you too, Symes. I need my sleep.'

They all trooped down behind Phyllie, with Jake bringing up the rear, as though they were herding the visitors, which in a way they were. Joe stayed behind in the kitchen for a moment. 'I'll be back in an hour, to guard her majesty,' he said. 'Tell her I'll be downstairs, so's not to bother her unless she needs something. But Ron?' he muttered, an eye on the back door, in case Mrs Symes had suddenly developed extraordinary hearing.

'Jake and I are seeing him this evening, and the decision will be his, though there will be house rules.'

Joe's face split in a smile. 'That'll please her upstairs; so you best nip up and let her know. I gather Mrs Speedie is coming this afternoon to prepare tea, which is when I'll nip off. They're a good lot, and don't mither on too long. You've a bit more colour in your cheeks too, girl. Shame you have to keep it quiet that you're back at school; darned authorities.'

There was a knock on the door, and this time it was Andy who stuck his head round, when she had expected it to be Dr Nicholls. 'Come on, Dad, let the girl spend some time with Miss F, she's got a school to run now.' He grinned at Phyllie and she saw the likeness to Joe for the first time. It was in the way the skin crinkled round their eyes when they smiled. Andy was smiling much more, too.

Miss F was dozing, as Jake and Francois sat by her bed. Jake watched Miss F, and Francois watched Jake. Phyllie sat alongside the boy and pondered Francois' reaction to Ron full-time. Well, it would have to work out, and that was that.

After school, Phyllie made the offer in the kitchen of Myrtle Cottage, sitting around the table over mugs of cocoa. Ron coloured, looked at his hands tightly clasped around his mug for a long time, but said nothing.

Jake murmured, 'We've started clearing your room, me and Dan. You can help after school tomorrow if you like, then you can decide where you want your bed. Mr Andy lifted the heavy stuff for us.'

'How long will I be able to stay?' Ron asked. His mousy hair was long, and flopped in his eyes. He was pale and drawn.

Phyllie pushed the plate of honey biscuits towards him. 'For as long as you like, Ron. We have rules, of course, but we want you here. You helped Jake, and that cancels out anything else.'

381

There was silence, except for the ticking of the clock. Ron said, 'Yes please. I'll try to be good.' His smile brought his face alive.

The next evening Andy and Joe gave both boys time off from the horses for 'more important work'. Dan met them in the kitchen as Phyllie prepared an egg custard for Miss F, with eggs from Atticus, who was one of the two hens Mr Milford had given them, along with a hen house. All three boys pounded upstairs and scraped furniture across the floorboards, until Miss F banged the walking stick that Joe had given her to attract attention, Phyllie hared up the attic stairs, as fast as Charlie would allow, suggesting that they lifted things, and making a mental note on the way down to deal with Joe, and his walking stick, in the fullness of time.

There was already a bed in the attic, and the mattress had been well wrapped and was adequate. Over the next few days the WI members brought various pieces of linen. The next Saturday, on the day Ron moved in, they put together the final touches. Ron found a spare oil lamp in a cupboard up there and this was placed on the bedside table. At the windows Phyllie hung blackout blinds, although Jake, Dan and Ron called, together, 'Miss F said not to stretch.'

'Don't tell her, then,' Phyllie puffed. 'Now for the rug.' She followed them downstairs, to find the rug that Andy had brought, along with some vegetables. He had left it in the front room, which was never ever used.

She followed the boys in, and they hesitated at the darkness caused by the drawn curtains. There was a smell of old age, gloomy heavy wallpaper, the equally heavy furniture. 'Blimey, miss,' whispered Ron, 'we could get a fair whack for this.'

'Ron.' Her tone was thick with warning.

He turned. 'I didn't mean nothing. Honest I didn't.'

She thought she believed him, but saw that Jake and Dan were wondering too. Yes, she thought to herself, it will take time. She smiled. 'Let's just take the rug, and leave the room as it is. Miss F will know when she wants to do something with it, if ever. That's the time to call on your ideas, eh, Ron?'

'It's a deal.' He was pulling the rolled-up rug onto his shoulder, and turned, almost knocking an ugly dog off the sideboard. Jake grabbed the dog, while Dan caught the end of the rug. After supper and when the boys were in their respective beds, she kissed Ron on the forehead. He flinched because it was something totally foreign to him. She just smiled.

She helped Miss F downstairs for the first time later that evening, to listen to the news on the wireless. Miss F felt dizzy, but that was only to be expected, and the poultice slipped as she eased herself into her chair. 'There, that's better.' She changed her mind as they heard of the Japanese advances in South East Asia, the continued bombing of British cities

'Switch it off, Phyllie dear. I will fight them on the beaches when my cold is better, but not now. The war will have to wait.'

They both laughed quietly. 'How will it go, do you think?'

Miss F raised her eyes to the ceiling. 'Our grubby angels, I suppose you mean?' Phyllie shifted to get comfortable. Charlie was kicking. 'I feel it will be good for them both,' Miss F went on. 'A bit of rough will toughen Jake, and a bit of smooth will soften Ron. Incidentally, I heard what was said about my furniture. He's right, you know. Why on earth am I hanging onto it all? It was Mother's, you know. She had me – and no husband – and the village closed ranks, and I had no idea until I was about to be married, during the Great War. She thought I'd be an old maid, but I was choosy and waited until I was thirty for Robert. It was then she felt I should know, and my husband-to-be as well. Robert couldn't have given a toss, bless him. He was never found and is still out there, like your Sammy; neither with a grave. Not one that we can visit, anyway, but we don't need that, do we? They're always here.' She touched her chest.

Phyllie asked, 'Tucked inside your poultice?'

They laughed together. 'Exactly. The difference is that I didn't have a Charlie, but I have a Ron and a Jake, to share with you, and soon a Charlie. But, of course, you will marry again, and then you will take your brood, and I will be a granny, visiting. When that day comes, you will go with a light heart. Now help me up, I've had quite enough for one day, though you'll be pleased to hear I'm on the way to being fighting fit.'

'Oh Lordy,' Phyllie muttered, easing herself up, and going to the aid of Miss F who said, 'I heard that.'

Together they made their way upstairs.

Chapter Twenty-One

Sunday 29 March 1942, Little Mitherton

The school children were on a rota to feed the lambs but Phyllie lay in her bed, while the boys were in the kitchen, supposedly doing homework. Miss F informed her that in fact they were pacing like a pair of worried fathers. Phyllie couldn't give a damn who was pacing where, she just wanted this over. Another longer pain came, and the midwife called, 'Breathe.' Phyllie feared she would slap the woman if she said it again. It had been hours, and she was tired. At last the pain faded, but almost immediately there came another, and she felt she must push.

'Don't push, not yet.' Good grief, the woman was a monster; it was like trying to stop a runaway train.

'I must.'

'You must not.'

She didn't.

'Pant, don't push.'

Phyllie groaned, sweat pouring from her. Miss F patted her shoulder. 'It will be all right, it's all perfectly natural. Think of those lambs, they drop like a cake mixture off a spoon, no trouble at all.'

Phyllie stared at her. 'Shut up,' she shouted, because she'd slap her too. What did she mean, no trouble at all, when she was being torn apart? Why hadn't anyone warned her? She gasped out the question.

'Don't be silly, dear,' the midwife told her, 'you'd never have believed us.'

Here was another pain, and she had to push. The midwife was shouting, 'Yes, push, come on, Phyllie. Push.'

Why didn't she make up her ruddy mind? But this thought faded, as the pain grew and became like a huge wave, and there was only that, and the pushing, and if any man came anywhere near her ever again, she'd cut it off, too bloody right she would. The push faded, the pain too. She wept. 'I can't, I'm too tired.'

'Nonsense, it's only been twenty-four hours.' It was Dr Nicholls, entering. He had his bicycle clips on, of course.

Miss F said, 'If you're coming anywhere near her with those filthy hands you can think again. Go and wash this minute.'

'Just observing, dear lady.'

Phyllie looked wildly from one to another. The pain and the push began again, and she heard Dr Nicholls tell Miss F that Joe and Andy had arrived. Oh God, they should sell tickets. She groaned, and suddenly saw Sammy, just as he had been on the platform, his face, his smile, and she felt his kiss, and now she cried because he should be here to see Charlie. He should be here. For the next twenty minutes she pushed and groaned and wept, and hated herself for making a fuss, but when Dr Nicholls took her hand with his freshly washed one, she groaned, 'Sammy should be here.'

He said, 'I know, my dear child, but we're all here to stand in for him.' It was almost enough.

Charlotte was born at three twenty-three on 29 March 1942, six weeks or so after Japan had taken Singapore, though a British convoy had broken through the blockade around Malta and delivered supplies. There would have been submarines there. God keep them safe, she thought, as she held her daughter in her arms, a daughter who even at this early age looked very like her father. She gazed through the window and up at the sky. It was a fresh blue, and a bird flew across her field of vision.

The midwife left, and Dr Nicholls also. Miss F fled the room for a moment, to bring up the boys. Jake and Ron stood in the doorway, their eyes big.

Phyllie smiled. 'Come in, say hello to your sister.'

Their socks were down round their ankles. Had they lost their garters again? Their knees were grubby, and bits of straw were tangled in their hair. Jake's hair was so dark, and Ron's a light chestnut and no longer looked mousy. Charlotte's was dark, just as Sammy's had been. They tiptoed across in their plimsolls, and looked down. Ron said, 'Ain't she small, Miss Phyllie?'

'She's red,' Jake added. 'And look at her little hands.' He held his finger against hers. 'See, she's tiny.' Her fingers unfurled and gripped his. The boys looked at one another, grinning. 'She's strong.'

Miss F stood behind them, smiling as though her face would split in two. 'They say that they can hang from your fingers, and take the weight, even when they are a few hours old. They're like little monkeys.'

Ron frowned. 'She ain't like a monkey; she's pretty. I reckon your Sammy would be right pleased if he could see her, don't you, Miss Phyllie? I wonder if she'll play table tennis. I reckon he'd have been good, with me teaching him.'

Phyllie leaned forward and stroked first Ron's cheek and then Jake's. 'I think he'd be really pleased if he could see my family, including Miss F, and you know what, I think he can. And Isaac, too. I just feel it.' That lump was back in her throat, her voice sounded strange. Oh, Sammy.

Charlotte sneezed and released Jake. The boys nodded. Jake said, 'Mr Andy was downstairs. He was really worried, and Joe had to tell him to sit down or he'd drive him right bloody mad and wear the flagstones out.'

Miss F was shooing them out now, saying, 'Phyllie needs some rest.'

As Ron was leaving the room he said, 'Mr Andy left when he heard you were all right and the baby was too. Joe wanted him to stay, but he said he had to look after the sheep, and besides, you wouldn't want a lot of people poking their noses in.'

Jake said from the landing, 'I said that Mr Andy wasn't people, but he still went. He left you some flowers, so he did. Joe put them in a jam jar. They look funny, just stuck in that...'

His voice faded as Miss F herded them downstairs, and Phyllie heard her say, 'Phyllie will be really tired for a while, but you can talk to her again soon.'

It was Joe next. He didn't come in but stood in the doorway, his cap off for once. He was twisting it in his hands. 'You've got a grand tiddlin there, lass.'

She eased herself on the heaped pillows. 'Don't stand there, come and say hello to Charlotte.'

He tiptoed across, his socks still full of holes. Someone needed to get out a darning needle, she thought, and soon. When were the pair of them going to get their act together? He peered down. 'Reckon she's a belter. Reckon your Sammy'll be right pleased, cos he'll know, lass.'

Her eyes blurred. 'I hope so, I feel he will, but sometimes I forget his face, Joe. I can hear his voice, but I forget his face.'

Joe reached out and touched Charlotte's cheek. 'Their skin is always so smooth. With our Andy I couldn't feel his skin, it was so bloody smooth.' She thought he hadn't heard what she had said, but now he focused on her, not the baby. 'It's to make room for the rest of your life. That's not to say you'll forget him, no, not at all, and you'll never stop loving him, but there'll be room for others. It'll be different, but there'll be room. You see, Phyllie...' He hesitated.

She prompted him, 'Go on.'

He tiptoed to the window now, looking out over the fields behind them, as though he was seeing them for the first time. Well, he probably was, from this bedroom. 'You see, I was thinking about our old bag.' He stopped as the stairs creaked and Miss F called, 'Time up, Joe. The girl needs her sleep, they both do. Put Charlotte in her basket,

389

for Phyllie, and come on down, at once.'

Joe sighed, and came to Phyllie. 'God has spoken.' He scooped Charlotte from her arms. 'Don't you be fretting, lass, I've picked up so many young 'uns, she's safe with me.'

Phyllie said, 'But the others were animals, Joe.' He ignored her, and placed Charlie into the bassinette that stood on a stand by the bed. It was as though he was born to it. 'Farmers are good with tiddlins; you just remember that, and forget any other nonsense I talk.'

He fled from the room; yes, that was the only way of describing it. Phyllie looked down at Charlotte. 'Do you think he'll ever actually ask her, Charlotte, or are we going to have to do something about it ourselves?'

Mrs Otis and Miss F managed together until Phyllie was back on her feet, then Phyllie took Charlotte in with her, snug in her pram in the staff room, with Francois on guard. The three women worked well together and all the while the secret had to be kept or the authorities would be round. Every weekend, and often in the evening, she would push the pram, which used to be Andy's, to the farm to perform her duty at the old barn. April turned to May, by which time the hawthorn was a white cloud, and the wheat was growing, the oats too. The children worked with the Scouts and Guides to earth up the potatoes, and Joe scared off the official who dared to suggest another try with the land girls. As these months went by Ron, Jake and Dan grew thick as thieves, and the horses had never gleamed as they now did. Dan had grown to enjoy them too, with not a sign of his hives. Even Charlotte was feeding every four hours, and sleeping contentedly.

Life had achieved a pattern, and all was calm.

Chapter Twenty-Two

June 1942, Little Mitherton

Miss F and Phyllie stayed glued to the *News at Nine*, the boys chatted together, up in the attic, into which Jake had moved his bed to be with Ron. Francois slept on the rug between them. The good news was that the blitz over British cities had eased, along with the pulverising of Malta from the air, but now they heard the calm voice of the BBC newsreader explaining that Rommel was still pushing the allies back in the Libyan desert, which Ron worried about, sure his father was in danger.

Phyllie lifted Charlie onto her shoulder, and rubbed her back, hoping that all the wind escaped and she would settle better than she had last night. 'We can either tell him the truth – that his father is safe and it has all been a lie – or share his concern and leave the illusion in place.'

Miss F had decided in the early days of her recovery that in order to listen to the nine o'clock news she needed a good 'belt' of Joe's homemade elderberry wine. She sipped thoughtfully. 'For illusion, read lie, but it must be the "comfort" option, and Joe agrees.'

Charlie burped. 'Quite, Charlie.' Phyllie laughed. 'There does seem to be a great deal of "Joe says" or "Joe agrees" these days. Well, of course I totally agree too, and when you think about it, Miss F, it's too early to upset the apple cart again, when Ron's settling into the boy he always could be. Andy thinks so too, though I only say that because he has more to do with them than either of us in many ways. They basically *live* there after school, and are becoming real horsemen. They even handled the hay carts. Weren't they marvellous, Miss F?' Phyllie felt again the flush of pride that she had experienced when Jake and Ron had each driven a cart into the field as a surprise two weeks ago. She added, 'They've really missed him while he's been away having a more advanced hook fitted. That one he got from the local place just didn't fit properly, did it?'

Charlie burped again. Miss F raised her glass to the baby. 'My thoughts entirely, Charlie; Andy says, eh? But yes, the boys were marvellous. So, we're agreed, we say nothing. When is Andy back?'

'Perhaps tomorrow, apparently he promised the boys that he'd try to make it for sports day.'

Miss F switched off the wireless, and settled down to the timetable of the school sports day that would take place tomorrow, rain or shine. Phyllie kissed her daughter, and heaved herself up from the sofa, saying, 'Time for the pair of us to get some sleep, before two o'clock comes and it's the usual wake-up call.'

She held Charlie out for Miss F's hug and kiss, before reclaiming her daughter and heading for the door. It was then Miss F said, 'Remember that the ghastly Grimes might turn up, complete with homburg. One of the children is quite likely to mention that you are teaching, though the parents are determined to do a flanking movement every time he gets within speaking range.'

The day dawned dry and warm. The sky was blue, the birds were noisy and busy, and in the field adjoining the mown meadow the adolescent lambs clipped the grass. Soon they would be washed, ready for shearing. The last two evenings the older children had been out marking up the field for the races. The women of the village had donated clothes for the dressing-up relay race, and by eleven o'clock, were out in support. The children had made paper Union Jacks, and stuck them onto sticks, and those not participating in a particular race would line the track, and cheer on the others.

Younger unmarried women between the ages of twenty and thirty were liable for call-up now, so the supporters were mums, or men and women of a certain age. Some mothers had managed to come down from London for the day, or even to stay over. Ron's mother could not come, yet again, but he seemed untroubled and he, Jake and Dan, along with the rest of the class, rushed around, organising the piles of clothing at either end of the track. They then checked the precious hard-boiled eggs for the egg and spoon race. Phyllie 'unofficially' organised the children, with the help of Miss F, Mrs Otis and Mrs Whitehead, who had decided that retirement didn't suit, and had been taken back on by Mr Grimes as an occasional teacher. Mrs Symes, Mrs Speedie and Miss Deacon had taken a break from jam making for the day, to prepare lunch.

There was no Bryan at sports day. He had gone to a distant aunt, and his family had followed soon after. Eddie was in a borstal where the discipline would do him a great deal of good, Constable Pringle had informed them grimly.

Joe stood near the starting line with Phyllie and Francois, guarding Charlie's pram. At eleven thirty Andy arrived, his shirtsleeves rolled up, his new hook gleaming, and Phyllie was relieved to see him laughing as she said to Joe, 'Look, he's made it, and his sleeves are rolled up. That's new.'

'Aye, he's getting there,' Joe murmured, waggling his fingers at Charlotte.

Joe and Phyllie watched Miss F ticking off the names for the first race, and lining them up. Joe added, 'Though it seems to me that them boys of yours 'ave done him as much good as he has done them. Mark you, getting away can make a difference. I reckon being at the unit for a bit'll have put the cap on getting his bonce around things. Or perhaps 'e'll have got his arms around a pretty nurse, which'll do 'im a sight more good.'

Phyllie took the clipboard Miss F had just brought, shouting as only she could, 'Phyllie, take over, there's a good girl. I can see that ghastly little man Grimes traipsing across the field. Avoid him, at all costs. I'm off to head him away from all of this.'

Phyllie saw him now, wearing the same suit and hat. She left Joe with Francois and Charlie, and

394

hurried towards the children gathered in their class groups at the side of the track. Some were sitting cross-legged on the rugs, others were chatting in groups, their shorts and white tops pristine; a day in a hay meadow would soon put paid to that. She called out the names for the race; the children collected their spoons while Ron, Jake and Dan, with another two girls from their class, laid the hard-boiled eggs in the spoons. She grinned as she heard them warn, 'Try not to drop them; Mrs Symes wants them for sandwiches. If you do drop them, you might get Miss F's finger.' The look of horror on the children's faces told the story.

Phyllie then melted into the group of chattering women lining up alongside the track. She said, 'Any minute now we'll have them teetering along, scared to death in case they drop the egg. Loud cheers, ladies, please.'

They laughed, but one said, looking over Phyllie's shoulder, shading her eyes against the sun, 'Watch Mr Grimes, he has a nose like a beagle. He's heading this way.'

Phyllie moved swiftly through the women, who closed ranks behind her, and found herself next to Andy who had taken over Francois and the pram from Joe, and was rocking it. She felt ridiculously pleased to see him. 'Has she been crying? I'm so sorry, Andy.'

He said, 'Hello to you too, Phyllie. Yes, I had a good time, and my hook is much more comfortable now, thank you.'

She flushed. 'I'm sorry, I'm just trying to avoid the wretched Mr Grimes.'

He laughed. 'It's not a problem.' She tucked herself next to him, on the side away from Grimes, watching Charlie sleeping, but peering round Andy frequently. Mr Grimes was being successfully rounded up by Miss F and led firmly to the starting line where the WI committee surrounded him, although corralled him might be a better description. 'It's ridiculous that I can't be in evidence and cheer on the children in case he puts two and two together.'

'You don't have to be down there, Phyllie. They can see you here, and for all that man knows we're parents cheering on our children. Nice dress you're wearing.'

'Mrs Symes made it from some old cotton curtains. I should be draped in a window somewhere.'

'Roses become you, or so someone once sang, didn't they?'

She looked down at the big pink cabbage roses that festooned her. They were summery and cheerful. Children appreciated cheerful, and so did adults, it seemed from the smile on Andy's face. She grinned back. Had he missed her, as she realised she had missed him? She said, 'You once mentioned that we seemed like the only young people in the village, and today, I think you're quite right.' She crossed her arms, and laughed, in tune with him. 'Was it really worth it, were they kind to you?' What did she mean by that? Their arms touched, she stayed put.

He rocked the pram again as the cheering for the egg and spoon race startled Charlie. 'Very very kind, and yes, the hook is lighter, and the curve not so extreme. It makes it easier.'

Francois was looking from the noise of the cheering to her. 'Go on, then, daft dog. Go and find Jake,' she said. Very kind? What did that mean? She clapped. 'Well done, Sandra.'

Her class collected up the eggs and spoons for the next heat, running down the lanes to the starting line. Mrs Symes and Jack Thompson collected up the finishing tape. 'Look at the boys,' Andy said, pointing while he used the hook to rock the pram. 'Thick as thieves.'

She nudged him. 'Please don't say that.'

Andy roared, and Charlie threw her arms open, woke, stared, then rammed her fist in her mouth and slept again. 'Phew, that was a close one,' he said.

'I take my life four hours at a time.' Phyllie was watching the line-up, and saw her two boys and Dan doing Mrs Otis's bidding with Francois at their heels. 'Who would have thought it?' she murmured. 'You've done a wonderful job with them, Andy. What do you mean "very very kind", by the way?'

She shut her mouth but it was too late. He looked down at her. 'I'll answer the first one, and then the second. The boys are not just my doing. The whole village has shared in the care of these two lads, but you and Miss F have borne the brunt. The second answer: the doctor was kind; he took more time than was strictly necessary, I would say, and Sister Newton took great care of me. Her home is not too far from here, and when she next comes home, she will probably visit. I said we might well send her back with eggs. Not these, though.' He nodded towards the egg and spoon race, which was just coming to an end.

They clapped.

'Oh,' Phyllie said, feeling as though the day was flat, but only momentarily because Sandra rushed up. 'I'm in the final, miss.'

Phyllie crouched down. 'You ran so fast. I think we'll be able to put your name up on the board as the winner of the first heat, and who knows, run like the wind and we might have you as the all-round winner.'

Sandra pulled at her white ankle socks, which were now smeared with grass stains. 'Thank you, miss.' She rushed back to the group that clustered around Miss F. But if Miss F was there, alone, where was Mr Grimes? She peered round Andy again, and there he was, just a pace or two away, waving as though he was flagging her down. She gripped Andy's arm. He detached himself, and slipped his arm around her instead, pulling her close. 'Mr Grimes, I believe,' he called. 'Are you enjoying sports day?'

Mr Grimes didn't smile back, but looked only at Phyllie. '*Miss* Saunders, we've met before, have we not?'

'Yes, indeed we have, as you well know.'

'And this is the cause of all the problems, is it?' He peered into the pram.

'She's not an it and certainly not a problem; she's a delight,' Andy said, before Phyllie could speak.

Mr Grimes nodded. 'Yes, children are very precious, of course.' His glasses were black-framed, and she couldn't remember if he'd been wearing any last time. He continued, 'Which is why we have to keep an eye on the common good.'

He seemed embarrassed, and Phyllie found herself feeling sorry for him. After all, she was the pariah; an unmarried mother and therefore a disgrace. In the warmth of this village, and amongst these people, she had forgotten the real world. She could find no words.

Mr Grimes looked from one to another, and then at Phyllie's hand. 'I see you are engaged?' He was pointing to Sammy's ring.

She said, 'It's Sammy's, Charlie's father. He's dead.'

Mr Grimes shook his head. 'Oh no I think not. I think this engagement, for all that anyone knows or would feel they must report, is current, do you not agree?' He looked from Phyllie to Andy, then cast his hand around in an expansive gesture. 'Amazingly, Miss Saunders, one is given ears with which to hear and one does listen. The common good is always at the forefront where children are concerned, as I have just said, and one does not want more than one in a borstal, does one? One wants children to continue to be reclaimed, especially in a world in which tomorrow is uncertain, and our culture threatened. Who knows where the jackboot will tread next?'

Phyllie couldn't look at Andy, not after what Mr Grimes had said, but she stole a glance all the same and he smiled down at her. Who knew what the future would bring?

The children were cheering the next race. Mr Grimes turned to watch, but only for a moment. He continued, looking closely at Phyllie, 'Foundations have to be built to withstand whatever might come. I think good work is being carried out here at Little Mitherton School, don't you? I gather that Mrs Whitehead is only part-time, and I wonder if you would be prepared to be her "other half", officially.' He tilted his hat at them, as Phyllie nodded.

'I'd love that.'

'Do you know, I think she might not continue for too long, so you might consider full-time in due course?' Phyllie nodded again. Mr Grimes smiled. 'I fear I won't have time to stay for sandwiches but before I leave, may I wish you both the very greatest happiness possible, for you and your expanding family.' His gimlet eyes were on Ron and Jake who were running towards them.

Ron was shouting, 'We're in the final, Phyllie.'

And Jake yelled, 'Andy, Andy, you're back in time. I knew you would be.'

Chapter Twenty-Three

In July 1942 Andy invited Phyllie to walk in the woods as he had heard a nightingale. She was welcome to bring Charlie, he said, but Miss F insisted on babysitting. They walked the woods for two hours on a balmy evening, but heard no nightingale. It didn't matter. What mattered was that they talked of the beauty of the evening, the development of the boys, the, plans for Charlie's christening in August.

400

'Will you ask your mother and brother?' he asked carefully.

She smiled. 'I'll ask but they're probably busy. I'll also ask Mr and Mrs Williams. They have a right to be there.'

The village came to the christening. Her mother and brother could not: too busy, her mother had said on the telephone. 'Forgive us, but you can imagine how turbulent it is here. So many in jeopardy and crisis.'

'Indeed,' Phyllie had said. 'We will think of you.'

Her mother had sounded surprised. 'How nice. And how is ... er?'

'Charlotte, or Charlie as we call her.'

'Phyllis, I remembered her name. I just wasn't sure which to call her. You received our letter, with some money after her birth?'

'Thank you. I have bought nappies, which are so hard to find. I did write. And now I have to go. I have to write to Sammy's parents. Perhaps we will see you soon.'

'That would be nice,' her mother had said.

Phyllie had no idea if she meant it, but it didn't matter.

In August Jack Thompson christened Charlotte Williams with Mr and Mrs Williams in the front pew, and the godparents in attendance. Miss F was a godmother. Miss Deacon and Mrs Speedie had tossed a coin to be the second, and it was heads. So it was Mrs Speedie. The godfather was Andy. Miss F had suggested it because Phyllie would never be able to choose between Ron and Jake. She had explained the situation to Andy, who had taken her hand and said as they stood outside the old barn, 'I would rather it was because you trusted me to love and support your daughter.' He had kissed her then. He was not Sammy, but it was as lovely. She had kissed him back, and then again.

In September they were a couple, but only after they'd asked Jake and Ron how they would feel if they walked out together. The two boys had laughed. 'We thought you would, but you've taken long enough. Andy is like a dad to us, like a dad to Charlie,' Jake had said. 'Sammy will like to think that Charlie is looked after by him. He'll know you haven't forgotten him, because I can see you haven't.'

Ron said, as he polished Desmond's bridle, 'I think Sammy will like Andy to look after you. And I think that once you are married, Miss F and Joe will get hitched too. We think, don't we, Jake, that they're waiting to see you happy before they make a move. They love you, Phyllie.'

The boys stopped work and nodded to one another. Phyllie said, 'He hasn't asked me to marry him.'

Jake shook his head. 'Oh, Phyllie, he's waiting to get us on side and then he will.'

In October he did. She accepted, and felt completely happy, with his arms around her.

In December, just before Christmas, Jack performed the wedding service for Phyllie and Andy, with Ron singing the solo. Joe gave her away, in spite of the fact that her brother and mother had arrived unexpectedly, with half an hour to spare, clearly expecting Father Francis to fulfil this role.

Instead, they had been firmly led by Jake, acting as usher, to the front pew, on the bride's side. They joined Sammy's parents, who had written a fulsome acceptance and had brought linen with them as a gift. Mrs Saunders brought a hat for Phyllie to wear, as she was only wearing a suit. Phyllie wore it for half an hour, but it didn't look right, and spoilt the photographs, Mrs Williams said, who had no idea Mrs Saunders had brought it.

In the second pew on the bride's side, sat Phyllie's real family: Miss F, Charlie, Jake and Ron, with Dan alongside, and Miss Deacon, Mrs Symes and Mrs Speedie. Joe led the groom's contingent, which comprised an aunt and uncle, a million cousins and half the village. The other half of the village sat on Phyllie's side. Ron's solo, 'O for the Wings of a Dove', brought tears to the eyes of more than one person. As she left the church Phyllie threw the bouquet of late-winter roses, and myrtle for remembrance. Joe caught it and tossed it to Miss F. The three boys nudged one another and laughed.

Her mother and brother had asked to be booked into a guesthouse in town. At their reception in the village hall, and catered for by the WI, she explained to her mother that a taxi would call for them at the end of the reception to transfer them to their accommodation. Her mother, wearing a brown felt hat, and looking old and tired, said, 'Well, at least you have finally married, and to a respectable young man. I presume you will stop teaching now that you do not need the money?' Father Francis winced at his mother's side, but said nothing.

Phyllie jiggled Charlie, who was restless, while she tried to think of a reply, but she had no need, for Andy gripped her hand, and said, 'Sammy was a fine young man who loved and provided handsomely for your daughter. He sacrificed his life for his country, and if either of you wish to continue to see us, then you will acknowledge that and never disparage him in front of us or his daughter Charlie again. We value your presence in our family, so I do hope that you feel you can accept what I say, on behalf of Phyllie and myself. Phyllie has opted to continue working. Even if it is for only three days a week. She is the most wonderful teacher, and loved by her pupils.'

Phyllie squeezed his hand, even harder than he was gripping hers. It was not how Sammy would have said it, but it was *what* he would have said. She still wore Sammy's engagement ring, but her wedding ring was Andy's. She loved them both, but differently and always would.

After the chicken casserole, the speeches were delivered, short and sweet, which Joe said would be almost the only thing that was sweet this afternoon, to a roar of laughter. Later, the cardboard wedding cake was lifted from around the small sponge cake, which was rather dry, but at least it was a cake in these times of increased rationing. As the fiddlers grouped together and began to play, Phyllie and Andy danced the first waltz together, and his arms were strong around her. She held his hook, feeling his calloused hand on her back.

Sister Newton was there, and had turned out to be fifty and the motherly type, but Andy said he had wanted to spark a reaction.

When the waltz was almost over, Miss F and Joe joined them on the floor. Miss F had whispered as she had caught Joe's bouquet that she and Joe would be following them down the aisle. Consequently, the whole village had heard the news and cheered the old 'uns, now. Phyllie and Andy left the floor, and thanked Mrs Symes who was guarding Charlie's pram. They pushed it out into the village, Jake, Ron and Francois joined them while Dan stayed to dance with Monica, a new evacuee who had arrived from the Midlands. Together they strolled back to the farm, where they all now lived.

In September 1944 French tanks had led the Allies into Paris and Ron received a letter from his mother. He brought it through to Phyllie and Andy, who was having his breakfast in the small kitchen after returning the cows to the field after milking. 'It's from my mum.' His astonishment was clear. He laid the other envelopes on the table for Andy. They looked like bills. Jake was with him, looking concerned because he knew, just as well as Phyllie and Andy, what the newspapers were saying.

Phyllie exchanged a look with Andy, who continued to sop up his egg with a piece of bread. She knew from the muscle working under his chin that it was the envelope they feared, because the government was releasing some of the prisoners who had been interned as a risk to the state, and though Mr Cummins had been found guilty of grievous bodily harm, he was also a member of the BUF.

It was Saturday, there was no school for Phyllie or the boys, but there was ploughing to be done and she still couldn't get over how big and strong these young lads had become, and closer than any brothers. Ron read the letter in silence while Phyllie continued to feed Tommy, her new baby, who sat in the high chair and clearly liked the porridge. There was another letter enclosed, in an envelope with a crown stamped on the back. He read this, and then wordlessly passed it to Andy, who wiped his hand on his trousers and took it.

Phyllie laid a hand on his shoulders, and read it with him as Tommy mithered for more food. She held out the bowl to Jake, who took it and continued to feed him, looking from the letter to Ron, his worried scowl in place.

Sir,

I am directed by the Secretary of State to inform you that the Restriction Order made against you under Regulation 18A of the Defence (General) Regulations 1939, has now been revoked.

I am, sir, your obedient servant.

'Mum says now Dad's back, I can go home because he can give me a good bashing if I give her any gip.'

Andy coughed slightly, and returned the letter. 'I'm sorry; we should have told you he wasn't in the army.'

Ron shook his head and looked straight at Jake. 'I'm not daft, you know. I knew other children got letters when their dads were in North Africa but I never did. I asked Jake when I was ready to know.'

Phyllie went to him, put her arm round him, and led him to the table. 'Do you want to go home?'

Ron looked at the table, and played with some crumbs that lay on the oilcloth. 'That's not my home any more. This is. I just want to stay.' Jake handed Tommy's bowl to Andy, and went to stand with Ron. 'He can, can't he? He's fifteen with a mind of his own, so why does he have to do what they tell him?'

Tommy was crying for his food and Charlie was whimpering, picking up on the atmosphere. While Andy hoisted Charlie onto his lap, he handed the bowl back to Phyllie who resumed feeding Tommy. She said, 'What do you think, Andy? What's the best way of handling this?'

He kissed the top of Charlie's head and said, 'Well, they are his legal parents, but we'll write to them, and if you write a note too, Ron, let's see what happens. We all want you to stay. You are our son, just as much as Jake.'

That night, in bed, Phyllie lay in Andy's arms, and they decided that the only thing that would work with Mr and Mrs Cummins was money. They wrote, offering £200 if they would leave Ron in their keeping, to learn a trade as a farmer, though payment must never be mentioned to their boy. A reply was received, one to Ron, one to Mr and Mrs Bartlett. To Ron they said that they would miss him, but that they had a few more questions for his foster parents, after which they'd decide.

Andy and Phyllie's letter contained a demand for another £100.

This Phyllie and Andy had worked into their original equation. They sent it, knowing that this would be an expense that would pop up from time to time, because people like the Cummins always wanted more. Andy held her gently, and kissed her forehead the night after they had posted that letter. Within the week, they had an agreement. They told the boys immediately that Ron was their son for as long as he wished.

The boys flung themselves out of the house, to harness the horses. Andy said, 'The lad's worth every penny they get out of us, and more. I love them both, so much.'

Phyllie leaned against him. It was what Sammy would have said. They didn't have to worry about any extra expense for long because the V1 rocket campaign waged by a dying Nazi state hit the Cummins' local pub and killed Ron's parents. Ron barely grieved; instead, he seemed relieved.

As summer ended, Andy was on a trip to London and heard the news of the liberation of Majdanek concentration camp by Russian forces. He was pale when he arrived home, and though he smiled, Phyllie knew instantly that there was something very wrong.

The moment the boys left for the old barn, which they now helped to supervise, Andy told her the news. She said, 'Shall I speak to Jack Thompson? He might know what's best to do. I don't know whether we should shield Jake from this or be honest. It's so appalling I can't believe it can be true.'

Andy just shook his head. 'I don't know, I simply don't. All I do know is that if it is true, darling, what other camps are going to be discovered as the Allies advance?'

Phyllie cycled to the vicarage, where she had talked to Jack and Sylvia about whether to shield Jake from this news, but as Jack said, 'We can't know that he won't see this somewhere else. Perhaps to maintain trust, it should come from you and Andy.'

That evening, when Ron was saying goodnight to his favourite, Doris, as he always did, Phyllie and Andy talked to Jake about the discovery. He said little, but every so often came to one or other of them, and laid his head on their shoulder and whispered, 'She could still be safe?'

'Yes,' they had decided to say. 'We must hope.'

On 1 December 1944, Miss F and Joe married. They lived in Myrtle Cottage, though Joe still cycled to the farm for early-morning and late-afternoon milking, and everything in between. As Christmas approached there was no more news about Jake's relatives: his mother, Uncle Otto and Aunt Rosa Kaplan. Had they survived? Well, the war wasn't over yet, and every conversation about them seemed to end with, 'there is still hope'.

On Christmas morning, Miss F and Phyllie cooked in the big farm kitchen while the men continued the chores and Mr and Mrs Williams played with Charlie and Tommy in the sitting room. As usual Frankie and Mrs Saunders were unable to be with them, but had sent presents for all four of the children, with an affectionate card, written by Phyllie's mother, which pleased everyone, especially Phyllie.

As they prepared the vegetables, Miss F decided they needed more sprouts. Phyllie groaned. 'It means putting my boots on and slogging out to the vegetable patch.'

'Don't be dramatic,' Miss F said. The two women laughed. Phyllie had suggested at Miss F's wedding that now she was Mrs Bartlett, she should be called Audrey, her first name. Somehow it hadn't worked, and everyone had reverted within the week to Miss F, except Joe, who tended to call her 'the old bat'.

The track to the vegetable patch was muddy and across the field she saw the gulls following the ploughs, and her men creating straight furrows. Her heart was full of love and gratitude.

She looked up at the sky. 'Not bad, eh, Sammy?' Sometimes she wondered what her life would have been like with the love of her life, and knew that he and Isaac would have built a business of which to be proud. But she had been the most fortunate of women, because her life contained the memory of one splendid man and the actuality of another. Could one have two great loves? Well, yes, was the answer. She picked the sprouts from the stalks, with cold fingers, throwing them into the basket.

At midday lunch was served, but before Andy carved, he tapped his fork against his glass for silence. Phyllie looked around the table at their ever-expanding family. As Andy talked of their hopes for the New Year and their gratitude for the past year, she smiled at Miss F and Joe. They sat between Tommy in his high chair, and Charlie, who was perched up on a cushion. Tommy was a mixture of Andy and her, though Charlie grew more like Sammy every day. Phyllie exchanged a look with Ron who was checking that Charlie wasn't slipping off the cushion, proud of this handsome young man in a way she had never thought possible on Waterloo Station all those years ago.

Across from her sat Mr and Mrs Williams, Sammy's parents. Next to them Jake was holding his glass, looking at Andy. He was as tall, handsome, and a carbon copy of his father. He was her Jake, her lovely Jake. His father would have been so proud.

Miss F smiled at her, reaching across the table. Phyllie squeezed her hand. 'We're both so lucky,' Phyllie whispered, as the others toasted the company of family and friends. 'And surely the war is almost over.'

'We are indeed lucky, dearest Phyllie, and pray God it is the end, soon,' whispered Miss F, as only she could. Everyone heard, and everyone laughed, as they always did.

Andy said, his glass raised high, 'To absent friends.'

The publishers hope that this book has given you enjoyable reading. Large Print Books are especially designed to be as easy to see and hold as possible. If you wish a complete list of our books please ask at your local library or write directly to:

Magna Large Print Books
Magna House, Long Preston,
Skipton, North Yorkshire.
BD23 4ND

This Large Print Book for the partially sighted, who cannot read normal print, is published under the auspices of

THE ULVERSCROFT FOUNDATION